*—How young and foolish you are.—*

The intruder entity's distant and superior amusement was obvious. **This entity has come to make this new land completely ours,** it said. **Your entity is so new that you still perceive yourselves as individuals rather than as a whole, a fact which should clearly indicate how much greater this entity is than you. You will therefore respond at once to the question which has been put to you.**

*As you have requested a response, you shall have it,* the Rion entity said, feeling the agreement of his diverse parts. *Take your flesh forms and depart this land never to return, or we will destroy you.*

**You refuse to do as this entity commands? How can you not know that refusal is not permitted? Possibly you have not yet learned how truly helpless you are. Should that be so, then a lesson is clearly in order.**

A roiling began inside the intruder entity.

And then the Rion entity was struck so hard that he nearly lost all sense of center and balance . . .

## Other Books by Sharon Green

*The Blending Enthroned*

*The Blending*

# SHARON GREEN

# DESTINY

## Book Three of THE BLENDING ENTHRONED

*An Imprint of HarperCollinsPublishers*

EOS
*An Imprint of* HarperCollins*Publishers*
10 East 53rd Street
New York, New York 10022-5299

Copyright © 2002 by Sharon Green
Excerpt from *The Fresco* copyright © 2000 by Sheri S. Tepper
Excerpt from *Memory of Fire* copyright © 2002 by Holly Lisle
ISBN: 0-380-81295-9
www.eosbooks.com

First Eos paperback printing: April 2002

Eos Trademark Reg. U.S. Pat. Off. and in Other Countries, Marca Registrada, Hecho en U.S.A.
HarperCollins® is a trademark of HarperCollins Publishers Inc.

Printed in the U.S.A.

10 9 8 7 6 5 4 3 2 1

Last but certainly not least, this one is for
Debbora Wiles, a great partner
and an even better friend.

# DESTINY

# ONE

Driffin Codsent entered the living quarters of the warehouse with more relief than he would have wanted to mention aloud. He hadn't gotten much sleep lately and tiredness dragged at him, but lying down was out of the question. He simply didn't have the time for rest, and wouldn't have been able to sleep anyway.

"Still nothing?" Edmin asked from where he stood beside the table, the man's frown showing deep concern. "What can possibly have happened?"

"I don't believe *this* is happening," Idresia said from where *she* stood in the cooking area of the room. "How can something affect every single High talent in the city?"

"I wish I knew," Driff answered the both of them as he walked to a chair near Issini Randos, who also looked deeply disturbed. "Every High talent in the city has somehow been put into a kind of stasis, and it just isn't possible to reach through to them. They're all in perfect health, except for the fact that they can't move or talk or probably even think."

By then Driff had collapsed into the chair and covered his eyes with his fingers, and Issini patted his arm.

"Their not being able to think is a good thing, Driff," Issini told him in a reassuring tone. "If they were aware of what was going on, they would probably be very upset."

"Going crazy would be more like it," Idresia corrected as she came closer, and then she, too, touched Driff's arm.

1

"Here, drink this tea while your food is cooking. If you're not going to rest, then at least you have to eat."

Driff lowered his hands to see the cup of tea Idresia had put in front of him, and he reached for it gratefully. His body did need the stimulation right now, not to mention the food that was cooking. There was still so much to do . . .

"What about the Middle Blendings?" Edmin asked once Driff had taken a good swallow of the tea. "Do they think *they* can do anything?"

"It was all I could do to talk them into taking over some of the routine duties the Highs were seeing to," Driff answered, finding it impossible to keep the annoyance out of his voice. "They're afraid that they could be next to be struck down just the way the Highs were, and can't seem to understand that that could happen anyway. I had to point out that even the uninvolved Highs were taken the same, so just sitting around was no guarantee of safety."

"What we need is for *you* to be able to take charge completely," Idresia said with matching annoyance. She'd gone back to the stove, and now waved the large wooden spoon she held. "If you were part of a Blending you could *tell* people what to do, not waste your time talking them into it."

"Driff doesn't like the idea of being part of a Blending," Edmin commented, studying Driff from the chair he'd also taken. "I wonder if I might be so bold as to ask why."

Edmin's expression was no longer the complete neutrality it had been when Driff had first met him. There was open curiosity in the man's eyes, but the words he'd used would have allowed Driff to refuse to answer the question if he really needed to. Driff smiled to himself, then let part of the smile show through.

"It's not the act of Blending itself that I dislike," he replied, sending his tired smile to Idresia and Issini as well. "You may not understand just how close a bond there is between Blendingmates, but I do. I simply can't see myself Blending with others who don't include Idresia—or you and Issini, for that matter. If you aren't careful about who you

Blend with, I've been told, you end up with less than you had alone rather than more."

"Yes, but—" Issini began, but a knock at the door cut her short. After the knock the door opened, and a man Driff didn't know put his head in.

"Sorry t' interrupt, folks, but this here's kinda important," the man said with a disarming smile. "Idresia, c'n I talk t' ya a minute?"

Issini left the table immediately to take the spoon Idresia held, which left Idresia free to go to the door. She stepped outside with the man, and it was possible to hear the words of a low conversation through the partially open door.

"The man's really excited about something," Edmin said softly to Driff. "Have you any idea what that can be about?"

"I don't even know who he is," Driff admitted after taking another sip of tea. "He's probably part of Idresia's spy network, and I can only hope that his news isn't bad. I don't think I can take much more bad news."

"No, I'm fairly sure it isn't *bad* news he's brought," Edmin said, now studying the doorway. "And there seems to be more than one something. Idresia was more surprised over the first something than the second, and now she seems to be giving instructions."

"I'm sure we'll find out what's going on as soon as she's through," Driff said, amused by Edmin's open curiosity and running commentary. Edmin was not the same man Driff had met only a short while ago, not as . . . controlled and repressed. Once Edmin had decided to join them, he'd done so wholeheartedly.

"I wonder if I might ask *you* a question, Edmin," Driff added as the thought occurred to him. "You seem to be doing better with your talent than other Middle talents in Spirit magic that I've met, and I'd like to know why that is. You haven't managed to join one of the training classes, have you?"

"I wish I could," Edmin answered ruefully with a touch of wistfulness. "Whatever facility I may have comes only from years of using my talent to survive among my former peers.

It's been quite some time since I've been able to release the power, but I've somehow been able to . . . shield my doings from others with Spirit magic. I really have no idea how the thing *should* be done, so I would welcome the chance to correct any mistakes by attending one of the classes."

"You're shielding your efforts," Driff repeated, staring at Edmin and only just resisting the urge to gape. "You're completely untrained, but you *can* shield."

"Yes," Edmin replied, obviously amused by the way Driff—and Issini—stared at him. "That, I believe, was why the Noll woman had no qualms about allowing her brood to touch my father so blatantly. Am I to assume that my lone efforts are rather commendable? You two seem somewhat impressed."

"Rather commendable, he says," Driff commented to Issini with a small laugh, shock turning to delight. "I think it's a good thing he told *us* about this in private. If any of the Highs had heard him say it, he'd be running so many training classes that it would be years before we saw him again."

"Training classes?" Edmin echoed, his amusement gone behind confusion. "Whyever would *I* be running—You can't possibly mean—"

"I think he understands now," Issini said with her own amusement as Edmin floundered while looking back and forth between the two of them. "Yes, my dear, what we mean is that no one else has managed to . . . shield their efforts from others of the same aspect. Can you explain how you do what you do and how it works?"

"I'm not certain I can," Edmin answered, his brows high as he obviously struggled to accept what he'd been told. "What my shield does—I think—is keep others from knowing that I'm touching the power and actively using my ability. Other Spirit magic users know I have the same talent, but they don't seem to—Are you *certain* that no one else has developed the same ability?"

"No one I've ever heard of," Driff answered, speaking gently to soothe the shock he could feel in Edmin. "But the lack of others isn't all that surprising. Don't forget that commoners were forbidden to use their ability except for certain limited and well-defined tasks, and the nobility seemed to consider using talent as beneath them. Most of your former peers didn't *have* much ability, I'm told, so that's probably why they were happier not using it."

"Then I do have something of value to offer the new regime," Edmin said, sudden delight replacing his former distress. "Anyone can plot and plan, but my ability at subterfuge was all I had to offer—until now. You have no idea how relieved I feel."

"That's what *you* think," Driff told him with a small laugh. "Until I found out how strong a healing ability I had, I felt exactly the same way. But the question still remains: Do you think you can explain how you do that shielding thing?"

"I don't know," Edmin replied, the delight fading. "I've been doing it for so long that it's become pure habit. I'll have to think back to when I first developed the shield, and try to remember exactly what I did."

"I was about to offer the help of a High in Spirit magic," Driff said, his own good mood disappearing as he remembered their most serious problem. "Gensie would have loved to get involved, but she's as unliving as every other High. But that does remind me: I'll have to have someone check on that residence for the disturbed that some of the Highs were running. We can't afford to have those people walking around without supervision."

Issini seemed about to comment or ask a question, but that was when Idresia came back into the room and closed the door behind her.

"It certainly does help to be prepared, but it will be a while before we know how *much* it helps," Idresia commented. She'd apparently been about to return to the stove, but seeing Issini coming with a plate of food for Driff sent Idresia to the table instead to sit with the others.

"We've been waiting to find out what that man wanted," Driff said, nodding his thanks as Issini put a plate of cheese omelet in front of him. "And once you tell us *your* news, we'll tell you ours."

"There's definitely news," Idresia agreed, her expression puzzled as she looked around to see that all of her companions were amused. "But what news can *you* possibly have?"

"We'll tell you later," Driff said around a mouthful of eggs. "You first."

"Since the first part of this is really important, I won't argue about going first," Idresia said after the briefest of hesitations. "It looks like our renegade noble is starting to make his move."

"What is he doing?" Edmin asked at once, speaking the words Driff would have used if his mouth hadn't been filled with food. "Is there any indication of what his objective is?"

"He's started to send his men out from those other locations in groups of three, six different groups of three to be precise," Idresia answered. "Two of each group are fairly large in build, but the third is either short or slender or both. You remember that I added to the number of people watching Noll's men when we heard about the Highs being in trouble. I assumed that the Middle Blending helping us would be needed elsewhere, and I didn't want us to be caught short. I had twenty of my people in place, so twelve of them paired up and followed each of the renegade's groups."

"For pity's sake, Har, stop dragging it out and tell us what happened," Issini protested. "Or don't you know any details yet?"

"Four of the groups went to taverns, and the last two went to dining parlors," Idresia replied with an apologetic shake of her head. "I'm sorry to drag it out so badly, but the story is worth telling in detail. One of the two big men of each group went into the tavern or dining parlor alone, and a few minutes later the second big man joined the first. One of my two shadows was already inside the place, having gone in after the first man.

"When the second renegade's man walked in, he pretended that he and the first man were friends who hadn't seen each other in a while. The third, smaller man came in right behind the second one, but he pretended not to know either of the other two. The third man sat or stood by himself while the first two went through how-have-you-been and how-are-things conversations.

"After a couple of minutes, the first two started to tell each other how badly they were being taken advantage of by the new government. They were a couple of innocent victims being ground under the heel of uncaring tyrants, and their voices were loud enough that everyone in the establishment heard what they were saying. That, of course, was when the 'stranger' stepped forward to agree with what they'd said."

"The 'stranger' being the third of their group, of course," Driff said angrily, this time beating Edmin to the comment. "Don't tell me that the people listening believed them."

"Apparently the people listening were seriously concerned," Idresia confirmed, but she herself looked a good deal less than disturbed. "I still don't believe the good luck I had in picking people as watchers, but apparently the inside person did the same thing in every instance. He or she announced that the three 'victims' must be leaving out some important details, because no one else seemed to be having anything like the same trouble. Then he or she turned to the rest of the patrons in the place, and asked if *they'd* had anything like the same trouble or knew of anyone who had. That was when the listeners realized that no one else *had* had the same trouble."

"How did the three 'victims' take being interfered with?" Issini asked, a small frown creasing her brow. "They couldn't have been happy to have their little act ruined."

"They *weren't* happy, but there wasn't much they could do," Idresia replied with a headshake. "A hothead from one of the groups seemed to be ready to beat up our man who interrupted whatever they were trying, but luckily there were off-duty members of the guard present. When the guard members got to their feet and stepped forward, the hothead changed his mind and simply stalked out of the tavern. Our man left by the tavern's back door, just in case the hothead was waiting outside for him."

"I believe *I* know what they were trying, but I have a question first," Edmin said, his expression thoughtful. "Did the groups return then to where they came from, or did they make another attempt elsewhere?"

"Actually, they did try their acts a second time," Idresia confirmed, looking at Edmin curiously. "My people switched places, so the groups weren't interfered with by the same man or woman. But they *were* interfered with again, so none of them tried a third time. They were so frustrated that they simply went back where they came from, probably to report and ask for new instructions. So now tell us, what do you think they were after?"

"In my opinion, they were trying to make people believe that the new government isn't as helpful and benign as everyone now thinks," Edmin said, looking around at all of them. "Noll has most likely decided to spread rumors that will circulate throughout the entire city, rumors calculated to cause unrest and doubt. Once the rumors and accusations have spread far enough, he undoubtedly plans to have rabble-rousers go out and fire up the populace to the point where they can be led in attack against some important point, like the palace. His own people will be hidden among the innocent, directing the attack without anyone being aware of it. Once the important point is taken, it will be *his* men who hold it."

"And that's something we can't let happen," Driff said, agreeing completely with what Edmin had told them. "There would have been trouble stopping a frenzied mob even with the help of Highs, but without them . . . If we don't want innocent people on all sides getting hurt, we have to stop Noll's plan as quickly and thoroughly as we can."

"I think I may know how we can do that," Issini said slowly, her gaze thoughtful and inward. "It all depends on how many people Har can produce, and how brave they are."

"Actually, I now have more than fifty men and women who are willing to help," Idresia said, her brows high. "Some of them are in it for the silver, but the rest just want to help us all keep what we have now. Most of them are as brave as they need to be, but only a few can be considered

good enough fighters to hold their own against the renegade's men. I'm sorry, Ran, but sometimes bravery just isn't
enough."

"Fighting ability will have very little to do with my plan,"
Issini said, her hand gesturing dismissal as she smiled. "I
just realized that our best defense against what the renegade
is trying will be the worst thing you can do to a man. As
soon as I get a few more details ironed out, I'll tell everyone
what I have in mind. In the meantime, what was the other
thing that man told you?"

"Oh, yes, I almost forgot about that," Idresia said with a
small start. "I don't know if I've mentioned it, but I have
people watching the various approaches into the city. The
renegade lost a lot of men when more than half of his force
deserted him, and I didn't want to get caught unawares if he
managed to replace those men."

"That was really good thinking, Idresia," Driff said with
his brows high. "I hate to admit it, but the thought never
would have occurred to me. I'll have to remember to give
myself a commendation for putting you in charge of our spy
force, but first I'd like to know how many more men the
renegade now has."

"So far he doesn't have *any* more men, Driff," Idresia answered with faintly embarrassed amusement. "My people
were watching for reinforcements, but instead they wit-
nessed the arrival of two members of the nobility. It was a
man and a woman on horseback looking somewhat worse
for wear, but my people were certain about their origins.
Forgive me, Edmin, but there's no mistaking the unconscious arrogance that members of the former nobility carry
themselves with even when they're dirty and tired."

"No apology necessary, Idresia," Edmin answered with
his own amusement. "Issini and I were both aware of the
problem, which is why I agreed to that disguise as an old
man. Shuffling along bent over was the only way to disguise
my usual . . . thrust through life's unimportances. I take it
that you're going to have the two people watched?"

"Actually, I arranged to have them intercepted and

brought here," Idresia replied, a trace of uncertainty now in her gaze. "We can't afford to assume that they won't make trouble, not now with everything else going on, and if they happen to join the renegade and his family he'll have the worst kind of reinforcement: more and possibly better thinkers and planners. That would be worse for us than his getting more men."

"Yes, I'm forced to agree," Driff said after thinking about Idresia's decision for a moment. "At first I was going to say that we can't just arrest and detain those people when they haven't done anything illegal, but that rule applied before we lost all our High talents. No one can argue that we're in a state of emergency now, and if we're going to hold things together we'll have to bend a few of the rules."

"Bend the rules, yes, but not break them completely," Idresia said, her gaze now showing more certainty. "If those people have no interest in making trouble either alone or with the renegade, I mean to turn them loose again. I hope you two men will be able to tell me whether or not that's a good idea."

Driff exchanged a glance with Edmin, seeing the former noble's brief startlement before pleased pride took its place. It was fairly obvious that Edmin still wasn't used to being trusted, but his reaction clearly said that he *intended* to get used to that state of affairs.

"Well, Edmin and I aren't much when it comes to talent, but we'll certainly do our best," Driff said to Idresia in as pitiful a way as he could manage before turning to the other man. "Isn't that right, Edmin? We'll do our pitiful best?"

"Yes, we certainly will, Driff," Edmin agreed, apparently trying to sound as humble as Driff had. The problem was Edmin didn't know *how* to sound humble, so all his effort produced among the group was laughter.

"As long as you two meager talents are willing to try," Idresia said with amusement while Issini laughed aloud. "We do have to work with what we have, you know."

"Speaking of what we have to work with, we still haven't

told Har our news," Issini pointed out then. "We don't want her thinking we're holding out on her, do we?"

"Aha, so you *are* holding out on me!" Idresia pounced with a mock frown so fierce that the rest of them chuckled. "Well, come on, out with it."

"You'd better brace yourself," Driff warned Idresia, only partially joking. "While you were getting your report on outside doings, those of us in here learned that Edmin can . . . shield his working with talent in some way. He's going to try to remember what he did to gain the shield, and then he's going to tell *us* how to do it."

"That sounds like a very useful thing to know," Idresia said, her brows still high even though she had stopped staring at Edmin with her mouth open. "Can we do anything to help you remember faster, Edmin?"

"I think I'll need a time of undisturbed quiet," Edmin answered, his amusement tinged with very faint embarrassment. "I considered asking for the help of another Spirit magic user, but I think we must first decide whether or not we want word of a shield to get out. Until things settle down and we have the High talents back again . . ."

"Until then we'll need all the help—and secret weapons—we can get," Driff agreed with a sigh. "I think your caution isn't overdone, Edmin, so let's—"

A knock came at the door to interrupt Driff, and Idresia rose to go and answer it. Driff quickly finished the last of the food on his plate, and only just in time.

"Our two newly arrived nobles weren't far from here when my people went to get them," Idresia said, still standing by the open door. "They'll be here in another moment, so let's get all meager talents ready, shall we?"

Driff joined the others in nodding agreement, even Issini losing her usual friendly and easygoing manner. Edmin was the only one among them who hadn't been to a training class, but he *had* had training in life when it came to dealing with the nobility. Now it was time to see if any of their training had been wasted.

In no more than the specified moment, two people were escorted into the room. They both looked dirty and very tired, but the man looked considerably more worried than the woman did. The woman held a large bundle close against her body, and the man's arm circled her protectively. The man took a quick look around, and then he glared at Idresia and Driff and the others.

"What's the meaning of this?" the man demanded, his voice harsh with fear-tinged outrage. "You people aren't the authorities, so I demand that you release us immediately."

*Yes,* Driff thought with a sigh. *Definitely members of the old nobility. Just what we needed . . .*

# TWO

Kail Engreath looked around at the outskirts of Gan Garee as he and Asri rode into the city. It was the same city he remembered so well—along with its bad memories—and he couldn't decide how he felt about returning to it. He wasn't the same man who had left this city, and hopefully that would produce more pleasant events to have memory of in the future.

"I suddenly feel very odd, Kail," Asri said from where she rode to his left, her infant son, Dereth, held close against her right side. "As soon as you suggested that we return here to Gan Garee, I somehow felt that that was what we *had* to do. Now the feeling has intensified in some way, as if something very important to us is about to happen."

"I hope the something turns out to be a place where we can live our lives in peace," Kail told her with a smile, reaching out to touch her arm. Day by day during their trip from Astinda, Asri had begun to share more and more of her thoughts and feelings with him. From time to time her "feelings" had kept them from running into people who might ask the wrong questions, so Kail had come to rely on her opinion.

"Now that you mention it, I have the strangest feeling that something *is* going to happen that will affect our lives," Asri told him, her gaze a bit unfocused the way it became from time to time. "Whatever it is might not be pleasant at first, but it's definitely necessary."

Kail made a sound of agreement and interest, the only thing he could do when Asri made comments the way she just had. She didn't do it often, happily, but Kail wondered if it would be possible to find help for her somewhere in the city. Kail had decided that Asri's cryptic statements were attempts to make herself useful in some way, a definite reaction to not having any talent. He knew he'd have to work harder to make her believe that her lack of talent was unimportant to him, otherwise her inner anxiety could well get out of hand . . .

"I think we need to look in the poorer neighborhoods for a place to stay," Asri said after a moment, the distraction mostly gone from her gaze. "People in the better neighborhoods might recognize us for what we are—what we *were*—and that would bring nothing but trouble."

"You're right, and I'm glad you thought of it," Kail said with a smile, already having had the same thought himself. "We still have most of the gold we brought with us, so we shouldn't have trouble surviving until I can take a good look around for something to do to earn a living. Do you have any preferences in the way of a poorer neighborhood?"

"As a matter of fact, I do," Asri answered with a smile, mirroring Kail's own smile. "I like the idea of going *that* way."

Asri had pointed to a street to the left, and since it made very little difference Kail immediately agreed. There were really too many people around on the street they now rode along, so turning off was a good idea.

The street they turned off into was a narrower one than the street they'd come from, but it was still possible for them to ride side by side. After a few minutes the worn old houses they'd been passing were replaced with large buildings that must be warehouses of some sort. Most of the warehouses looked really run-down, and Kail was about to suggest that they turn back to where actual houses could be found when people suddenly materialized around them.

"Just take it easy—no one's going to hurt you," the man who held Kail's horse's bridle said quickly and soothingly as Kail got ready to defend himself and his woman. "There are some important people who want to talk to you, just talk. You aren't going to force us to do something unnecessary, are you?"

The man's glance touched Asri briefly, letting Kail know how things stood. Four of the people around them were Water magic users just as he was, and all four were Middle talents and touching the power. If Kail started a fight he would find himself outnumbered, and there was a good chance that Asri might be hurt. Since he couldn't allow the woman he loved to be hurt, Kail had no choice but to surrender.

"All right, you win," Kail growled, hating having to back down. "Who is it who wants to talk to us, and where are they?"

"You'll find out who they are when they tell you themselves, and they aren't far away," the man holding Kail's horse's bridle answered with a brief smile. "We appreciate your being reasonable, which you really shouldn't regret. Please step down now, and we'll see to your horses while you're busy talking."

Kail frowned as he dismounted and then went around Asri's horse to help her down. They were now committed to doing as these people said, but Kail couldn't help wondering how the ones who wanted to "talk" to them could be close enough to walk to. Was there a building of offices somewhere among all these run-down warehouses?

Kail kept his questions to himself as the group that had stopped them led the way to one warehouse in particular. The place looked as rickety as the rest from the outside, but once inside it was possible to see a difference. The warehouse looked much more solid and well cared for on the inside, but there didn't seem to be the offices he'd been expecting. He and Asri were led toward the back of the warehouse to a door standing open, and once he reached it Kail's suspicions flared. Through the doorway was something that looked more like living quarters than an office, and that shouldn't have been.

"What's the meaning of this?" Kail demanded as he

stopped in the doorway, his arm automatically tightening around Asri. "You people aren't the authorities, so I demand that you release us immediately."

"Looks can be deceiving," a pretty woman who stood by the door said gently while a small man seated at a table sighed. "Right now we're just about as official as it gets, but we mean you no harm. You both look like you could use some tea while we talk."

"I would *love* a cup of tea," Asri said before Kail could demand again to know what was happening. "It really has been a very long day, Kail."

"It isn't a good idea to accept things from people before you know what they want," Kail said in answer, trying to explain things gently to Asri. "Let's find out first why we were brought here, and then we can think about tea."

"No, it's all right," the woman interrupted when Asri actually started to argue what Kail had said. "His request isn't unreasonable, especially since I would feel the same way. We had you brought here because you were recognized as members of the group that used to be called the nobility. We wanted to know if you've come back to the city to regain your former positions."

"If you only knew how terrible a suggestion you've just made," Kail said at once with a short laugh that had no amusement in it. "Our 'former positions' in this city were living hell, and if we thought we had to return to them we never would have come back. All we want is to live our lives in peace, and I'm willing to work any honest job that will let us do that. If you thought we could be used in some scheme you might have in mind, you can forget about it."

Kail hadn't meant to be quite that blunt, but something had made him speak without reservation. As soon as the words were out he put his arm around Asri again, afraid that he might have put both their lives in danger. If these people wanted something that they now knew they'd never get, he and Asri—and the baby—might have just become unnecessary burdens.

"I'm delighted to say that our guest has just told the absolute and complete truth," the slight man at the table told his companions, his smile warm and real. "Reviving the nobility isn't any part of their intentions, so we can now let them go about their own business."

"I'm really glad to hear that," the pretty woman said with her own smile. "I apologize for having had you brought here, and you're now free to go. But if you'd like that cup of tea first, by all means have a seat at the table."

"We took their horses to that empty lot to graze," the man who still stood behind them said. "Do you want me to have them brought back here right now?"

"Only if they've changed their minds about the tea," the woman answered, then looked at Kail. "I'm Idresia Harmis, by the way, and the choice of staying or leaving has now become yours."

"I don't understand any of this," Kail said, having decided to stick with being blunt. "You used force to bring us here, but now you say we can leave. What's going on?"

"We're what you might call unofficial officials," the woman Idresia said with a small and gentle laugh. "Our job is to keep an eye open for possible troublemakers, people who are determined to bring back the bad old ways. We already have one like that to contend with, so we didn't want to add to the problem. Now that we know you *won't* be a problem, we have no reason to detain you."

"You're willing to take my word for it?" Kail asked, still more than a little suspicious. "If I were in your place, I'd need a bit more proof than that."

"We have the proof," Idresia said, still speaking gently. "One of our people has Spirit magic, and another Earth magic. They've both confirmed that you're telling the truth, so nothing else is needed."

Kail looked toward the table then, really seeing the three people who sat there for the first time. The woman was very pretty and wore a smile like Idresia's, and the slight man nodded his support of what Idresia had said. The other man—

"You're Lord Edmin Ruhl!" Kail blurted, suddenly more than a little disturbed. "Am I supposed to believe that *you're* working for the new government?"

"Yes, because that's exactly what I'm doing," Ruhl answered, the evenness of his tone doing little to mask the way he'd flinched. "If there were any doubts about this man's attitudes before now, my friends, they can be forgotten. Our guest hates nobles more than any of *you* ever did."

"If you'd gone through what we did, you would feel the same hatred," Asri said calmly before Kail could reply. "Those people were often worse to their own kind than they were to commoners, which is why our hatred is greater."

"Yes, we've heard that," Idresia said as she put her own arm around Asri, supportive understanding clear in her voice. "Come and have that cup of tea, and let it wash away all those bad memories. We won't let those bad times come again; we've pledged our lives to the promise."

Kail watched as Asri walked with Idresia to the table, surprised by the trust Asri showed. Asri was usually friendly, but giving trust was another matter entirely.

"We really don't charge more for sitting down," the slight man at the table said to Kail, his smile filled with understanding. "Why don't you have a cup of tea and tell us where you've been—or not tell us, if you feel you'd rather not say."

The last of the man's words had been hurried, as if he knew that Kail had felt a stab of alarm over the suggestion of talking about where they'd been. Kail didn't want *anyone* to know that they were escaped slaves, not when someone could decide to send them back . . .

"You really don't have to worry about being betrayed," Ruhl said when Kail continued to hesitate. "If these people were the sort to indulge in the kind of games our former peers loved to play, I would hardly be sitting here among them. And please don't use the title 'lord' again. I've become something much more important than a lord, a position I had no idea existed. I've become a trusted friend."

Kail stared at Ruhl for a moment, but it wasn't the man's words that convinced him. It was Ruhl's smile, the kind of smile Kail had never before seen the man wear. The former lord really did seem changed, and before Kail knew it he was at the table and sitting in a chair near Asri.

"If you two are hungry, I can throw something together for you," Idresia said as she came back to the table with two cups of tea. "Is the baby all right? He or she looks so beautifully sound asleep."

"His name is Dereth, and he's gotten used to sleeping with all sorts of things going on around him," Asri said with a smile as she unwrapped her son just a bit. "I fed him just before we reached the city, so he should be fine for now."

"But you two aren't, so I'll have something for you in just a minute," Idresia said, her briskly decisive tone refusing to hear any argument. "Do you have any objections to omelets?"

"If that's a fiendish plot to keep us here, it pains me to say that it worked," Kail offered, hoping the feeble humor would lighten his mood. "We haven't had eggs of any sort for much too long a time, and I've started to dream about them."

"Then omelets it is," Idresia said when Asri agreed with a gentle laugh. "Why don't all of you introduce yourselves while I'm cooking."

"That's a good idea," the slight man said. "I'm Driffin Codsent, the lady is Issini Randos, and Edmin Ruhl you already know. Would you care to share your own names?"

"I'm Kail Engreath, and my companion is Asri Tempeth," Kail answered with a sigh. "I'm still feeling the urge to say nothing on any subject, so if I sound a bit surly I hope you'll forgive me."

"There's really nothing to forgive," the woman called Issini said with a very attractive smile. "When it's just you against the world, friendless and alone, there's no other way *to* feel. Edmin probably understands that better than any of us."

"In point of fact, I do," Ruhl responded, his smile having turned wry. "I also know how marvelous it feels to no longer *be* alone, a truth you'll hopefully find out for yourself. I ought to mention that I remember you as well, Engreath, and recall thinking that you would never fit in with your father and brothers. Right now, that's the best endorsement anyone in our position can possibly have."

"I'm really glad to hear that," Kail said, not as surprised as he would have been only a few moments earlier. "And you're right about my not fitting in with my father and brothers, a state I've always been happy about but never happier than now. By the way, someone mentioned that there's another of our former peers here in the city who doesn't seem to look at things the way we do. Would you mind telling me who it is?"

"Since the matter isn't much of a secret, it shouldn't hurt anything to mention their names," the man called Driffin said when Ruhl glanced at him. "We're currently trying to keep Sembrin and Bensia Noll from taking over the city."

"Him!" Kail couldn't help exclaiming, and then he realized that Asri had said, "Her!" at the same time. Kail looked at Asri questioningly just as she did the same with him, and Ruhl made a sound of amusement.

"You both seem to know and dislike the family," Ruhl observed, looking from one to the other of them. "Would you care to share why that is? The more we know about the Nolls, the better our chances of ruining their plans."

"It wouldn't be quite accurate to say I *know* Sembrin Noll," Kail responded with a grimace when Asri hesitated. "My father once tried to get me an appointment with the government, and Noll intruded in the matter. Noll somehow knew that I wanted nothing to do with the position, and mentioned the fact to a number of advisors—along with his opinion that I would be useless anyway. He told everyone that I would be useless at whatever I tried to do."

"Noll's brother, Ephaim, put him up to that, I think," Ruhl said, his gaze obviously searching past memory. "The post was one that Ephaim wanted for his own candidate, so he had his brother, Sembrin, block the only other candidate. But it was Sembrin's choice as to how to do the blocking, so he chose the way he liked best. Ruining people's reputations seemed to be a hobby of his."

"The more I hear about Noll, the better I like him," the woman Issini said dryly, then she turned to Asri. "And what did the Noll woman do to *you*?"

"She . . . was very cruel," Asri answered hesitantly, and then she seemed to brace up as she looked directly at the other woman. "She said it was lucky that I had no talent at all, or my prettiness wouldn't have helped me. Men of real importance disliked stubborn women, but they were willing to overlook the stubbornness if there was nothing in the way of talent behind the attitude."

Kail felt startled that Asri would mention to these strangers the one point of her life that disturbed her the most. Asri looked almost defiant, as though she waited to be rejected because of her lacks. Kail was prepared to put an arm around Asri in support, but he suddenly found himself startled for the second time.

"Lack of talent?" Driffin echoed with abrupt and unexplained interest as he exchanged glances with the others at the table. "Did you all hear that? Asri supposedly has no talent, but I'm now remembering that Idresia's man said these two were found not far from here. They 'just happened' to locate the neighborhood of the only people in the city who could give them a true welcome . . . Would anyone care to guess how unlikely that is?"

"That's an excellent point, Driff," Idresia said from where she stood near the stove, her expression seemingly filled with delight. "I'll bet Asri was the one who wanted to come in this direction. Isn't that right, Kail?"

"Well, as a matter of fact, she *did* say we ought to come this way," Kail admitted without thinking, completely confused about what these strangers might be talking about. "But that doesn't really mean anything, any more than her lack of talent makes Asri less of a person. She—"

"Less of a person!" Driffin echoed again, now looking really amused. "You've been away from the city a *long* time, haven't you? You obviously missed the great revelation, so it gives me quite a lot of pleasure to tell you two that Asri doesn't lack talent at all. She's clearly someone who has the sixth talent, and wasn't taken in with the others because she was a member of the nobility."

"What are you talking about?" Kail demanded, disturbed over the way Asri now sat staring at Driffin as though what she'd heard was too good to be true. "If there was a sixth talent, the Astindans would have told us about it. I don't know what you think you're playing at, but—"

"Engreath, the Astindans don't yet know about the sixth talent," Ruhl put in gently, and Kail could feel himself being calmed. "Driff told me that it was the sixth talent that let our Seated Blending defeat the Astindans when they came here to destroy the city. The sixth talent is Sight magic."

"Those with Sight magic hid out among the supposedly untalented," Driffin added just as gently while Kail sat with his mouth open, gripped in mild shock. "They were afraid to let anyone find out about their talent, since they knew without doubt that the nobles would have made slaves of them. The current Seated Blending somehow managed to have a Sight magic member as one of them, and after they won against all comers the people with the sixth talent revealed themselves."

"And now it's time for you two to eat," Idresia said as she put plates in front of Kail and Asri. "Revelations sit better on full stomachs."

"Is what you just said really true?" Asri asked the others, ignoring the plate of food in front of her. "I'm really not useless and I do have a talent? I don't have to give up my baby because he isn't untalented either?"

"No, my dear, you're really not untalented," Driffin said with a warm and reassuring smile. "The fact that you're sitting here being told about it ought to be proof enough of *that*. If you were an ordinary talent I might not be certain about your son, but since you have Sight magic the chances are excellent that he has the same. We'll have to wait until he gets old enough to speak before we can be certain, but I'm very optimistic."

Asri began to cry then, but the way she laughed at the same time kept Kail from being overly disturbed. Her tears were ones of relief, and if Kail didn't understand exactly how she felt, no one in the world did.

"The Astindans are still requiring 'the untalented' to give up their equally 'untalented' children?" Ruhl asked after a moment, faint surprise in the question. "I would have thought that they'd learned the truth by now."

"They don't seem to have," Kail confirmed as he began to give his omelet some attention. "I suppose I might as well admit now that we were sent to Astinda with the rest of our former peers, but we did well enough that we were given the chance to earn Astindan citizenship. I was in the midst of doing just that when Asri was told that she would be best off giving up her 'untalented' son. That's when we decided to come back here."

"What sort of thing were you doing there?" Idresia asked as she returned with more tea for everyone. "Is it anything you could do here as well?"

"I'd love to do the same here," Kail answered ruefully after he swallowed a delicious bite of omelet. "A group of us were looking into new uses of talent, and we came up with a number of good ideas. If you know of any High talents who would be willing to help out, I'll be glad to share what we came up with."

"We'll accept that offer, but not right now," Driffin said after exchanging odd glances with the others. "Among other things, we have the Nolls and their plans to worry about. Those renegades have almost a hundred and fifty men to do their dirty-work for them, and we don't want to see any innocents hurt by their hired bullies. If you'd like to give us a hand with *that* project, we'd be happy to have you."

"I suddenly have the feeling that we'll be of more help to you than you expect," Asri said, the food on her fork ignored as she stared elsewhere. "Does the feeling have anything to do with my . . . talent?"

"It certainly does," Driffin agreed at once as he leaned forward with obvious interest. "That's what Sight magic is— being able to see into the future. Do you see any details to go along with the feeling?"

"Not really," Asri answered, sighing as she now looked at the forkful of food. "Obviously my talent isn't as . . . full as I'd hoped it would be."

"That's what *you* think," Driffin disagreed as quickly as he'd spoken a moment ago. "Being able to see into the future at all is nothing less than incredible, so being disappointed that there aren't all sorts of details to go along with the sight is downright silly. *You* might not think you're doing much, but you have to remember that it's a lot more than the rest of us can do."

"I knew there was a reason I would like you," Asri said to Driffin with a warm smile and a bit of amusement. "Thank you for saying that."

"Believe me, it's my pleasure," Driffin returned with his own amusement as he watched Asri begin to eat with as much enthusiasm as Kail already showed. "But if I recall correctly, Issini said she had a plan we could use against Noll's men. I'd like you to listen to that plan, Asri, and then tell us if you get any 'feelings' about it."

Asri nodded her agreement as she chewed, clearly enjoying the omelet as much as Kail was. Idresia was a really fine cook, and the food was excellent.

"I don't yet have *all* the details of my plan, but here's the outline," Issini said with a smile for everyone. "If one of you has a suggestion or something you'd like to add, please speak right up. The only thing I haven't really thought of a way to do is see the renegades' faces when they hear about what we mean to arrange."

At first Kail considered that an odd comment to make, but once he heard Issini's idea he quickly agreed. It *would* be worth quite a lot to see Noll's face when he learned what his plans had come to, or rather what they *would* come to. Kail finished his food quickly as he began to apply himself to the task of refining Issini's plan, and even Asri joined in with complete eagerness. The talk went on for quite a while, but Dereth's waking up hungry put a temporary halt to the discussion.

"Do you two actually have a place to stay?" Idresia asked

as Asri began to soothe her son. "If not, there's another empty apartment here in the warehouse. Edmin and Issini have all but moved in, so you two—or three—might as well do the same."

Kail exchanged a glance with Asri, seeing the smile and nod he'd expected to. He mirrored Asri's smile, and then turned to Idresia.

"We haven't even been here two hours, but for some odd reason I feel completely at home," Kail said, looking around at the others as well. "I believe Asri agrees with me, so we'll happily accept your offer. I'll admit I never expected anything like meeting you four, but I'm very glad that we did."

"And *we're* glad we kidnapped *you*," Driffin said as the others smiled. "Your suggestions about Issini's plan will make the plan stronger, and we'd better not wait to put it into effect. Since the renegade can move on to the next stage of his own plans at any time, we need to be ready."

"I'll show you both to the apartment, and you can get some rest," Idresia said as she stood. "When I've gotten my people arranged into groups, we'll meet again and see if any of us have come up with additions or changes to the plan."

Kail joined Asri in nodding agreement as they stood, and then the two of them followed Idresia out. He hadn't been lying about how comfortable and safe he felt, and that despite his suspicions when they'd first arrived. These people were not lying or intending to use Asri and him—Kail was willing to bet his life on that opinion. He'd had to leave his good new life in Astinda, but it looked like he might have traded something good for something incredibly great.

# THREE

Lord Sembrin Noll sat in his study, enjoying the book he'd decided to read. He'd been enjoying quite a lot of things these past days, not the least of which was the return of his ability in Spirit magic. His ability wasn't all that strong, but having even a weak talent was better than having none at all.

Just a short time ago the thought of having had to do without his talent would have enraged Sembrin, but he'd had a number of days of pleasure which had soothed his need to feel rage. His loving wife, Bensia, and their children had kept him under their control for quite a long time, but Sembrin had gotten his hands on some of the drug Puredan and now had his devoted family under *his* control.

"And they've all paid quite a lot for what they did to me," Sembrin murmured, the memories making him smile. He now used Bensia every time the mood took him, her own interest being entirely secondary. And he did what he pleased to her, a good deal of which she most certainly did *not* enjoy. That last was a terrible shame, of course, but Bensia had no choice about cooperating. The Puredan saw to that . . .

"And my darling children are *much* more polite these days," Sembrin murmured again, enjoying *those* memories as well. He'd punished all of them, more harshly than had ever been done, and now they gave him every courtesy as well as complete obedience. Sembrin's family life had finally become a delight, and his public life would surely soon become the same.

A knock came at Sembrin's study door, pulling him out of his thoughts. When he called out permission to enter, the door opened to show Jost Feriun, the commander of the men Sembrin had brought with him to help gain control of the city.

"All the men have now reported back, my lord," Feriun said as he entered and closed the door behind himself. "I've spoken to them, and have their reports for you."

"Your expression isn't the victorious one I was expecting, Feriun," Sembrin observed aloud as he put his book aside. "Did something keep the men from putting on their little plays in the taverns and dining parlors? Too many city guards around, perhaps?"

"No, my lord," Feriun said, stopping in front of Sembrin's desk without making an effort to sit in one of the chairs. "Each set of the men was able to . . . put on their play in two of the chosen locations, but the reaction they got was so far from the expected one that they decided against trying a third location before reporting back for orders."

"How different could the reactions have been?" Sembrin asked with a frown. "When people complain about being taken advantage of with a large crowd around them and someone else pipes up to agree, there will always be *some* fool in the crowd who also agrees. All that agreement makes the rest of the crowd think, and they believe what they heard even if they've experienced the exact opposite of the claim themselves."

"I'm afraid it didn't work like that at *any* of the locations," Feriun returned sourly. "Instead of some fool in the crowd coming forward to agree with our men, the fool in each instance came forward to *dis*agree. And to make matters worse, the fools forced the rest of the crowd to agree with *them* instead of our men. Since the fools didn't have to get anyone to change his mind, the agreement they got was a lot more certain and forceful."

"And none of your marvelous men thought of accusing the fool of being a tool of the government before knocking him unconscious?" Sembrin demanded, hearing the growl his voice had become. "Do you have any more excuses about why *your* men ruined what I'd *thought* was a foolproof plan? Obviously, incompetents have the ability to destroy *any* plan, no matter how good."

"One of my men *did* try to stop the fool from the crowd," Feriun stated, all but interrupting Sembrin in mid-tirade. "He would have stomped the fool into the floor, but there were off-duty guardsmen in the tavern who made it clear what would happen if my man did as you suggested. Did you really want him to be arrested and questioned by members of the government?"

"Since his being arrested would have helped us enormously, of course I didn't want him to be arrested," Sembrin returned dryly, leaning back in his chair to study the commander of his forces. "The other two men could then have pointed out that the guardsmen were arresting people to keep them from speaking against the government, and the only one being protected by the guardsmen was the tool of that very government. If you'd chosen intelligent men the way I'd ordered you to, they wouldn't have missed the opportunity."

"You consider it an opportunity to put one of our people in the hands of the government?" Feriun came back, and the man actually had the nerve to sound disdainful. "If you do, I could always send a letter to the authorities telling them exactly what we're trying to do. That way the authorities will have the same information without our having to sacrifice one of our very few men."

"How dare you be sarcastic with me when you're admitting that one of your men would betray us?" Sembrin demanded, his anger rising. "You weren't supposed to send out anyone weak, and now you're telling me—"

"Where have you been, Lord Sembrin?" Feriun demanded in turn, actually having the nerve to interrupt his superior. "The government has Highs in Spirit magic, people who can make *anyone* tell everything they're involved with. If one of our men was taken, the man would talk no matter *how* strong and loyal he was. You can't tell me you didn't know that."

Sembrin wanted to snap at Feriun in the same way the
man had done with *him*, but sudden unease kept him silent.
Of course he'd known that the government had High talents,
but for some reason he'd dismissed the knowledge. For
some reason he'd been picturing anyone arrested being
questioned in an ordinary way, possibly with the help of
someone with Earth magic to apply a bit of coercion. Then it
came to him why he'd dismissed the matter.

"Feriun, you've just demonstrated why you're no more
than hired help," Sembrin said with a haughty sneer, making
the words as cutting as possible. "Using a High talent to
force people to talk is something *we* would do, but the peasants in the government are much too wholesome and pure to
do the same. In their own eyes they're *good people,* and
good people don't do awful things like invade the privacy of
others. I thought you would have realized that by now."

"Depending on the government having that kind of outlook doesn't strike me as being wise, my lord," Feriun answered after something of a hesitation. "If even one of the
people in charge doesn't care about being considered 'good,'
then we'll be betrayed even if the man involved has no desire to betray us."

"Why don't you let *me* worry about that, Feriun?" Sembrin said, now trying to soothe the man. "And while I'm doing the worrying, you can be getting other men together to
try the plan again. And this time choose men who are adapt-
able, men who can think on their feet. I want the necessary
rumors circulating throughout the city before we go to the
next step of the plan. Do you understand me?"

"Yes, my lord, I understand," Feriun said, sounding and
looking as though he would have preferred to say something
else entirely. "I'll choose the men, and send them out again
tomorrow."

"Good," Sembrin said with a smile. Feriun performed a
small bow before turning and leaving, and once the door was
closed Sembrin lost his smile.

"The man's a damned fool," he growled under his breath,
feeling the urge to break something. "Imagine, someone like

him trying to do the thinking for someone like me. If I had
anyone at all I could put in his place . . ."

But there *wasn't* anyone to take Feriun's place, no one all
the men would take orders from the way they did with *this*
man. Sembrin knew he would have to put up with Feriun's
old-womanish fears until the plans worked, but afterward
would be a different story. Feriun would pay for the disre-
spect he'd shown today, not to mention the way he'd ruined
Sembrin's good mood. Now Sembrin needed something to
retrieve that good mood . . .

"And I think I know just what that should be," Sembrin
murmured, rising from his chair as soon as the thought came
to him. "Bensia will certainly be delighted to help me, and
the diversion will put me in an even better mood."

Sembrin left his study with the intention of asking the servants where Bensia was, but asking quickly became unnecessary. The large sitting area near the dining room contained
Bensia and their oldest son, Travin, the two standing and
talking. Part of the orders Sembrin had given his family was
to behave as normally as possible, and it pleased him to see
how well they obeyed.

"Bensia, my dear, how fortunate to find you so easily,"
Sembrin said as he approached the two, which immediately
drew their full attention. "Travin, I'm sure you have tasks to
occupy you, so please go on about those tasks. There's a different chore your mother needs to see to."

"Of course, Father," Travin agreed at once before turning
and walking away. That obedience in itself gave Sembrin
pleasure, but not as much as Bensia would.

"Come along, my dear," Sembrin said before turning
away. In past times Bensia would have demanded to know
what he had in mind, but right now all she did was follow
him like a sweet lamb. And following behind him suited her
*so* well . . .

Bensia stood beside her eldest son as they watched Sembrin walk off without a backward glance. She couldn't keep
from smiling, especially when Travin chuckled.

"At first I thought it a pity that I'm not old enough to take over for him," Travin said softly, obviously still watching his father's back. "Now, though, I've changed my mind. Seeing him prance around thinking he's in complete charge is an amusement I don't seem to tire of. If we weren't blocking him from picking up *our* real emotions, I wonder what he'd think about the amusement."

"The only thing he'd think about it would be what he was told to think about it," Bensia answered, turning to smile at her son. "Exposure to our talents was quite clearly strengthening his own talent, and it was only a matter of time before he broke loose from control. Taking control of him and then letting him believe that he gave us Puredan was our only option, aside from disposing of him. I wouldn't have minded having him out of our way, but we still need him as a figurehead. Once we're in control of the city, however, I mean to tell him the truth before we toss him out into the street. He can suffer over living with his shame while begging on some corner."

"He deserves at least that for daring to even imagine what he thinks he's done to *you*," Travin said, no longer even faintly amused. "The man is an animal, and I find it difficult to believe that he could be my father. But I was just starting to tell you what Feriun told Father when he interrupted us."

"Yes, you were," Bensia agreed with a gentle, encouraging smile. "Please go on."

Travin let himself be distracted from his previous thoughts as he repeated what he'd heard of Feriun's report. Bensia listened carefully, but part of her attention was on the question of whether or not to tell Travin the truth. The boy *said* he was ashamed that Sembrin was his father, but men were so strange. How would he feel if he learned that his father was someone else entirely . . . ?

". . . and so they're going to try the plan again tomorrow, supposedly with men who are brighter than the previous ones," Travin finished. "I nearly walked in and reminded them that it was peasants they were discussing, so how bright did they expect those men to be?"

"They must be hoping for unusual luck, but they'll certainly be disappointed," Bensia said, letting Travin see her complete agreement. "Sembrin keeps forgetting that it's peasants we have to deal with, not members of the nobility. And you said that Feriun thought our men could be made to talk by the commoners in charge? What utter nonsense."

"Of course it's nonsense, but Father almost agreed with the fool before he remembered what he'd been told," Travin said with a snort of disdain. "We have nothing to fear from the commoners 'in charge,' and he should have known that without having to be told. Do you want my brother and sisters and me to accompany those men going out? *They* may not be able to make the crowds believe them, but we surely can."

"No, it doesn't pay to have you and the others risk yourselves," Bensia decided after a moment's thought. "If there was only one group of men going out, you and the others would be able to go with them. But with six or more groups going . . . No, I'd rather save your efforts for another time. If this current plan doesn't work, we'll have to find something that will."

"Father has a plan he means to follow this current plan with," Travin reminded her. "Do you know what it is, or do we need to ask him about it?"

"I believe I know what he has in mind, but we might as well ask just to be on the safe side," Bensia said, and then an amusing thought came to her. "In fact, I think I'll go and ask him right now, while he's . . . relaxing. Watching him doing things with thin air is more than simply amusing. It pays the man back for all those times he betrayed me with peasant whores."

"Betrayal *deserves* to be punished," Travin said solemnly, and then he leaned down to kiss her cheek. "You go ahead, Mother, and I'll tell the others what's happening."

"Thank you, Travin," Bensia said, returning his kiss warmly before walking away. It was marvelous to have sons who were devoted, and it was just too bad that those sons couldn't be had without needing to put up with the foolishness of a husband. Of course the children *could* be had without the efforts of a husband, just as Bensia had arranged matters, but appearance was *so* important . . .

Honrita Grohl made sure she wasn't being followed when she returned to Holdis Ayl's hideaway. His rooms were in a deserted area of the city, and the door leading into the building was opened by pulling on a torch sconce on the outside wall. Honrita stepped through the doorway and closed the door again behind herself, then continued up the hall to the door to Ayl's quarters. Ayl opened that door before she reached the end of the hall, his expression speaking to her before his words.

"Tell me you were able to reach him," Ayl said very flatly, and then he saw *her* expression. "No, you needn't bother answering, I can see that you've failed again."

"The failure still isn't mine," Honrita replied, making no effort to keep her annoyance out of her voice at the way Ayl had turned away from her. "The Fire magic user we want for the Blending is sick in bed, and since I've never met him I have no way of visiting him even for a moment. I can make someone *believe* he and I are old friends and get in to see him that way, but to what purpose? Until he's well enough to be up and about, having him join the rest of us will do nothing more than let us catch what *he's* got. Isn't there anyone you can replace him with?"

"No, he's the one I want and the one I mean to have," Ayl answered as he turned again to glare at her. "You will take our Earth magic user to him, and the Earth magic user will cure him."

"He's already *had* an Earth magic user in to work on him," Honrita said as she moved to the stove to make herself a cup of tea. "There's an infection of some kind in the man's blood, and the healer was only able to make the sickness a bit less severe. The Fire magic user's own body has to overcome the infection, and until it does the man will stay sick. The man's mother doesn't remember that she told me those details, and the healer doesn't remember that I confirmed the facts with *him*. If there's no other Fire magic user that you're willing to accept, all we can do is wait until the man is healthy again."

"I detest the need for such a delay," Ayl said as he sat himself in a straight-backed chair, the only sort of chair his rooms had. "So far nothing has been able to stand in my way, and now . . . *this*."

"There may be a good reason for this delay," Honrita quickly pointed out, her talent telling her that Ayl was on the thin edge of losing his sanity entirely. The man was extremely unstable, and only his "purpose" had so far kept him from complete raving madness. If he began to doubt that purpose . . .

"What reason, good or otherwise, could a delay like this possibly have?" Ayl countered, but with less stiff-necked arrogance than usual. "As I'm meant to rule, I should be able to do so quickly."

"It's just possible that this is the wrong time for us to attempt to put your puppets on the throne," Honrita said, using the excuse she'd thought up on the way back here. "The others and I have to learn to Blend and also have to learn how to use our Blending. Then we'll use our Middle Blending to take over a High Blending, one member at a time. If all of that goes as quickly and easily as we know it will, we won't have a reason to delay our plans. It could be your own destiny that's causing this delay, to make sure that we strike only at the very best time."

"My own destiny, protecting me from failure," Ayl murmured, his gaze inward as he considered the idea. "Yes, now I see your point and I believe you may be correct. As I am destined to rule behind my puppets, I must be kept from moving at the wrong time."

Ayl nodded just a bit to silently add to his agreement, obviously having no idea that *Honrita* had added to his belief with her talent. Ayl thought—no, *knew*—that no one could touch him with talent without his being aware of the effort, but that knowledge was part of the arrogance of his madness. Ayl could be touched even more easily than normal people, as Ayl was one of those who were able to judge ability in others but had no ability of their own. Ayl now believed in Honrita's loyalty completely, just as she wanted him to.

*And he'll keep believing in my loyalty until the moment I push him aside and take over,* Honrita thought as she turned back to the stove to see if the tea water had begun to boil yet. *My father died before I could get even with him for rejecting me the way he did, but Ayl is just the way my father was. I can get even with my father by ruining Ayl's plans, and when he sees me ruling in the place he thought was his he'll be looking at me with my father's eyes.*

That concept was a warming one for Honrita, so much so that she prepared two cups against the time that the tea was ready. Ayl was going to make her ruler of the empire of Gandistra; the least she could do in return was share the tea she'd meant to make for herself alone . . .

Holdis Ayl sat straight in his chair in the proper way, seeing the Grohl woman only out of the corner of his eyes. The faint smile he wore was the same smile he always wore, which meant that the woman was unlikely to know the direction of his thoughts. The woman was even more of a fool than other women, but she was considerably more useful than those others.

*Yes, my dear, I believe what you said but not because of your talent,* Ayl thought, his smile no more than a faint reflection of his feelings. *Your talent slides past me in a way that most of my former "peers" were unable to match, with only the trail of your attempt left to show for the effort. You mean to betray me in the moment of my ultimate success, having no idea that I am aware of your intentions and am therefore on guard against the betrayal.*

But one thing the woman had said *was* the truth. It was indeed his destiny that now protected him, just as it was his destiny that had brought the woman to him in the first place. He'd grown impatient waiting for the *right* Spirit magic user to appear, and so had tried to use the one most easily manipulated. The man had been a total disaster and failure as a tool, but the fool *had* been the means by which the proper Spirit magic user had come within his reach.

And now that he had almost every one of the proper tools, his plans would go forward as soon as his destiny thought that the time was right. He would have his own Blending to use, and even though they were all Middle talents they would have no trouble taking over High talents one by one. And as soon as the High Spirit magic user was his, the fool of a woman who thought to steal his destiny would be put in her proper place.

*And her proper place will be unlike that of the rest of the populace,* Ayl thought, his inner smile wide and wild. *For daring to presume, the Grohl woman will serve me on her knees with unquestioning love in her heart. The others will be permitted to stand and simply bow, but she . . .*

Ayl felt his outward smile grow the least bit, and for that reason put all thoughts of future justice out of his mind. The time would come, and when it did his smile would be very visible indeed . . .

# FOUR

Feeling uncertain wasn't a familiar state for any of us, but I definitely felt the emotion and I was convinced that my Blendingmates did as well. Borvri Tonsun, the invader of Gracely that we'd questioned, had told us things that suggested his "leaders" were a lot stronger than my Blendingmates and I. We'd already suspected that the possibility was a fact, and having the guess confirmed didn't do any of us any good. After questioning the invader from West Tallvin, the six of us moved a short distance away to talk privately.

"Okay, what do we do now?" I asked when no one else spoke up. "That man said his country had High Blendings when those 'leader' people showed up, but their Blendings didn't keep them from being taken over. If we face the rest of these invaders toe to toe we'll probably lose to them, and I don't like the idea of losing."

"None of us likes the idea of losing, Tamma," Jovvi said with a sigh that Naran joined. "Personally, I almost wish we could just turn around and go home, but I have the definite feeling that running now will mean the end of everything. After the invaders have taken Gracely, they'll come after *our* country next."

"Yes, the probability of that is very high," Naran confirmed, looking as though she wished she didn't have to agree. "From what little I can See, our turning away from this problem leads to nothing but dead ends and total defeat for everyone. The only chance our side has is if we fight those people, which may mean we'll think of something to help us win. At least I hope that that's what it means."

"Well, I can't see us runnin' anyway unless innocent lives were at stake," Vallant said after taking a deep breath. "Turnin' to run only gives your enemy a chance at your back, and we don't have to wonder if this enemy will take advantage of that kind of chance. That means we have plans to make that don't include travelin', and the first thing we have to decide is what to do with all those invaders we captured."

"We can't kill them," Lorand said at once, his tone as serious as the look in his pretty brown eyes. "Those people are slaves rather than villains, and they don't even really know what they're doing. Killing them for being victims would make us just as bad as those 'leaders' of theirs."

"Would it be wise to free them from control, as we did with that Borvri Tonsun fellow?" Rion asked, his brow creased in a small frown. "I dislike the thought of leaving *anyone* in the complete control of those who care nothing about their true welfare."

"I don't think that turning them all loose would be a good idea right now," Jovvi said, a definite sadness in her expression. "I agree with Lorand that we can't kill them, but we really should ask ourselves whose side those men would be on—if anyone's."

"What do you mean, whose side would they be on?" Vallant asked, just about taking the words out of my mouth. "Wouldn't *you* be against anyone who had put you under their control and made you kill?"

"I think all of *us* would be frothing at the mouth to get even, yes," Jovvi agreed, the sadness still with her. "That doesn't mean these men will react in the same way, though. Borvri Tonsun was even afraid to talk to us, remember, for fear that the 'leaders' would kill him for giving away their secrets. Some people don't have the courage to stand up to their oppressors, and there are about a hundred men in this group. Even if only half of them are as afraid as Borvri Tonsun, what will we do with them? Send them away with the refugees and the people of this village? What if they're too afraid to run? What if they either go right back to be conditioned again, or try to hurt some innocents to keep their 'leaders' from hurting *them*?"

"I hadn't even thought of that," Lorand said in a mutter while the rest of us stood silent, watching him run his hands through his hair as he avoided everyone's eyes. "I was all ready to ask our associate Blendings to free them the way Tonsun was freed, but we can't do that now, can we?"

"No, I fear we must think of something else to do with them," Rion agreed in a tired voice, as though he were consigning those innocents to death—or worse than death. "To allow others to come to harm because of our own needs and prejudices would be inexcusable."

"Not to mention the fact that we don't want them warnin' our enemies," Vallant pointed out with a headshake. "At the moment I'd say there's only one thing we can do with those men, and that's scatter them through the woods along the road to this village. We may end up needin' their help when those 'leaders' of theirs get here."

"To fight fire with fire," I said, a sudden idea coming to me. "You know, this won't help against Blendings that are stronger than we are, but it's come to me that we didn't do everything we could against these invaders while they were protected from our talent. We tried to touch *them*, but we never tried to affect the world they moved through. How many people would they have been able to kill if the ground had collapsed under them, throwing them into a deep pit?"

"Not many, especially if the pit was suddenly filled with water," Vallant said, now looking a good deal happier. "I wonder how we missed thinkin' of that sooner?"

"We probably missed it because the first thing a Blending entity does is try to control individuals," Lorand said, also looking less depressed. "When we discovered we couldn't reach those invaders, all our attention went toward breaching their protection."

"Which we now know will gain us little or nothing," Rion said, clearly agreeing as much as the others. "And that may well be the answer we need for besting those 'leader' people. If they find themselves unable to breathe, how strong will their Blending entity be?"

"That will work only if they haven't already formed their Blending," Jovvi pointed out, but she wasn't really arguing. "What we need is a closer look at our enemies, one that will give us some desperately needed answers about them. Borvri Tonsun told us that the force coming behind his is about a day and a half from reaching here. The first thing we have to do is get all these innocent people out of this village, and then we can discuss how to get our closer look at the enemy without letting them know we're there."

"And I'm afraid we'll have to put Tonsun back under control," Vallant said, speaking the words that I, personally, hadn't wanted to speak. "We can't afford to have him runnin' around loose, not when we don't know what he'll do once his owners get here. If he was the kind of man who was willin' to fight them, he wouldn't have needed our help to tell us what was goin' on."

"Vallant, you'll have to have our associate Blending put him back under control," Jovvi said, her expression more vexed than apologetic. "Just as I couldn't free him by myself, I can't now put him under strong enough control that his leaders won't be able to take him right back. For all our sakes, he needs to be held as tightly as possible."

"I'll see to it right away," Vallant said, looking just as vexed as Jovvi. "And I'll also get the rest of them hidden in the woods where they can feed themselves, with orders not to show themselves unless specifically directed to do so. We don't want them poppin' up at the wrong time."

There was nothing any of us wanted to say to that, so Vallant moved a few feet away to speak to the Blending entity that waited to give us what help we needed. The rest of us just stood there in the dark of very early morning, all but huddled around the light I'd kindled to let us see where we were going and what we were doing. The air was more cool than cold, middle-of-the-night cool that made you think about the comfortable blanket waiting for you in your bed. We hadn't had our own beds for a very long time, and now it looked like getting back to those beds would take even longer.

"I really wish this was over," Jovvi murmured, her arms wrapped about herself. "Back in Gan Garee I thought that being 'stuck' in the palace was a terrible fate, but right now even a small farmhouse would look good if we were going to be staying there for a while. I never knew I was such a . . . homebody."

"I'm really glad you said that," Lorand told her as he folded his own arms around hers. "I'd pretty much decided that I was the only one who was tired of being constantly on the move, so I didn't mention the feeling. Now I feel a lot less alone."

"You're even more not-alone than you know," I put in, touching his arm briefly. "I've been dreaming about being back in my house, and every time I wake up to find that I'm not really there . . ."

"The disappointment is almost crushing," Rion finished when I didn't, a wry smile turning his lips. "I've had my share of the same dream, and it was *your* house I dreamed about. Once Naran joined us there, it was the happiest time of my life."

"And of mine," Naran said with a better smile as she took Rion's hand. "I've spent most of my life on the move, never staying in one place too long, so it's no wonder that I consider Tamrissa's house as the haven I never had before. If we were back there now, I'd be incredibly content."

"Naran, are you saying that you've also dreamed of Tamma's house?" Jovvi asked, a small frown on her face. "And what about you, Lorand? Have you been thinking about the house you grew up in, or being back in Tamma's house?"

"Actually, it *is* Tamrissa's house that I've been missing most and dreaming about," Lorand answered, his own frown matching Jovvi's. "And now I'd like to hear Naran's answer."

"Yes, of course it was Tamrissa's house I've been dreaming about," Naran said with a small headshake. "How could it be anywhere else? And why are you all looking at me like that? I've just done the same as everyone but Jovvi and Vallant."

"You can't exclude Jovvi from the group," Jovvi said, obviously trying to lighten a situation that had grown heavy with some kind of portent. "I've also had the dream of being back in Tamma's house, and this is too much of a coincidence for it to *be* a coincidence. Would anyone like to bet gold against the possibility that Vallant has had the same dream as well?"

"That would be like betting gold against a complete certainty, so stop trying to cheat us," I said, and the words managed to bring a brief smile to everyone. "Instead, why don't you tell us what this could possibly mean?"

"Sure," Jovvi responded with a sound of ridicule that was totally unlike her. "It means we're all homesick for the safety and comfort we found in your house, even if it *was* only for a short while. What else could it possibly mean?"

We all shook our heads at her, I, at least, hating the way she'd said she had no idea of what the dreams meant. It was another really annoying mystery to add to the rest, and when Vallant suddenly rejoined us he looked at each of us with a frown.

"What's happenin' now?" he asked, and there was almost accusation in his tone. "I leave the bunch of you alone for no more than five minutes, and you find somethin' else to worry about as soon as my back is turned. So what is it now, and just how dangerous will it turn out to be?"

"Before we answer *your* question, you have to answer one of ours," I said, doing the honors this time. "Have you been dreaming of being back in my house?"

"As a matter of fact, I have," he said, and his frown had deepened. "Is that supposed to mean I'll be messin' up in some way because I don't really want to be here?"

"What it means is we now have confirmation that all of us have had the same dream about being back in Tamma's house," Jovvi said, her smile a good deal less soothing than it normally was. "We would love to know what the dream means, but so far nothing has come to us."

"And please don't say that it might not mean anything," Lorand put in when Vallant parted his lips to speak. "If all six of us are having the same dream, I'll bet everything I own that it means something very specific."

"I was *goin'* to say that just because we don't know what the dream means, that doesn't mean we won't find out at some time," Vallant told Lorand with just a trace of injured feelings. "I was also goin' to add that the invaders are bein' taken care of by our associate Blendin's, but there's somethin' *we* need to look into. One of the associates told me that there was a fairly heavy stir of activity over by the place where the Gracelian assembly members were watchin' the goin's-on. No one has gone over to find out what happened, so we'd better take a look."

"And after we find out what they've done wrong this time, I hope we can get some more sleep," Naran said with a sigh. "The next time I wake up I'm going to make a concerted effort to break through that flux that's been keeping me from Seeing more than bits and snatches. I'm tired of being surprised by everything but what we absolutely have to know."

"You know, that's exactly the way it *has* been," I said, distracted from her first, out-of-character statement by a flash of revelation. "You haven't been able to see much of anything beyond the completely essential, and that can't possibly be a coincidence either. Someone has to be deliberately blocking you."

"Could the enemy really be strong enough to reach all the way here to block Naran without us being aware of it?" Lorand asked, worry widening his eyes. "If they are, we have even more trouble than we thought."

"It can't possibly be the invaders," I said while everyone else just came up with exclamations of worry and startlement. "Naran's had this trouble since before we left Gan Garee, and if the invaders are *that* strong we might as well just stand here and let them take us over. No, someone else is responsible for blindfolding us, and I'd really like to know who that is."

"Who *could* it be?" Vallant countered, but not in a challenging way. "I'd be willin' to believe that Ristor Ardanis, leader of those with Sight magic, is behind the blockin', but he and most of his people are a long way away from here. Naran, are you absolutely certain that the people in your link groups are workin' *with* you rather than against your breakin' through?"

"Normally I might not be absolutely certain, but once I'm part of the Blending there's no doubt," Naran answered with a nod. "My people are trying as hard as I am, but something is keeping us from breaking through."

"It certainly can't be the Gracelians," Jovvi said, her distracted gaze saying that her mind searched for an answer. "The Gracelians don't *have* anyone with Sight magic, so they can't possibly affect it. Who does that leave?"

"No one but the Highest Aspect," I said, finding it impossible to keep the dryness from my tone. "If the enemy isn't doing it, the Gracelians aren't doing it, and Ristor Ardanis's people aren't doing it, there's no one left."

"But there *is* someone left," Rion disagreed slowly, his gaze as distracted as Jovvi's had been. "We haven't mentioned the fact in quite some time, but there's still a mystery in our lives that we haven't solved. Those 'signs' the Prophecies spoke of . . . We've denied that they ever happened, but they did happen and we still don't know who was responsible for causing them."

"And we don't know who was responsible for bringing us all together," Lorand took his turn to point out. "A minute or two ago we were refusing to accept all those dreams as a coincidence, but we never questioned the even bigger coincidence that we all ended up in the same residence. We are each of us the strongest practitioner of our respective talents, and we all just *happened* to end up in the same residence and made into a Blending? If you can believe *that,* then you must also believe that the Highest Aspect leaves a copper coin under our pillows as a reward for having gone through the five-year-old tests successfully."

"It looks like someone's been makin' a *lot* of things happen around us," Vallant observed, vexation showing on his face as strongly as I felt it inside me. "So there's some group, large or small, makin' these things happen, but we don't know if they're friend or foe. Until we find out just what their aim is, we can't call them one or the other."

"Well, one of their aims *was* to bring us together," I suggested, thinking about it even as I spoke. "If they're friends of ours, they did it so that we could win the throne and get rid of the nobility. If they're enemies, they did it to put us all in the same place so we could be gotten rid of with a single effort. If *we* get taken down, everyone knows that no one else is as strong as we are and so they might not even put up a token struggle. By winning over us, the enemy would win over everyone else at the same time."

"I see a flaw in that logic," Lorand said, another of us almost lost to distraction. "These unknown someones have obviously known about us since before we got together in Gan Garee. Putting us all together just to conquer us at the same time makes no sense, not when they could have killed us one at a time before we knew what we were doing. If they had, there would *be* no 'others' to worry about, only the Middle Seated Blending the nobles picked out. Even an arrogant enemy would never go to such lengths just to best six people."

"I'm forced to agree with that," Vallant said even as Jovvi nodded her own agreement. "What's the sense in havin' almost a dozen more enemies, when killin' a few people will give you no enemies to speak of at all? These invader leaders just rolled over all opposition until it was crushed, and then it took over the people and used them for their own purposes. That means there's definitely someone else in the game."

"And we're being used by them," Jovvi said, closing the circle that I seemed to have opened. "There has definitely been someone interfering in our lives, and that fact suggests that the someone is also interfering with Naran's talent. There are things about to happen that they don't want us to know about in advance, but it shouldn't be because they're our enemies. If they weren't on our side, we would hardly be standing here discussing the matter now."

"That idea isn't very flattering," I had to point out when no one else said anything in response to Jovvi's conclusion.

"Keeping us in the dark suggests that we do better reacting to a situation as it happens than we do after we think about the circumstance. If they're trying to tell us that we're not built to think, I'm definitely feeling insulted."

"I really don't believe that that's what Jovvi—or our mysterious others—are saying," Naran told me with a laugh that had everyone else joining in. "It's probably just a matter of their wanting our entity to do the reacting and thinking rather than us as individuals. Our entity does things that sometimes horrifies us afterward, and if we knew about the need in advance we might be able to influence the entity against doing what was needed."

"That makes sense to *me,* at least," Lorand said, looking a bit shamefaced. "The rest of you have found it easier to accept what we've sometimes needed to do, but the horror of some of it still disturbs me. I feel the urge to say that we ought to have a choice about whether or not to add to that horror, but there's too much at stake here. If we don't do something necessary because of my tender sensibilities, a lot of innocent people will pay the price for my squeamishness."

"It isn't squeamishness, Lorand," Vallant said, and it seemed that he'd taken the words out of Jovvi's mouth this time. "Tamrissa, Rion, and I seem to be the most aggressive ones in this group, and in my opinion we *need* people with real consciences to balance us out. That balance consists of you, Jovvi, and Naran, so there's a good chance that Naran isn't bein' allowed to See very far because she would want to do what *you* would. Which means I'm wonderin' if you really should try forcin' your way through that flux again, Naran."

"I've been wondering the same thing for the last few minutes, Vallant," Naran answered, her pretty face showing the ghost of disturbance. "Let me think about the matter for a while, and then we can all discuss it again before I do any forcing."

"That's more than sensible and reasonable, so we'll table the discussion for a while," Vallant agreed with one of those smiles I like so much. "Meanwhile, let's go and find out what's happenin' with the Gracelian assembly people."

Jovvi and Rion made sounds of surprise, leading me to believe that they'd forgotten about the Gracelians just as I had. The mystery had distracted us all, but since there was nothing we could do about solving it right now it only made sense to go on to other things.

Vallant and I—along with the light I'd kept burning—led the way back into the village and through it. Vallant suggested that we stop to check on the new Blending members on our way, but one glance told us that it would be a waste of time to stop. All twenty members of the new Gracelian High Blendings were dead asleep, which really came as no surprise. They'd used all of their strength removing the protection from half of the invaders, and they'd probably let themselves collapse once they saw that *we'd* taken over to handle the rest.

"There won't be any wakin' them before mornin'," Vallant said as we walked past the unmoving bodies. "I remember how much I needed sleep when I was in *their* place, more than I needed almost anythin' beyond breathin'. Too bad *you* don't remember feelin' the same way."

"Don't rub it in," I grumbled, finding it impossible not to laugh at the same time. Back when *we* were in the same position, Vallant had fallen asleep when he was supposed to stay awake and make love to me. I'd been so hurt and disappointed that I'd been ready to swear that I'd never speak to him again, and he'd had to come up with a really wild story to get me past the feeling. We'd long since gotten the matter completely straightened out, but remembering the time was still enough to make me blush with thinking how innocent I'd been.

I hadn't been that innocent for quite some time, so when we finally reached the camping place of the Gracelian assembly members and everything seemed quiet I felt more suspicion than relief. If the previous disturbance had been bad enough for our associate Blending to call it "heavy," then everything shouldn't be peaceful and quiet now.

"I hope you've come to tell us that you've found a way to defeat the invaders," Antrie Lorimon said as she and Cleemor Gardan came toward us out of the dark. "After everything that's happened, we could use some *good* news."

"No, unfortunately, we haven't found any magical ways to defeat those invaders," I answered, finding it impossible not to notice how really weary both Antrie and Cleemor looked. "We're here because we were told there was some trouble. Is it anything we can help with?"

"Probably not," Antrie answered, and there were tears in her eyes as if she were crying without knowing it. "Thrybin Korge is probably going to die, and Zirdon Tal will be the one who killed him."

# FIVE

"We've been discussing whether to execute Tal before Korge dies or after," Jovvi heard Cleemor Gardan say as she stared at the two Gracelians in surprise. "There's also the problem that the attack against Korge was due to Korge's playing games again, so the matter could almost be considered suicide. If having someone plunge a knife into your back can be looked at as suicide."

"What kind of games was Korge playing?" Jovvi asked as Lorand hurried off after exchanging a glance with her. Lorand was going to see what *he* could do for the victim, and it was Jovvi's job to speak to Antrie and Cleemor and try to calm them.

"Tal told us that Korge tried to talk him into killing *your* group," Cleemor said with a sigh, responding to Jovvi's soothing without seeming to be aware of it. "Tal pretended to be uninterested, but once you'd all Blended and your bodies were unprotected, he took a knife and went after you. He said he'd almost reached you when the truth finally came to him. *You* weren't the ones this country had to be protected from, the real villains were those of us who still pretended to be leaders. He turned around and came back to kill all of *us,* and Korge was his first target."

"The rest of us were Blended and watching what was going on with the invaders," Antrie said after taking a deep breath. She'd stopped crying, which meant that she was also responding to Jovvi's soothing. "We noticed nothing, of

49

course, but Zirdon had apparently forgotten about Thrybin's former Blendingmates. They couldn't Blend without Thrybin, but they were trying to follow what was going on by individually using the power the way we do in challenges. Korge was doing the same, so he had no idea that Zirdon was near him until Zirdon plunged that knife into his back. When Thrybin screamed, his former Blendingmates in Spirit and Earth magic took control of Zirdon."

"Well, at least Tal started with the proper victim," Tamma said with a headshake. "It was an absolute guarantee that Korge would make trouble for *someone,* so isn't it nice that the someone turned out to be himself? If Korge didn't deserve it, no one in this world does."

"How can you say that?" Antrie put to Tamma, the Gracelian's distress clear enough to see even without Spirit magic. "You sound as if you think we ought to be pleased that Thrybin is dying, but that just isn't possible. The man was a colleague of ours, another human being even if he *wasn't* everything a man should be. Being attacked like that shouldn't happen to anyone, not even Thrybin Korge."

"That has to be one of the most ridiculous things I've ever heard," Tamma stated flatly, looking at both Antrie and Cleemor. "Korge wasn't just attacked, he brought the attack on himself and you know it. He wasn't an innocent victim, he was someone who should never have been allowed near *any* kind of power. He shouldn't have *been* a colleague of yours, and Zirdon Tal shouldn't have been one either. The bunch of you let those two twisted fools get into positions of power and authority, and they were almost responsible for *your* destruction as well as their own. If you refuse to do the right thing, you can't complain when tragedy strikes."

"And you were supposed to have Tal under control," Vallant pointed out before Cleemor could come to Antrie's defense. "You can't claim you didn't know how unstable Tal is, not and still be tellin' the truth. You also knew how frantic Korge was, especially once his Blendin'mates refused to Blend with him again. Anyone with half a brain would have *known* that Korge would try to make trouble, but the bunch of you just let him go his way and do anythin' he pleased. Now you stand here cryin' about how Korge is a human bein' and didn't deserve to have a knife plunged into his back. If you'd sent him back to Liandia after the first time he tried to play games, if you'd done somethin' really effective with Tal, none of this would have happened."

"But the truth of the matter is, you people would rather play politics than be effective," Rion said, once again forestalling Cleemor. "You know exactly what *should* be done, but fear of having the same thing done to you in retaliation holds you back from doing as you should. There should never *be* retaliation for doing the necessary, but those who live their lives playing politics find that impossible to understand."

"But that won't be going on for much longer, will it?" Antrie asked bitterly, looking from one to the other of her accusers. "Our positions of power will soon be gone, our way of life about to be forced into something else entirely. We may be guilty of many things, but destroying the lives of people who never did anything to *us* is a charge that can only be leveled against *you* wonderful people."

"I'm sorry, Antrie, but you can't put the blame for that on us," Jovvi said, deciding it was time she aired her own thoughts. "You and the rest of your innocent people were given the chance to make the right decision. If you had, your lives would have changed only a little in response to the threat of the invaders. But instead of doing the intelligent thing, you chose to cling to your old ways which had already been proven totally ineffective. You chose the familiar over the absolutely necessary, still playing politics even when people's lives were in danger. If you refuse to change with the times, you can't complain when you get left behind."

"And weeping over a fool only shows how ineffective you really are," Naran said, surprising the others as much as she did Jovvi. "The only reason you wish Korge was unharmed is because you're afraid the same thing could happen to the rest of you. You're incapable of changing enough to defend yourselves, so your only answer to the danger is to wish it away. Unfortunately for you, the real world doesn't *let* us wish things like that away."

"You all think you know so much," Cleemor said, speaking as bitterly as Antrie had. "Changing isn't nearly as easy as you make it sound, and maybe someday *you'll* be unlucky enough to find that out. You'll try to cling to what *you* think is right, and the real world you're so fond of will plow you under in the same way that's being done to us. You'll understand us a bit better then, but the time will be far too late to offer us your apologies."

"We understand you well enough right now that I can guarantee there won't be any apologies offered," Lorand's voice came, and then Lorand joined them with Olskin Dinno and Satlan Reesh coming up behind him. "We know how you feel, Gardan, because we watched the nobles in our own land behaving in the same way. Anyone with eyes would have seen that the nobles were heading for disaster, but they just kept blithely on, playing their games the way they always did. If the day ever comes that we refuse to change our ways in response to something necessary, we'll deserve to be plowed under as much as you deserve it right now."

Cleemor glanced at his two countrymen who stood behind Lorand, but Jovvi knew well enough that neither Dinno nor Reesh would try to argue on Cleemor's and Antrie's behalf. The two newcomer Gracelians felt sympathy for their embattled colleagues, but a definite lack of agreement kept the men from defending the others. It took a moment for Cleemor to realize that Dinno and Reesh would remain silent, but once he did he took Antrie's arm and the two of them simply walked away.

"I really feel sorry for those people," Reesh said with a sigh once Cleemor and Antrie were gone. "They aren't bad people, you understand, just trapped by their private lives. Antrie is afraid of what people will say about her, and Gardan . . . He's afraid that his wife won't stay with him if he loses his place in the assembly, but if he goes along with the new ways she might leave him anyway. I never thought I'd be saying this, but I'm beginning to believe that being disliked by those around you gives you an odd kind of freedom."

"You don't have to be disliked to have that kind of freedom," Dinno said with a faint smile as he clapped Reesh on the shoulder. "You just have to understand that you can't please everyone in the world, so you might as well do what's right and in that way please yourself. Lorand tells us that you've captured that group of invaders, but you don't consider it an accomplishment. Do you really think that the next group of invaders will be too strong for you to handle?"

"It's not the ones who do the killin' who worry us, but the ones who direct them," Vallant said with a shrug. "We have reason to believe that they may be a lot stronger than we are, which means they'll be stronger than everyone else as well. Is Korge healed enough to be moved? Your groups and the villagers will have to leave this area, just in case we can't stop the next invaders."

"Korge is a good deal better, now that Lorand has worked on him," Dinno said with a wry smile. "I've never seen a healer as good, but I do feel rather foolish. Lorand asked why I hadn't used my Blending to increase my strength in healing, and the only answer possible was that I just didn't think of it."

"None of us is used to thinking about our Blendings in that way," Reesh said, obviously trying to reassure Dinno. "Assembly protocol denied us the right to Blend except under certain very strict circumstances. That made us used to acting alone rather than with the others, so your reaction is completely understandable."

"But still not very smart," Dinno said, his smile taking the sting out of his words. "If I don't change my own way of thinking, I can't very well stand here and criticize anyone else. I assume you want us all to start leaving at first light?"

"No, actually, I think it would be best to get as many people goin' now as we can," Vallant said, answering the question that had been put specifically to him. "The roads will be clogged as it is, and havin' everyone tryin' to run away at the last minute won't help to keep them safe."

"Then we ought to start with the people who are up and around," Reesh said with a thoughtful frown. "After that we can start to wake people and let them pull themselves together before we send them on their way."

"Try not to let any of them stop until you reach the city," Tamma said, her tone more gentle and concerned than usual. "If we have to retreat as we fight, we don't want to have to worry about running over any innocents."

"Just telling everyone that more invaders are coming ought to keep them going," Dinno said with a sigh and a nod. "It's a good thing we aren't all that far from Liandia, but it's also a bad thing. If the entire population of the city has to run, I have no idea where they'll all go."

"When you get to the city, try to put together a few more High Blendin's," Vallant said softly. "We'll do the best we can out here, but you'll need some protectin' in case our best isn't enough."

Both Dinno and Reesh stared at Vallant for a moment before nodding, and then the two Gracelians turned and walked away. Neither one said anything about wishing them good luck, but Jovvi knew that that was because of how frightened the men were. Intellectually they knew that their champions could well lose the fight, but emotionally they weren't able to even consider the possibility.

"And now we have to start sending people on their way," Jovvi said with a sigh, mostly to break the uncomfortable silence. "But it occurs to me that we ought to try to get the Gracelian High Blendings their own link groups. Some of those who had no interest in being part of a true Blending might be willing to act as part of a link group."

"I don't believe we missed thinkin' of that," Vallant said with a groan that more than one of their Blendingmates echoed. "And I was foolish enough to think that we'd be able to get some sleep soon."

"Vallant, we *have* to get some sleep soon," Rion pointed out almost immediately. "There are things that have to be done before the next invaders get here, and they won't be accomplished if we're falling off our collective feet. Our

Blending and Holter's are the two strongest among us. Both of our groups will have to sleep while the others take care of the details."

"He's right, love," Tamma told Vallant gently before Vallant could voice the protest clear in his lovely eyes. "You know I prefer to be in charge whenever possible, but there are certain times when being in charge will do more harm than good. This is one of those times."

"You're both right, so I surrender," Vallant agreed with a tired smile. "We and our link groups will be needin' all the rest we can get, and it's time the other Blendin's got to do some of the work anyway. I'll let everyone know what the plan is, and then we'll get out of the way."

Jovvi could tell that Vallant was still faintly reluctant to leave overseeing the details to others, but he still walked off to speak to the others. That meant they would all soon be able to lie down, and Jovvi was looking forward to the time more than a little.

"You look really tired, love," Lorand said softly to Jovvi as he put an arm around her shoulders. "When Vallant gets back, I'm going to suggest that we take Rion up on his offer to provide private places for us to sleep in. Not only do we deserve some privacy, but I'm almost as reluctant as Vallant to let others be in charge of our safety. If I can't see what's going on, I won't have any choice but to let go for a while."

"How did you know about Vallant's reluctance?" Jovvi asked, sudden curiosity distracting her from weariness. "And did you notice how oddly Naran and Tamma have been behaving from time to time? Naran said things to Antrie and Cleemor that would have been more fitting coming from Tamma, and Tamma was actually patient and supportive when she spoke to Olskin Dinno, Satlan Reesh, and even Vallant."

"Yes, I noticed both of those things," Lorand replied, his headshake one of mystification. "I don't understand why they acted that way any more than I know how I know about Vallant's reluctance. And you can add another oddity to your list: the calmly firm way that Rion spoke to Vallant. It was almost as if they'd swapped places while we weren't watching."

"There's so much we really need to think and talk about, but there just isn't any time," Jovvi said, faint annoyance suddenly growing stronger. "I'm beginning to believe more and more strongly that those mysterious someones we were talking about are playing games with us. If that turns out to be true, I think I'm going to get really nasty when we finally find them."

"Now *you're* sounding like Tamrissa, and I'm feeling like Naran," Lorand said with another, stronger headshake. "I have the feeling that we *will* find those someones, but the meeting won't be anything like what we might picture."

"I'm really much too tired for this," Jovvi said, closing her eyes briefly as she echoed Lorand's headshake. "And to make my position even more clear, I don't know when I *won't* be too tired to face all this."

"Personally, I've decided to ignore it all for now," Tamma said, obviously having heard the exchange. "But when we do find those someones, I'll be the one who handles the nasty."

"Not without me," Lorand said, just as Rion put in, "Along with *my* help." That made all of them look at each other while Jovvi groaned silently. Naran's expression of firm agreement made them *all* look and sound like Tamma, and that was really more than Jovvi could bear.

"All right, everythin's set," Vallant announced as he reappeared. "Holter's Blendin' didn't like the idea any more than we did, but they also aren't arguin' . . . What's goin' on? You're all agitated and roilin' on the inside."

Jovvi closed her eyes again while a couple of groans were voiced, but Lorand just sighed.

"If you ask yourself how you knew we were all agitated, Vallant, you just might be able to answer your own question," Lorand said. He sounded as tired as Jovvi felt, and Jovvi didn't have to wonder why. "We seem to be borrowing each other's attitudes and talents, and we can't figure out why it's happening—or how."

"If we live through all this, I just may take a trip to Astinda to visit our former nobles," Vallant said, his anger too overshadowed by weariness for the emotion to really be in control. "Beatin' up some chosen few of those people may not accomplish anythin' to speak of, but it will sure as chaos make *me* feel better."

"I know I don't need to say that you won't make the journey alone, but I'll say it anyway," Rion pronounced. "Now, however, I believe it's time we retired. If we end up being bested, I would really dislike being too tired to appreciate the manner in which it's done. Where would we be best off putting our privacy areas?"

Rather than pointing out the oddness in Rion's being sarcastic, Jovvi joined the others in looking around. They were much too close to the far side of the village, an area that almost everyone would be leaving through.

"I think we ought to set up near the Gracelian High Blendings," Lorand said after a moment. "That's close enough to the other side of the village that we shouldn't be in anyone's way, and we'll also be closer to the road that the invaders will arrive on."

Everyone agreed with that, so they trooped back to the place they'd come from. Going back also let them reclaim their sleeping pads, and once they'd positioned the pads in pairs with a discreet distance between the pairs, the rest of them stood back while Rion stepped forward. Jovvi expected it to take Rion at least a short while to produce their privacy areas, but an instant after Rion stepped forward there were three dark oblongs blocking sight of the sleeping pads.

"Shouldn't we have been on the inside before you did that?" Vallant asked as he stared at the oblongs. "Gettin' in and out without your help might be a problem."

"I didn't harden the air, I merely made it opaque," Rion answered with a smile. "We all have blankets to protect us from the cool of the night air, and maintaining simple opacity will be easier for the others as well as for us. If for some reason any of us needs to leave the sleeping area for a brief time, leaving won't require the aid of someone with Air magic."

"Good thinking, Rion," Lorand told him with a smile, and then he turned to Jovvi. "Come on, love, let's get you bedded down."

Jovvi had no need to be asked that twice, so she went along with Lorand while Tamma went with Vallant and Naran with Rion. They were finally back to their original pairings, with Naran and Rion no longer separated by misunderstanding. The arrangement was a relief to Jovvi, but one other thing wasn't: Lorand and Vallant were still showing faint traces of jealousy, and Jovvi was very much afraid that those feelings would bring trouble at the very worst of times . . .

"Why are you just sitting there?" Lorand asked, and Jovvi came back to awareness to realize that they were in their privacy area and she was sitting on her sleeping pad. The fact that she didn't remember walking in and sitting down would have been upsetting under other circumstances, but with everything that had been going on it was a miracle that she even remembered her name.

"I was just appreciating how nicely dim and private it is in here," Jovvi temporized as she looked around, not in the mood to explain the truth. "We don't have as much room as we did in the tents, but we do have privacy enough for me to get out of these clothes. I'll enjoy sleeping a lot more without them."

"Yes, that's a good idea," Lorand agreed, and then he began to undress the way she was already doing. Jovvi merely folded her clothing in a pile near her sleeping pad, and once she put herself under her blanket she became aware that Lorand's shadowy face was turned in her direction.

"Is something wrong?" she asked, reaching out to touch the face that seemed to be studying her even though they were nothing but shadows to each other.

"No, it's nothing," Lorand replied, and Jovvi could almost feel the faint, humorless smile curving his lips. "I was just waiting for you to be ready so that I could put my arms around you before you fell asleep."

"Is that the only thing you have interest in doing?" Jovvi asked, moving closer to him. "Just holding me while we both sleep? We could have done that without a privacy area."

"Do you really think I'd take advantage of you when you're this tired?" Lorand countered, sounding slightly offended and torn both at the same time. "You nearly emptied yourself of strength trying to break through the conditioning on that invader Borvri Tonsun, and now you need to sleep to regain your strength. We can make love again when you're feeling up to it."

"Our associate Blending returned a good measure of my strength, and I think you're forgetting something," Jovvi said, making sure that a smile was clear behind her words. "I may not be able to touch you and the others, but I can still tell what you're feeling. You have no more interest in going straight to sleep than I do, my love. You don't intend to make me force myself on you, do you?"

"That would be impossible, my love," Lorand returned, and now there was clear amusement in *his* words as his arms went around her. "For you to be able to force yourself on me I would have to be unwilling, and unwillingness is the only thing I'll never be able to give you. As long as you're sure I won't be taking advantage . . ."

"You'd never take advantage, and I know that even if you don't," Jovvi assured him as she moved even closer. The feel of his body against hers was as marvelous as it always was, but there was something the least bit odd about the contact. Lorand lowered his face to begin a kiss, and Jovvi joined him so quickly that all oddness disappeared. Being held in Lorand's arms had always been a magical experience for her, and this time was no different from the others.

Jovvi's rising desire quickly enhanced Lorand's, and they kissed and touched as though for the first time. After a very short time it was Lorand's burning need that fed Jovvi's, which meant that she was more than ready for him when he rose to his knees and began to enter her. Having Lorand in her possession was pure delight for Jovvi, and she was just about to give herself over to nothing but bodily sensations when Lorand ended their current kiss and put his lips right next to her ear.

"I may be fond of our sisters, my love, but I'll never feel for them what I feel for you," he murmured, the words more unthought-about than deliberate. "I've waited forever to have you back in my arms, and when the time comes for you to be gone again, I don't know how I'll bear it."

Lorand went back to kissing her then, and Jovvi wasn't able to do anything but respond to what his body did to hers. They shared love for a very long time, and once they'd both found release Lorand fell asleep almost immediately. Jovvi lay in his arms, expecting to find sleep almost as quickly, but the words he'd spoken kept echoing in her head.

*I may be fond of our sisters, but I'll never feel for them what I feel for you,* he'd said, and now that Jovvi could think again she also felt disturbed. Jovvi loved Lorand as much as she always had, but that oddness she'd felt when their bodies had first touched . . . She now knew the oddness stemmed from the fact that she felt just the same being held by Vallant or Rion. She still loved Lorand as much as she had, but somehow she'd started to feel the same about their Blending brothers.

But that wasn't the disturbing part. Jovvi felt Lorand's warmth where her hand lay on his arm, but an odd chill began inside her. For some reason *her* emotions seemed the proper ones, emotions she was meant to feel. But Lorand had said that he would never feel the same, and that idea kept her awake much longer than it should have. Something bad would happen because of it, somehow she *knew* something bad was going to happen . . .

# SIX

When Rion left the privacy area he'd created, the surrounding village struck him as odd. Even in the darkness he'd been aware of the presence of large numbers of people, many of whom were completely out of sight. Now . . .

"You feel it too, don't you, Rion?" Tamrissa's voice said, and he turned to see her approaching him. "We and all of our people are still here, but this village still feels empty and deserted."

"The evacuation seems to have been a complete success," Rion said after nodding his agreement. "But I did expect to see more Gracelians than just our four new Blendings. Weren't we going to get them link groups?"

"There weren't enough High talents to form link groups for even one of the new Blendings," Tamrissa said with a sigh. "Our associate Blending told me that Dinno and Reesh offered to round up High talents in Liandia and send them back to us, but until they get here we'll either have to share with the Gracelians or let them go it alone. Which we do will depend on what happens with the invaders."

"Has anyone checked on how close the invaders are now?" Rion asked as Naran left the privacy area to join them. "And is that breakfast I smell?"

"Yes, that's breakfast in spite of the fact that it's closer to lunchtime," Tamrissa answered with a smile. "And, no, no one has checked on the invaders yet. That's *our* job, as soon as the rest of our Blending is up and about."

"I take it Jovvi and Lorand haven't yet made an appearance," Rion said after glancing around again. "I see Vallant over by the cooking fire, but they're not with him."

"Jovvi came close to draining herself, and Lorand did a lot of healing," Naran pointed out before Tamrissa was able to reply. "It's not much of a surprise that they're still asleep."

"And since the invaders aren't supposed to get here until sometime tomorrow, there's no reason to wake our sister and brother," Tamrissa added with a smile for Naran as well. "I'm currently enjoying this quiet time, but that's because I've already eaten. Once you've had your breakfast, you might be able to do the same kind of enjoying."

"At the very least, I need a cup of tea," Rion said as Tamrissa began to lead them over to the cooking fire. "I've discovered that I'm able to face quite a lot as long as a cup of tea is available to sustain me."

"If Rion ever becomes conditioned, we'll probably be able to break him out of it by offering him tea," Naran said, making Tamrissa chuckle. "I can't imagine anything being able to keep him away from the drink."

"Don't forget that he's not alone in that," Tamrissa pointed out to Naran while Rion took his turn at being amused. "The rest of us usually yearn after tea at least as much as Rion does, and the only thing that draws half our Blending more is the thought of a bath."

"The female half of our Blending," Rion said after joining in the general laughter. "We men enjoy being clean, but not nearly as much as you ladies do. We need to spend some time today giving ourselves clean clothes, so that tonight we can also enjoy Vallant's version of a bath."

"Yes, we do want to be clean when meetin' those invader leaders for the first time," Vallant said as they stopped near him, obviously having heard what Rion had said. "Or maybe we shouldn't be clean. If our Blendin' entity can't best theirs, maybe our body odor will overwhelm them."

"I'd like that idea more if it didn't mean passing up the chance to bathe," Tamrissa said while everyone else chuckled. "Rion, isn't there some way to . . . save the odor, so to speak, and use it as a weapon without having it used on us at the same time?"

"Using an odor as a weapon," Rion mused, taking the suggestion a lot more seriously than Tamrissa had meant it. "It just might be possible to do something like that, but there are better odors to use than the ones *we* produce. Once, when I rode through the woods with *that woman* in our carriage, we were forced to go past part of a deer carcass that had been . . . perfumed by a skunk. I never felt so ill in my life, and that woman actually threw up. Once we got home she also fired our carriage driver, as if driving through the woods had been his idea rather than hers."

"Well, I seriously doubt if she's doing any hiring or firing *these* days," Tamrissa said just as Rion's emotions came perilously close to depression—just as they always did when he thought of that woman. "The woman who claimed to be your mother was sent to Astinda along with the rest of her exalted noble friends, and all of them have been working to bring the land alive again for quite some time. She's probably become quite mellow by now, don't you think?"

"Hardly," Rion said with a sound of scorn that wasn't meant for Tamrissa. In his mind's eye Rion was almost able to see Halina Mardimil, dressed in cheap and colorless clothing, her hair hanging tangled and sweat-soaked as she used what looked to be a hoe on a section of burned-out ground. The woman's mind was filled with growing fury, and after another moment she straightened and threw the hoe away from her.

"I am Lady Halina Mardimil, and I refuse to be treated like this any longer," the woman announced in cold and haughty tones as she glared around. "One of you will run and *immediately* fetch me a cold drink, which I will sip while my carriage is brought around. I will then go home, and none of you peasants is ever to come near me again."

"I'm Vistern Lankers, who used to be a High Lord, and you're a fool," a nearby man said after wiping his brow on the back of his arm. "If you can't stay in touch with reality, woman, just keep your fantasies to yourself. And pick up that hoe and get back to work. The rest of us don't want to be late for supper because you still think you're too good to do your share."

"But my back hurts and my hands are covered in blisters," the woman answered, fighting not to sound as shaken as she felt. "I don't like this dream, and I want to wake up now."

"Waking up would be a good idea," another voice said, this time a female one. "Even I've been able to separate reality from fantasy by now, so *you* have no excuse. Pick up your hoe and get back to work."

The woman looked in the direction the female voice had come from, and found Eltrina Razas staring back at her. The two of them had hated each other almost forever, and that made it easy for the woman to hold her head up high.

"*You* are and always have been a nothing," the woman informed the Razas female. "I, on the other hand, am the most important woman in the world. My father always told me that, and I've never been given any reason to doubt the truth of the claim. With that in mind—"

"You really do have to wake up," another, more kindly voice interrupted the woman, this time another man. "Your father told you what many fathers tell their daughters, and in their own hearts they aren't lying. You'll find all this easier to accept if you make yourself understand that your father simply failed to make himself clear. You were the most important woman in the world to *him*, but not to anyone else."

"Most especially not to these Astindans," a third man put in with nothing in the way of kindness. "To our captors you're no more or less than the rest of us, except that you do less work than we do. Now pick up that hoe and stop ruining things for us."

"But I don't want to," the woman said, frustration rising higher and higher. "I don't want to do this anymore, I don't want to, I don't want to!"

By now she was screaming rather than speaking, her fists clenched tight as she stamped her feet and shrilled out her demands. She'd never in her life been denied anything, and now she refused to accept *their* refusal. She would just scream and stamp her feet until she got her way, and the tactic would be just as successful as it had always been . . .

Except that this time it wasn't the father who loved her who came to see what the problem was. This time it was one of those Astindan peasants, who did something to her mind. The screaming and stamping stopped, she went and picked up her hoe, and she was forced to start working again even in the midst of the humiliation of having those around her laugh as they went back to their own work. Halina hated having that done, but they kept refusing to give her what she demanded. She hated it *all*, but was being forced to work even while she hated. If only she could wake up from this horrible dream . . .

". . . wake up," Rion heard, and suddenly he no longer saw what surely had been purely imagination. "We can eat and drink tea until then, and afterward we'll be able to take a good look around."

"You're right, it *shouldn't* be too long before Jovvi and Lorand wake up," Tamrissa said, agreeing with what Vallant had just said. "In fact, I have the definite feeling that it won't be more than five minutes or so before they're here."

"Stop stealing *my* talent," Naran said to Tamrissa, but Rion's beloved smiled as she spoke. "As far as I can tell you're right about Jovvi and Lorand, so stop stealing my talent."

"Now that's really interestin'," Vallant said, looking back and forth between Tamrissa and Naran. "Knowin' things *is* Naran's talent alone, but I'm feelin' the same certainty that Tamrissa just spoke with. And somehow I also know that you and Rion are feelin' very satisfied, Naran. We seem to have been borrowin' each other's talent lately, at least the non-physical talents. Is that supposed to happen, or are we doin' somethin' wrong?"

"A better question would be will we also get to the point of sharing the physical part of the talents?" Tamrissa said, her tone musing. "Whether or not this is *supposed* to happen doesn't matter. As long as it *is* happening, we have to cope with the situation."

"I do a better job of coping on a full stomach," Rion said,

heading off what promised to be a long discussion. "Naran, my love, would you care to join me in fortifying the inner practitioner? We can get back to discussing things we have no control over after we see to something we do have control over."

"A delightfully practical suggestion, my love, and it would be my pleasure to join you," Naran replied with her usual lovely smile. "And we might as well wait to have the discussion until Jovvi and Lorand have joined us. That way if we get any brilliant ideas, we won't have to repeat them for our brother and sister."

"You really are an optimist, Naran," Tamrissa said with amusement as Rion guided his love to the man who was ready to fill plates with food for them. "I wasn't expecting any of us to *get* any brilliant ideas, so I didn't think about having to repeat any."

"I'm really wounded," Vallant said to Tamrissa, one hand placed in the middle of his chest. "Are you sayin' you don't even expect *me* to get any brilliant ideas? Such lack of faith is very painful."

Tamrissa laughed and went over to soothe Vallant's supposed pain, which meant that Rion was able to choose his breakfast with undivided attention. In truth there wasn't much to choose, only how much of the eggs and potatoes and venison and bread he thought he could eat, but Rion still felt a good deal of inner satisfaction. He and Naran were back to being able to show their love for each other, he was part of a group that was closer than a family, and he had all the true freedom he could want.

*Unlike that woman,* Rion thought as he accepted the plate with his breakfast. What he'd seen in his mind's eye couldn't possibly be what was really happening with the woman who had tormented him all of his life, but thinking that the situation might be close to the truth was a lovely kind of revenge. The woman *would* hate not being able to get her way any longer, a situation her former victims would certainly have been willing to pay gold to see.

Naran chose a bit of grass to sit down on with her breakfast, and Rion sat beside her. They had barely begun to eat when Jovvi and Lorand appeared, looking well rested and as satisfied as Rion felt. But as the last of his Blendingmates went for their own breakfasts, Rion had the distinct impression that Jovvi's satisfaction was only on the surface. Something bothered his sister, but Rion made no effort to rise and question her. He *had* learned the meaning of discretion, which meant it would be far better to wait until later before speaking to her privately.

Lorand and Jovvi wasted no time in getting their breakfast plates, and a moment later they had joined Rion and Naran on the grass. The meal went quickly because of the general silence, and by the time Rion had finished his tea everyone was through eating.

"So, are you sleepyheads ready to do some work yet?" Tamrissa asked as she and Vallant stopped near where Rion and the others were sitting. "I'm getting bored just standing around."

"Boredom is soundin' better than it ever used to," Vallant added dryly with a glance for Tamrissa. "I'd take the feelin' happily if I didn't already know it wasn't likely to last, so we really should get on with it."

"Unfortunately, I can't argue with that decision," Lorand said with a sigh before finishing the tea in his cup. "I'm not looking forward to finding out more about the people we'll be facing, but *not* knowing about them can only hurt us. Shall we Blend right here?"

Rion and the others agreed with the suggestion, so Tamrissa and Vallant sat down and joined them. Once everyone was settled comfortably, Jovvi initiated the Blending.

The Rion entity formed as easily as ever, and it took only a moment's thought before a decision was made. To float back along the road would be a tedious process, especially when floating was unnecessary. The entity's flesh forms had gone a considerable distance up that road, therefore the entity knew enough about the area to flash rather than float. Flashing covered distances in an instant, at the same time conserving strength.

It was clear to the Rion entity that the enemy had not as yet reached the village which had been attacked, therefore the Rion entity flashed to the village. The area now appeared to be completely empty, all human life-forms either ended or gone away. Animal and insect life-forms abounded, of course, yet nothing of the human remained.

Using the road as a guide, the Rion entity floated in the direction from which the enemy would come. It would be necessary to be fully alert to keep from being detected, as the distance was far too great for any meaningful battle. The closer to its flesh forms, the stronger the entity would be, and it had been clear for some time that the enemy would require all the strength the Rion entity was able to generate. A pity the alternate arrangements were so far unavailable . . .

The Rion entity floated quickly up the road, and in time it was possible to detect the presence of flesh forms up ahead. Nothing in the way of independent thought could be sensed in the minds of these flesh forms, which told the Rion entity that the first of the enemy had been found. Now was the time to exercise caution, which the Rion entity proceeded to do.

A memory had come to remind the Rion entity that the more it attenuated its being, the less detectable its presence would become. At the same time the Rion entity would find it possible to cover a larger area in its search for knowledge, which was the entire purpose of this foray. It took but a moment to turn thought into deed, and a much larger, thinner entity spread itself and looked about.

The enemy flesh forms were in even greater numbers than those which had been captured by the entity's flesh forms. Twice the number led what appeared to be a procession of sorts, with a matching number following behind. In the midst of the procession was an odd arrangement of five covered litters being carried by four flesh forms apiece, with an additional ten flesh forms walking close beside each of the litters.

*Obviously each is a Blending talent with its tandem link groups,* the Rion entity heard. *There are, however, only five of them.*

*A piece of information definitely worth the having,* the Rion entity replied. It had been the Tamrissa part of the Rion entity which had spoken, just as had happened the previous time. *It would also be valuable to know exactly how strong their entity is, which cannot be known until the entity forms.*

*It would be unwise to seek knowledge at this time which would bring more harm than benefit,* another part of the Rion entity said, this time the Jovvi part. *It has been perfectly clear that these invaders will be the stronger, possibly only for a time. What benefit in proving what is already known?*

*No benefit,* the Rion entity replied just as its Tamrissa part agreed in the same manner. *There is nothing further to be done until the enemy has approached a bit more closely. I will now return to my starting point.*

The Rion entity flashed back to the village where his flesh forms waited, and then it was Rion alone back inside his own body. He sat up just as the others did, and smiled at the astonishment on Jovvi's face.

"This time it happened to me, too!" Jovvi exclaimed as she looked back and forth between Rion and Tamrissa. "I was the entity, but I heard the two of you speaking inside my head and knew who you were."

"I think I've got another surprise for you," Vallant said to Jovvi with a wry smile. "There wasn't anythin' for me to say so I kept silent, but I definitely heard the rest of you. I was the Blendin' entity, and I heard parts of myself speakin'."

"I'm trying to decide whether to be jealous or relieved," Lorand said as he looked around at the others. "I was also the Blending entity, but I heard nothing in the way of conversation, inner or otherwise. How about you, Naran?"

"I'm in the minority right along with you, Lorand," Naran answered with an odd but reassuring smile. "Have we decided yet what this development means? And did anyone else catch the entity's passing thoughts about how we seem to be missing something? I'm not even certain what it is that we're missing."

"It was something about alternate arrangements and strength," Rion supplied, remembering having had the thought. "I would love to say that I know exactly what that means, but I'm afraid I haven't the slightest idea."

"I do remember, though, what Jovvi said," Tamrissa put in, looking extremely thoughtful. "She said that we knew the invaders would be stronger, 'possibly only for a time.' Is that supposed to mean that there's a way for *us* to be stronger if we're bright enough to figure out how to do it?"

"I think that's exactly what it means," Naran responded slowly before Jovvi could speak, Rion's beloved's distraction showing that she gazed upon things kept hidden from the rest of them. "I didn't really see the point until we were Blended, but now I can remember seeing it. There's a clear possibility that we'll win the ultimate confrontation—but only if we figure out how. The rest of the possibilities show us losing, in some instances even dying."

"And the ones showin' us dyin' aren't the worst," Vallant said grimly, indicating that he, too, remembered the Sight. "If we let those people get their hands on us, they'll *use* us instead of killin' us. Personally, I'd rather be dead."

Rion waited for someone to protest that outlook, but no one did and that included himself. Rion knew from personal experience that death wasn't the worst that could happen to a person. Being enslaved without the hope of breaking free was worse, and he would never willingly allow that to happen to him again—or stand by while it was being done to his beloved family.

The six of them sat in silence for a short while, and then there were people all about asking if they'd gotten a look at the enemy. Vallant stood and began to tell the others what little they'd seen, and Jovvi rose and headed back toward the cooking fire. She seemed intent on getting another cup of tea, and Lorand had risen and gone with her. Rion was about to follow their example when Naran put a hand on his arm.

"Rion, I need to tell you something that also needs to be passed on to most of the others," Naran murmured, her face showing a smile that suggested she spoke of personal if not intimate things. "When I agreed with Lorand a few minutes ago, I lied. I *was* aware of the inner conversation when we were Blended, but just like Vallant I kept silent because I didn't have what to say."

"Which means that Lorand is the only one of us who hasn't reached this new point," Rion murmured back, fighting to keep from frowning. "Are you able to see anything of significance surrounding the lack?"

"Only one thing," Naran answered, a hint of fear now showing in her lovely eyes. "If we don't figure out what's wrong and fix it, that possibility covering our winning disappears completely."

*Marvelous,* Rion thought with an inner groan. They didn't even know what was wrong, but unless they fixed it they would lose the coming battle. That day might have started out being fairly nice, but it was rapidly going very much downhill . . .

# SEVEN

Deslen Voyt walked into the tavern he was beginning to know rather well. He and Brange had taken to meeting in the tavern every night, just as friends often did. Deslen and Brange *were* friends, but the matter wasn't as simple for them as it seemed to be for everyone else. Or at least it still wasn't that simple for Deslen. Brange sat at their usual table looking completely unbothered, and when Deslen walked up to him Brange smiled.

"How's it going, Voyt?" Brange asked as Deslen sat down and signaled the serving girl for an ale. "You still enjoying the classes as much as I am?"

"Actually, I can't remember enjoying anything more in my life," Deslen answered, the question distracting him from the usual unease. "I'm still a Low in Water magic, but I'm beginning to have real control of my talent. And no one has even *looked* as if they consider me a waste of good living space."

"And I'm doing better in Earth magic," Brange agreed, giving the serving girl a smile as she set a flagon of ale in front of Deslen and then hurried off. "If you want the truth, I've been *looking* for people who might consider me a waste of good living space. I expected to find some, just the way I always have since I became a man, but these people are different somehow. They really want to help me become the best I can be, and they aren't surprised that we have jobs with the city guard waiting when we finish our classes.

72

Walking away from that fool noble was the smartest thing we ever did."

Deslen glanced around when Brange mentioned the noble, but no one seemed to have overheard the low-spoken comment. He and Brange—and a large number of others—had been brought into the city by the noble to help the noble take over control from the new government. When Deslen and Brange had found an opportunity to walk away from the noble and make something decent of their lives they'd jumped at the opportunity, but they hadn't left alone. They'd managed to get almost half of the rest of the men to go with them, and the noble had been too busy with reorganizing the men he had left to find it possible to hunt those who had escaped.

"I've been talking to some of the others, and they're also glad we all walked away," Brange said, still speaking softly after sipping at his own ale. "Three of the ones who left with us are gone from the city, but the rest are either already in a training class or have signed up for one. And only a handful or so plan to join the city guard with us. The rest have plans of their own that they've never before had the chance to try. Can you see some of those fools as shopkeepers?"

"If that's what they really want, sure I can," Deslen said with a faint smile. "The only thing I keep worrying about is what's going to happen if someone finds out that we came here in the first place to make trouble. They'll never believe that we changed our minds, and if they do find out it will mean the end of all our dreams."

Brange frowned and was about to answer Deslen, but the words were never spoken as a third man joined them at the table. The man was Chelten Admis, one of those who had left the noble at the same time Deslen and Brange had. Admis was easily as big as Deslen, but the blond Low Air magic user always wore a cheerful expression that made him look a good deal less dangerous than he really was.

"Voyt, Brange," Admis said with a pleasant nod for each of the men as he settled into his chair. "How are you two coming with your classes?"

"We agreed not to get together in large groups, Admis,"

Deslen said, ignoring the question Admis had asked. "If we start to hang around together, people will wonder how all we strangers know each other."

"Three men at a table in a tavern can't be considered a large group," Admis pointed out, obviously more amused than insulted or disturbed. "Besides, I have something to tell you. We've been asked if we'd like to help out, but we don't have to if we don't want to. If we decide to volunteer we'll get paid, but nobody says we *have* to volunteer."

"What are you talking about?" Brange demanded just before Deslen was able to say the same thing. "*Who* asked us to volunteer, and for what?"

"I keep getting the feeling I'm dreaming," Admis said with the strangest smile Deslen had ever seen the man wear, answering something other than Brange's question. "Do you know how worried most of us were that someone would find out what we came to this city to do? That our one chance to lead normal lives would be gone if the truth ever came out? I would have done anything to keep the secret, but now I don't have to. What we were never *was* a secret, and they really do want us to have our chance."

"Admis, tell us what you're talking about," Deslen said, hearing the way his voice had become a growl. His insides had also knotted up, a perfect match to the growl. "*Who* knows about us, and how did you find out?"

"Someone came to talk to me," Admis said, his smile fading a bit when he saw how agitated Deslen and Brange had gotten. "The man said he worked for the 'unofficial officials' of the city, and they've been watching Noll ever since the man and his family got here. When we all left Noll to become ordinary citizens of the city, we changed our status from enemy to friend. They *want* us to make good, if for no other reason than to prove it can be done. When we do make it, we'll be their 'shining examples.' "

"What makes you think they were telling the truth?" Brange said while Deslen sat silent and numb with shock. "You're just Air magic, Admis, so how would you know?"

"The man came and spoke to me while I was with

Folden," Admis said, his smile warming again. "Folden has Earth magic the way you do, Brange, but when he joined a class he had to admit that he's a Middle instead of a Low. *I* might not be able to tell if someone was lying to me, but Folden can and he said the man told us nothing but the truth."

"I don't believe this," Deslen found himself saying, confusion turning his mind into a whirling mess. "Why would a bunch of strangers care what happened to us? Why wouldn't they just throw us out of their city to make *sure* we don't do damage? It's happened often enough before, so why isn't it happening again?"

"Maybe it's because those 'unofficial officials' aren't solid citizens any more than we are," Admis said, and again the man looked amused. "Or at least they never *were* solid citizens, not until this new government took over. The new people running things are willing to give a chance to anyone who wants one, but they're not pushovers. Anyone who tries to play smart instead of straight gets booted out fast, and they're never allowed to come back again. They even did it to a couple of High talents, just to prove that they're not kidding."

"So we've been worrying for nothing?" Brange asked, looking as confused as Deslen felt. "They know all about us, and are still willing to give us our chance? Why did they suddenly tell you about it?"

"The man said they were going to tell all of us once we finished our classes, but something came up sooner than they expected," Admis explained. "They'd like our help with the something, but we really don't have to give it. You two will probably want to, considering the fact that you'll be working for the city guard once you've finished your classes."

"What has the city guard got to do with anything?" Deslen said, while Brange put in, "Aren't *you* going to be working for the guard along with us? I thought you were."

"*I* thought there would be nothing for me *but* the guard," Admis said, answering Brange first. "Then I got to talking to someone in a dining parlor about cooking, which I always considered fun to do but not very important. With more and more people having silver to spend on a good meal, the city is very short of people who can produce that good meal. I ended up cooking my two favorite dishes in that dining parlor, and now I don't have to wait until I finish my class to get a job. I already have one."

Deslen joined Brange in staring at Admis in silence, finding it impossible to think of what to say. Admis was one of the most dangerous men Deslen had ever worked with, and *he* had taken a job *cooking*? The world really was turning itself upside down.

"And what all this has to do with the city guard is this," Admis continued, looking even more amused. "Those people who know about us and Noll tell me that Noll is starting to put his plans into motion. They could take Noll right now and send him and his wife to Astinda after the rest of their friends, but they've decided to let Noll make his play instead. This way, if any of Noll's friends happen to be watching, they'll know what to expect if *they* try anything."

"A horrible example instead of a shining one," Brange said with a thoughtful nod. "That's probably a good idea, but I don't understand what they want *us* to do. Are we supposed to pretend to go back to working for Noll?"

"No, almost the opposite," Admis said, now showing a grin. "It sounded like so much fun that I decided I wanted a part of it, so any cooking I do for a short while will be out on the street. Let me tell you what they need us for, and then you can decide if you also want a piece of it."

Deslen leaned forward in order to listen more closely, and only distantly noticed that Brange had done the same. The two of them listened to what Admis had to say, and by the time he was through his listeners were grinning just as broadly as he was.

"I can't see *any* of us refusing to go along with that," Brange said at last, a chuckle behind the words. "The only problem is, I also want to see Noll's face when he finds out about it. *That* show ought to be almost as good as the one *we'll* be a part of."

"They promised to watch Noll *for* us, and tell us what he says and does," Admis said with a laugh. "Are you both in?"

"You'd better believe it," Deslen confirmed with a smile he thought might crack his face. "Just tell us when and where."

"I'll get word to you just as soon as they tell *me*," Admis said and then got to his feet. "I've got to talk to more of us, so I'll see you both later."

Deslen joined Brange in nodding his understanding, and once Admis was gone Deslen looked over at his friend.

"You know, I thought the day we left Noll was the best day of my life, but now I know that today is," he said. "The cloud that was hanging over my head is gone, and I can sit back and enjoy life. They know all about us, but they still want us to be with them."

"I think I agree with Admis that we have to be dreaming," Brange answered with a shake of his head that did nothing to chase away the man's smile. "But if we *are* dreaming, I never want to wake up."

"Our one chance is for real, and there's nothing that can keep us from taking advantage of it but ourselves," Deslen said, feeling his amusement being replaced with grim determination. "I will *not* lose this or mess it up, not even if my life depends on it. I'd rather be dead than go back to watching other people's happiness from the outside."

Brange remained silent, but the expression on his face told Deslen that his friend felt exactly the same way. They would both rather be dead than mess things up for themselves; now all they had to do was make sure it stayed like that . . .

Idresia Harmis sat drinking a cup of tea, enjoying the fact that Issini and Asri had taken over the cooking chores for the day. It was nice to have others around who could produce a meal that wasn't guaranteed to poison them, which Driff's efforts—and Edmin's—would certainly have done. The two men were willing, and Asri said that Kail was just as willing, but willingness doesn't automatically produce a good cook. Besides, Idresia had other things to think about besides cooking, and being able to do her thinking without distraction was another treat.

"You look more satisfied than just sitting around would account for, Har," Issini said to Idresia from where she stood by the stove. "Would you care to share what's making you smile?"

"I wanted to wait for the men to get back, but they're taking too long," Idresia answered as she looked over at the two women. "Since Kail already knows the city, I thought that giving him a look at our arrangements would be a quick trip. But since they're not here . . . I've made new arrangements centering around our renegade."

"What new arrangements?" Issini asked while Asri showed a faintly surprised expression. "Have you changed your mind about my idea to counter what will probably be their next move?"

"No, I haven't changed my mind about liking your idea," Idresia quickly assured her friend with a smile. "As a matter of fact I *love* your idea, and I've already had some of my people get started with making sure that no one will be hurt because they went along with the idea. But the thought came to me that the renegade wants and needs a proper basis to build on before he goes to the next stage of his plans. That realization made me believe that he'll try to put on his show in taverns and eating parlors again."

"If he does, then your people can just stop the show the way they did the first time," Issini said with a shrug. "That second failure should push the renegade into the next step of his plans from anger if for no other reason."

"But what if he decides instead to do something we haven't thought of?" Idresia countered, verbalizing the way her thinking had gone. "We can't let him do something we're not prepared for, not at this stage of the game. What we *can* do, though, is make him think that everything is working out, so he'll definitely commit himself and his men to the course of action we're ready to counter."

"How can we make him believe that everything is working out without letting trouble develop?" Issini asked, her frown looking odd next to Asri's faint smile. "His people won't report success unless they actually *have* success."

"That's not quite true," Asri said, sharing a brief moment of amusement with Idresia before turning her full attention to Issini. "I think that what Idresia did was arrange some way to make the renegade's men *believe* in their success, whether or not they actually have any."

"But how could she do *that*?" Issini started to ask, and then her expression changed. "I'm an idiot! Of course she could do it, and rather easily."

"Well, I know she did *something,* because I Saw it," Asri said, now looking less amused. "What I don't understand is *how* she did it, but you obviously do. Can you tell me what was done, or is the process a secret you'd rather not share?"

"There's nothing secret about the process itself," Idresia said when Issini hesitated over answering. "I had Driff find me a Middle Blending, and they're with my people who are watching the renegade's house. If another group of troublemakers is sent out, the Blending will convince the troublemakers that whatever they've been told to do will work out just the way it's supposed to. What will actually happen is their act will be done so woodenly that no one listening to them will be fooled in the least. That way there's no danger of their actually making trouble, but I'm not happy about what had to be done to get us the help we needed."

"What do you mean?" Issini asked, her frown back as Asri digested what she'd been told. Asri knew almost nothing about Blendings, so her question hadn't been a true surprise. "What did you have to do to get the help you needed?"

"It wasn't what *I* had to do, but what Driff had to," Idresia said with a shake of her head. "Driff had to talk to more than half a dozen Blendings before he found one that didn't have 'more important' things to do. With all the High talents completely out of touch, too many people in the Middle Blend-

ings are 'seriously concerned' with the lack of leadership.
I'm not suggesting that all those people are insincere, just
that they're too narrow-minded to see everything involved.
They're so worried about the picky little things that have to
be done that they're completely ignoring the really important things."

"I have a feeling I know why that's happening," Issini said
with a sigh. "Those people in the Middle Blendings are
probably frightened to death of making a mistake, so they're
concentrating on unimportant things where mistakes won't
matter so much. It's too bad we don't have a Middle Blending of our own, so to speak, one that will do just what *we*
need done. Having them would at least make life easier for
you and Driff."

"It certainly would," Idresia agreed fervently. "I have
more than one job for a good Middle Blending, and by
'good' I mean people with a little imagination who aren't
afraid to take a risk. If you refuse to take any chances, how
are you supposed to get anything worthwhile done?"

"Oh, now I understand," Asri said suddenly, but her attention didn't seem to be on Idresia or Issini. "If I knew more
about Blendings then I would have understood sooner, so I
guess I'll just have to make a point of learning."

"What is it that you would have understood?" Idresia
asked, trying to pay close attention in spite of her confusion.
"Are you Seeing something that we need to be told about?
But don't worry about learning things. Driff is going to find
you someone with Sight magic to help train your talent."

"I already know that, and also that he'll find someone
soon," Asri told her with a smile that showed she'd returned
from Seeing. "But to answer your more important question,
there *is* something you need to know about. It's a way to
have exactly the Middle Blending that you need."

"I'm definitely listening, even if blackmail is involved,"
Idresia said, leaning forward across the table just a bit. "I'll
have to draw the line if it's torture that's involved, but threats
aren't necessarily out."

"You really won't have *anything* like that to worry about,"

Asri said with a chuckle while Issini laughed. "The Middle Blending you need is the one you'll belong to."

Idresia felt her own frown growing to match the one Issini showed as they both stared at Asri. It was almost as though the two of them had stopped understanding spoken language, but then Idresia realized what the problem was.

"I think we're still having a bit of trouble with your understanding concerning Blendings," Idresia told an Asri who looked perfectly calm and unbothered. "I don't know anyone well enough—or like them well enough—to want to Blend with them. That means I'm not *going* to be part of a Blending, so whatever you Saw has to mean something else entirely."

"But of course you know people well enough and like them well enough to Blend with them," Asri contradicted with a warm smile. "Kail and I felt as though we'd known the four of you forever, and that only a few minutes after we met. Now that it's been almost an entire day, there's a closeness among us that I've never in my life experienced before. Or don't you and Issini agree with what I'm saying?"

Idresia felt so stunned that words refused to form in her mind. All she could do was stare at Issini, who looked as if she'd been poleaxed. The two of them sat or stood with mouths open as they stared at Asri, but Issini pulled out of the shock only a moment later.

"That has to be the best idea I've heard in a very long time," Issini stated, looking first at Asri and then at Idresia. "We do have a complete Blending among us, Har, one that feels really complete now that Asri and Kail are here. Why *can't* we Blend?"

*Possibly because Driff doesn't* want *to Blend,* Idresia said, but only to herself. *I love that man too much to join any group that doesn't include him, but something seems to bother him about Blending that he hasn't mentioned out loud. If the something is too serious for him to get around, we won't replace him even if we find someone as good as he is. I won't turn my back on him no matter what, so if he doesn't change his mind then there will* be *no Blending for us.*

"There . . . might be a problem with your and Asri's idea that has nothing to do with Kail and Asri," Idresia said slowly, forcing herself to say the words. "Let me tell you how things are, and then maybe one of you will have an idea about how to handle the problem."

The meal Issini and Asri had been making seemed to be at the point where it just had to cook, so the other two women came and joined Idresia at the table. Idresia *would* tell them everything, and then maybe one of them would find a way to make something wonderful happen—if only they were able to change Driff's mind . . .

# EIGHT

As Edmin reentered the warehouse with Driff and Kail, he realized that he'd really been enjoying himself. Driff seemed to be a strong, steadying influence in almost any situation, and Kail, although less sure of himself, seemed determined to behave honorably at all times. Walking about parts of the city with the other two men had been oddly liberating, and not only because he no longer had to worry about being found by Noll's men. For the first time in his life Edmin was in the company of people he considered his equals, not just those who had been born into his social class.

". . . so if you two ever run into trouble, those are some of the people you can go to for help," Driff was saying to Kail—and also to Edmin. "They know you both now, and they'll either hide you or give you whatever help they can if it's help you need. Do you think you'll be able to find them again?"

"It shouldn't be *too* much of a problem," Kail answered with distraction. "At first I didn't recognize the neighborhoods at all, but then I found a familiar landmark and the rest all fell into place. My father considered my occasional trip into this part of the city a waste of time, but it looks like that was something else he was wrong about. Are we going to be able to help personally against Noll's efforts? Is that why you showed us all those places?"

"I'm not the one you have to ask that question of," Driff said with amusement that Edmin knew was really a great amount of pride. "Idresia is in charge of our campaign against the renegade, and considering how well she's done so far I won't even *try* to second-guess her. If she thinks we can be of use in the campaign, then we'll be helping out personally."

"Is there something in particular that we can use to bribe her?" Edmin asked, knowing Driff would understand that he was joking. "If nothing else, I want to be part of the effort when Noll is finally taken down."

"I think she understands that we all want to be there when the renegade finally realizes that he's lost," Driff said, the curve of his lips showing his amusement. "I'll make sure of that, of course, and if I'm wrong *then* we can think about what to use to bribe her."

"You have no idea how good it feels to be among people who don't simply give their women orders," Kail said with a small shake of his head. "My father and his friends had only three uses for women: as something to enjoy in bed, as something to bear their children, and as something to show off like any of their other possessions. Women were never *people* to them, not unless the woman had more power than they did. Then the woman was either an enemy or an ally, never just a woman. The Astindans weren't like that, and neither are you."

"My own mother never felt as much concern for me as she did about what my father thought," Edmin put in without realizing that he was about to speak. "My brother and I were raised by nurses, and if our father was in the same room with all of us, our mother never even glanced in our direction. We were just something unimportant to her that she'd given to her husband, like a cup of tea or an inexpensive gift."

"My mother was too . . . distracted to protect me from my father," Kail said, and the very neutral words hid an inner pain much like the one Edmin felt. "She had a long string of men she gave all her attention to, mostly because my father usually ignored her. When he didn't ignore her he simply gave her orders, and she never made any effort to disobey him—not even to help my brothers or me. Her charm would *not* have protected her if she'd tried to cross my father about something he considered important."

"You know, you two have done something I never thought was possible," Driff said, pausing a few steps from the door leading to the living quarters to look at his companions. "You make me glad I grew up on the street instead of as part of a family. Being part of *some* 'families' isn't worth the pain and heartache, is it?"

"You don't know the half of it," Edmin said while Kail simply smiled without humor. "No one admitted to *knowing* what many of our peers were doing with their children, but gossip was always a favorite pastime. Listening to the gossip often made my blood run cold."

"But right now I'm getting something a lot more pleasant than gossip," Kail said after sniffing the air. "If that aroma is from the meal waiting for us, what are we doing wasting time standing out here?"

"It's too bad we don't have to find something to bribe Kail with," Driff remarked with a smile as he began to walk toward his living quarters again. "After all the time he and Asri spent on the trail coming back here, a nicely cooked meal would buy us anything we wanted."

"*Almost* anything," Kail corrected with a laugh while Edmin grinned. "I may be a slave to my stomach right now, but I do still have *some* standards I'd refuse to betray. You'd never get more than half my blood for a three or four course meal."

They were all laughing as they entered the apartment, and Edmin's companions continued with their amusement. He, on the other hand, was immediately aware of a tension behind the pleasant or neutral expressions the three women wore, and he quickly discovered that he'd lost all sense of discretion.

"What's wrong?" Edmin asked without an instant's hesitation. "Why are you three so disturbed?"

"It's all right, Edmin, nothing bad has happened," Issini said at once, her smile soothing and calming. "While you men were gone we tripped over a revelation, and we're not sure how you'll take it. Will it help to say that we women think it's a great idea?"

Issini's question was addressed to Idresia and Asri, but all she got in return was a smile and two shrugs. The smile came from Asri, Idresia's concern being too strong to let her do the same.

"What's wrong, love?" Driff asked Idresia as he moved closer to his woman, somehow apparently sensing her mood. "What did Issini mean about a revelation?"

"Asri made a really good suggestion, Driff," Idresia answered, taking Driff's hand as he bent over her where she sat. "The only problem is . . . We don't know if *you'll* think it's a good idea."

"All of us, or just me?" Driff asked, again showing that incredible insight that was so much a part of him. "I have the feeling you mean just me, but I don't understand why that is."

Idresia took a deep breath as she stared at Driff, her hand closing more tightly around his. Edmin felt her very great reluctance to go into details, but her inner strength was enough to overcome any weakening emotion.

"We were discussing how nice it would be to have a Blending that was just ours to use," she began, doing nothing to avoid Driff's stare. "Ours to use for anything that we felt was necessary, without having to spend all kinds of time talking the Blending members into going along with us. That's when Asri pointed out that *we* six could Blend, and then we'd have what we need."

Edmin's surprise was so strong that he almost missed the reactions of the other men. Kail's matching surprise turned almost at once into full agreement, but Driff . . . Driff's expression showed nothing, but on the inside the man was floundering in fear and distress.

"But you don't *want* to Blend, do you, Driff?" Idresia said, showing the same insight that Driff usually did. "You don't think that Blending is a good idea at all."

"You don't understand," Driff said, shaking his head as he

released Idresia's hand and straightened. "It's not that I don't *want* to Blend with all of you, it's just—"

Driff's words broke off as he gestured vaguely with one hand, an effort to show that he couldn't put his feelings into a form that others would understand. Edmin felt confused for a moment, but then suddenly, without warning, everything came clear.

"You're afraid to Blend because you're afraid to be part of something that's closer than a family," Edmin said, this time speaking deliberately. "Too often families aren't what they're supposed to be, and you're afraid you'll be trapped in a nightmare. That's it, isn't it, Driff?"

"That's exactly it," Driff agreed, his slight frown almost lost behind the extreme distress that now showed clearly on his face. "You're really good, Edmin, but I don't see how knowing what the problem is will help. I . . . *can't* agree to being part of something that might trap me forever."

"I think the key word there is 'trap,' " Asri said when everyone else remained silent, their emotions roiling. "I had almost the same reaction when I first understood that we could make a Blending. I was born into a family that put me directly into a trap, and I was kept there until they opened the trap so that the husband they chose for me could put me into *his* trap. For a long time I believed that there was nothing I could do to escape, and then I realized that it was the child I'd been who was helpless. The woman I'd become was far from helpless as long as I refused to go along with my captors, which I did as soon as I understood my true position. They might have been able to kill me, but from the moment I understood the truth they were never able to own me again."

"I learned the same lesson, but sooner," Idresia said with a nod and a faint smile for Asri. "I was only twelve when my mother brought home a new boyfriend, but I'd had years to learn that no one on the street was able to push me around unless I allowed it. When my mother's new boyfriend tried to . . . 'show me how much he loved me,' I broke a heavy pitcher over his head and then ran away from home. My mother was prepared to let him do anything he liked because she was afraid of not having a man around to lean on, but I didn't need *anyone* to know I was strong. I stayed independent until I met *you,* Driff, and then I happily agreed to stop being a loner. But only because your strength added to mine, rather than trying to displace mine. And that's what a true Blending is supposed to be, my love. Something to add to your strength, not ruin it."

"Don't you think I know that?" Driff came back, but his words were more haunted than hostile. "I've always felt stronger with you beside me; Issini and Edmin bolstered that strength, and now we have Kail and Asri to add even more. We all seem to *belong* together, but the fear inside me isn't rational. It makes me think that if we Blend I'll be trapped, and there isn't enough strength in the world to let me face something like *that.*"

"If you're serious about wanting to get around the problem, there are two things we can do," Edmin said slowly, hating the taste of the fear that turned Driff helpless in its grasp. "*Are* you serious, or would you rather I minded my own business?"

"You might say that this *is* your business," Driff answered slowly after a moment, now studying Edmin with a hint of suspicion and uneasiness. "What did you have in mind?"

"Nothing you won't be able to refuse to agree to," Edmin replied firmly, doing nothing to avoid Driff's gaze. "In fact, the first part of my suggestion is nothing but words. Would you like to hear them?"

"I've been successfully resisting people's words for a long time now," Driff said with a faint smile, almost as though he were thinking aloud. "Go ahead and say what you like."

"What I have to say is more of a narrative," Edmin told him, then gestured to the table. "Why don't we all sit down and get more comfortable, and then I can start."

The suggestion wasn't one to put anyone on his or her guard, so Driff joined Kail and Edmin in taking chairs around the table. Idresia and Issini got up and went into the kitchen area, and in a moment they'd returned with cups of tea for the three men. After thanking Issini for his own cup, Edmin turned back to Driff.

"You probably don't know this, but I had the chance to . . . *look* rather closely at the last noble Blending," Edmin began after taking a sip of his tea. "Since no one knew I was doing it, there was no reason not to indulge my curiosity. What I discovered made me believe that the reign of my peers was about to come to an end, because those five people who were supposed to be closer than a family actually disliked each other intensely."

Driff, Idresia, and Issini made sounds of surprise, but Kail and Asri didn't share the emotion.

"I would have bet gold on that point," Kail said, Asri showing a wry expression at the same time. "I knew almost all of those people and even tried to warn my father about some of them, but my father was too arrogantly sure of himself to listen. When the five of them were put together, it was obvious to anyone with eyes that they hated the idea of being together and only later did that change."

"It changed because three of the other four were put under Kambil Arstin's control," Edmin said, and this time it was Asri, Issini, and Kail who looked surprised. Driff and Idresia seemed to know about that, which helped a small bit. "Deep down those people hated to *be* together, but they were still able to work together."

"If your point isn't that they were High talents, I don't understand," Driff said after sipping again at his own tea. "What difference does it make whether or not they liked each other?"

"My point is that they didn't really like each other, but they were still able to Blend," Edmin said, speaking rather slowly to let Driff actually hear what he was saying. "If you don't like someone but agree to work with them, you aren't trapped you're compromising. And from what I've heard, toward the end the five weren't even working together. That means it's possible to refuse to Blend, which in turn means that Blending isn't the trap you seem to think it is."

"You're right about their not Blending at the end," Idresia said just before turning to a frowning Driff. "You know that yourself, Driff, so you can't argue the point. If something happens in the Blending that you don't like, you can always refuse to Blend again."

"In my head I understand that point and agree with it," Driff said, his expression wry. "The trouble is, my reluctance is more in my gut than in my head. My head understands your point and agrees with it, Edmin, but my gut seems determined to refuse to listen to reason."

"Then this is where my second suggestion comes in," Edmin said, knowing there was no sense in delaying. "If your head really wants to do this thing, I can help you overcome your . . . gut. But I won't do it unless you really want me to. I respect you too much to tamper with your beliefs."

This time there was nothing but silence and expectation to greet Edmin's words. All eyes were on Driff, but Driff's gaze was lost to the distance as he frowned at whatever he saw. Confusion still roiled as heavily as ever in Driff, with apprehension now added to the rest.

"Driff, do you understand what Edmin is saying?" Idresia murmured after a very long moment as she took her man's hand. "You don't have to fight your fears and win over them without anything to help you. Edmin can make it possible for us to Blend the first time, and if you don't like what happens you can refuse to do it again. If he meant to force you into cooperating he would have already done it, so you don't have to worry that it will happen the next time. And you really ought to know that you might not be the one who refuses next time."

"What?" Driff said, blinking back to the world around him. "What do you mean, I might not be the one to refuse next time? I thought that everyone really wanted the Blending."

"Well, speaking only for myself, I have no idea what Blending is like," Idresia told him, her lips curved in a very unsteady smile. "I'm willing to try it if *you're* one of those I'll be Blending with, but being willing to try something once doesn't mean I'll want to do it again. I've . . . heard that Fire is supposed to be the most important talent in a Blending, and I don't understand that—or particularly like the idea. If we're all supposed to be equals in a Blending, why would the Fire talent be so important?"

"Fire is the talent that guards the Blending, attacking or defending as needed," Kail said, surprising everyone including Edmin. "Very frankly, Idresia, I can't see you *not* guarding and defending under any circumstance at all. The protectiveness is part of you, not something you'll have to go looking for."

"How do *you* know about Blendings, Kail?" Driff asked before Edmin could put the same question. "I know you're right, but how do you know so much?"

"I was trained in the use of my talent in Astinda," Kail answered, his open expression matching the same emotion on the inside. "After we finished the training class, the last thing we were told was how to Blend. In Astinda they *expect* people to go on to wanting to Blend, and making sure everyone knows how to do it is a way of being certain that the information doesn't become restricted to a small group the way it happened here."

"That's one of the reasons the information is spread far and wide here now," Driff said with something of a nod. "No one wants to give a new nobility the chance to own us again . . . No, I still can't agree on my own, even though a part of me really wants to. The rest of me is still a frightened little boy, so it looks like I'm going to have to take you up on your offer, Edmin."

"Are you sure, Driff?" Edmin asked quietly, more than aware of the man's inner reluctance. "I can tell how unhappy you are at the thought of being 'forced,' and I really don't want to do that to you."

"But you'll be doing it with my permission, which makes all the difference as far as *I'm* concerned," Driff answered, and then he drew a deep breath before laughing just a bit. "Besides, if I actually do it, I won't have to put up with every other High talent I run across making the effort to talk me into trying. It may also help me to work harder to find a way to wake them all up."

"Since the Blending will increase your ability, that might be the key to ending the problem," Kail said with a small frown. "And since you said that every High talent in the city was affected whether or not they were in a Blending, we don't have to worry that Blending will put *us* at risk."

"You know, I missed that point," Driff said with brows high, his inner turmoil actually easing enough for Edmin to notice. "Being part of a Blending *will* give me a better chance to bring the Highs back to themselves, so what are we waiting for?"

"Actually, we're waiting for someone to tell us how to do this thing," Idresia said dryly as the rest of them chuckled. "We *were* waiting for some blockhead to make up his mind, but now that the blockhead has seen the light we just need instructions."

"I guess Kail and I can supply the instructions, but the blockhead hasn't yet seen enough of the light," Driff answered with shamefaced amusement. "Edmin, if you'll help me out here, we can get started today instead of some time next year."

"Of course," Edmin answered with a smile, and then reached toward the man. Soothing the roiling conflict inside Driff was actually almost effortless, now that Driff had a reason of his own to want to Blend. Edmin had thought that he might actually have to control Driff, but soothing seemed to do the trick.

"Yes, that's much better," Driff said as he got to his feet, showing a wide smile. "I *am* going to try this, and if I don't like it I just won't do it again. Let's all stand over there."

Driff had gestured to the space between the door and the table, so Edmin joined the others in rising and walking to the spot. Both Driff and Kail directed everyone into standing in a group, with Idresia first, then Edmin and the rest lined up loosely behind her. Kail and Issini stood sort of to either side of the line, but both of them looked at Asri with perplexity.

"So where is Asri supposed to stand?" Kail asked Driff. "The Astindans don't *have* anyone with Sight magic, so the point was never covered."

"It's not that they don't *have* anyone with Sight magic, they just don't know about it yet," Driff corrected in a distracted way. "We do know about it, but all the High talents I spoke to added the member with Sight magic after they'd already Blended. That means I don't know where the Sight magic user is supposed to stand for the first try, but it doesn't make much sense to ask Asri to wait. Since we know she *can* Blend with the rest of us, she might as well join our first effort. Asri, why don't you come and stand in front of *me*."

"Yes, that feels right," Asri said after a brief hesitation that seemed to be more a checking of possibilities than true hesitation. "At least I can't See anything to suggest that I shouldn't be standing there."

As Edmin watched the pretty woman move to a place behind him, he smiled to himself. As soon as Asri had found out that her "feelings" were actually a talent, she'd started to use that talent more and more. The change in her should have happened in many days rather than just one, and Edmin couldn't help wondering if the process should be considered more than just impressive . . .

"All right, now we're all standing where we belong," Driff said, and his concentration on procedure seemed to be enough to keep his mind from other worries. "I'm told, Edmin, that you have to . . . reach out to the rest of us with your talent in some way, and when we feel you reaching toward us we have to do our own reaching out toward *you*."

"Yes, that's the way it's supposed to work," Kail confirmed from where he stood. "Spirit magic reaches out toward the rest of us, and when we feel his touch we also reach out toward him."

"Let's try it, then," Edmin murmured, making the effort to picture doing what they'd said. But first it was necessary to touch Driff again, a bit more firmly than before. Driff did want to know if Blending would allow him to help more people by increasing his ability, but his fear of being part of something very like a family had begun to reassert itself. Edmin's heavier touch calmed Driff, so it was time to get on with the experiment.

At first Edmin had difficulty with reaching out in all directions, but after a moment he realized that he was doing it wrong. Something seemed to . . . click inside his head, and then he knew exactly what he was supposed to do. He *reached* to the others, and one by one he was able to feel their return touches. All but Asri, the only one, in addition to himself, who hadn't been trained in any class.

But Asri *was* there and trying to reach him, so she just needed a small bit of help. Another moment showed Edmin how to use his touch on her to guide her own touch back to him, and once that was done Edmin felt the urge to stagger. They were connected, all of them, as though they'd been holding hands just before all their flesh began to melt together. But their connection wasn't physical, which was quickly proven.

*We've done it!* came in a silent voice that just had to be Kail's. *The first step is surface bonding, and we've done that.*

*Yes, we have,* came in Driff's tones, as clearly as if he'd spoken aloud. *Now we need to take that one step more, the one we should all be feeling a need to accomplish. Once we've actually done it, Edmin, you have to break the connection rather quickly. I'm told that Blending the first time is very draining.*

Edmin only thought about nodding, but the thought reached all the others. The need he felt to go one step farther was nearly overwhelming, so he took that step . . .

And then it was the entity who looked about itself. It was a newborn entity and therefore rather limited, but it was whole and strong in ways that other, even stronger entities were not. It felt that it could do many things and was eager to begin, but its first moments of life must be short in order to spare its flesh forms. The next time it came into being, it would begin to see to some of the many chores awaiting its maturity . . .

Then it was suddenly Edmin again, but an Edmin who felt the urge to sit down where he stood. The others were also making sounds of weariness, but the exultation Edmin felt was also holding everyone else in its excited grasp.

"That was incredible!" Issini exclaimed, her smile and delight child-deep. "I've never experienced anything so—so—"

"So close and wonderful," Idresia said with her own childlike smile. "What do *you* think, Driff? Was it anything like the trap you were expecting?"

"Actually, it was more like a very special freedom," Driff said with his own strange smile, moving closer to Idresia to take her hand. "When I was part of the entity, I knew that nothing would be able to hurt me ever again. But why didn't you and Issini mention that you'd been to a class? As soon as we were surface Blended it was perfectly clear that your talents were trained."

"We . . . didn't want to make Edmin feel bad," Idresia said with an apologetic glance for Edmin that Issini joined in. "He *would* have taken a class if he could have, and we didn't want him to feel left out because circumstance had made him miss the opportunity. But Asri hasn't taken a class yet either, and strangely enough neither of them felt particularly . . . weak or lacking in any way."

"No, they didn't," Driff said, turning to study first Edmin and then Asri. "They've both obviously been holding to the power long enough that they can't release it, and that has increased their strength. They may be untrained, but they're not all that far behind the rest of us."

"Actually, I had the feeling that they may be ahead of some of us," Kail said ruefully, but his gaze on Asri was filled with pride. "Edmin seems to have a *lot* of strength, and when we were Blended I could see a string of . . . situations where we'll need to act. Or should I say I Saw it? That *was* your talent, wasn't it, love?"

"I guess it was," Asri answered with delight clear in her smile as well. "I've always seen things in that way, but most of the time I tried to ignore what was there. I thought it was a mental sickness of some kind, not a talent."

"Well, it *is* a talent, and now we have to take the next step if we're to be as effective as we need to be," Idresia said briskly with some kind of hidden amusement. "Should we change bed partners tonight, or simply lie with those that we must?"

Edmin was so shocked that he felt the definite urge to babble out a demand for explanations, and Asri seemed almost as surprised. The others, though, were looking more rueful or faintly embarrassed, as if they knew just what Idresia meant.

"I think Asri and I need some explanations," Edmin finally managed, fighting to speak rather than babble. "I, personally, have no qualms about accommodating these lovely ladies, but . . . why will we be doing that accommodating?"

Without actually meaning to, Edmin had been speaking to Driff and Kail. Ignoring Idresia was rude, Edmin knew, but this was one subject he felt incapable of discussing with Idresia without blushing like a child.

"In order for a Blending to be properly bonded, the members of the Blending need to lie together," Driff answered gently, as though aware of how . . . almost distraught Edmin felt. "This is one of the things about Blending that disturbed me, but not any longer. I know now that I won't be betraying Idresia by lying with Issini and Asri, not when they're . . . almost parts of her, can I say? Just as you and Kail are now almost parts of me. We all belong to each other, but oddly enough with nothing of ownership involved. Blending really does have to be experienced to be understood."

That was the point Edmin realized that Driff no longer felt the fear that had ruled him only a few moments earlier. The act of Blending had soothed Driff's fears permanently, and then Edmin realized something else as well. He'd been wanting to hold Idresia in his arms from the moment he'd met her, but now he felt the same about Issini and Asri. It *was* almost as if they were all one woman, a woman who was also a part of himself. And the two other men were included in that, in a way that was as far beyond friendship as friendship was beyond the solitary life he'd been forced to live until now.

"Having to lie with the husband my parents chose for me was what I consider hard," Asri said while Edmin stood in what was nearly a stupefied daze. "Lying with Driff and Edmin will be nearly as much pleasure as lying with Kail has become. But let's sit down and eat first, or I may not survive the pleasure."

Everyone laughed at that comment, and Edmin found himself joining in the laughter as well as joining in the group movement back to the table. Idresia's question about procedure could be answered later, once they'd taken care of the hunger they all seemed to feel. After that . . . after that they'd be a true Blending, which would bring a happiness that Edmin felt he'd never be able to explain in words to anyone else, especially not to his father . . .

# NINE

Sembrin Noll, sitting behind the desk in his study, waited impatiently for his guard commander, Jost Feriun, to report. Feriun had sent out eighteen other men to work on the plan that hadn't been handled properly the first time, and the men were due back to report. If Feriun's men had fumbled the effort a second time, Sembrin intended to be extremely hard on the man. He wasn't completely certain what he would do, but Feriun would definitely—

A knock at the door interrupted Sembrin's thoughts. He called out his permission to enter, and Feriun stepped into the room looking grimly pleased.

"The men have reported back, my lord, and this time they found nothing but success," Feriun said even before he stood in front of Sembrin's desk. "Each group of three visited all four of the locations they were given, and in every instance the reaction was the same: the fools were outraged and incensed despite the fact that most of them should have known better."

"Excellent, Feriun, truly excellent work," Sembrin said, both delighted and relieved. "I knew that the plan would work if you just used the proper men. Tomorrow you're to send the same men to the other side of the city, and if they have the same success a second time then the following day we'll move on to the next part of the plan."

"By then, having men speaking openly against the government on street corners should be perfectly safe," Feriun said with a distracted nod. "If any of the city guardsmen try to stop our men from speaking, they'll be inviting a riot on the spot. If they *don't* try to stop our men from speaking, there will be mobs converging on the palace from every direction of the city."

"And every time one smaller mob joins another, we'll have a larger and even angrier mob," Sembrin said, his satisfaction growing. "Make sure that most of our people are mixed into the final mob, ready to take over as soon as the citizens get them into the palace. In just three days we will be dining in the palace, Feriun, all of us enjoying what's rightfully ours. Will you enjoy being a noble, do you think?"

"I mean to enjoy it *very* much, my lord," Feriun answered, hardness clear behind the cold amusement in the man's eyes. "This time, though, we'll really have to do things the right way. Branding and collaring the 'people' will let them know exactly what they are to us, and if any of them try to protest or fight, we execute the loudest and punish the rest brutally right on the spot. That will make the rest of them fall into line, and more than that, *stay* in line."

"I do believe I like the way you think, Feriun," Sembrin told the man with a small laugh. "You're perfectly right about us needing to do things the proper way once we take over, and the more brutal we are, the less trouble we'll have. You and your men will have your pick of the women, of course, but right after me. I've missed having a pleasant variety in my life."

"Yes, I'm fond of that kind of variety myself," Feriun said after joining Sembrin in a laugh, but then the other man lost his amusement. "I wonder, my lord, if you have a plan yet to handle those people who are now considered to be the Seated Blending. They may be out of the city now, but the day will come when they show up again."

"By then the peasants will be under our complete control, so those freaks won't have the sort of help they had the first time," Sembrin said, losing much of his own amusement. "We know they won't hurt their precious supporters, so we'll just use those very peasants to take the freaks down.

But we won't try to make them our prisoners. I want those people dead as soon as they show their faces back here."

"I'm glad to hear you say that, my lord," Feriun muttered, looking more relieved than glad. "Your . . . former peers tried to use those people instead of putting them to death, and now men and women who were once noble are less than nothing. I'd really hate to have that happen to *us*."

"I believe I'd hate that result even more than you would," Sembrin said, rising to his feet. "I'm going to give you a bonus in gold for your men, and when you hand out the gold make sure the others know that the same will be theirs once we've won. Wait outside in the hall for me."

Feriun hesitated very briefly before nodding his agreement and leaving, which made Sembrin smile to himself. Feriun already knew that some of his employer's gold was in the study, but the man didn't know just how much or exactly where it was. Feriun had probably been feeling the urge to do a bit of searching, but had wisely decided against throwing away his future for a few gold coins in his hand right now.

*Still,* Sembrin thought as he went to the sideboard behind which the gold had been hidden, *it might be a good idea to give Feriun a bonus as well. Gold will help him to remember who is in charge, and will also add enthusiasm to whatever he says to the men. Until the Throne is mine, I do still need the fool.*

And Feriun *was* a fool, something Sembrin knew without doubt. When brutality and death were all that people had to look forward to, they sometimes decided to make their death count by making a gesture. If that gesture resulted in harm to those who had taken charge of everyone's life, the purpose would be achieved. Sembrin had no desire to end up maimed or dead, so Jost Feriun would *not* be part of his new nobility once he was firmly seated on the Throne. There were other ways than brutality to have people in your complete control, and those were the ways that Sembrin would use.

After counting out twenty pieces of gold, Sembrin returned the rest of the coins to their hiding place. It was a good thing that Bensia was no longer in a position to show her displeasure, otherwise Sembrin would have been given difficulty over handing out gold. This was *their* gold that he distributed so freely, but it did happen to be in a worthy cause. And in three days' time they would have more gold than even the old Bensia would have been able to spend . . .

Sembrin gave Feriun the gold out in the hall rather than calling the man back into his study. Feriun was more pleased than he should have been to get two gold pieces when his men would get only one apiece, showing that the man was petty and greedy as well as a fool. Sembrin watched Feriun stride away, and once the man was gone Sembrin decided to find Bensia. There was cause to celebrate, and no reason not to celebrate in his very favorite way . . .

Bensia Noll was annoyed. She'd seen the man Jost Feriun going into Sembrin's study, but by the time she'd found her son Travin the meeting was over.

"So this time we'll just have to ask Father what he was told," Travin said with a shrug when Bensia pointed out the obvious. "If I could have overheard the conversation it would be unnecessary to bother, but we just didn't get here in time, Mother."

"I don't like the idea of interrupting his daydreams, Travin," Bensia answered, her annoyance growing. "He'll stay under our control unless something shakes him out of it, so providing that something ourselves would be foolish."

"Simply questioning him won't bring him out of it, Mother," Travin disagreed with entirely too much amusement. "His strength may be close to ours, but there are still more of us than there are of him."

"That isn't the point, Travin," Bensia pointed out with forced patience. "If I hadn't noticed what he was doing just before we took him over, we might be the ones who were under control instead of him. We're too close to success right now to take any foolish chances, which is what turning your father loose at this time would be."

"Very well, Mother, we'll do it your way," Travin agreed,

but the put-upon tone in his voice accompanied by a sigh nearly made Bensia speak to him sharply. But this was also not the time for her to quarrel with her most loyal supporters, so Bensia forced herself to smile.

"Thank you, Travin," Bensia said as she put a hand to her son's arm. "I know you take the idea of risks in stride, but I'm just a woman so I worry. You won't regret indulging my concerns."

"Indulging you is always my pleasure, Mother," Travin responded with a smile of his own and a small bow. "Let's go and find out what Father was told."

Bensia thanked him with a small nod, and then took his arm for the short walk to where her husband stood. As long as she remembered that Travin was a male first and her son second, there was no difficulty at all in controlling him even without the use of her talent.

Bensia had, in a manner of speaking, frozen Sembrin in place. Her talent had made him lose himself in more than usual daydreams, and now he stood awaiting her and Travin's arrival. The man wasn't really aware of their presence, which was all to the good. Bensia nodded to Travin, to show that he was to do the questioning while she maintained her hold on Sembrin.

"Commander Feriun was just here speaking to you, Father," Travin said softly as he also used his talent. "Tell me what the man had to say."

"Today's attempts at swaying the peasants worked just the way they were supposed to," Sembrin answered, the words dreamy and distant. "They'll do the same thing tomorrow in another part of the city, and the day after that we'll have rabble-rousers forming mobs all over the city. When the mobs are fired up hot enough, we'll combine them and lead them in an attack on the palace. My men will be there to take over the palace once the mobs have gained them access, and they'll kill every member of the 'government' they can find. Then I'll go to the palace myself, and once the peasants are quieted I'll be Seated on the Throne."

"That sounds lovely, Father, and it will come just in time,"

Travin murmured with a smile. "We're all beginning to feel very cramped in this tiny house. Did you give Commander Feriun any other orders?"

"I told him to pay the men involved a bonus in gold," Sembrin answered, speaking with as little reluctance as he had earlier. "I also gave Feriun gold, to make sure he did pay over the bonus. He's to tell the men that there will be even more gold, and for all of them, once we're in the palace and in charge."

Travin simply nodded when he heard that, but Bensia's reaction was quite a bit different. Simply giving away gold to commoners went against her nature, unless it happened to be someone else's gold. In this instance it had been *her* gold that was given away, and her anger rose high enough that she was drawn into thinking thoughts of revenge against this fool she happened to be married to. He'd known she'd never approve of his giving away her gold, and that was why he hadn't told her about it . . .

"You can go back to what you were doing, Father," Travin said, the amusement in his voice drawing Bensia part way out of her anger. "And do keep up the good work."

"Of course," Sembrin said, stirring back to life and motion. "Come along, Bensia."

Bensia stood beside her son and watched her husband move off toward the stairs. The fool obviously intended to indulge his fantasies again, but this time Bensia found the intention offensive rather than amusing. She'd lost her hold on Sembrin a pair of moments earlier, but that didn't really matter. What mattered most was that the pretense was almost over. In three days it would be possible to let Sembrin know the truth, and then watch as he was chained at the foot of *her* throne. She and her children would be the ones who ruled the empire, her will controlling whatever was done.

But before then she would have to have a serious talk with Travin. It had almost seemed that he'd stopped controlling his father simply because he thought that *she* was doing the controlling. Since anger had made her lose her hold on Sembrin, they could have had a serious problem if Travin really

had released all control. But happily he hadn't—this time.
Bensia led Travin away to find his brother and sisters, and
then she would make sure that they never came this close to
trouble again.

Sembrin Noll felt oddly ill at ease as he led his wife into
their apartment. He continued on into their bedchamber and
held the door for Bensia, wondering what could possibly be
wrong. When Bensia began to fade into nothingness and
then disappeared entirely, Sembrin found himself badly
shaken. But it wasn't simply Bensia's chilling disappearance
that disturbed him. There was something more, something
important . . .

"By all the talents in the universe, none of this has been
real!" Sembrin suddenly whispered to himself, the truth
forcing itself from his lips. "I didn't give them Puredan, *they*
put *me* under control!"

Sembrin began to totter to a chair to collapse into it, but
before he sat fury flared and raged all through him. The
burning emotions kept him on his feet, curled his hands into
fists, and nearly had him scream at the top of his lungs. None
of the pleasure he'd had was real, none of it, and his sense of
personal safety had been just as much of an illusion.

The need to scream grew greater, but some still-sane part
of Sembrin forced him to deny the need. His loving family
couldn't possibly know that he'd escaped their grip, otherwise they would have already reclaimed him. It would have
been very satisfying to scream out his rage, but that would
simply bring him to Bensia's attention. He had no idea how
he'd managed to throw off the control, but it must have been
his luck or their carelessness. If he depended on the same
thing happening a second time . . .

But he wasn't fool enough to depend on the same thing
happening a second time. He had to take advantage of its
happening *this* time, but as he ran his hands through his hair
he couldn't think of a way to do it. But there *had* to be a way,
otherwise he was as good as lost.

Sembrin sat down in the chair he'd kept himself from collapsing in, leaned forward with his hands still in his hair, and began to think with all the energy of desperation behind the effort.

Honrita Grohl glanced from one to the other of most of the members of her future Blending. She had these people well enough under her control that they could now meet in Ayl's shabby little hideaway and discuss their plans. The fools all thought that being part of the group was their own idea, and that was exactly the way Honrita wanted it. As long as they all continued to be under her control they could believe anything they cared to.

". . . and I stood outside the window of his house without anyone knowing I was there," Kadri Sumlow, their Earth magic user, was saying to everyone. Kadri was a heavy woman with dull, dark hair, but she always carried herself as though she were the queen of the universe and utterly beautiful. "The man is still sick, but he's making a slow but full recovery. Another few days and he'll be up and around."

"It's about time," Stelk Faron, their Water magic user put in with his usual stiff disapproval. "We can't Blend until we have a Fire magic user, so this delay is wasting the time of all of us."

Faron was a tall, thin man with narrow-faced features that seemed to be set in a perpetual frown. He was also the fussy kind of man that Honrita had trouble putting up with, but circumstances had forced her to make an exception. At least the man sat quietly when she wanted him to . . .

"Dom Faron is perfectly right," Seeli Tandor said, showing her own frown of disapproval. The Air magic user was a tall, plain woman who didn't seem to have a personality of her own. Whenever she spoke it was as if she were borrowing the personality of one of those she sat among, most often the last person who had spoken. "We *are* all having our time wasted, which shouldn't be allowed to continue much longer. After all, we do have a rather special purpose that has brought us together."

"And our purpose *will* be served, in the time it's destined to be served," Ayl said, showing them all his faint smile. "The last of your group will soon be with us, and then your Blending can be born."

"What about our Sight magic user?" Sumlow put in, her regal expression showing a small bit of contempt for the obvious oversight. "Our Blending won't be complete without a Sight magic user."

"That is a lie," Ayl said, his faint smile disappearing as his voice went cold and distant. "There *is* no such talent as Sight magic, else I would be able to detect it. The lie has been put out to fool the people into believing what isn't so, but the claim hasn't fooled *me*. We will never discuss this subject again."

Honrita joined the others in exchanging glances without meaning to, so menacing had Ayl's tone been. The man found it impossible to admit that there was a talent he couldn't detect, so he'd decided that there *was* no such talent. For all Honrita knew, the man could be right. It was possible the idea of Sight magic *was* a ruse of some kind, but it didn't really matter. Her Blending would not be needing Sight magic, not once they had control of a High Blending.

"I want all of you to think of ways we can use to gain access to the palace," Honrita said, firmly changing the subject. "I went by there yesterday, just to take a quick look around, and discovered that no one was being admitted without an appointment. In order to reach a High Blending we need to be inside the palace, so—"

"There are any number of ways into the palace," Ayl interrupted, that faint smile back on his face again. "You can all apply for jobs, or go in as maintenance people of some sort, or even use your talent on the guardsmen. Aren't *those* enough options for you, Dama Grohl?"

"They would be, except for one or two small problems," Honrita replied, gazing at Ayl with the most neutral expression she could manage. "After all the times your former followers entered the palace as workers, no one is hired or even allowed through the front entrance until they've been thoroughly investigated. As for using our talent to gain entrance, a number of the guardsmen are Middle practitioners of Spirit magic themselves. Those people are on the alert for anyone trying to influence the rest of the guardsmen, so acting alone is out. If we use our Blending to influence those people, we can't walk inside. If you Blend, you can't walk around. If you want to walk around, you can't Blend."

"Must I do all the creative thinking myself?" Ayl put in after a long moment, that smile still there but a bit more distant. "If it becomes absolutely necessary, we'll simply wait for one of the Blending members to come out to us."

"How are we supposed to tell a Blending member from any other High talent?" Honrita countered, beginning to get a bit of pleasure from taunting Ayl. "I'm sure *you* can tell the difference, so please share the method with the rest of us."

"The difference is easily seen, less easily described," Ayl said after another long moment, only the suggestion of a smile left to him. "When the time comes, I'll point out the desired target."

"Why won't we be able to simply take someone over and ask?" Kadri Sumlow put in, looking back and forth between Honrita and Ayl. "Getting the answer from someone who knows what we need to find out would take the guesswork out of the effort, wouldn't you agree?"

Honrita watched Ayl stiffen at Sumlow's patronizing tone, and pleasure touched her again. Ayl seemed to be used to people falling all over themselves to worship him, just as she had pretended to do at first. But worship, she'd discovered, was extremely boring, whereas baiting seemed to be a never-ending enjoyment. As long as she used her talent to keep from going too far, there was no real need to be bored.

"There, you see?" Honrita said to a still-silent Ayl with an open smile. "When you ask the right people for suggestions, you tend to get what you need. I can see now why you chose these people, Dom Ayl."

"Yes, I did choose them, didn't I," Ayl said, as though he were thinking out loud. "They are, in effect, my creatures, and what one of mine does is merely an extension of my own efforts. The matter is now clear to me, and I approve."

Ayl sat looking as though he certainly did approve, and Honrita caught the glances exchanged among the others. She'd made sure to tell *her* people about Ayl's madness, and to explain that the man was needed to put *them* in power. Once they were successful, he would no longer be needed. Ayl had told Honrita that he'd chosen the strongest Middle talents in the city for his own private Blending, and that Honrita did believe.

"So that point is settled," Honrita said, looking around at everyone with the same pleasant, open smile. "When the time comes, we'll have no trouble finding the ones we want. Taking over even one High talent will give us the rest of them through the efforts of our puppet, and then we'll have *them* walk us into the palace. Does anyone see a problem with that plan?"

"Not with that one, no," Stelk Faron said, his stiff disapproval still very much in evidence. "I must, however, return to the problem of our fifth member. His recovery is taking much too long, and we must do something to hasten it."

"If I were able to get closer to him, I might be able to help out with that," Kadri Sumlow said with a thoughtful look coloring her haughty attitude. "I am, after all, a much better healer than the one treating him. I simply can't do my best from a distance."

"She shouldn't be *expected* to work at a distance," Seeli Tandor stated, showing just as much haughtiness as Sumlow had. "Using her talent in such an unproductive way is tantamount to wasting it."

"Since our fifth is up and about, there's no reason why Dama Sumlow and I can't go and visit him," Honrita said as though considering an idea that hadn't come to her sooner. "I'm sure I can . . . convince him to let another healer work on him, and that way he can be among us more quickly."

The others murmured immediate agreement, not to mention approval of the idea. Honrita had saved the suggestion specifically for the meeting, to show everyone who the real leader of the group was. Ayl hadn't made a single useful suggestion, but she, on the other hand, had come off looking rather well.

Honrita glanced at Ayl, and was somewhat surprised to see his usual faint smile. The man should have been annoyed, but instead he was feeling extremely pleased about something. And even as Honrita watched, the pleasure inside him was . . . submerged, somehow, as though it had never been. If she hadn't been watching so closely with her talent, she would have missed knowing anything at all about the emotion.

It took only a moment of thought for Honrita to realize that Ayl had plans he hadn't mentioned to her or anyone else. Honrita had found another Guild member, one who was as high up as Ayl used to be, and discovered that she couldn't put the man under her control. Her talent seemed to . . . flow past the man, which meant that nothing she'd tried—or wanted to try—with Ayl affected him.

That made for something of a problem, but one that would continue only until she had a Blending of her own to work with. Not even Ayl would be able to resist a Blending entity, and then she would find out what the madman was up to. He obviously thought he could escape her just retribution, but that would not be happening.

She *would* get even for everything done and not done, she *would*!

# TEN

Everyone but Rion and Naran had moved away from the grass we'd been sitting on to do other things. I just sat there thinking about the enemy we'd only gotten a glimpse of in the flesh. We still didn't know what their entity was like, and that bothered me. When you know exactly what you have to face, it's possible to be brave even if your opponent is bigger and stronger and very frightening. But if you have no idea what your opponent will be like, fear goes wild along with your imagination . . .

"Tamrissa, we need to speak with you for a moment," I heard Rion murmur. When I looked up I saw that both he and Naran had moved closer to me, and both of them looked worried.

"What's wrong?" I asked, knowing for a fact that there was definitely a problem. "Did I miss seeing something happen?"

"No, it isn't something that you could have seen," Naran said, actually answering for herself. She'd been doing a lot of that lately, a definite improvement. "When I agreed with Lorand that I wasn't aware of conversation when we were Blended, I lied. I heard everything just the way Vallant did, but I didn't want Lorand to think he was all alone. Was I wrong to support him? Is there anything you can think of that we can do to help Lorand?"

"Naran has also told me that we must discover what the problem is and correct it," Rion put in, looking really disturbed. "If this particular problem isn't solved, we won't have to worry about any of the others."

"Why does every problem we face have to be a matter of survival or extinction?" I asked the world at large, my growing anger making me really want an answer. "Why can't we have an unimportant problem for once, one we can ignore without worrying that the world will end because we didn't take care of it?"

"We're just lucky, I guess," Naran answered with an odd smile. "Someone or something doesn't seem to want us to grow bored."

"I've decided I agree with Vallant about boredom," I stated, showing Naran that her comment hadn't amused me. "I can learn to really enjoy boredom, if someone or something would only give me the chance to do it. Well, no sense in wishing for something we aren't going to get. You two take Lorand aside and make a bunch of guesses as to why he and Naran haven't experienced what the rest of us have in the Blending. I'll get Vallant and Jovvi together and pass on the problem, and maybe one of *them* will think of what we can do."

The two of them agreed immediately before getting to their feet, so I sighed just a little before doing my own standing. The anger I'd felt earlier seemed to be growing, as if there really was someone to be angry at. If it ever turned out that there *was* someone behind everything we'd been going through, they would enjoy my discovering who they were as much as I was enjoying what we were being put through . . .

"What's wrong now?" I heard Vallant ask, and looked up to see that he'd left the people he'd been speaking with to come over to me. "I could feel your temper burnin' all the way over there."

"Don't worry, it's nothing personal, but I'm going to act as if it is," I told him in a mutter. "As soon as Jovvi is alone I'm going to stalk over to her, and when you follow to hear me complain about you I'll tell the both of you what the problem is."

"I'm glad you warned me," he muttered back with a scowl

that hid amusement. "If you really started bein' mad at me again, I'd probably go hide instead of followin'. I don't think I'm strong enough to go through war with you again."

"Poor baby," I murmured with my own pretend scowl, giving him a wink only he could see. "Then I guess I'll have to do the arguing for both of us."

And with that I turned with a haughty toss of my head and strode off toward Jovvi, who now stood alone sipping tea. Vallant lost no time in following me, and by the time we reached Jovvi her brows were raised high.

"What's going on?" she asked at once, looking back and forth between Vallant and me. "My eyes tell me that you two are in the midst of feuding again, but my talent says you're doing no such thing."

"It's all *his* fault!" I said in a moderately loud voice, then lowered my tone to keep the "complaint" private. "Actually, your talent is right. I have to talk to the two of you, and pretending to complain about Vallant is the easiest way to do it. Naran and Rion told me that she lied when she said she didn't hear the rest of us in the Blending. That means Lorand is the only one who's cut off, and Naran also says we have to solve his problem otherwise we don't have a chance against the invaders. Do either of you have any idea what's wrong, or what we can do about it?"

"Lorand seems perfectly normal to me," Vallant said with a frown that wasn't acting. "He's just the way he always was, so I don't know what the trouble can be."

"What you just said may be the very thing that's causing trouble," Jovvi said to Vallant with a worried expression creasing her brow. "Lorand *is* just the way he always was, which means he's been hiding jealousy instead of talking about it or showing it. But possibly understand the situation better than I do, Vallant. I've been able to detect jealousy in you as well."

"No, it's not really important or even relevant," Vallant said at once with a glance for me as his skin darkened just a bit. "It's a silly private thing that I'm havin' trouble with, and it's really not important."

"Please, Vallant, tell us what it is," Jovvi urged as I stood there without anything to say. "Even the smallest scrap of information could mean the difference between helping Lorand and leaving him to flounder. And we're quickly running out of time. The enemy—"

"All right, I know how little time we have," Vallant said sharply, then shook his head. "I apologize for cuttin' you off, Jovvi, but I've been feelin' guilty about this for some time now . . . Tamrissa, I really do love you, but—I also love Jovvi and Naran. That makes me a low, miserable dog, doesn't it?"

"If it does, then I'm the same," I blurted, more relieved than I ever expected to be. "I love you too, but I also love Rion and Lorand. I had no idea how to tell you about it without hurting you."

"But that's wonderful!" Vallant said with a big smile, putting one hand to my arm. "We both feel the same way about it, so there's nothin' of a problem."

"*You* have nothing of a problem," Jovvi corrected with gentle understanding, drawing our attention. "Lorand is still in the same position, so can you please explain why you felt jealous if you really weren't?"

"I was jealous of Rion, mostly," Vallant answered with what looked like a small boy's discomfort. "He seemed just as devoted to Naran as ever, and I was hatin' myself for not bein' the same with Tamrissa. Lovin' her only a little bit more than lovin' you other ladies seemed like nothin' short of betrayal."

"I think we're *supposed* to feel like that, since most of us do," I offered with a warm smile for Vallant. "Is it possible that Lorand is feeling the same kind of guilt and jealousy, but in his case it's keeping him from . . . I don't know . . . merging with us completely, maybe?"

"But the feelings didn't keep Vallant from . . . merging with the rest of us, so I don't think that's it," Jovvi said, a small headshake joining her concern. "That means his problem has to be different, and the only way we'll find out what it is will be by asking him."

"Naran and Rion are talking to him right now, to distract him from *this* conversation," I said with a sigh. "Maybe they all figured something out, and the problem is solved without the rest of us."

"I certainly hope so, but I'm not counting on it," Jovvi said with her own sigh. "Let's go over there and find out."

Vallant gave me a glance that said he'd rather just stand and talk for the rest of the day, and I knew exactly how he felt. Personal interrelations between the members of our Blending had always been more than complicated, but we had no choice about getting involved again. If our Blending was growing again in some way, we all had to grow with it or the rest of us were wasting our time.

Lorand was still deep in conversation with Rion and Naran when we walked over to them. Jovvi led the way, and when she reached Lorand he put an arm around her shoulders.

"Hi, love," Lorand said as he kissed Jovvi's cheek. "We were just trying to figure out why Naran and I are the only ones who haven't experienced this new thing in the Blending. We haven't gotten very far, so maybe the rest of you will come up with something that makes sense."

"Lorand, love, the problem isn't exactly what you think it is," Jovvi told him gently as she touched his face with one hand. "You need to know that Naran *did* experience what the rest of us did. You're the only one who hasn't, so things are more complicated than we thought."

"But . . . Why did you say you didn't experience it when you did, Naran?" Lorand blurted, agitation giving him a bewildered expression. "Were you trying to fool me into something?"

"I didn't want you to feel left out, Lorand," Naran said at once, her expression so full of commiseration that it was impossible to doubt her. "I know much too well what feeling left out is like, and I'd only wish the feeling on my worst enemy. Not on someone I care so much about."

Lorand went silent as his skin darkened, and suddenly he wasn't able to make eye contact with any of us. I thought it was just embarrassment over his having accused Naran of something underhanded, but Jovvi seemed to know better.

"What you're feeling right now relates directly to the problem, love," she said, her tone relentless despite the compassion on her face. "Tell me why your discomfort is ringed with so much guilt. And I'd also like to know what all that jealousy inside you is about."

We all waited to hear what Lorand would say, but he stood silent as he continued to look down at the ground. The silence dragged on for a very long moment, and then I got the strangest idea.

"Lorand, we once had a discussion about how you felt about Jovvi being a courtesan," I said slowly, trying to get my thoughts in order. "You said you hated the idea of her lying with other men, but that can't possibly relate to her lying with Vallant and Rion. They're not other men, they're part of the whole that makes up our entity. It would be like resenting your own lying with her."

"And I seem to recall a time not long ago when you happily went with Naran while I paired with Jovvi," Vallant said when Lorand made no comment on what I'd said. "You told me you weren't bothered at all, and you were also actin' like it. You can't mean you were lyin'?"

"I wasn't lying, not really," Lorand blurted, finally looking up. "I knew in the beginning that we had to lie with each other to make our Blending bond strong, and that time you're talking about was to help out a brother as well as a sister. But now it looks like we'll have to lie with each other on a regular basis, and that's not the same thing at all. It's just not the same."

Once again Lorand was looking away from the rest of us, while *we* were busy exchanging glances. Vallant had obviously been right to say that Lorand was the way he had always been, and that *was* the whole trouble.

"So Naran and I both love you, but you don't return the feeling," I heard myself saying to Lorand, and somehow a trace of hurt ran through the words. "You haven't merged with the rest of us in the entity because you don't want to be a part of us the rest of the time."

"But that isn't true," Lorand said at once, his expression now stricken. "Of course I love you and Naran, or I couldn't have lain with the two of you. That's not what's . . . disturbing me."

"I believe *I* see the point of disturbance," Rion said, a small bit of revelation in his tone—along with something else. "Your lying with Tamrissa and Naran is perfectly acceptable, but Jovvi's lying with Vallant and myself is not. Would you care to explain how that can be? You've used the term 'brother' at least as often as I have, but obviously the word has a different meaning for you than it does for the rest of us."

"But—don't you see that it doesn't *matter* if I consider you brothers?" Lorand said, his brows having risen with surprise. "I had brothers at home, too, but I didn't share a woman with them. No man shared his woman, because doing something like that just isn't right."

"No, Lorand, this time *you're* the one who isn't right," I said quickly, annoyed with myself for not having seen the truth sooner. "It's clear now that you may have left that farm district physically, but inside your head you're still living among those narrow-minded provincials. The rest of us have grown, but you're still a little boy who worries what the neighbors will think."

"What Tamrissa means is that you're not lookin' at the matter in the proper light," Vallant added hastily as Lorand actually frowned at me. "Sleepin' around, especially after you pair up with a woman, isn't acceptable behavior in my hometown either, but men boast about doin' it and women pretend they never indulge. If a woman is caught sleepin' around, her reputation disappears instantly. But, Lorand— haven't you noticed that we're not sneakin' around behind each other's backs? We're not playin' sex games, we're doin' what we have to in order to make our Blendin' as strong as it can be. And we only do it in our merged pairs—

or at least that's all the rest of us do. Are you sayin' you indulge with women other than our three?"

"Of course he doesn't, but not for the reason the rest of us don't go looking," I said while Lorand tried to babble out a very embarrassed denial. "*He* doesn't go after other women because he's still a little boy who worries what a bunch of people he doesn't even like may say about him. And more than that, he worries about what those stupid people will say about Jovvi, the woman he considers his. If *he* gets caught with one of the other women in our pairs, he can grin while his loutish friends congratulate him in private. But if Jovvi is caught with you or Rion, Vallant, he'll be humiliated in front of everyone. After all, we all know what people think of *sluts* and the men who associate with them."

"It was Korge who did this, wasn't it, Lorand?" Jovvi said, shock staring from her gaze. "Tamma is right about the way you feel, and it all stems from that act Korge put on to keep the members of the other council Blendings from lying together. No one else took him seriously, but his attitude threw you right back into your original way of looking at things. You're ashamed of all of us, and ashamed to be considered one of us."

"And that's why you haven't merged with us in the entity," Naran said while Lorand stared at Jovvi silently with a stricken expression. "You think it's wrong to do what we do, so you've held yourself back."

"And you'll probably continue to hold yourself back, which is fine with me," I said, the words hard as I interrupted whatever else Naran may have wanted to say. "Since you're such a better person than the rest of us, you can relax from now on. If anyone ever suggests that I lie with you again, I'll burn them to ash just to show how firm my refusal will be."

After having told him exactly the way I felt, I turned and walked away from all of them. It had been impossible to miss how hurt Jovvi felt, and her pain had fed my anger to the flaming stage. At one point I'd thought we were all through with being hurt by anyone but outsiders, but obviously I'd been wrong.

"Tamrissa, wait," Vallant called from behind me, his voice filled with disturbance. "Lorand isn't feelin' things like that on purpose. He's just reactin' to the way he was raised, which is always the hardest battle we ever have to fight."

"Garbage," I countered with a very rude sound, pausing to turn and glare my disdain. "Rion and I also had to fight the way *we* were raised, but we managed it because we didn't consider ourselves morally superior. *He* does, and if I ever need my life saved again and you let *him* do it, I'll never speak to you again. I'd rather be dead than be saved by someone so . . . *good*."

The shock on Lorand's pale face said he knew I wasn't lying or just speaking to hear the sound of my own voice. I meant every word I'd said, and I was *glad* he knew it. What I didn't understand was how I could have ever considered that man a friend and more . . .

I began to take another step away from the group when I became aware of something that anger had kept me from noticing sooner. One of our associate Blendings had their entity on watch, and some part of me knew exactly where that entity was. Which meant that the entity I now sensed probably wasn't one of ours. I didn't know *exactly* where the new entity was, but there was no doubt about its being very near.

The enemy was right on top of us, and our strongest Blending members were barely speaking to each other, not to mention being totally unready to fight!

Lorand swam in confusion and helplessness. It had been something of a shock to learn that he was the only one who hadn't . . . merged during the last time they'd Blended, but the following conversation had made things worse rather than better. He hadn't known himself precisely what he was feeling, and he'd been horrified when Tamrissa actually put those feelings into words. It wasn't possible to deny what she'd said, and then she turned and started to stalk away.

"Tamrissa, wait," Vallant called, saving Lorand from having to fight to say the words himself. "Lorand isn't feelin' things like that on purpose. He's just reactin' to the way he was raised, which is always the hardest battle we ever have to fight."

"Garbage," Tamrissa denied with a snort, pausing to turn and stare at Lorand with disgust. "Rion and I also had to fight the way *we* were raised, but we managed it because we didn't consider ourselves morally superior. *He* does, and if I ever need my life saved again and you let *him* do it, I'll never speak to you again. I'd rather be dead than be saved by someone so . . . *good.*"

Lorand felt as though someone had stabbed him in the chest with a very long, sharp knife. Tamrissa had been his friend almost from the first day they'd met, and since then she'd become something a good deal more . . . complex in his life. He loved Jovvi with every fiber of his being, and when Jovvi had looked her pain at him it had been almost more than he could bear. Now Tamrissa had added to his anguish, in a way that a simple friend could never have done. The beautiful Fire magic user was vitally important in Lorand's life, and now she had taken herself out of it.

And what was happening was all *his* fault! He'd thought he'd outgrown the provincial attitudes he'd been raised with, but it had suddenly been made clear to him that he'd simply buried those prejudices. Intellectually he knew that he and the others weren't just not doing wrong but were doing what was necessary, but some mindless part of him refused to accept that. That mindless part *knew* right from wrong, just the way his former neighbors in Widdertown did. Right was what *they* thought it was, no matter the opinions of others . . .

"Is anyone else sensing what I am?" Rion suddenly asked in a very soft voice. "Please answer quickly."

For an instant Lorand had no idea what Rion was talking about, but then an awareness pushed its way through the chaos in Lorand's mind. There was a Blending entity not far away, but it was too tenuous and . . . *stealthy,* for want of a better word, for it to be one of their associates. It looked like *they* were being scouted in the same way they had scouted the enemy earlier.

"We've got to take care of this," Jovvi said, visibly pulling herself together. "Are all of you ready?"

"What about Tamrissa?" Vallant protested, then he shook his head. "No, never mind. I can see that she already knows about our visitor, and she's ready and waitin'. That means there's nothin' keepin' us from doin' it."

*Nothing but me,* Lorand thought very briefly before the rest of his thoughts were submerged into the entity.

# ELEVEN

The Rion entity looked around as soon as he was formed. There was an intruder in their midst, something his flesh forms had become aware of in a very satisfying manner. The Rion entity was pleased, knowing that his maturation was proceeding in a proper manner.

But maturation was hardly the most important consideration at the moment. More to the point was the intruder, which had thinned itself to so diffuse a state that the Rion entity's associate entities had no idea that it was present.

*I think we ought to attack it, to teach it not to do this again,* the Rion entity's Tamrissa part said at once. *Making it cautious can only help us.*

*The probabilities counsel against such an action,* the Naran part put in as a response. *The results of such a doing narrow our options far too much.*

*Yes, you're quite right,* the Rion entity agreed as he, too, studied the probabilities. *It seems that an attempt to communicate would be the least restrictive action.*

*I agree,* the Jovvi part of the Rion entity put forth. *We may even get some useful information.*

*Before the rain begins,* the Vallant part added. *Once the rain does begin, all flesh forms involved will be less flexible.*

*Less willing to listen to reason,* the Rion entity clarified for his own sake. *Very well, let us attempt communication.*

It was very difficult to perceive the intruder entity in its present state, but knowing of its presence let the Rion entity float forward almost a foot of distance before he directed a thought at the intruder.

—*For what reason have you and your flesh forms invaded this place?*—the Rion entity sent.—*We are fully aware of your presence, therefore you need not remain silent.*—

—*You surprise this entity,*—the intruder responded, a superior amusement to be felt behind the communication.— *Those others have no idea that this entity is present, which should be the case for you as well. You will be useful to this entity once you have been properly subdued.*—

—*We will never be yours to command,*—the Tamrissa part of the Rion entity responded at once, disdain clear in the thought.—*Even an incomplete entity such as yourself should find that truth clear.*—

—*You are aware of the fact that this entity is incomplete?*—the intruder put just as quickly.—*As that is so, you must inform this entity at once as to what it lacks and how it may obtain that thing.*—

—*You have not responded to our own query,*—the Jovvi part of the Rion entity put before the Tamrissa part might comment again.—*With that in view, it would be illogical to expect a response from us.*—

—*How young and foolish you are,*—the intruder entity responded, distant and superior amusement clear.—*This entity has come to make this new land completely ours, just as the old lands are. Your entity is so new that you still perceive yourselves as individuals rather than as a whole, a fact which should clearly indicate how much greater this entity is than you. You will therefore respond at once to the question which has been put to you.*—

—*As you have requested a response, you shall have it,*— the Rion entity put, feeling the agreement of his diverse parts.—*Take your flesh forms and depart this land never to return, or we will destroy you.*—

—*You refuse to do as this entity commands?*—the intruder entity demanded after a long moment of silence, most likely a silence the intruder had expected to be filled with the information it sought.—*How can you not know that refusal is not permitted? Possibly you have not yet learned how truly helpless you are before this entity. Should that be so, then a lesson is clearly in order.—*

By then most of the Rion entity's associate Blendings had put forth entities to join his, and yet the intruder entity seemed to dismiss their presence entirely. A . . . roiling began inside the intruder entity, and then the Rion entity was struck so hard that he nearly lost all sense of center and balance. The Rion entity's defenses were just able to withstand the assault, but it wasn't possible to respond in any way.

At the first sign of the intruder's attack, the Rion entity's associate Blending entities attacked in return. The Rion entity was able to perceive those counterattacks, yet was, unfortunately, also able to perceive the fact that the intruder entity remained mostly unharmed. That the intruder entity suddenly flashed away beyond all perception seemed to be more a matter of choice than of necessity, but once it was clear that the intruder was gone it was suddenly Rion alone again.

"That *hurt*," Tamrissa's voice came while Rion tried to stop the dizziness twisting him about. "I've never felt anything like that before even though it seemed familiar in some way, and it was all I could do to protect us. What in the name of chaos did that thing use?"

"Whatever it was, respondin' just wasn't possible," Vallant put in, his voice sounding as strained as Tamrissa's had. "If the others hadn't attacked and distracted the intruder, we might not be sittin' here complainin' right now."

"I think I could have taken *one* more blow like that first one," Tamrissa said, and Rion opened his eyes to see that she sat among them. Something seemed odd about that fact, but Rion's head hurt too much for him to want to think about anything that wasn't absolutely essential.

"One more blow, but not two," Jovvi put in, stating rather than asking. "I had that same impression, which gives us another bit of information to add to the others. The fact that the intruder is stronger than we are isn't something I really wanted to have confirmed, and now that we know for certain . . ."

"Now that we know for certain, we'll have to do something about it," Lorand finished for Jovvi firmly, apparently surprising the others as much as he did Rion. "Yes, I know why you're all looking at me like that, but you don't have to. When the intruder hit us like that, I think the blow jarred loose some of the rock that has been lining the inside of my head."

"What do you mean, Lorand?" Jovvi asked at once, her gaze fixed anxiously on his face. "Are you saying that you were able to merge with the rest of us inside the entity?"

"No, I still couldn't hear anyone's thoughts but my own," Lorand replied, bleakness flitting briefly through his own gaze. "But that was before the attack, so it's possible that I might . . . merge the next time. You see, it finally came through to me that right and wrong don't matter when it comes to all of *you*. For an instant I thought you might all be killed, and I simply couldn't live with that idea. I couldn't bear the thought of any of you dying or even of you being hurt, and my own survival or ending was an insignificant and unimportant point that wasn't any part of the situation. You're all more important to me than my own individual existence, something I thought I understood before this. Now I *know* what you all mean to me, and I'll never let anything make me forget again."

"Talk is cheap," Tamrissa put in, but not as brashly as she usually spoke. Rion's sister of Fire magic still looked more than a bit pale, suggesting that the pain she'd mentioned still hadn't left her.

"Talk is cheap, so let's just wait until the next time we Blend before we congratulate Lorand on having grown up," Tamrissa said, the words a bit breathy. "Until then, I think I need to lie down for a while."

"What you need, you beautiful but obstinate mule, is to borrow some strength from your link groups," Lorand replied rather dryly. "Your strength was drained too badly by that attack, and the pain you feel won't go away until you have most of the strength back again. And when you find out that I meant what I said, I'll expect an apology from you."

"Just keep on expecting it," Tamrissa muttered, but then she closed her eyes for a long moment. During that time she actually began to sit straighter, and when she opened her eyes again the shadow of pain was gone from them.

"All right, now I'm more in the mood for a discussion than a nap," she said as she looked around, pointedly not thanking Lorand for his suggestion. "The first thing I'd like to discuss is how the intruder could not know why it was incomplete. Didn't it pay any attention at all to the composition of our entity?"

"That question just raises another," Jovvi said with a small shake of her head. "It's possible for *us* to know when a Blending entity doesn't have Sight magic as part of it, but is it possible in any way to separate out one of the six talents for a Blending that doesn't possess all six? That, I think, is the first question we need answered."

"Askin' our associate Blendin's won't do any good, so let's ask the new Gracelian Blendin's," Vallant suggested. "We've never gone into what the rest of us look like to *them*."

"That's a good idea," Rion said, feeling considerably better after he had also borrowed some strength from his link groups. "The Gracelians don't seem to be Blended any longer, so let's call them over and ask."

No one spoke up with an objection, so Rion stood and walked over to where the new Gracelian Blending members had arranged themselves in groups. Most of them remained sitting, but some few members had risen to their feet to pace back and forth. They gave Rion their immediate attention, and then all rose to follow him back to where his Blending-mates still sat.

"You people are really incredible," Rangis Hoad, the Spirit magic member of one of the Blendings, said as he and the others arranged themselves on the ground around Rion's Blending after Rion resumed his own place. "When the enemy struck at you we could almost feel it, and if *we'd* been struck directly the blow would have flattened us for good. How did you develop the ability to withstand the use of so much power?"

Rion began to explain that greater strength developed the longer a Blending practiced together, but an exclamation from Tamrissa cut him short.

"Yes, *that's* what it was!" Tamrissa said excitedly after having straightened where she sat. "I knew there was something familiar about what was done, and that has to be it. They didn't strike at us with talent, they used *power*."

"You didn't know?" Rangis Hoad asked, looking around at all of them. "We all noticed that you don't use power the way we do, but we thought it was choice on your part. You can't mean you don't know *how* to use power instead of talent?"

"Using power wasn't part of our initial training," Tamrissa explained briefly, looking distracted. "But I accidentally stumbled across the way to do it, using one of the patterns we taught you. Do you find it easier using power *without* using the pattern?"

"No, not in any way at all," Hoad answered while exchanging glances with some of his countrymen. "Using the pattern gives us the kind of control we've never really had before, but it takes practice to work *with* the pattern instead of without it. Even so, we still can't match the kind of strength *you* show."

"The longer you touch the power continuously and work as a Blending, the stronger you'll get," Tamrissa said in a reassuring way. "Right now I'm just wondering how much practice *we'll* need before we'll be able to use all that extra strength as easily as we now use talent."

"I'm afraid I don't quite see the benefit in using power in the place of talent," Rion said, suddenly deciding to voice his doubts. "Power may provide raw strength, but talent gives us finer control of our *individual* strengths."

"But that seems to be the whole point, Rion," Tamrissa objected before anyone else could speak. "When *I* used power, it manifested as my own talent but greatly magnified. We know we can't take *in* any more power, but there doesn't seem to be anything keeping us from *using* power instead of taking it in. Do you See anything to disagree with that idea, Naran?"

"Truthfully, I'm having trouble understanding the difference," Naran replied, looking almost as confused as Rion felt. "I have the definite impression that this is something we really do need, but that doesn't help me to understand what it is."

"Okay, let's see if we can start from the beginning, so to speak," Tamrissa said, her brow creased with concentration. "In order to make our talents work, we have to first touch the power. Once we do that we can use our talents to the extent of individual ability, and there are patterns that let us use our ability in a definite, concentrated way instead of just throwing it out at large. Does everyone follow that?"

"The patterns help direct whatever ability we have," Naran said with a nod. "I understand that and have even learned to use the patterns, but what I don't see is how we can use power *instead* of our ability. Isn't that like eating food to give us strength to throw rocks, and then trying to throw the food instead?"

"No, because we aren't really throwing the food," Tamrissa said after joining everyone else in chuckling. "The pattern I'm talking about is like a stove, and it turns raw food into cooked, which is much easier for our bodies to handle. Here, look at the pattern *I* used, and see if it makes the idea easier to grasp."

Suddenly a flaming pattern hung in the air in the middle of their circle, one that could be applied to Air magic with just a few minor changes. Rion vaguely remembered having seen the pattern before, but now it made a lot more sense to him. If he adapted it to Air magic and used it instead of the patterns he now used . . .

"Oh, I see now," Naran exclaimed after a moment, apparently reacting just as Rion had. "The pattern has to be changed for *me* to use it, but once I make the changes it ought to increase my ability. The other patterns let me *eat* the food, so to speak, but this one lets me *absorb* the food directly."

"I think I've gained some weight from all this talk about food and eating," Jovvi commented with a smile as a chuckle ran through everyone again. "I remember seeing this pattern once before, and also remember seeing how it can be changed to work for *me*. What isn't clear right now is why we never tried to do anything with this pattern before now. Why did we just see it and then forget about it?"

"Possibly we forgot about it because we didn't need it," Vallant suggested, but the hint of a frown showed on his face. "Usin' a mountain to crush an ant doesn't make much sense even if you *can* move the mountain if you have to. Simply steppin' on the ant is so much easier."

"And the stepping makes more sense if you're in the middle of chaos," Lorand put in, also looking faintly disturbed. "That explanation sounds so reasonable, I'm wondering why I feel as if I shouldn't believe it."

"Possibly because you have the ability to tell truth from lie, just as I do," Jovvi said, gazing at Lorand in a speculative way. "There isn't any real, *outright* lie here, but there's some kind of evasion involved that I don't understand at all. *We're* not involved in the evasion, but that doesn't seem to matter. It's still here."

"You seem to be saying that there *is* someone standing in the shadows, causing all these things that are happening to us," Tamrissa stated, and Rion saw the hint of flames in her eyes that he hadn't seen in quite some time. When Tamrissa grew really angry, her Fire talent seemed to grow almost beyond her control . . . "If someone *is* using us as handy puppets, I don't think they're going to like my reaction when I find out who they are."

"If there *is* someone like that out there, I'd venture to guess that they aren't controlling everything," Rion put slowly as he thought the matter through. "To believe that someone would encourage—or allow—the deaths of hundreds or thousands of innocent people in this invasion merely to put *us* in the middle of it is quite insane. We may have been rather important to the people of our own country, but we simply aren't important enough for something like that."

"I have to agree with Rion," Vallant said as Lorand added

a sigh and a nod. "We've been feelin' as if the world revolves around us, but it just isn't so. Every now and again we might be important to those around us, but no one in the world is important enough for somethin' like what's happenin' now to be done on purpose."

"But it doesn't necessarily *have* to be something that's being done on purpose," Jovvi said, looking more thoughtful as doubt began to quiet the flames in Tamrissa's eyes. "Do you remember the way Ristor Ardanis, the leader of those with Sight magic, kept testing us before he came forward to tell us about his people? Somehow this feels very much like another test situation."

"Who would be mad enough to test us when there are so many lives at stake?" Lorand asked as he showed the same confusion Rion had begun to feel. "And to add to the question list I just started, what would be their purpose in testing us? Not to mention asking how they can stand apart and do the testing in the midst of all this insanity."

"Is it possible that we're imagining things?" Tamrissa asked, her doubt clearly having grown. "I know I tend to be arrogant most of the time, and arrogance does encourage a feeling of self-importance. Is it possible that my arrogance has rubbed off on the rest of you, and that's why we all feel that someone is doing something?"

Rion joined most of the others in conceding that Tamrissa's suggestion *might* be true, but Naran simply shook her head.

"No, I don't think that that's possible," she said, her gaze on the distance rather than on anything around her. "This new pattern lets me cut through quite a lot of the fog that's been keeping me almost blind, and I'm getting a hint of a larger picture that's been kept from me before this. There's more involved here than just a simple invasion, and there's the suggestion of other forces on the fringes of what I can See. We seem to be walking a tightrope among the probabilities, and if we fall off we won't have another chance to survive."

"Somehow I get the feelin' that more than our own sur-

vival is at stake," Vallant said, a frown creasing his face
again. "I don't know why I'm feelin' that, but there's no
doubt surroundin' the notion."

"I don't know how you're doing it either, but you're
right," Naran answered with a faint smile, her gaze still distant. "More than our own survival is definitely at stake, but
the number of probabilities covering that fact is too large for
me to see them all. Now it's not just Tamrissa who's stealing
my talent, brother. You're doing the same."

"Although I brought one of the matters up myself, we really don't have time to worry about shadowy figures or odd
thievery," Jovvi said, apparently feeling it was time to
change the subject. "What we do have to worry about is
practicing with the new pattern so that we'll be ready for the
intruder the next time we meet. One of the things we need to
find out is whether to use the pattern at all times, or only at
certain times."

"Hopefully, practice will show us that," Rion said, agreeing that it was time to return to the matter at hand. "And perhaps our Gracelian colleagues will assist us in learning the
truth."

"We'll definitely be glad to help any way we can," Hoad
agreed as all the others either nodded or spoke different
words of agreement. "But I'm still a little confused. Am I
wrong in believing that you asked us over here for a different reason entirely?"

"No, as a matter of fact you're right, and once again
we've been diverted from our original purpose," Rion said,
definitely feeling foolish. "I have the distinct impression
that a good deal of the difficulty we have is due to our being
too often diverted from our original purpose. What we
wanted to know was, when your Blendings look at ours, are
you able to see which of the six talents is missing in your
own Blending?"

"No, not really," Hoad said after exchanging glances with
several others. "We can see that your Blending is larger,
stronger, and more complete than ours, but we can't tell
what's missing in our own."

"Well, that answers our original question," Vallant said with a nod. "The intruder may know there's somethin' missin', but it can't tell what that somethin' is. Okay, people, let's get on to the practicin' now. I'm sure you've all realized that we'll be better off takin' the fight to the invaders rather than lettin' them come to us. We'll need room to run if runnin' becomes the only thing left, so we don't have much time."

There was a disturbed murmur in reaction to Vallant's comments, but Rion's reaction was more internal and a good deal colder. They *would* have to go after the invaders and see what could be done against them, but Rion had the definite feeling that their attempt would not be as successful as they were hoping it would be.

But Rion kept that opinion to himself. He, too, seemed to be sharing Naran's talent, and as he ran a hand through his hair he admitted to himself that he would have been happier without the knowledge . . .

# TWELVE

If Lorand hadn't been quite so hungry from the practicing they'd been doing, he knew he'd probably have nothing in the way of an appetite. He sat among his Blendingmates as they all ate, but he had the impression he also seemed to be sitting alone. Practicing with the new pattern had been individual efforts for all of them, but in a short while they would be trying the new technique as a Blending.

It was only a short time past noon, but the coming rain had put clouds all over the sky and lowered the temperature more than was comfortable. Lorand felt a definite urge to shiver and wrap something around himself, but he wasn't certain that the chill he felt was entirely physical. He'd loudly announced a few hours ago that he was a changed man, but now that boast felt more like wishful thinking than fact. Was he really changed, or would he still find himself barred from merging with the others?

After muttering something about getting more tea, Lorand got to his feet and went over to the cook fire. He somehow felt less alone over here, even though he'd left the midst of the people most important in the world to him. He *did* love them all and living without them would be impossible, but . . . Just how much *could* you change the way you'd been thinking since you were a child? Enough to let you get over the prejudices that would ruin your life?

"I thought you wanted more tea?" a soft voice commented

132

from his right. "Standing here staring at the pot won't fill your cup, love."

Lorand smiled as he turned to Jovvi, who stood to his right.

"How did I ever manage to earn the love of a woman who's always there when she's most needed?" Lorand asked as he put a hand to Jovvi's face. "If I stop to think about what I might have done to deserve you, I tend to notice all the things I've done to accomplish the exact opposite."

"You've never done *anything* to destroy the love I feel for you, Lorand Coll, and you'd better never say you have," Jovvi countered fiercely, her expression making Lorand want to chuckle. But he knew better than to do more than smile and shake his head.

"See what I mean about how wonderful you are?" Lorand told her, leaning down to kiss her cheek. "But I have to say that I think you've been spending too much time with Tamrissa."

"Tamma has been rubbing off on all of us including Naran," Jovvi returned, her own smile full of amusement. "At first I worried, but now I've decided that it's really for the best. There are times when it helps quite a lot to show a bit of temper . . . Lorand, you're worried about whether or not you'll merge with us the next time we Blend. If you worry about it *too* much, your anxiety might bring you the opposite of what you really want. What all of us want."

"I know that, but I can't seem to help myself," Lorand replied ruefully as he moved forward to use the provided cloth to pick up the teapot. "Left to myself, all I can do is worry and fret. Maybe if you talk to me for a while, I can start to think about other things. Would you like more tea?"

"Yes, please," Jovvi answered, holding out her cup, and once Lorand had poured tea for both of them she studied him. "If you need something else to think about, let's try this: The intruder entity said that we were backward because our own entity thought of itself as 'we' rather than as a single being. Does that mean the intruder is Blended but not merged?"

"What else *can* it mean?" Lorand asked in turn, waiting

until he replaced the teapot before he shrugged. "When this individuality thing first started in the Blending, even we were wondering if it was a step forward or a step back. But I have a different question. If the intruder entity is older than our own, and I think it's fairly obvious that it is, why hasn't *it* progressed to individuality—if the individuality really is progress?"

"Maybe it's the lack of a Sight magic user," Jovvi said, her expression growing thoughtful. "The intruder entity isn't complete, so it can't grow beyond its present state no matter how old it is. The Gracelian Blendings had entities older than ours too, but the Blendings were so unbalanced—and also unfinished—that they were pale in comparison to us and our associates."

"I hate to say this, but I have the definite feeling that there's another difference between us and the intruder entity that will keep us from equaling them," Lorand said, the sudden conviction forcing him to voice it. "I can't imagine what that other difference is, but I also can't get past feeling certain."

"And *I* hate to say it, but I feel the same certainty," Jovvi agreed with a sigh. "There's still something we're missing, something we're doing wrong maybe, and that something will keep us from winning. I just hope we have the chance to figure out what we're not seeing or doing."

"You're not the only ones feelin' that, so I've taken steps," Vallant's voice came, and then he stood with them in their small group. "Naran brought up the matter first after you two walked away, so I did some thinkin' and then spoke to our associate Blendin's. The farther away from here we keep those invaders, the longer we'll have to get where we're supposed to be strength and technique-wise. When we go to try ourselves against the intruder entity, our associates will do some attackin' against their army people."

"Which ought to delay their advance at the very least," Lorand said with a nod of understanding. "But we ought to be ready to leave this place fast if we have to. There's no sense in losing any of our people just to make a useless gesture of defiance."

"That one's been taken care of since last night," Vallant assured him, one hand coming to close gently and briefly around Lorand's arm. "We can move out of this village almost as soon as we decide we want to, so hopefully you and the other Earth magic users won't have any extra healin' to do."

"That's good to know," Jovvi said as Lorand felt the weight of an unnoticed worry lift from his shoulders. "But if we're all finished eating, we really should get on with trying to delay the invaders."

"I'll be with the rest of you as soon as I make sure that everyone else is finished too," Vallant said, and then he moved off in the direction of their associates. Lorand joined Jovvi in walking back to the place the rest of their Blending waited, and Tamrissa sent Lorand an evil smile as he and Jovvi reclaimed their sitting places.

"We're about to Blend again, Lorand," she said, reminding Lorand of the fact he hadn't really forgotten about. "I've decided that if you don't merge with us *this* time, I'm going to do something really horrible to you afterward."

"What sort of something horrible?" Lorand asked as he blinked in confusion. "What can you possibly have in mind?"

"I'm not going to tell you that," Tamrissa answered, her smile turning even more evil. "The something won't be painful, but it will be so embarrassing and terrible that you'll never live the episode down. The idea came to me suddenly, and you'll never guess what I have in mind no matter how hard you try."

Lorand blinked again but kept silent, his mind already working on what Tamrissa could possibly have decided to do to him. Not painful, but still embarrassing and terrible. There were any number of things that Lorand would find embarrassing, but what could she mean by terrible? Lorand didn't doubt that she knew what terrible was, but how would that relate to *him*?

"All right, let's do it," Lorand heard Jovvi say, and he had just enough time to look up and discover that Vallant had rejoined them before Jovvi initiated the Blending. And then it was the Lorand entity who looked about, seeing his associate entities as well as the newly born entities of the flesh forms belonging to the place in which they were. All were prepared to seek out the intruder entity and its captured flesh forms, and all knew the location where the invaders would be found.

—*We will flash to a point just short of the invaders' position,*—the Lorand entity told his associates and the new ones.—*Those who were designated earlier as emergency protection for those of us engaged in battle will remain somewhat behind. It would be redundant to speak in detail of the need for caution.*—

And with that the Lorand entity flashed to the point he had previously decided on, to find that the invaders' advance had been temporarily halted.

*They have apparently stopped for midday nourishment and rest,* the Vallant part of the Lorand entity thought. *It would be best to wait for them to resume their march before we proceed.*

*Yes, that would clearly be best,* the Lorand entity agreed as his other parts spoke matching words of concurrence. With agreement complete the Lorand entity prepared himself to wait, but the time was very short. The invaders got to their feet only moments after the Lorand entity's arrival, and their column began to march in the direction of where the Lorand entity and his associates waited.

—*The time to begin is at hand,*—the Lorand entity informed his associates, and then they all floated forward. One of the associate entities spread insubstantial "hands" under the road the invaders walked, and a moment later that road and the dirt beneath it abruptly disappeared. More than fifty of the invader flesh forms fell out of sight into the pit that had been formed, a deep pit that was just as suddenly filled with water.

There had been no indication of the presence of the intruder entity, but an instant later the intruder was there. The water in the pit disappeared as quickly as it had formed, and then the intruder had turned to the Lorand entity's associates.

—*No*,—the Lorand entity sent, floating quickly to place himself between his associates and the intruder.—*We are here to face you, not them.*—

—*You may face this entity, but you shall not prevail,*—the intruder sent with familiar arrogance.—*You will fall before me as you should have done when last we met.*—

And then that odd roiling began in the midst of the intruder again, but this time the Lorand entity knew what the roiling was. The intruder reached to manipulate the power itself, which flashed through the intruder's individual talents to strengthen them far beyond what they would be normally.

When the attack reached the Lorand entity he was able to withstand it a good deal more easily than he had the first time, but once again he was unable to respond. It took all of his attention and ability to simply hold off the attack, which he did until his associates indicated that they had done everything they could. At that point the associates held in reserve attacked the intruder at the same time, and when the intruder withdrew just a bit the Lorand entity and his associates were able to flash back to where their flesh forms waited.

"That was a lot better, but it still wasn't what we need to win," Tamrissa said as soon as Jovvi dissolved the Blending. "But one thing of value *was* accomplished: Welcome to adulthood, Lorand."

"How would *you* know what adulthood is like?" Lorand countered with a wide grin, hearing the others chuckle. "I'm delighted to say that I've now caught up to the rest of you, but I'd still like to know what you threatened to do to me if I failed. I've been wracking my brain, but I can't think of a single thing."

"That's because there *isn't* anything I would have done," Tamrissa answered with a laugh. "I knew you were worrying about whether or not you would make it, so I decided to distract you with nonsense to keep your own worries from interfering with the merge. Obviously, my idea worked."

"It certainly did, but I'm going to have to get even for that threat," Lorand said after he and the others had added their own laughter. "Knowing what you're capable of, I was already blushing hot enough to start a fire by the time we Blended . . . But we did make a much better showing this time, even though none of us was entirely successful. I feel like a traitor saying this, but I'm glad the intruder was able to keep all those men from drowning. They may be our enemies now, but if we win against the intruder then we can free those slaves of theirs."

"It isn't being a traitor to want to save innocent lives," Jovvi told him with a gentle smile and a touch of her hand, then the smile disappeared. "I'm just not sure if those men *were* saved, since Vallant expected the intruder to interfere with our attack. Let's find out how things went for our associates before we decide it's time to feel relieved."

Lorand glanced over to see that Vallant now spoke to someone who crouched near where the Water magic user sat, and the two of them conversed in low tones. Neither man seemed pleased with what they discussed, at least not happy-pleased. The pleasure was more on the grim side, which meant they were in for partially bad news. Lorand tried to brace himself, but he wasn't quite ready when the other man left and Vallant returned his attention to his Blendingmates.

"The invaders now have only half the men they did before we attacked," Vallant said without preamble. "Once the intruder turned to face us, our associate Blendin's replaced the water in that pit and then kindled a fire for some of the others to walk into. It isn't possible to *touch* those army members with fire, but lettin' them walk into it is another matter entirely. Our associates also put another pit all around the road, so the intruder will have to circle all the way around to keep comin' at us. We've bought some time, but that's all we've done."

"I won't ask why we couldn't destroy *all* of the intruder's people," Tamrissa put in with a sigh. "I could feel the protection around the ones closest to those litters the intruder members travel in, and it would have taken too long and too much effort to break through the protection. Do you think there's a chance the intruders will turn around now and go back the way they came?"

"They can't afford to do that," Vallant said with a shake of his head. "They're workin' with the theory that they can't be stopped or resisted, so retreatin' is completely out of the question. Once they back off from anythin', their claim to inevitable victory turns too shaky for anyone to take seriously. As long as they keep comin', people will continue to fear them."

"So *we* have to continue to fight them, and also find a way to win completely," Tamrissa said with a nod and a sigh. "Just chasing them off will let people think they might be back, and that will give the intruder the victory if we aren't here to face them. Since I'd rather not move to this country permanently, we have to make sure that the intruder *can't* come back."

*But we still don't know how to do that,* Lorand thought as the others remained silent. And that was when the rain began, adding to the overall depression. The small victory they'd gained from their attack was no victory at all, it had simply cost the enemy some lives. But those weren't the lives they'd needed to take, and Lorand couldn't help wondering if they'd find the way to take the right lives in time for it to do any good . . .

Thrybin Korge was as furious as his weakened condition allowed him to be. He'd been put on a litter suspended between two horses front and back, with two blankets under his face and one covering him. He lay on his face to spare the wound in his back, and only by looking over his left shoulder was he able to see where the horses were headed.

*And the place we're headed and have almost reached is Liandia,* Thrybin thought, seeing the city through the light rain coming down. *I was supposed to return here a hero, not an unimportant burden the others dragged along behind them. My failure is all Tal's fault! If not for him, I would have thought of something to set matters right!*

Sullen fury burned inside Thrybin, a hatred possessing full knowledge of everything that had been stolen from him. Zirdon Tal wasn't the only one who had stolen Thrybin's destiny, but Tal had done the most damage. He had taken away Thrybin's last chance to overcome all the back stabbing and intrigue leveled against him, using literal back stabbing!

"I'm glad you're still alive, Korge," a soft voice came, and Thrybin's attention left the city they approached to see who rode beside him to his left. That one was Zirdon Tal himself, a true madman who was bound in leather to keep him from escaping his just due.

"You won't be glad I'm still alive when I give evidence against you at your trial," Korge whispered, knowing Tal would probably hear him. "I also intend to insist that I be allowed to attend your execution."

"I'm glad you're still alive, Korge, because now I get to kill you a second time," Tal murmured back with a smile that froze what blood Thrybin had left in his body. "They think they have me safely neutralized, but they're entirely wrong. You and they will find that out the hard way. If the empire is to survive, you and those others must die."

"You're insane, Tal, completely insane," Thrybin whispered, too terrified even to move. "Don't you know that it's those Gandistrans who are the real danger to this empire? They're the ones who have destroyed everything we had, including your own talent."

"The Gandistrans are risking their lives to save everyone in this empire, including your own useless self," Tal came back, proving that he really was a madman. "Even if your Blending members took you back, you would have no hope of even matching the invaders, let alone besting them. You refuse to admit that very obvious truth, and that makes *you* the true danger to this empire. If you were in charge you would fall and take the rest of us down with you, but you just can't see that. All you can see is your own desire to be important, no matter how many lives are lost putting you in that position."

"Denying what Tal just said would be a waste of time," another voice put in before Thrybin was able to sneer at that stupidity, and then the fool Satlan Reesh moved up to ride to Tal's right. "Tal told you the exact truth, and you can't even entertain the idea for a moment. You want what you want, and nothing anyone can say will make you understand that this time you can't *have* what you want."

"I'm not surprised to hear you agreeing with a madman, Reesh," Thrybin said, making the effort to speak a bit more loudly so that the fool would hear him. "A useless follower like you needs *someone* to agree with, just to feel that he actually belongs somewhere—which you don't."

"You really *are* stupid, aren't you, Korge," Reesh said with the sort of disdain Thrybin had never heard the man use before. "Someone with intelligence would have noticed by now that that line of nonsense doesn't affect me any longer. So let me repeat what Tal just said: You *cannot* have what you want this time, no matter how much you want it. You aren't smart enough or capable enough to run this empire, so you never will."

"Well, we'll just see about that, won't we," Thrybin returned, hating the fact that he was too weak to really tell the fool off. "I'm not without my resources, and once I'm back on my feet we'll see who's smart and capable and who isn't."

"Don't waste your time trying to bring him in touch with reality again, Reesh," the madman Tal actually had the nerve to say to the fool Reesh. "Korge won't ever be back on his feet again to ruin this empire, so there's no need to worry. But that doesn't leave the field clear for you and the others. The rest of you are just as bad for the empire as Korge is."

"Dinno and I have already come to that conclusion," Reesh said with a sigh, sounding as if he really spoke to the madman instead of just avoiding an argument as he should have. "The Gandistrans are right to say that the assembly needs to be composed of High Blendings, without Blending members being constantly replaced. Things are going to change radically in this country even if the invaders are stopped. Our companions don't want to hear that, but in a very short time they won't have any choice but to go along with the changes."

"You can't be certain of that," Tal replied, and oddly enough some of the blaze in the madman's eyes had died down a bit. "Lorimon and Gardan have more than a little influence in the assembly, and they can delay the changes long enough to ruin everything."

"But the changes won't come through assembly action, Tal," Reesh said gently, as though explaining the facts of life to a boy. "Dinno and I will probably be the only assembly members who step aside voluntarily, but that won't make a difference. When the High Blendings get here, they'll *tell* the assembly members to step aside. They won't have the patience to ask nicely and then wait for the request to be complied with."

"You may be right, but I'm not certain you are," Tal said, his brow creased with indecision. "Killing Gardan and Lorimon will probably be necessary just to be sure."

Reesh shook his head with another sigh, then urged his horse to a faster pace. Tal retreated into himself, which let Thrybin return to his own thoughts. Blocking all changes in the assembly would hardly be as difficult as the fool Reesh thought, especially if the members of those High Blendings were killed as soon as they approached the city. Gardan was terrified of losing his place in the assembly, so Thrybin knew the man could be made an ally with very little effort. And since Thrybin was the actual assembly member, he'd be able to replace his Blending members with the same minimal effort. After that . . .

After that, Thrybin would take over the assembly as he'd planned to do all along. The empire of Gracely would be *his* to run as he saw fit, and if those Gandistrans ever showed up again he would have them executed before they knew what was happening. Yes . . . That picture of the future was so pleasant that Thrybin was easily able to fall asleep as he viewed it with eager eyes.

\* \* \*

Satlan Reesh kept his horse moving until he rode beside Olskin Dinno, who rode a short distance behind Antrie Lorimon and Cleemor Gardan. Lorimon and Gardan headed their column, and they rode as though unaware of anyone behind them.

"Korge is still plotting and planning, and Tal seems incapable of seeing any kind of reason," Satlan murmured to Dinno. "You and I *might* have been crossed off Tal's list of future murder victims, but our colleagues just ahead there—as well as the balance of assembly members—are still firmly on it."

"I was hoping that Tal could be talked around," Dinno replied with a weary shake of his head. "We really can't execute him until we find out if the Gandistrans can neutralize whatever was done to him. Since his efforts were Korge's doing to begin with, Korge can't really complain about the plot turning around and biting him."

"Of course Korge can complain, and he will," Satlan disagreed with a faint smile. "The man is still determined to be the ruler of this empire, and has no idea that we mean to throw him out of the assembly as soon as we return to the city. He won't just sit back and take any of our plans without screaming."

Dinno was about to say something, but the words were lost as he—and Satlan—both noticed a large number of people coming out of the city on horseback. In a moment it was possible to see that Frode Mismin led the group, and he held up his hand to halt the column he apparently had come out to meet. Lorimon and Gardan both pulled their mounts to a halt, so Satlan joined Dinno in riding close enough to find out what was going on before they also stopped.

"I'm sorry, Exalted Ones, but you can't enter the city without a heavy guard," Mismin said as soon as he reached the column and came to a stop near them. "In fact, it might be best if you didn't enter the city at all."

"Why not?" Lorimon asked at once, heavy concern in her voice. "Frode, you look terrible. What's been happening?"

"I'm afraid that the six of you who left the city are the

only assembly members left alive," Mismin answered heavily, looking like a man who had died but still hadn't lain down. "The rest of the members were killed in their homes, virtually all at once so it wasn't possible to guard anyone after the first death. I managed to locate two of the assassins, but *they* were killed before I could question them. I have no idea who's responsible for what happened, but I do have the definite feeling that the insanity isn't over."

"Insanity," Dinno echoed while Lorimon and Gardan made sounds of horrified surprise. "That reminds me of what the Gandistrans made Tal tell us about Ebro Syant's involvement in what went on before we left. I think, Mismin, that you're going to have to use your Spirit magic on Tal to see if we can get any definite details on what Syant might have arranged."

"And there aren't *six* of us left," Satlan corrected mildly as Mismin stared at Dinno in confusion. "Tal no longer has any talent, and Korge is to be expelled from the assembly as soon as possible. That leaves only four of us, and I have the impression that hiding out won't do any good."

"I agree," Dinno said at once, ignoring the way Gardan patted the shoulder of a very distraught Lorimon. "What we need to do is find out who's behind the killings, and then the threat won't be hanging over our heads. Besides, staying outside the city could well end our lives even sooner than the attempts of assassins."

"You can't be saying you failed against the invaders," Mismin stated, shock actually animating rather than freezing him. "How could those people have possibly stood up to six Blendings, not to mention to the strength of those Gandistrans?"

"It's a long, ugly story," Dinno answered with a shake of his head. "The short of it is, those invaders are even stronger than the Gandistrans. None of our assembly Blendings stand a chance against the invaders, not when our Blendings have only a single High talent. The Gandistrans stayed behind to do what they can against the invaders, but that may not be enough to stop them. And we already have hundreds of refugees right behind us, desperate to find shelter in the city. You'd better do something to make room for them."

"If the Gandistrans do manage to stop the invaders, it won't matter that we only have one High talent in our Blendings," Gardan said, his gaze somewhere between Lorimon and Dinno. "We won't have to change the way we do things just because foreigners think we should."

"Gardan, give it up," Dinno said, weariness thick in his voice. "If the Gandistrans are successful, those High Blendings they put together will be here to take over. If the Gandistrans fail, there won't be anything *left* for anyone to take over. The world we lived in will never be the same again, so pretending it is will do no one any good. If you can make yourself understand that, you can make your last days as an assembly member really mean something."

Gardan made no effort to answer and Lorimon stayed just as silent, so Mismin took over and arranged his guardsmen around the four remaining assembly members and they all headed for the city. Satlan rode as quietly as everyone else, but his thoughts were busy. He and Dinno had promised to find other High talents and send them to help the new High Blendings, and that was something that *had* to be done. With the invaders so close to the city, assassins actually had to take a second place on the list of things that were most important.

And that realization made Satlan smile. Even if Gardan never came around, at least *he*, the very unpopular Satlan Reesh, would make his last days in the assembly count. How much more could a man ask of a life that had gone so badly before now? Real acceptance by real people would have been nice, but that possibility was actually more frightening than the thought of death.

Satlan heaved a private sigh, and then he smiled very faintly. Whatever happened would happen, and the new Satlan Reesh might even be able to cope with it . . .

# THIRTEEN

Antrie Lorimon had been doing a lot of thinking while she and the others rode back to Liandia. Frode's announcement about the deaths of the remaining assembly members had been shocking, but for some reason the shock had faded rather quickly. Now that Frode was beside her again, her thinking seemed to clarify even more. It would take almost an hour to actually reach the city, and the time would best be spent in making plans.

"Frode, a lot of things have happened since we last saw each other," Antrie began, speaking as quietly as possible to keep the conversation private. "Will you be upset to learn that I won't be an assembly member for much longer?"

"I would be upset only if you were, and I don't seem to be getting that impression from you," Frode answered with a frown. "Have you simply decided to retire, or do you expect to lose in the next competitions?"

"Neither," Antrie answered with a mirthless smile. She then told Frode a shortened version of what had happened and continued with, "So it will definitely be the High Blendings who take over running the empire. I'm part of the old guard, so to speak, and the time has come for us to step aside."

"But I don't understand," Frode protested. "Why can't you simply join a High Blending yourself? You do have the experience of being part of the assembly, so—"

"Frode, it isn't that simple," Antrie interrupted, fighting to keep control of her feelings. "In order to be most effective, the members of the Blending have to lie with each other. I . . . really don't see myself being able to do something like that."

Frode absorbed that bit of information silently, and Antrie wished she had *his* talent. Knowing what he happened to be feeling would help quite a lot . . . Then he looked up and gave her a faint smile.

"You seem to be picturing bedding a lot of strangers," he said, an odd expression in his eyes. "You might not feel the same if you knew and liked the people involved, but that's for you to say rather than me. If we survive everything we're in the midst of, possibly we can make a start on putting together a Blending of our own . . ."

When Frode's voice trailed off, Antrie realized that he'd made an offer that might or might not be one of marriage. Antrie had been raised to believe that marriage was the only thing she might honorably look forward to, but everything that had happened—and all the thinking she'd done—might just be starting to change her mind . . .

"Yes, let's discuss that idea once we're no longer in the midst of chaos," Antrie agreed, reaching over to pat Frode's hand. "In the meantime, we need to discuss some of the thinking I've been doing. First on the list is the fact that there are only four assembly members left, and we need to be protected while we see to the defense of the city. I think our defense will be most easily seen to if we're all in the same place."

"Yes, that *would* be the best idea," Frode agreed. "If you're willing to have houseguests, your house would be the easiest to defend."

"Why can't it be *my* house?" Cleemor put in abruptly before Antrie could respond. "Why are you offering to guard her house instead?"

"I'm afraid, Exalted One, that your house could well prove to be *too* large," Frode replied, speaking with clear deference. Cleemor sounded so out of sorts that Frode had apparently decided to soothe the man. "Your house is also . . . odd in its layout, which would make guarding people extremely difficult."

"And you know that Tenia would hate having her household disrupted by so many people," Antrie said to a frowning Cleemor. "She could well decide that guards were entirely unnecessary, and demand that they be removed. What would you do then, Cleemor?"

"I would do what any reasonable man would, Antrie," Cleemor answered, his tone more stiff and formal than she had ever heard it. "I would look into the possibility that she might be right. After all, what real proof do we have that—"

"Cleemor, stop it!" Antrie snapped, desperately hoping that *something* would be enough to get through to the man. "I've never spoken to you like this before, but maybe I should have. If Tenia really loves you, she'll stay with you no matter *what* happens. If she doesn't love you, nothing you say or do will keep her now. In a very short while none of us will be assembly members any longer, and that's a fact you'll be forced to accept even if you don't want to. Isn't it better to make the most of the time we have left by doing the best we can for the people of this empire? If you worry about nothing but Tenia, you'll lose everything else in your life."

"If I lose Tenia, I don't *have* anything else in my life," Cleemor muttered, a wild look now in his eyes. "But I *won't* lose her, not if there's anything in this world I can do to stop it."

"Standing in the way of the changes ahead won't get you anything but run over," Frode put in without any of the deference he'd used a moment ago. "It's time you woke up, Gardan, and stopped acting like a fool. There isn't anyone in this city who doesn't know that your wife will be gone the instant you no longer have the standing she demands of the man in her life. It's position she wants, not you, and another man would have had the stones to throw her out a long time ago. If you're that determined to play slave to a woman, there are plenty of other women you can do it with."

"How dare you speak to me like that?" Cleemor demanded, his face white with shock and dismay. "You know nothing about my situation, and the entire city certainly knows the same nothing! You're fired, Mismin, and I want you out of my sight this instant!"

"I'm sorry, Gardan, but you can't fire Frode," Olskin Dinno put in from where he rode behind them. "With only we four left as assembly members, Reesh and I will stand with Antrie to outvote you. *You* may prefer death to having to stand up to that wife of yours, but the rest of us aren't as eager to be killed."

"But you and Tenia will still be welcome in my home, Cleemor," Antrie put in quickly when her longtime friend seemed almost about to lose control of himself entirely. "Why don't you leave it to Tenia to make the final decision about what will happen? Come to my house with everyone else, and then send her a note asking that she join you. If everyone is wrong and Tenia really does love you, she'll respond to your note and come to join us."

"Tenia prefers her own home, and there's no reason she shouldn't," Cleemor muttered, his gaze on the road ahead rather than on Antrie. "Asking her to move to someone else's house is unreasonable, so her refusal would *not* mean—"

"Yes, it would," Satlan Reesh's voice interrupted from where the man rode beside Olskin Dinno. "This is an emergency situation, and anyone with sense will know it. If the woman insists that you come to her instead, which you obviously expect her to do, her demand would prove that you mean nothing to her. Making excuses for the awful way other people treat you is pathetic, Gardan. If *I* don't know that then no one does."

This time Cleemor made no answer, and that disturbed Antrie more than his previous anger. Tenia meant everything to Cleemor, and it could prove more than possible that he *would* choose death rather than lose the woman. Antrie parted her lips to speak to Cleemor again, hoping that if she kept at it she might be successful. But before she could voice any part of her feelings, Frode's hand closed around her arm. When she looked at Frode he shook his head, telling her silently not to speak. Well, he was the one with Spirit magic, after all. If he thought it was best to stay silent, Antrie was forced to abide by the decision.

It was a very quiet group that finally reached the gates of Liandia. Frode had brought Zirdon Tal forward to ride with the rest of them in the midst of the guard force, and with very good reason, Antrie knew. Zirdon was the only one who might be able to stop the assassins, by telling them who was in charge. If Zirdon was accidentally killed or badly hurt . . .

The thought of attack brought Antrie memory of how the Gandistrans handled the matter. Rion had confided at one point that he sometimes hardened the air around his Blendingmates as a precaution, finding it foolish to wait until they were actually under attack. Antrie wasn't very large physically and she certainly couldn't be compared to Rion in strength, but she remained a High talent in Air magic. That meant she hesitated only an instant before using her talent to cover those who rode beside and around her with an invisible wall of hardened air.

And the effort was made just in time. The guards at the head of their column rode through the gates without a problem, but as soon as Antrie and the others did the same there was a sudden *whoosh!* as gouts of flame came at them from what seemed like all sides. The horses went frantic at the first indication of fire and they all had to fight for control, but that was the extent of the difficulty. No one was touched by the flames at all.

A moment later the fire was gone, and there was a stir in the crowds to both sides of the road. People were being held by other people, and some were flat on the ground.

"Most of the members of those 'crowds' are *my* people," Frode murmured as the horses settled down. "I've also recruited other than Spirit magic users, so we'd know at once when the other talents are being used. Let's get to your house as quickly as possible."

Antrie considered that suggestion the best Frode could have made, and no one else showed any inclination to argue either. Instead they all increased the pace of their horses, looking around carefully as they rode. Antrie kept her shield in place even when her house came into view, and unfortunately the effort wasn't wasted.

"Look out!" Frode shouted as heavy waves of water tried to engulf them. They had just entered Antrie's driveway, which was lined with shrubs and bushes. Frode's shout had no effect on the water, but people suddenly appeared from inside the house and around to both sides. The newcomers weren't attackers, however, as a round of yells from the shrubbery proved. Those in hiding who were doing the yelling abruptly showed themselves, and showed as well that *they* were now under attack.

The true attackers turned to face Frode's people, and Frode touched Antrie's arm.

"Now that those people are distracted, you and the others have to get to the house," he told Antrie urgently. "Don't worry about your horses, just leave them where you dismount. My people will take care of them later."

Once again no one argued, so just a few moments later Antrie and her companions quickly dismounted near the steps leading to her front door. Men now stood guard around that door, and they hurried everyone inside to be met by other men on guard. After Antrie and her associates came their Blendingmates, and for a short time there was a great deal of confusion. Then Antrie pulled herself together enough to direct the Middle talents to the other side of the house before she led her associates to her study.

"Ah, a tea service!" Olskin Dinno exclaimed as soon as they were in the room. "Antrie, you're the best of hosts. May I help myself?"

"Let's all help ourselves," Antrie said with the best smile she was able to produce in the midst of chaos. "Once we all have some tea inside us, we can decide which of our Blendings will assist Frode's people first. Our entities should have little or no trouble locating any other attackers."

"That's a very good idea, Antrie," Satlan Reesh said with a smile and a nod as he gestured Antrie to the tea service

ahead of him. "If no one else has a burning need to hunt attackers immediately, I'll volunteer to go first. We may not
have been very effective against those invaders, but this is a
different situation entirely."

"I agree," Dinno said, also stepping aside for Antrie at the
service. "We need to be able to gather High talents as link
groups for the new Blendings, and we can't do that if we're
held prisoner in this house."

"I think we need to speak to Mismin about that as soon as
possible," Reesh said to Dinno while Antrie poured herself a
badly needed cup of tea. "Those link groups are needed *now,*
and Mismin may be able to shorten the process of gathering
the High talents."

"Which means we might do best taking our tea with us,"
Dinno concurred, stepping up to the tea service as soon as
Antrie moved away. "After that trip I'd love to sit down and
put my feet up, but if I save relaxing until later I might actually be able to enjoy the time."

Reesh's sound of amusement was also complete agreement, and as soon as both men had cups of tea they left the
room. Antrie had gone to the chair behind her desk, and
when she looked up she saw that Cleemor Gardan simply
stood where he'd stopped when they'd first come into the
room. The big man looked so helpless and lost that Antrie's
heart ached for him.

"Cleemor, why don't you get a cup of tea and then sit
down," Antrie said gently. She'd meant the words to be
soothing, but Cleemor still jumped as if he'd been hit.

"I need something stronger than tea right now," he
growled in answer, but the tortured expression in his eyes
turned his response pitiful as he looked at her. "I've been
trying to understand how you can have changed your stance
so drastically, Antrie, but I'm not having much luck. How
can you act as if you now approve of having our world completely destroyed?"

"I spent the trip back here thinking, Cleemor, and I was
forced to admit that the Gandistrans had some very good
points." These words weren't easy for Antrie to speak, but

Cleemor needed to hear them. "I found that playing politics *is* a terrible vice, and one that often gets to be so much of a habit that you forget how to act in any other way. I *was* upset over the fact that I could have been attacked just as easily as Korge was, but instead of saying that, I pretended to be bothered for Korge's sake. I managed to lie even to myself, and that realization bothered me deeply."

"Playing politics is part of our way of life," Cleemor returned, his tone having turned stubborn. "It's what the civilized do to keep from being constantly embroiled in wars of disagreement."

"Even when you're already *in* a war, and with people who have no interest in talking to you?" Antrie pursued, not about to let her old friend lie to her. "Playing politics in a situation like that is criminal, and also quite probably suicidal. If Korge hadn't been stabbed, he'd be spending his time right now trying to take over instead of helping the common cause. Are you saying he'd be right to do that?"

Antrie could see that Cleemor wanted to say just that, but not even his current mood allowed him to approve of a man like Thrybin Korge.

"Cleemor, we both know what the real problem is," Antrie said, and this time her tone was only partially gentle. "You know you'll be given no choice but to join a High Blending or lose your place in the assembly. Tenia won't stand for either action, and she'll demand that you keep things just as they are. Why are you so worried about a woman who really does care more about her own whims than she does about your life?"

"She's the one who makes my life worth living," Cleemor whispered, looking as though he were about to cry. "I don't know how I got along before I met her, but I do know that if I lose her my life is over. She's everything I want in a woman, everything any man would want . . ."

"Nonsense!" Antrie snapped, bringing a startled expression to Cleemor. "Before you met Tenia, you were more interested in a woman's mind than in her face and body. As soon as Tenia appeared, how she looked was suddenly the only thing you could think and talk about. And you said you wanted children. How many children has Tenia given you?"

"She . . . thought it best that we wait to start a family," Cleemor muttered, discomfort sending his gaze away from Antrie. "As soon as things settle down and return to the way they were—"

"That's right, things aren't *going* to settle down and return to the way they were," Antrie said when Cleemor's words ended abruptly. "And even if they did Tenia would still refuse to have children, and I think you know that. Does she have Spirit magic, Cleemor? I don't believe you've ever mentioned her talent."

"Well, yes, she does have Spirit magic," Cleemor grudged, now showing a frown. "She asked me not to mention the fact because of all the coarse jokes that have gone around about women with Spirit magic. You can't blame her for that, Antrie, not when you're a woman yourself."

"Of course I can't blame her for that," Antrie assured her old friend immediately, keeping her expression mild in spite of the nasty idea that had just come to her. "I think I'd better see how my staff is coping with this emergency. Get yourself a cup of tea, Cleemor, and then sit down for a few moments. I'll be back in a little while."

Cleemor nodded wearily and went toward the tea service, so Antrie left her emptied cup on her desk and headed out of the room. She made sure to close the door firmly behind herself, and then she went looking for Frode. She found him in the front entrance hall, speaking to his men, and as soon as he was through he came over to her.

"Satlan Reesh and his Blending will soon be on patrol," Frode said, looking as though he wished he could touch her. "That will make things incredibly easier and safer, especially when we start to gather High talents."

"The first thing we have to do is question Zirdon Tal," Antrie responded with a nod. "If he knows who's behind these attacks, we can get them stopped for good and all. But first I have a question to ask you. What level of talent does Tenia Gardan have in Spirit magic?"

"I'd say she was a strong Middle at the very least," Frode answered with something of a frown. "She never seemed to use her talent when I was around and never mentioned her Guild rating, but every now and then I'd get an impression of sorts from her. Why do you ask?"

"I ask because I think she's been using her talent on Cleemor," Antrie responded flatly. "The idea leaves a bad taste in my mouth, but it occurred to me a few minutes ago that Cleemor never *used* to be the kind of man to . . . enslave himself to a woman, as you put it. And Tenia also made him promise not to mention what her talent was."

"I don't like the sound of that at all," Frode said, his frown having deepened. "We have very strict laws against controlling people, but if you're the beloved wife of a powerful assembly member you might decide you have nothing to worry about. I tend to keep my own talent away from people unless I'm working on something they're involved with, but I think it's time I took a closer look at your friend."

"I would appreciate that," Antrie said with all the relief she felt. "Can we . . . do that before we question Zirdon?"

"I think it might be better if I do the looking alone," Frode said before Antrie could lead the way back to her study. "If you'll wait here, I should be through in just a few minutes."

And with that Frode walked away, giving Antrie no chance to protest. She had no idea why Frode would exclude her like that, but when he came back a few minutes later she found out the reason.

"He had a rough time of it, but after he rests for a while he should be all right," Frode said as he stopped near her. "Gardan *was* under all sorts of orders and requirements, and my stripping them away wasn't easy for him. But I do have to apologize for not having gotten suspicious myself. Most people are more reasonable than Gardan was, especially in emergency situations."

"Easy or not, at least he's now free of control," Antrie said with a good deal of relief. "And you knew it would be even harder for Cleemor if I happened to be there to see what was done. You're a beautiful man, Frode Mismin, and I'm very glad you were as brave as you were a short time ago."

"So am I," he agreed with a wide smile, obviously knowing she meant the time he'd asked to come courting. "But now we have another task to see to, and this time I'd very much like to have you with me."

"Not as much as I want to be there," Antrie returned, her own smile turning grim. "It's more than time that Zirdon Tal made up for some of the harm he's caused. Do you know where he's been put?"

Frode nodded and led her deeper into the house in the direction of the servants' quarters. In that area there was an unused storage room that had no windows, and that was where Zirdon Tal was being kept. There were also three of Frode's men standing guard inside the room, and when Frode gestured them out they left without a word.

"Insulting me like this won't save your life, you know," Tal said as soon as he saw Antrie. The former assembly member sat on the floor leaning against a wall, his arms bound behind him. "Trying to make me feel inferior won't do a thing to weaken my resolve."

"Your resolve," Frode echoed, staring at Tal intently. "Yes, I can see now where that resolve comes from, but the conditioning doesn't look intentional. I also think I can remove it."

Tal began to frown at Frode, but then he gasped and threw his head back as his body arched. He held the pose for almost a full minute, and then he released it with a groan as his head came forward and his chin touched his chest.

"That should do it," Frode said as Tal gasped in breath after breath of air. "With someone else I would have been a lot more gentle, but you've done nothing to deserve gentleness, Tal. In fact you deserve just the opposite, so I hope you refuse to answer this question: What's the name of the man you hired to put Ebro Syant's plans into action?"

"I don't have to tell you anything," Tal gasped out, glaring hatred at Frode that would have frightened Antrie if she were the one being looked at like that. "I demand to speak with my father, and what's more—Oh!"

"You're a talentless criminal, Tal, so your father won't want to have anything to do with you," Frode countered with a distant smile. "That ... push I just gave you was very small and not very painful, but my patience is now all gone. Answer my question, or I'll *make* you answer me."

"It's against the law to control people, Mismin," Tal sneered in spite of the unease Antrie could see in his eyes. "Trying to control an assembly member can get you executed, so you just go ahead and—"

"Zirdon, wake up!" Antrie interrupted, deciding it was time to help. "You are *not* a member of the assembly any longer, and never will be again even if your family doesn't desert you. Denying that fact won't do you any more good than it's done Korge, but if you want to insist on being a member of the assembly we just might let you do that. Out on the street, away from all protection."

"But I could be killed out there!" Zirdon protested in outrage, staring up at Antrie. "You'd never be able to live with yourself if you did that, and if I were dead I certainly couldn't answer your questions. That means you're just bluffing, so—"

"Wrong again," Frode said, taking his turn at interrupting. "Antrie might be too kindhearted to put you out in the street, but I'm not. If I have to force an answer out of you that's exactly what I *will* do, and then it won't matter if you end up dead."

"Yes, you'd do that, I know you would," Zirdon muttered, the look in his eyes terrified. "All right, I'll tell you what I know, but first you have to promise not to send me out there. I don't want to be the last one killed by those madmen."

Antrie stepped back and watched Frode assure Zirdon that he would be kept in the house if he told everything he knew. Antrie had the feeling that Frode now used his talent to make Zirdon speak without the former Fire magic user knowing what was happening. If for some reason Zirdon wasn't executed for the things he'd done, he'd certainly try to make trouble for everyone he could. Better to let Zirdon believe that confessing was his own idea.

And confess Zirdon did. Frode got the necessary name first, and then he and Antrie were forced to listen to what seemed like a thousand reasons why Zirdon had been right to act as he had. Frode quietly slipped out of the room after a few minutes, and Zirdon didn't seem to realize that he was gone. The man just kept talking, and when the three guards came back into the room and Antrie left, Zirdon didn't seem to notice that either. He just kept talking and talking and talking . . .

"Is he still at it?" Frode said as he rejoined Antrie in the hall. "I've sent some of my people to find that man Tal told us about. Once we have him we'll go after the assassins he hired, and my people will be very thorough in finding out the identity of all of them as well as information on any other plans. We don't need this nonsense distracting us from our serious problems."

Antrie felt the urge to smile at the way Frode called assassination nonsense, but she couldn't quite manage a smile. The invaders *were* a more serious problem, and at the moment they could do little more than fervently hope the Gandistrans were successful against them.

# FOURTEEN

Olskin Dinno watched Satlan Reesh approach him in the sitting room where he'd found a place out of the way. Olskin had never seen a man change as much as Reesh had, at least not in a positive way. Reesh had always been the sort of man Olskin avoided whenever possible, but now he actually looked forward to sharing the man's company.

"There were four other attackers waiting for their chance to approach the house," Reesh announced with a smile as he stopped near Olskin. "My Blendingmates and I had very little trouble locating them and changing their minds, and now Mismin's men have the four. Are those sandwiches for us alone, or are we supposed to share them with our people?"

"Our people have been given other sandwiches, I'm told, so these are ours," Olskin answered with a small chuckle. "We've all been promised a more substantial meal for supper, but it will have to be buffet style. There are too many of us for a proper sit-down . . . How sure are you that there aren't more than four attackers lurking about?"

"As sure as possible after checking a full half-mile radius," Reesh answered as he moved closer to the plate of sandwiches and appropriated one. "There are a lot of people out there who have nothing to do with the attacks, so a half mile was the best we could do. Do you know whose turn it will be now that mine is over?"

"The next turn is mine, but I'm not going to start immediately," Olskin answered after sipping at his tea. "If I wait a short while, I might catch some attackers sneaking up in place of the ones *you* caught. But first we need to give those people a chance to realize that some of their assassins are gone—and maybe even be gone themselves."

"I take it that Mismin got the information he needed from Tal," Reesh said after sitting down. He hadn't even tasted his sandwich yet, but he seemed more curious than hungry. "That should help quite a lot, especially if Gardan suddenly decides to run home without telling anyone."

"I don't think Gardan is going to be running anywhere," Olskin said, and then made up his mind to share the rest of what he'd been told. "Antrie let me know privately that Gardan's lovely wife has been breaking the law with her Spirit magic, but Mismin was able to pull him out of it. We're leaving Gardan alone for a while so he can gather himself together, and after this we won't mention the incident either to him or to anyone else. Unless *he* mentions it, of course."

"Do you really think Gardan will let the woman get away with controlling him?" Reesh asked, looking more concerned than curious. "I know for myself that I can make enough mistakes on my own. I have no need whatsoever of someone else adding to my efforts."

"I suppose it depends on how much Gardan really cares for the woman," Olskin replied with a shrug. "If the love he felt was *all* her doing, she won't be very happy with his reaction now that he's free."

"I have no sympathy for someone who tampers with another's mind," Reesh said with his own shrug, raising the sandwich before clearly remembering something else he wanted to mention. "Oh, yes, before I get down to eating, I ought to tell you that my Blendingmates and I did some additional healing on Korge. The fool was put in a room in the servants' quarters, and he's been complaining nonstop. We've taken away most of the fool's pain, so the servants may not have to kill him to get some peace and quiet."

"If they do kill Korge, I won't find much to complain about myself," Olskin said with a chuckle. "If, on the other hand, the servants decide to leave instead of doing a killing,

I'll have a lot to complain about. After my Blendingmates and I do our own patrol, I'll also see about additional healing. The sooner Korge is healthy enough to leave, the happier I'll be."

"The happier we'll *all* be," Reesh corrected around a mouthful of sandwich, which made Olskin chuckle again. *Yes,* he thought, *Reesh has definitely become someone worth knowing. If it weren't impossible, I'd wish the same change would come on Korge. But maybe coming so close to death will change Korge. An outcome like that would be well worth the hoping for . . .*

Thrybin Korge lay on his side in the shabby little room those fools had consigned him to. He now lay on a bed rather than on a litter, but he'd shouted himself hoarse and no one had come to see what he needed. Lorimon's inept servants hadn't been able to do anything for him the two or three times they *had* come in, but that didn't mean they had any right to ignore him. Especially now that he was feeling so much better . . .

Korge eased himself down on his back, and even that didn't bring back the crippling pain he'd been feeling. For some reason he seemed to be healing much faster than he'd expected he would, which certainly proved how superior he was to everyone else. As soon as he could walk he would be out of that house, and then he'd be able to continue with his plans. He would spend half his time making people outraged over those new High Blendings, and the other half of his time would go toward lining up powerful people to back his claim of still being an assembly member. The other assembly members would certainly support him, once he pointed out how insecure their own positions would be if they didn't.

"And I'll have to find out what all that fuss was about when we entered the city," Korge muttered, anger turning his voice to a growl. "The nerve of those idiots, refusing to tell *me* about what's going on! Tal was taken to the front of the column, but they left *me* all alone and in the dark knowledge-wise. I'll have to remember to return the favor, at least until it's time to displace those morons. Then I'll certainly tell them all about it . . ."

Thrybin spent a few very pleasant minutes picturing the time when he would take control of the entire assembly, but then another thought occurred to him. He hadn't tried to see if he could stand and walk, and with the servants ignoring him he wasn't likely to find a better time to experiment. If the pain came back he would simply demand that the servants pay some attention to him, but if there *was* no pain . . . Yes, this would be the perfect time to leave.

Sitting up carefully was Thrybin's first effort, and although there was a small amount of pain it wasn't anything he couldn't bear. Being out of that house and back in his own was a more important consideration, so he next got shakily to his feet. There was a moment of dizziness and a small increase in the pain he felt, but nothing he couldn't cope with for a short time. He was now standing and would soon be walking, but only until he found a coach for hire. After that he would ride, and after *that* . . .

Thrybin Korge, the man destined to rule the Gracelian empire, smiled as he slowly made his way out of his enemy's house. He would be back there one day, he knew, but only when it was time to take the house away from Lorimon. And it would be broad daylight when he did that, not late afternoon as it was now. But now, late afternoon with its very convenient shadows was much more useful . . .

Cleemor Gardan looked up at Antrie Lorimon where she stood, and somehow found it possible to smile at her.

"I can't decide whether I ought to be furious or miserable, so I suppose I'm all right," he said in answer to the question she'd put. "I thought I'd married a woman who loved me, but instead I got . . . Tenia."

"If you weren't such a wonderful person, we might have seen what she was doing a bit sooner," Antrie told him as she took a chair opposite his. "If you were mean and nasty and ugly on top of it, we would have wondered how you two

could be so 'in love.' As it is, though . . . Have you decided
what you'll do now that you know the truth?"

"Yes, I think I have," Cleemor answered, only faintly surprised that he *had* made a decision. "Tenia gave me no true
chance to fall in love with her, using her talent instead to
make me *think* I was in love. She was the one who made the
choice to cheat rather than behave fairly, so now fairness
gets to be given to *her*. As soon as we're out of here, I'm going to have Frode arrest her."

"Since Frode hasn't yet come back from going after the
man behind the assassins, we still have some time yet,"
Antrie pointed out with a sigh. "If you think about the matter and then change your mind, I'll certainly understand. But
whatever you do, you can be certain you'll have my full
support."

"I appreciate that, dear friend," Cleemor said with the best
smile he was able to produce, meaning every word. "We've
supported each other for years now, but this was a decision I
had to make alone. My first urge was to forgive Tenia, just as
I would have if she'd been sneaking around with another
man. But this is much more serious than a simple affair, and
I can't let her get away with it. She deliberately went after a
man with power in the assembly, and she got what she
wanted. Now it's time she learned that the other side of
power is responsibility."

"And you consider yourself responsible for seeing that
she doesn't get the chance to do the same again to someone
else," Antrie said with a nod of understanding. "I admire
you, Cleemor, but I certainly don't envy you. I don't know if
I would be strong enough to do the same . . . I ought to ask,
though: Where do you stand now on the question of High
Blendings? You do know that our time as leaders is coming
to an end?"

"Yes, and now that I can think clearly again I have to
change to *your* stance," Cleemor said, but not very happily.
"I still abhor the idea of losing everything I've worked for,
but the time is very close when my personal preferences

won't matter. If I can't find a High Blending of my own to join, I'll simply step aside."

"But in the meanwhile you and I and Reesh and Dinno are what's left of the government," Antrie pointed out. "In my opinion that means we have to work toward survival in case the Gandistrans can't find a way to defeat the invaders. If we have to abandon Liandia, do you have any idea where we can go?"

"Our only practical destination would be Gandistra, and from there to Astinda," Cleemor said slowly after considering the question. "If the Gandistrans fail to stop the invaders, that doesn't necessarily mean the invaders *can't* be stopped. It just means we'll need more time to find the method, at the same time denying the enemy as many of our people as possible. If we can take over or destroy the enemy's troops without letting those troops be replaced with our own people, finding a way to destroy the enemy Blending itself might be easier."

"If we can't find another way, we can just wait until the enemy Blending *has* to sleep," Antrie said just as slowly, her gaze distracted. "Even if we can't kill more than one or two of them, they'll still never be able to Blend again. That will make them a lot less dangerous and decidedly more vulnerable, and after that if we can't kill the rest then shame on us."

"I like the way you think, Exalted One," Cleemor said, feeling more amusement than he'd expected to. "Obviously women really are more bloodthirsty than men, and more practical as well. Shall we share our thinking with the others?"

"That's a good idea, but I'd like another cup of tea to take with me," Antrie said as she got to her feet and moved toward the tea service. "I asked my people to put another service in the sitting room where Dinno was when they had a moment, but I don't know if they've been able to get around to it. With so many . . . guests in the house, my servants will have to be given a triple bonus for taking care of us all once this is over."

"A triple bonus at the very least," Cleemor agreed, getting to his feet with a silent sigh and following Antrie's example.

"And once we have our tea, will we be calling on Tal and Korge as well? We owe those two some special and individual attention."

"No, I think we need to speak to Dinno and Reesh first," Antrie said, stepping aside to wait until Cleemor had his own cup of tea. "Formally expelling Thrybin Korge from the assembly will be the easy part, but we also need a unanimous decision about Zirdon. I'm going to ask the rest of you to agree to executing him as soon as the man he hired is caught."

Cleemor turned away from the service with his cup of tea to study Antrie for a moment, and then he shook his head just a bit.

"I was about to ask you to go into detail about why you want Tal executed, but I've decided to wait," he said. "There are only four of us left in the assembly, so we might as well all hear your reasons together."

"Yes, going through the matter once will be quite enough," Antrie returned with a sigh. "Shall we join our brothers now?"

Cleemor replied by taking her arm, and when they reached the door he opened it for her. The hallway was reasonably free of people with only two guardsmen in sight, so a few moments later they walked into the sitting room where Reesh and Dinno were.

"Well, just in time," Dinno said as he and Reesh rose from their chairs. "I was about to go and join my Blendingmates for our patrol, but you two look like you have something to tell us. Has Mismin gotten back with the man he went after?"

"No, not yet," Cleemor said as he guided Antrie to a chair and then chose one of his own. "At least he hasn't gotten back yet as far as we know. We're here to take care of official business, but I have a question first. Have you been able to make arrangements yet to send High talents to help the Gandistrans and our own Highs?"

"We're working on being able to start with that as soon as all the assassins are caught," Dinno answered, his mood sobering. "Reesh and I are chafing at the delay, of course, but we can't find a way to avoid it. If any of us are killed, that will just mean more work for the rest."

"It will mean a good deal more than that to *us*," Cleemor assured the man as they all took their seats. "But since we have a delay we can't avoid, let's take care of what doesn't *have* to be delayed. I move that Thrybin Korge be officially expelled from the membership of the assembly. Do I hear a second to the motion?"

"I second the motion," Reesh said before either of the others could speak. "And I notice officially that it's about time."

"All in favor," Cleemor said, doing nothing to hide his smile. Reesh was turning into a truly amusing fellow . . . "Four hands in favor, leaving none to vote against. The motion is carried, and Thrybin Korge is no longer a member of this assembly. Now on to other business. Antrie Lorimon has proposed that Zirdon Tal be executed as soon as the man he hired has been caught, but she hasn't yet spoken about the reasons behind her stance. Would you care to speak now, Antrie?"

"I wish I didn't have to, but there's no getting out of it," Antrie replied with another sigh. Both Dinno and Reesh had shown raised brows, but neither spoke against the proposal. "Zirdon Tal is directly responsible for the deaths of nine members of the assembly, and guilty of plotting against the rest of us. We all know that for a fact, but if we leave him alive his family could well decide to come to his defense. If they do we'll have a terrible fight on our hands, and I can't bear the thought of Zirdon getting away with what he's done. If he's already been executed, his family can argue and complain forever and I won't care."

"I think it's more than just not letting him get away with what he's done," Dinno said, his tone thoughtful. "If we leave Tal alive, he's certain to find *some* way to push himself forward again even if he no longer has any talent. Letting Tal live will be a terrible example to others, and we have enough trouble without that."

"And we owe the effort to those High Blendings who will

be in the assembly after us," Reesh pointed out, looking just as thoughtful. "Leaving the problem for *them* to see to will taint their first efforts, and that isn't fair. I move that we execute Zirdon Tal as soon as his main hireling is found and arrested. Does anyone second the motion?"

"I second the motion," Cleemor said, deciding to make his own position perfectly clear. He hadn't added any other words because he considered them unnecessary. He already agreed with everything the others had said.

"All in favor," Reesh said, then continued after a glance around. "Four hands in favor, leaving none to vote against. The motion has been passed, and Zirdon Tal will be executed as soon as his hireling has been found and arrested."

The last word had barely left Reesh's mouth when a knock came on the sitting room door. Since the door hadn't been closed, Cleemor turned to see who was knocking. Frode Mismin stood in the doorway, and a smile was clear on his face.

"Since the assembly has never before acted with such efficiency, I couldn't bring myself to interrupt until you were done," he explained as he came farther into the room. "Now that the vote is over, however, I'm here to tell you that we have the man Tal hired. We also have five of his last six assassins, so in a very short while you'll be able to get on with the rest of what you said you have to do."

"In a very short while," Cleemor mused while Mismin stopped near Antrie's chair. "Does that mean you know where the last assassin is, but just haven't put your hands on him?"

"We haven't put our hands on *her*, but we expect to shortly," Mismin answered after giving Antrie a wry smile. "We know the area she was assigned to watch, so my men ought to have her in just a few minutes. For that reason I put out the word on my way back here. In another hour or so the city's High talents ought to be showing up."

"And then we'll need to do some heavy recruiting," Dinno said to Reesh before getting to his feet. "But first we have an execution to attend, or at least the rest of you have one to attend. I have one to perform."

Cleemor felt a small jolt of shock as he stood, finally realizing something that Dinno had obviously known right from the start. As the only Earth magic member of the assembly left, it would be Dinno's place to put Tal to sleep and then to stop the man's heart. It might be necessary to execute someone, but there was no reason to be cruel about it.

"Yes, let's get this done and put behind us," Antrie said as she rose and took Mismin's arm. "You may be the one performing the execution, Olskin, but the responsibility for your actions lies with all of us. Taking responsibility isn't easy, but it's time we all learned how."

"More than time," Cleemor muttered to himself as he followed the others out of the room. A lot of people would·be taking responsibility for their actions in the next few days, and not all of them would be embracing the effort with a whole heart. But at least the Gracelian empire was about to start over again in the *right* way . . .

Zirdon Tal had gone from confusion to fury. It had taken a while for him to understand what had been going on, but he finally seemed to have it all worked out. Those miserable Gandistran peasants had done something to him, and because of that he'd been behaving like an ass.

*Not that I regret having tried to kill Korge,* Zirdon thought as he glared at the men who were obviously there to guard him. *Korge is an ambitious fool without a mind, and we would have been well rid of him. It's his fault as well that I'm now being treated like an animal.*

Or less than an animal, Zirdon realized. Not only was he being kept in what looked to be a storage room, but his hands were still tied behind his back. They all had a nerve treating *him* like this, but they'd soon be paying for their presumption. As soon as his family realized that *their* good name depended on *his* being exonerated of all charges, no one would be allowed to continue accusing him. He'd be free to take his revenge, and would make plans to do so immediately.

Zirdon had only just begun to formulate those plans when the door to the storage area opened. Olskin Dinno walked in first, with Reesh, Gardan, Lorimon, and Mismin behind him. Mismin dismissed the three guards, and once they were gone Zirdon sat up straighter.

"If you expect to get away with this, allow me to disabuse you of the notion," Zirdon told them all stiffly. "You had no right to treat me like this, and I demand to be taken home to my family."

"That's one of the reasons why we're here, Tal," Dinno answered with an odd and unexplained gentleness. "We wanted you to know that you'll be returned to your family in just a little while."

"It's about time," Zirdon said, triumph flashing through him. In just a little while he'd be back with his family, and then he'd be able to start getting even with those who had insulted him so badly. He knew exactly how his revenge would go, and as weariness began to take him over, Zirdon was able to picture the time. It was a very pleasant picture, and he never noticed when the picture abruptly faded to unrelieved black . . .

Thrybin Korge walked along the street in the shadows, looking for a carriage to hire. His back had begun to throb more vigorously, and he wanted nothing more than to get home and lie down. After a good sleep he would put the first of his plans in motion, the plans that would make *him* the ultimate leader of the empire. It had come to him that he didn't need to be part of a Blending himself to begin with. He simply needed to control a Blending at first, one that would take over everything for him. After that he'd be free to find the perfect Blendingmates, preferably the best looking women of strength in the empire . . .

A smile curved Thrybin's lips as he walked, an acknowledgment of the truth he'd inadvertently come upon. When he chose Blendingmates they all *would* be women, thereby making him the major talent again. After all, how could a woman be a true major talent? She couldn't be, of course, and everyone would know that as well as he knew the fact himself . . .

"Good evening, esteemed sir," a voice came, a soft and interesting voice. "Would you care for some dinner—and evening company?"

The woman who stepped out of the shadows was very attractive, much more so than the average woman who offered herself on the streets. Her smile would have raised Thrybin's interest immediately at another time, but at the moment he wasn't even able to regret the missed opportunity.

"The only thing I can use right now is a carriage," Thrybin answered, pausing with one hand against a building to rest. "Go and find one for me, girl, and you'll have earned a few coppers the easy way."

"I know an easier way to earn more than coppers, Exalted One," the girl answered with an odd smile. "You *are* a member of the assembly, aren't you?"

"Of course I am," Thrybin said, flattered that the girl actually seemed to recognize him. "But I don't understand what you meant—"

Thrybin's question was interrupted by the sound of shouting behind him, and he turned with a bit of difficulty to see what looked like some of Mismin's guardsmen running and gesturing. So they'd discovered that he'd escaped . . .

"Those men are undoubtedly coming after *me,* but they won't catch me," Thrybin told the woman hurriedly. "If you keep me out of their hands, there's silver in it for you."

"There are more of them coming from the other way, but you're right, Exalted One," the woman said as she stepped closer to Thrybin. "They may catch *me,* but they certainly won't get their hands on *you.*"

Relief and triumph flooded through Thrybin as he realized that he'd outsmarted his enemies again. He'd use this girl to get him away and hidden until the guardsmen were gone, and then he'd continue with his plans. Nothing could stop him, absolutely nothing—

Thrybin made a sound of pain when he felt the sharp stabbing in his chest, and the confusion was terrible. He had looked down to see a dagger sticking out of him, and even as he slipped to his knees he saw the girl who had stabbed him try to escape from the closing guardsmen. She had obviously thought she could run away from the two groups, but a third group appeared in her way. Then all three groups converged, and the girl was firmly in their custody.

*Good,* Thrybin thought, not having noticed that he'd fallen to his side on the ground. *They have her, so I'll be able to testify at her trial. But it's getting very dark now, so they'd better be quick about fetching a healer. I need a healer again, because I can't die now. I can't die when I'm so close, I can't, I just can't . . . I can't . . . I—*

# FIFTEEN

The day was windy and a bit cooler than Sembrin Noll would have liked, but not even pouring rain or mounds of snow could have ruined the day entirely. Sembrin was out of that house with no one but Jost Feriun, his guard commander, as escort, and the feeling of freedom was so heady that someone might have thought he'd been drinking.

But for the last day and a half, Sembrin hadn't had more than an occasional sip of wine to drink. After somehow getting free of the control Bensia and the children had had on him, he'd realized that his only hope of *staying* free was to pretend that nothing had changed. It had been a terrible struggle to make himself actually feel as unconcerned and satisfied as he'd been when under control, but he'd managed it because he'd had to.

And Bensia had apparently been taken in completely. The vile woman had smiled to herself and ignored him, and the children had done the same sort of ignoring they'd been indulging in for years. They all went about their business without giving him a second thought, showing only indulgent smiles when he took "Bensia" to their bedchamber for what was supposed to be pleasure. The only pleasure involved, however, had been the opportunity to relax for a while.

"We're almost there, my lord," Feriun murmured, bringing Sembrin out of his thoughts. "One of our men will be setting up on the corner just beyond this alley."

Sembrin nodded without speaking, the stench in the alley-way encouraging his silence. They'd left their horses some distance from where they now walked, and were in the process of sneaking around in an effort to remain unseen. Sembrin had discovered that speaking put the fetid stink of the alleyway into his mouth, but speaking was really unnecessary. Feriun already knew that Sembrin meant for them to follow the mobs the men gathered, which would put them into the palace along with their men.

A smile curved Sembrin's lips as he remembered that Bensia waited at the house to be told that they'd been successful. The miserable woman had smiled triumphantly as Sembrin left the house, certainly expecting to be escorted into the palace once it was firmly in their hands. Sembrin meant to have her taken to the palace, all right, but not with the children behind her and not with an escort. Chains would look particularly good on Bensia, especially once she'd been stripped naked . . .

"Ah, the men are about to begin, my lord," Feriun said softly with relish, and Sembrin looked up to see that they'd stopped at the mouth of the alley. The corner they meant to watch was only a dozen steps away. Once their man climbed up onto the box he'd brought with him, it would be possible to see the man even if the crowd grew larger than they expected it to.

"The other two men had better support the speaker if anyone in the crowd tries to give him trouble," Sembrin murmured, finding the air considerably fresher so close to the street. "Are the other two also prepared to take over if for some reason the speaker can't continue?"

"All three know what's supposed to be said, so there shouldn't be a problem," Feriun murmured in return, and then the guard leader straightened. "Yes, it's time, so they're going to start."

Sembrin felt a thrill of anticipation as he did his own straightening. All of the men, all over the city, would be starting their haranguing at the same time. In that way the various mobs formed would also be formed at the same time, making it much easier to gather the peasants into one large mob. The more peasants there were to hide among and behind, the better off Sembrin and his men would be.

The speaker had stepped up onto the box he'd brought with him, and a few curious passersby had already paused to find out what was going on.

"I'm here to tell you the truth!" the speaker shouted, looking around at everyone in sight. "If you have the nerve to hear the truth, come closer and listen!"

There were a lot of raised brows and exchanged glances among the peasants on the street, but most of those who had heard the speaker did come closer to where he stood.

"Do you people have any idea how unhappy most of your neighbors are under the new government?" the speaker demanded once he had an attentive audience. "You've all been told that life is better now that the nobles are gone, but is life *really* better? Don't you all know someone who didn't get that job he or she wanted, or someone who tried to speak up about the unfairness all around? Until now those who tried to speak out have been arrested and thrown out of the city, but it's more than time that you all heard the truth."

A mutter ran through the slowly growing crowd, a sound that meant the peasants were beginning to respond to the speaker. Sembrin tasted the feelings of the crowd and found them to be uncertain, which was really an excellent start.

"The truth is that the new government is out to help itself, not any of you!" the speaker shouted, pointing at the crowd as he spoke. "Getting rid of the nobles should have made us all rich, but has it? How many of you have gotten your share of the gold left behind by the people who had it all? *I* haven't seen any gold, and the government wants to keep it that way!"

"There's something wrong that I just can't put my finger on," Feriun said as the crowd muttered again, only louder. "More and more people keep coming over, but there's something—"

"Don't be a fool, Feriun," Sembrin snapped, hating the way the man always tried to ruin things that were going well. "My talent tells me that those people are starting to get angry, and angry is the way we want them. What could be wrong in *that*?"

Feriun simply shook his head, proving that Sembrin was wise to ignore him. Things were going just the way they were supposed to, and at this rate they would be in the palace in no time—

"If the government gave *us* all the gold, what would they use to pay the farmers for the food we need?" a woman in the crowd suddenly shouted. "I don't know about you, but for me eating on a regular basis has become a habit."

"If *we* had the gold, we could pay for our own food," the speaker returned almost at once, clearly ignoring the ripple of amusement that had gone through the crowd. "I don't know about *you,* but I'm not a child who can't look after himself."

"You're going to pay for a city's worth of food all by yourself?" the woman came back with a sound of ridicule. "Just how much of that gold do you expect to get?"

"I won't be the only one paying, so there won't be a problem," the speaker countered. "Or don't you think there are enough sensible people in this city to join me?"

"Where does sensible enter into it?" the woman asked at once, again sounding ridiculing. "You'd need to get everyone together and collect their gold, then you'd need to get in touch with the farmers. Then you'd have to pay the farmers and make arrangements for the food to be shipped. We might get a bit hungry waiting for all that to be done, and while we're starving we might ask ourselves why we're bothering. The new government is already taking care of the matter, a lot more easily than we could."

"You don't mind being enslaved as long as you have your meals on time?" the speaker scoffed, taking what Sembrin considered the proper attitude. "The point is that gold isn't the only thing being kept from us. The wonderful new government promised us new and better jobs if we did things their way, jobs that were supposed to lead to a better life all around. No one I know has seen a trace of that better life, and I'm willing to bet that most of *you* haven't seen it either!"

The muttering grew even louder, putting a faint smile on the face of the speaker. The man seemed to be confident that he had the crowd now, but as soon as the muttering died down a bit the woman spoke again.

"Maybe you and your friends don't have a better life because you're more interested in stealing it than in working for it," the woman stated. "You want *us* to demand gold that we would then give to you, knowing in our hearts that you would never cheat us. Is that because you've done so much for us already?"

Too many people in the crowd laughed at what the woman had said, a fact the speaker didn't miss. Sembrin saw his man's jaw tighten, and then the speaker gave one of his companions a small nod. One of the two men there to support and protect the speaker began to step forward to see to the woman, but suddenly there was a very large blond man standing beside the woman. The man who was supposed to support the speaker stopped short with what looked like confusion, and Sembrin heard Feriun curse under his breath.

"That's Chelten Admis, one of the men who disappeared a few days ago," Feriun snarled, staring at the big blonde. "I don't know what he's doing *here*, but none of my three will try to take him. In spite of that easy grin the man is wearing, he won't hesitate to kill anyone who challenges him. I told you something felt wrong, but what does it mean?"

Sembrin made no attempt to answer Feriun, primarily because he *had* no answer. He had no idea why his plans had suddenly started to go wrong, and then the woman in the crowd made things even worse.

"I think you're so concerned about us because you work for one of the nobles still on the loose," the woman accused the speaker abruptly. "Since we all know how much the nobles cared about us, we now know why *you* care. And you were able to talk so knowingly about slaves because you have personal experience with the state. It takes a slave to be a willing running dog for a fool who refuses to understand that his time is now past. Why don't you bark for us so we can all see the real you?"

The crowd laughed even harder, and Sembrin had no trouble feeling the panic his speaker experienced. Everything had gone terribly wrong, but getting to safety now had to be Sembrin's primary concern. After he'd hidden himself again he could take the time to figure out why his plan hadn't worked . . .

"Let's get out of here," Feriun muttered, speaking Sembrin's already-made decision. "If those aren't city guardsmen heading for our men, I've never seen the breed. We don't need to be here to see the arrest, or whether the rest of our men get away. And we can't go back to that house where your wife is. Too many of the men know about it, and at least one of them is guaranteed to talk."

Sembrin couldn't have cared less about Bensia's safety or lack of it in the house, so he nodded and began to turn with Feriun to retrace their steps through the alley. When Feriun stopped short Sembrin almost ran into him, but Sembrin's words of rebuke died before they were spoken. The reason for Feriun's abrupt halt was the presence of strangers behind them, people who looked far too amused for Sembrin's peace of mind.

"Surely you aren't leaving the party *already,*" a small woman said, all but smirking. "You've been wonderful guests so far, so good, in fact, that we won't hear of your leaving. We've been looking forward to having a long conversation with you, and we'd like to have that conversation *now.*"

"Unfortunately, madam, my friend and I have pressing business elsewhere," Sembrin said at once, ignoring the group of large men who stood behind the woman. "I'm sure you understand the problem, so please ask your companions to step aside and let us through. Going around the block will take far too long."

As he spoke, Sembrin reached for the woman's mind. He intended to use his talent to take control of her, and then *she* could get all those men out of their way. It might be possible for him and Feriun to go out into the street and lose themselves in the crowd, but there was no need to do things the hard way. All Sembrin had to do was touch the woman's mind . . . touch it . . . touch—

"Don't bother trying again, Sembrin," another voice drawled, this time a male voice. "*I'm* protecting the lady, so you haven't a chance of taking control."

And then Edmin Ruhl stepped out from behind the very large men, a sight that made Sembrin's blood turn to ice. Edmin ought to be hiding in the deepest hole he could find—if not gone from the city or dead—but instead he was here, making no effort to disguise his identity . . .

"That man is an escaped noble!" Sembrin blurted as he pointed, the only thing he could think of to say and do. "You have to take him into custody at once and turn him over to the authorities! There's bound to be an incredibly large reward for you all—"

Sembrin's words broke off when he realized that the men facing him were laughing, just as though he'd told them a joke. Edmin was laughing as well, and Sembrin couldn't bear it.

"I'm not lying, you fools!" he shouted, feeling the heat of embarrassment and anger in his face. "That man *is* an escaped noble, so why aren't you arresting him?"

"We aren't arresting the man because we were told you might say something like that," one of the large men informed Sembrin with a chuckle. "Accusing other people of what *you* are is an old trick, much too old for any of us to fall for it."

The blood that had been so hot and uncomfortable in Sembrin's face suddenly drained away, leaving behind the ice felt earlier and most likely a matching pallor.

"Well, *I'm* not an escaped noble, and some of you ought to know that," Feriun blustered while Sembrin stood silent and frightened. "I'm only an ordinary hired man who isn't responsible for what his employer does, so I'll just be on my way—"

Feriun had started to turn back to the street, and Sembrin wondered what had caused the turncoat's words to break off. A glance over his shoulder showed another group of men blocking the way to the street, which perversely made Sembrin glad. Feriun had been willing enough to share in Sembrin's victory; making the fool share defeat instead was nothing more than justice.

"You don't have to bother with throwing me out of the city," Sembrin said to the woman as he squared his shoulders. "I'm perfectly capable of leaving on my own, which I mean to do at once. Unless, of course, you happen to have room in your government for someone with my ability. I can be of more use to you than you can possibly imagine, and I won't ask more than a modest amount for my help. I can tell you—"

"Oh, spare me," the woman interrupted, no longer looking in the least amused. "I'd sooner have a rat from the sewers working for me, and in a short while we'll know everything *you* know without having to pay you even a copper. But after that you won't be thrown out of the city, which I'm sure you already know. You'll be taking a trip out into the country to see old friends, just not *our* country. Arrest them now, please."

A number of the large men began to step forward, but what really destroyed Sembrin was the look of delight on Edmin Ruhl's face. Somehow Ruhl had managed to protect himself, and the man's lack of worry showed that nothing Sembrin might say would cause Ruhl to be sent to Astinda with him. A scream began in Sembrin's throat and forced its way out of his mouth, but that didn't stop the large men from chaining him to a cursing Feriun.

It was over and they'd lost, they'd actually lost, lost everything . . . lost . . . lost!

Bensia Noll paced back and forth in the sitting room, much too agitated to read the way she'd been doing earlier. She knew she should have heard from Sembrin or one of his men at least an hour ago, even if they'd had a small bit of trouble at the palace. Everyone in the peasants' new government ought to be dead by now, so why hadn't someone returned to tell her that? Possibly she ought to send one of the guards left at the house to find out . . .

"And why aren't the children down here with me?" Bensia muttered, stopping to glare at the empty doorway. "I sent a servant to fetch them, so they should have been down here by now. Do I have to do everything myself?"

"Your pardon, lady, but there are callers here to see you," one of the servants appeared to say, making Bensia jump just a bit. "Shall I show them in?"

"Of course you're to show them in!" Bensia snapped, hating the stupidity those peasants always showed. Imagine, asking if they ought to show in men who were in this house until just this morning. "I've been waiting for those callers, so get them in here fast!"

"Yes, my lady," the servant said with a bow, and then he stepped aside. Bensia was all ready to demand that Sembrin's men tell her what had taken so long, but the first sight of her "callers" froze the words on her tongue. Instead of it being Sembrin's men who were shown in, the callers were three strange women, two strange men, and Edmin Ruhl!

"Well, Bensia, how delightful to see you again," Edmin all but purred as he and the others came farther into the room. "I must say you're *looking* fit, and that's a lucky thing. You'll soon need all the fitness you can get."

"Guards!" Bensia shrieked, both furious and frightened at this unexpected turn of events. "Guards! Get in here now!"

"You want your guards?" Edmin drawled as he and the others stopped only a few feet away. "Oh, what a pity. We didn't realize you'd want them when we put them under arrest, thinking they'd be much better off with the rest of their ilk. We have them all, you know, including their leader and your poor husband."

"Mother, what's going on?" Travin demanded as he and his brother and sisters came hurrying in. "Who *are* these people?"

"No one of any importance, dear," Bensia replied with a smile, relief flooding through her. "I'm afraid we've lost your father's services, but the assistance of *these* people will probably prove to be a good deal more valuable. Why don't we see if we can convince them to cooperate with us? There's a good chance they even have access to the palace, the place we'll be going next. The place we're destined to be."

"If they have access to the palace, they must be servants there," Travin said with a sniff, properly identifying the group as one of peasants. "But I think we can still make use of them."

Travin smiled then, and his brother Wesdin and sisters Solthia and Liseria smiled as well. Bensia's children were more than ready to assist their mother, but in another moment her smile began to waver. She had tried to reach the power at the same time her children did, but for some reason she couldn't . . . quite . . .

"Is something wrong?" that wretched Edmin Ruhl inquired as the children lost their own amusement and became as agitated as she felt. "I thought you were going to ask us for help of some sort."

"Really, Edmin, they need more than just a *little* help," the trollop on Edmin's arm drawled just the way he had earlier. "That woman is so thick in the head that she thought we would walk in here without taking precautions. I'm not surprised that those children are living in a fool's fantasy, but isn't *she* too old to do the same?"

"She *is* getting a bit long in the tooth," Edmin answered with an air of consideration while Bensia gasped with insult and outrage. "That means her actions aren't necessarily due to stupidity. They might be due to senility."

"How dare you!" Bensia demanded with furious mortification, but then she remembered something and forced herself to smile. "And how is your dear father, Edmin? Still going on as usual, I trust."

"Oh, he's doing quite well these days," Edmin answered blandly instead of falling into the rage Bensia had expected to see. "He's recuperating in the palace, coming back beautifully from a small accident he had. Driffin there was good enough to treat him, and he tells me the healing took only moderate effort."

"You're lying!" Bensia snarled, hating the way all six of the strangers—especially the one Edmin had gestured to—

were all but laughing at her. "But you've always *been* a liar, Edmin, so I'm not surprised that you're still at it. Now you and your peasant friends can get out of my house. My children and I will be taking tea soon, and—"

"Now, now, Bensia, we all know that this isn't your house," Edmin interrupted to wave a finger at her. "In fact it wouldn't be yours even if you'd owned it originally. All property formerly owned by those people known as nobles has been confiscated, and the nobles themselves finally given something useful to do. Very soon now, you'll be doing that same useful thing yourself."

"I'd rather die," Bensia stated as she drew herself up, speaking nothing but the truth. "You might find it possible to kill me, Edmin, but you'll never be able to force me to cooperate with peasants."

"I have no intentions of trying to do so, Bensia," Edmin returned as other strangers entered the room. "Our Astindan allies there will do any necessary forcing, and they're rather difficult to argue with. But you do need to learn that for yourself, so we'll be going now. Thank you so much for your hospitality."

Edmin and the two men with him performed ironic little bows, but the three women simply smiled. That *really* infuriated Bensia, but before she could think of something to say to the six peasants they turned and began to leave. And then the other peasants came closer . . .

"Mother, make them stop!" Solthia demanded shrilly as her sister and brothers simply made sounds of distress. "They're forcing us to obey them, but they're only peasants! I don't *want* to obey peasants!"

"Leave my children alone!" Bensia commanded, but instead of being obeyed she felt . . . *strength* being used on her. She was made to move closer to her children, and then all five of them were forced out of the room.

Bensia could never remember being as humiliated as when the five of them were taken past the peasants who had been their servants. The peasants laughed and applauded as their former masters walked past, the hold she and the children had had on them clearly gone now. Those peasants were enjoying the sight of their betters being brought low, but their amusement would be remembered and avenged. As soon as she escaped capture, she would find those peasants again even if it was the last thing she did!

Anger carried Bensia outside and a short way down the drive without her noticing anything else. The children were walking in front of her, and the sudden sounds of protest they made caused her to pay attention. Bensia had naturally expected that they would be taken to a coach, but an old, worn wagon stood in the driveway and *that* was what they were being told to climb into. Another wagon was already filled with her former guardsmen, but *they* were peasants so it made no difference.

"You can't seriously expect us to ride in this—this—*thing*," Bensia said as their escort helped her sons and daughters into the wagon. "We have two perfectly good coaches, and I *demand* that we be allowed to use them."

"You'll only be riding in this wagon to the place where the rest of your people are," one of the peasants commented without really looking at her. "Once we have you all together and out of the city, you'll spend most of the trip walking. Up you go."

Bensia found herself in the wagon with the children in a very abrupt way, with nothing to sit on but dirty wooden planks on both sides of the conveyance. The girls were protesting in outrage and the boys had their hands curled into fists with anger, but all four of them were sitting down on the left-hand side of the wagon. Bensia couldn't understand why they would cooperate like that, but when she found *herself* sitting on the bench to the right she understood only too well.

"This is *not* happening," she muttered, staring down at her tightly folded hands. "This is nothing but a nightmare that I'll soon be waking up from. This *cannot* be happening to me."

Bensia held firm to her belief even as the wagon began to move. The wagon with her former guardsmen had gone first, and when it reached the road it turned left. When their own wagon reached the road they turned right, and both drivers of Bensia's wagon glanced at the quickly disappearing first wagon.

"I don't envy our Gandistran hosts," their driver said to the peasant beside him, speaking only just loud enough for Bensia to hear most of what he said. "Our lot here will simply be put to work. What the Gandistrans have to decide is what to do with those others. If there's no way to reclaim that group as useful citizens, they may have to—"

"Yes, I know what you mean," the second peasant said rather quickly. "Even putting down a dog would be hard for me, but if there's no way to keep those men from hurting innocent people, they mustn't be turned loose. And I can't decide which would be worse, making sure those men *can't* hurt the innocent, or putting them down. You're right. I'm glad the problem isn't mine."

The two peasants went silent then, but Bensia's distress still increased. That peasant government couldn't possibly kill or neutralize *her* guardsmen. Somehow her men would escape and free her, somehow they *would*!

But no one had come to free her when the wagon turned into the drive of another house. It was beginning to get dark so torches had been lit along the drive, but the wagon didn't stop at the house. It continued on to the stables, and that was where it stopped.

"What fools these peasants are," Travin sneered as he looked around. "They don't even know that we should have been let off at the house. Now we'll have to walk back to it."

"You won't have all that far to walk," one of the peasants said as he put down the tailgate of the wagon, clearly having heard Travin's comment. "Come right this way."

Bensia had meant to stay in the wagon and refuse to move, but the peasant's words caused her to rise along with the children and let herself be helped down. Once they were all on the ground they were led toward the stables themselves, of all places, and walking inside brought even more of a shock.

"Aren't those people most of our former neighbors from the country?" Wesdin asked his older brother as he looked around with widened eyes. "If they also came to the city, why didn't they offer to help us?"

"I . . . don't think coming to the city was their idea," Liseria ventured, appearing as unsure as Wesdin did. "And we won't have any choice about what's done to *us* either, will we?"

"Nonsense, child, nonsense," Bensia said at once, looking sternly at her youngest daughter. "We are *nobles,* Liseria, and that means we have *every* choice. No one will ever be able to—"

"Guess again, you bitch," a voice suddenly interrupted Bensia, making her look quickly to the right. Just as she'd thought, it was Sembrin who had spoken, staring up at her from where he sat leaning against the wall of one of the stalls.

"You have no idea how glad I am to see you and the children again, Bensia," Sembrin went on with what looked like true enjoyment. "At first being captured was shattering, but once I had a chance to think it came to me that you and the children would be joining me in captivity. Picturing you and your precious brood toiling at your own labor will make mine infinitely easier and more pleasant. And, no, I didn't need the peasants' help to escape your control. I was already free when I left the house this morning, so *you* would have lost no matter *what* happened. I hope that thought comforts you in your hour of travail."

Bensia began to scream then, and the screaming didn't stop until complete darkness took her over.

# SIXTEEN

Idresia still felt wildly happy when she and the others got back to the warehouse. They were *all* laughing and giddy, in fact, looking and acting like children instead of adults.

"Did you see her expression when I called her stupid and old, Edmin?" Issini asked as they walked into the kitchen area. "The only way I could have bothered her more would be if I'd slapped her face. I *wanted* to slap her, and would have if the Astindans hadn't been there."

"Actually, it's a good thing our allies *were* there," Edmin answered, following Issini toward the tea service. "If they hadn't been, I probably would have hurt my hands rather badly showing her husband what I thought of him. If he hadn't been a complete fool, his wife would never have managed to make as much trouble as she did."

"He'll be paying for that foolishness in just a little while," Driff said as he joined the others in going toward the tea service. "In fact they both will, along with their children. I feel very fortunate that *we* aren't in their place. I'm not all that fond of working outdoors."

"But we have what might prove to be a harder job ahead of us," Asri said, looking less exhilarated than she had. "I took just a peek at the probabilities to see what we might be doing next, and now I wish I hadn't. We'll have to interview all those men our entity took over, and decide which of them can be saved and which can't."

"That decision won't entail what all of you seem to think it

186

will," Driff said, looking from one to the other of them where they'd stopped to stare at Asri with expressions of shock. "We'll definitely separate out the men who are willing to work at an honest job, but doing something with the ones who are lost won't be *our* problem. We'll only have to keep them quiet until the Highs are brought back to themselves."

"And then we get to dump the decision on the Highs," Idresia said with a nod of relief. "Since they're the ones with the stronger talent, it's only fair if they get the harder jobs."

"I . . . don't think that's exactly what Driff has in mind," Edmin said, faint disturbance creasing his brow. "We won't have to *do* anything to the men who don't measure up, but I think we'll be expected to make a recommendation."

"But if they take our recommendation, won't it be like disposing of those men ourselves?" Kail protested. "I mean, assuming we decide that the men should die. I don't think I *can* recommend that they be put under control for the rest of their lives. I had too much of that myself while growing up to be able to consider doing it to someone else on a permanent basis."

"And *I* think those men deserve whatever happens to them," Issini said with a shake of her head. "We all had it hard growing up, but none of *us* decided to get even with the innocent along with the guilty. A lot of those men just don't care about anyone but themselves, a fact that's clear enough to *me*. I can see, though, that the rest of you don't agree, so we'll have to talk it over. But only after Driff goes to work on the High talents and brings them out of their coma or sleep or whatever. After they're awake, they may decide they don't want our recommendations after all."

"Now *that* I would enjoy," Idresia said briskly, deciding it was time that someone took charge. "Let's have a cup or two of the tea we all obviously want, and then we'll go out to dinner. I think we've earned a small celebration, don't you?"

"At least a small one," Driff agreed with a chuckle. "Putting Noll's hired men under control before we had our people arrest the ones doing the talking was easier than I expected it to be, but I still feel almost empty."

"I've been feeling the same since our entity cut off Noll's children and wife from the power," Edmin said while the others just made sounds of agreement. "I suggest we have only a single cup of tea, and then get on to the food."

"Why don't we forget about the tea and just go out to eat?" Asri asked, holding up one hand. "If I weren't so fond of Kail I could broil and eat *him,* and since my son is in the very good hands of his new nanny, I won't feel guilty about leaving him behind."

"Yes, let's go right now," Driff said, glancing around to see that the decision was unanimous. "We don't know how long it will take us to bring the Highs back to themselves, so we ought to get an early start tomorrow."

"Why do we have to start *early*?" Idresia asked as they all turned back to the door. "We don't have anything else to worry about, so what if rousing the Highs does take an extra hour or two? What difference will it make?"

They all began to tease Idresia about her hatred of getting up early, but she was fully prepared to defend her position. After all, now that the renegades were accounted for, they *didn't* have anything else to worry about . . .

"Yes, do join us, my friend," Honrita Grohl said to Arbon Vand, their new Fire magic user. Vand was being led into the room by Stelk Faron, their Water magic user. The room was part of a small and shabby abandoned house that the group had taken over for its own use, and Holdis Ayl wasn't present. Too many people knew about Ayl, and his presence would only have made Honrita's job harder.

"Are you the one who needed to see me?" Vand asked as he looked first at Honrita and then at the room. "If the matter was all that important, why didn't you come to *my* house?"

Arbon Vand had brown hair and eyes and looked rather average, but that was only until he began to speak. Then his strong personality became obvious, supporting proof for the reason why Honrita hadn't tried to put him under her control from a distance. They needed Vand too much to take unnecessary chances with his enlistment.

"I didn't come to your house, Dom Vand, because there are too many people in and near your house for us to have a private conversation." Honrita had gotten to her feet as she spoke, and now she added a smile. "Please take a chair and I'll explain why I asked you here."

"Why does our conversation have to be private?" Vand asked as he stopped next to a chair rather than sit in it. "And who are those other women?"

Kadri Sumlow, their Earth magic user, and Seeli Tandor, Air magic, had just come into the room, and now the two stood next to Stelk Faron. Kadri looked even heavier and more ridiculous standing next to the taller and thinner Stelk and Seeli, but that couldn't be helped.

"I'll give you a more complete introduction to everyone once we've talked, Dom Vand," Honrita said with another smile. "Would you like a cup of tea? And I'm Honrita Grohl, by the way."

"No tea, thank you," Vand returned, his attitude firm rather than chilly as he continued to stand. "I'd rather get to the reason I'm here and then go home. I have fairly important tasks waiting for my attention."

"You consider teaching a class in Fire magic important?" Honrita asked as she sat down again and let a small part of her ridicule show through. "Surely you expected to do something *really* important when you finished your own class? A simple teaching job must be very much of a letdown."

"I happen to enjoy the idea of teaching," Vand came back, and oddly enough he was telling the truth. "Later on there ought to be other things for me to do, but right now teaching suits me. Was there anything else?"

"Yes, there *is* something else," Honrita said, ignoring his attempt at dismissal. "I asked you here today to offer you something more important right now, not at some nebulous time in the future. We would like you to join our Blending, a Blending we have very big plans for."

"I'm sure you do have plans, but I'm afraid I won't be a part of them," Vand said after glancing at the other three people in the room again. "If and when I do join a Blending, it won't be with complete strangers. Thank you for asking me, but I'll be going now."

And the miserable man actually began to walk toward the door! Honrita was furious that Vand hadn't responded to the subtle handling the other three had, making it necessary for her to take full control of him. Vand stopped short before he reached the door, of course, but his mind somehow tried to fight hers even as he obeyed her completely.

"He doesn't want to join us," Kadri Sumlow stated in that regal way of hers. "I take it that you're keeping him from leaving, but how will that help us? You can't *force* him to Blend with us, can you?"

"I should be able to force him to be more reasonable," Honrita said as she rose and walked over to inspect Vand. "It would be easier if Ayl found us another Fire magic user, but Ayl has already refused to do that. The man insists that we're all the strongest Middle talents in the city, and he won't hear of making substitutions."

"What about a Sight magic user?" Stelk Faron asked, stiffly disapproving as usual. "Ayl won't admit that there is such a thing, but the rest of us know better. If we don't have a Sight magic user, our Blending won't be complete."

"If you can figure out a way to sneak up on a Sight magic user, I'll get one for us," Honrita all but snapped at the fool of a man. "Until and unless you can do that, we'll just have to get along without Sight magic. People got along without it for hundreds of years, after all, so I think we can manage for a little while. Once we're in control, we'll have Sight magic users *begging* to join us."

"If you say so," Faron grudged, giving up the point only with reluctance. "How long will it take you to make Vand amenable?"

"I don't know, so I'd better get started," Honrita said after taking a short breath. "Why don't the rest of you come back in two or three hours? I ought to have our fifth fully docile by then."

"I hope you don't mean that literally," Kadri Sumlow put

in with her own disapproval. "A docile Fire magic user won't do our Blending the least bit of good."

"Yes, I do know that, so why don't you three go on about your business," Honrita said through her teeth without looking at Kadri. "The longer you take to leave, the longer it will take *me* to do what I have to."

There was a bit more grumbling from Faron and Kadri, but when Honrita refused to answer them they finally took Seeli and left. Honrita knew they would have gone a lot sooner if she'd been able to use her talent on them, but she had the definite impression that putting Vand under control would take all the strength she could muster. The Blending *needed* Vand so they would have him, and that no matter *what* she had to do to make it so.

Honrita made Vand go back to the chair he hadn't used and this time sit, and then she reclaimed her own chair. His mind continued to fight hers for the next hour or more, and then Honrita noticed something. If she put Vand under complete control without submerging his personality, she would have his obedience along with his strength. Until now she'd been trying to overpower his personality, which simply wasn't working. For such an average-looking man, Arbon Vand was incredibly tough-minded.

So Honrita changed tactics, and only then began to see some positive results. Vand still fought her control, but his . . . undermind, so to speak, became her slave. He definitely would not enjoy obeying Honrita, but he would have no choice at all in the matter.

By the time Honrita's other future Blendingmates returned, she was exhausted but triumphant. Vand sat glaring at her, and then he transferred the glare to the others.

"He doesn't look happy at all," Kadri Sumlow observed as she and the other two came closer. "Does that mean you weren't able to change his mind?"

"If he had the choice he would leave, but he isn't being allowed the choice," Honrita responded with a weary smile. "Tell us, Dom Vand: Do you still refuse to Blend with us?"

"You know well enough that I *can't* refuse," Vand replied in a growl. "I don't know what you people are up to, but don't expect any more cooperation from me than you can force."

"That should be quite enough cooperation to satisfy our needs," Honrita told him with the nastiest smile she could manage. "And you might even find yourself changing your mind. Now that you aren't able to speak about our intentions without my permission, I can tell you that we mean to rule this empire. Do you find *that* aim too far beneath your dignity to consider?"

"You're insane," Vand stated, obviously uninterested in being at all diplomatic. "I may be a strong Middle talent, but that's all I am. If the rest of you aren't any stronger, your marvelous plans are doomed even before you try to put them into effect."

"But we don't *have* to be stronger than Middles," Honrita countered, enjoying the process of deflating a know-it-all. "Our Blending entity will still be able to take over a High Blending member by member, and then we'll use *them* to put us in power. What's the matter, Dom Vand? Surely you still think we're insane."

"Your insanity is fairly obvious, so I won't comment on it again," Vand muttered, his mind roiling furiously. "I know it *sounds* as if you have a workable idea, but taking over can't possibly be as easy as you think. You'll find out about the snag only when you trip over it, and that will be the end of your grand intentions."

"But until then we'll be working as one," Honrita said with a small laugh. Vand would have brought up any overlooked points if he could have, and his failing to do so only proved there weren't any. "I would really love to Blend for the first time today, but I'm afraid that my strength isn't quite up to it. We'll have to leave Blending for tomorrow, then, but after that we'll truly be united."

"And more so after we've bonded," Kadri murmured, staring at Arbon Vand like a vulture looking at a dying body.

"Since bonding is absolutely necessary to a Blending for it to be as strong as possible—"

"You really are out of your mind," Vand told her with a strong sound of ridicule. "You people may be able to force me to go along with you, but there's no way you can force my body to enjoy the idea of lying with a skinny and overbearing old maid, a skinny and mindless near-old maid, and a fat fool. Even Earth magic can't accomplish miracles."

Kadri showed outraged insult and Seeli looked even more mindless than usual, but all Honrita felt was confusion—and mortification. *Her,* a skinny and overbearing old maid . . . ?

"What are you idiots talking about?" Honrita demanded, a bit more shrilly than she'd intended. "What do you mean by bonding, and what has that got to do with people lying with one another?"

"You never completed a class of your own, did you?" Vand said to her, a gleam of some sort in his dark eyes. "If you had you would have been told about everything that Blending entails and requires. Your pudgy friend over there knows that Blending members are supposed to lie together, but apparently you don't. What's the matter, *Dama Grohl*? Is the idea of lying with men too disgusting or frightening to consider? Well, it really doesn't matter because you're going to have to get along without the bonding anyway."

Honrita was very tired, but Vand's sense of amused ridicule came through to her clearly. As did Kadri's frustrated hunger and Seeli's trembling confusion. Stelk Faron stood as stiffly disapproving as ever, but his mind shuddered with fright and self-doubt and distaste. All that came to Honrita in a distant and distracted way, her own mind too numb with shock to form any true opinions or reactions.

*We're nothing but a bunch of misfits,* Honrita thought through the safety of distance. *Ayl didn't choose the strongest talents he could find, he chose the most twisted and incapable so we'd be easy to manipulate.*

But that idea enraged her so greatly, she was able to pull part way out of the shock. Ayl might *think* he could manipulate misfits, but she *knew* she could. And she would, as soon as she had a chance to think for a while.

"Since we aren't quite ready to Blend yet, discussion about related matters is a waste of time right now," Honrita announced as she stood, looking only at the three people by the door. "We'll all go home and say nothing of any of this to anyone, then meet back here again tomorrow morning. After we Blend, discussions will then be in order."

Giving her people orders made Honrita feel a small bit better, but she still hurried out of the old house on her way to the place she now called home. She knew she needed to sleep for a time, and once she'd regained her strength she'd be able to consider what she'd been told.

*I* will *be able to think about it,* she vowed silently, *I will, I will . . . !*

Deslen Voyt sat with Brange and Chelten Admis and some of the others in the tavern, all of them with tankards of ale in their fists and laughter in their voices.

". . . and those boys turned green when they saw it was *me* they would have to face," Admis was telling the others with a chuckle. "The little girl who did all the talking would have been easy to stomp flat, they thought, having no idea how hot Fire magic can make things even with a Low talent involved. I was just there to save the little girl some trouble when everybody started to laugh at those three. Getting laughed at is something almost nobody can take without getting wild."

"The ones at the corner where *I* was couldn't seem to understand why everyone wasn't getting all fired up," Deslen put in with his own chuckle. "The people were standing there and listening, but they all looked blank when the speaker mentioned all those rumors he thought were circulating. Then the man I was there to protect started to argue with the speaker, and in a couple of minutes everyone was laughing at the fool for trying to lie to them. The speaker really lost it then, and I had to quiet him down."

"With Water magic first and then a fist, I bet," Brange

said, showing a lot of satisfaction. "I heard you handled it really smooth, Voyt, but I'm not sorry I wasn't there to see it. I had a lot better show to watch, the one where Feriun and that fool noble were taken down."

"Did Noll really go foaming at the mouth?" Admis asked while some of the others put other questions. "And what did they do with Feriun?"

"Feriun and Noll were standing in an alley watching the speaker where *you* were, Admis," Brange answered after waving a hand for silence. "When they saw things starting to go really wrong they tried to disappear, but we were in the alley behind them and another group of us blocked the way to the street. Noll tried to tell everyone that Ruhl was also a noble, but we all knew that Ruhl had given that up to join a Blending. We pretended that Noll was lying about Ruhl, and Noll got so wild he actually started to scream."

"But what about Feriun?" Deslen put, firmly controlling his continuing hatred of the man. "He always acted like a noble himself, so he ought to get whatever they give to Noll."

"That's . . . probably not going to happen," Brange said slowly, now looking faintly disturbed. "From what *I* hear, we're more than a little lucky to have gotten out when we did. If any of the rest of the boys convince them that they want to come over to our side they'll let them, but they won't have the trust that we do. And for the ones that *don't* want to change their ways . . . Well, let's just say that Feriun might have some company when he's put down."

"Put down?" Deslen echoed, finding himself surprised. "Do you mean they might really do that to him?"

"That or put him under control for the rest of his life," Brange said with a shrug. "I don't know which I'd hate more, so I'm glad I don't have to decide."

Deslen joined the others in sitting quietly for a moment, disturbed in an odd way. Seeing Feriun put down would hardly bother him, but seeing the man controlled . . . Just as Brange had said, there was something hateful about watching a man being controlled. Being cleanly dead was an easier idea to accept . . .

"Well, it's time for me to be on about my business," Admis said after finishing his ale in a single swallow. "I have a number of meals to cook tonight, and the last one will be the most important. That little girl with Fire magic promised to come by to see what I can do. If she likes the meal well enough, she just might get curious about some of the other things I can do."

Everyone laughed as Admis got to his feet with a wide and open smile on his face, but Deslen felt a small twinge of jealousy. Admis had already found a woman to be interested in, but he, Deslen, hadn't taken that step yet. He'd been holding back because of worry over being found out by the government, but now that that worry was gone . . .

"I have to be on my way, too," Deslen said after finishing his own ale and standing. "I only have a couple of more classes, and then I'll be able to get to work as an official guardsman."

Brange and two others also got to their feet, and they left the tavern together to walk to the building where classes were held. On the way, Deslen remembered about that quiet woman who was in his class. She wasn't shy, just quiet, and even though she wasn't beautiful she was at the very least pretty.

*Maybe it's time to ask her if she'd like to have a celebration dinner with me once we finish the class,* Deslen thought. *Even if she says no, there's a woman I saw once in Brange's class. Maybe* she'll *want to have dinner* . . .

Deslen started to whistle as he walked along, and oddly enough he wasn't the only one in the group to do it . . .

# SEVENTEEN

It was still raining the next morning when Jovvi awoke. They'd all taken shelter in the abandoned houses of the village, and there was only a small bit of crowding. Some of the Blendings had had to double up or share their shelter with their link groups, but at least everyone was dry and fairly comfortable.

"I wonder if the enemy is enjoying this weather," Lorand said from where he crouched beside the hearth. He'd started a fire, and the room was already beginning to grow cozier. "Tents may give shelter, but they don't do well with keeping out the damp."

"But they travel in those litter things," Tamma put in as she moved closer to the growing fire. "They probably don't care how wet their slaves get, so they might be on the advance again. I think we ought to take a look."

"I agree," Rion said from where he still sat on his sleeping pad beside Naran and hers. "I have the definite feeling that they weren't delayed as much as we wanted them to be, and something needs to be done to slow them down again."

"He's right," Naran confirmed after yawning and stretching. "We do need to do something to slow those people down. If we have to run away from them, the probabilities will start to go against us."

"The Blendin' entity on watch agrees with all of you," Vallant said from where he stood. "I just got the report, and the invaders' entity managed to fill in just enough of the pit

197

we put in their path to let them all cross over it. They're comin' straight on again, and too many of our people are thinkin' about withdrawin'."

"Then we'd better get to it," Jovvi said, rising to her feet. "If you'll give me just a moment to visit the sanitary facilities, I'll be ready to initiate the Blending."

Jovvi wasn't the only one to use the sanitary facilities, but it didn't take long before they all sat on their sleeping pads again. They hadn't yet had their breakfast, but eating could wait until they knew the meal would continue uninterrupted.

When the Jovvi entity formed, she first checked with the lesser entity on watch to discover the location of the enemy in order to flash to the area. The Jovvi entity arrived to see the invaders in the distance, the various flesh forms moving along at a steady pace.

*They appear to be only a matter of hours away from us,* the Tamrissa part of the entity said. *We must make a more effective effort than our previous one.*

*The effort should also be more than simply a gesture,* the Vallant part of the entity said. *There must be true disruption and delay.*

*I have a thought about how we might accomplish that,* the Lorand part of the entity responded. *The flesh forms walking to either side of each litter could well be members of the enemy's link groups. If those members should be put in jeopardy, the enemy would need to pause to effect their rescue. If the effort the enemy had to make was strenuous enough, its flesh forms would also require a time of rest.*

*Yes, an effort such as that would certainly delay them,* the Naran part put in. *The delay adds greatly to the probabilities surrounding ultimate success.*

*Then let us proceed,* the Jovvi entity contributed to her other parts, already knowing the details of the plan mentioned by the Lorand part. The enemy entity remained unformed, therefore was there little difficulty for the Jovvi entity to do as was required. Air magic held a thin layer of road and side-of-the-road material in place while Earth magic removed the dirt below to a depth of thirty feet. The excavation was made ahead of the advancing slave life-forms in the shape of a large circle, and Air magic held the surface in place while the slave life-forms passed over the excavation.

When the five litters were carried into the circle, however, the surface layer was allowed to collapse. The litters remained untouched, but those life-forms walking to both sides of the litters disappeared rather abruptly. The bottom of the excavation had been filled somewhat with loose dirt to offer some protection to those who fell, but a thirty-foot fall still inevitably caused injury and distress. Some of those slave life-forms walking both ahead and to the rear of the litters also ended in the excavation, which had been made just wide enough to disallow an easy traversal by the litters.

The enemy entity appeared suddenly to roar all about itself as it assessed what had been done, and its anger and agitation pleased the Jovvi entity enough that she withdrew from the area. Then it was Jovvi alone again, to see Tamma's amusement.

"Did you all get how angry they were?" Tamma asked as she glanced around. "We didn't do anything totally harmful, and that seemed to be the enemy's main complaint. They can't just shrug and continue on, they have to rescue their people and then repair the road. But it's too bad we *couldn't* do something really harmful, and specifically to *them*."

"That would mean not facin' them, and we already agreed that we can't just wipe them out when they're not lookin'," Vallant pointed out as he stretched. "If we don't actually win over them, everybody will know it and they'll start livin' in terror waitin' for the next group to show up. And if next time there's more than one Blendin', people won't even try to fight."

"So we have to finish it the right way here and now," Rion agreed, getting to his feet. "But at this particular moment, breakfast is in order. I believe I'll try to see if my lessons in cooking have done any good."

There was a bit of stirring as Rion walked to the door leading to the house's pantry, but Jovvi noticed that no one spoke in spite of almost unanimous nervousness. They all knew that Rion had been taking cooking lessons, but none of them had ever tasted any of his efforts. Then Tamma left her sleeping pad and came over to crouch close.

"Lorand, you'd better let the rest of us eat first," Tamma murmured only loud enough for Jovvi and Lorand to hear. "If we end up poisoned, we'll need *you* to heal us. Talk about frustrated anticipation and distress. It took all of us to make the enemy feel like that, but Rion's managed to do it to us on his own."

"It looks like our individuals are more talented than the enemy's individuals," Jovvi murmured back as Lorand fought to hide his amusement. "I could feel the enemy entity trying to use Spirit magic to calm itself, but it hadn't gotten very far by the time we left."

"I'm surprised that they even *have* Spirit magic," Tamma said with a chuckle. "Spirit magic is supposed to be the talent that supplies a conscience, but that's one attribute they seem to lack."

"But they *have* to have Spirit magic," Lorand said with a wave of his hand. "Without a Spirit magic user, how would they Blend?"

"Well, how did the fourfold Blendings in our own empire Blend before they *had* Spirit magic users?" Tamma countered, and then she suddenly froze. "Wait a minute. Does that question sound as important to anyone else as it does to me?"

"Well, it's certainly interesting," Lorand granted after exchanging a glance with Jovvi. "But as far as important goes, I'm afraid I don't—"

"What's going on over here?" Naran suddenly interrupted to ask, Vallant right behind her. "A lot of layers of probability just disappeared, most of them concerning our failure. We're a large step closer to winning the way we have to, so what have you been talking about?"

"Tamma asked a question that she feels is important in some way," Jovvi explained while Lorand and Tamma stared at Naran. "Lorand and I can't see the importance, but maybe the rest of you can. Tamma, why don't you tell us all what you consider so important?"

"It's more a feeling than a certainty," Tamma began, her expression disturbed and partially distracted. "We were talking about Spirit magic and the way the invaders don't seem to have a conscience, and it occurred to me to wonder how the fourfold Blendings Blended without a Spirit magic user. With us, it's the Spirit magic user who always initiates the Blending."

"We do it that way for the simple reason that that's what we were taught," Rion said from behind Vallant and Naran, obviously having come over to see what the discussion was about. "Considering the fact that we were taught by people who didn't themselves know what they were doing, is it any wonder that the question was never covered?"

"I'm suddenly feelin' that it's a question we *need* to have answered," Vallant put in, his words slow and his tone thoughtful. "The invaders do have a Spirit magic member in their Blendin', but feelin' what their victims feel hasn't slowed down their maraudin'. We don't always act sweet and proper either, but as ruthless as our entity seems to *us* at times, it does have a point beyond which it won't go."

"And that's probably due to Jovvi's influence," Tamma said, nodding in agreement with Vallant's comment. "But if the Spirit magic member has so much influence, why wasn't that last noble Blending mellowed a bit? They destroyed everyone in their way almost without a second thought."

"That could be because their Spirit magic member was under the control of someone ruthless," Jovvi said, also putting forward her thoughts slowly. "That poor man didn't feel much about what he did because his grandmother wasn't letting him feel anything she considered unnecessary. So where does that leave us?"

"It leaves us on the trail back to my original question," Tamma said. "If the original fourfold Blendings didn't have Spirit magic to balance them and initiate the Blending, how did they Blend? And why would the nobles make us all believe that only a Spirit magic user *can* initiate a Blending? It doesn't make any sense."

"It does if you think about the aims the nobility considered most important," Rion said as he glanced around. He stood with his arms full of provisions and a pan, but he seemed to have forgotten his original intention. "The most important aim the nobility had was to stay in control, of everything and everyone including the Seated Blending. If they stressed the requirement that a Blending can only be initiated by a Spirit magic member, that requirement must have given them more control than any other arrangement."

"And there *has* to be other arrangements, or the fourfold Blendin' couldn't have Blended," Vallant said in agreement, an undertone of excitement now to be heard in his voice. "All we have to do is figure out what those other arrangements can be."

"I think I've just gotten a very strong hint about what at least one arrangement is," Tamma said, also glancing around. "Do all of you remember how you helped me accept the fact that Fire magic is considered the most important talent in a Blending? We were told that that was because Fire magic is both the guardian and strength of the Blending, but what if that's not the only reason? What if you get another kind of entity if the Blending is initiated by the Fire magic talent?"

"An entity that the nobles would *not* want their pet Seated Blending to know about!" Lorand exclaimed, clearly getting the same idea that Jovvi had just gotten. "An entity formed by an aggressive talent would probably *be* more aggressive, and that's the last thing the nobility would have wanted."

"So an entity initiated by a Spirit magic user would of necessity be less aggressive," Jovvi added, just to get the matter straight in her own mind. "We've all noticed that Naran, Lorand, and I are the mild ones in our group, so that could very well carry over when we Blend. And it could be the reason why we haven't found it possible to fight back against the enemy. We have the wrong talent coloring our Blending."

"The probabilities have just changed again," Naran said with a wide smile. "It still isn't absolutely certain that we'll win, but our chances just got a lot better."

"Let's try the new arrangement first thing after we eat," Rion said, apparently just remembering what he'd been about. "I'm simply going to throw some eggs and cheese and ham into a pan, so it won't take long before it's ready."

And with that he turned and headed for the hearth, obviously noticing nothing of the heavy silence and fearful stares that he left behind him. A moment earlier the entire group had been animated, but now Jovvi noticed how still they'd all grown.

"I think I made a bad mistake in not joining him in learning to cook," Tamma murmured to the group at large. "If I had, at least I'd be able to defend myself to a certain extent. Naran, can you check the probabilities to see how likely we are to die from eating what he gives us?"

"I'm sure he isn't that bad at cooking, really I am," Naran answered earnestly while Vallant choked and Lorand tried not to. "He's been watching and learning almost since we first began this trip, so I'm sure we'll all be fine."

"Which means you haven't yet tasted any of his cooking either," Tamma came back with a sigh. "But you can forget about checking the probabilities for our survival. That won't tell us if we'll need Lorand's help to continue living. Isn't there something we can talk about until it's time to face our destiny? I feel a very strong need to be distracted."

"I can oblige you there," Vallant said, swallowing his amusement. "If we're goin' to try Blendin' through *you,* we can't do it without lettin' the others watch what happens. If the enemy entity faces us and we win, we'll want everyone to know how we did it. If they have nothin' but our word that we won fairly, there will always be doubt about whether or not we told the truth."

"And then we'd have to come back if the enemy sends another Blending or two to replace this first one," Tamma said sourly with a nod. "I don't think I'd enjoy having to drop everything to run back here, so let's do it right the first time.

And I just had another idea. Let's make Rion take the first taste of what he produces. Knowing how finicky he is about food, if it doesn't kill *him* then it ought to be safe for the rest of us."

That produced general chuckling along with unanimous agreement, although Jovvi couldn't seem to get into the spirit of the thing, so to speak. She felt very down, but she wasn't left to the peace of brooding. Tamma's hand was suddenly on her arm, and when she looked up she saw Tamma wearing an odd expression.

"I'm not used to being the one to do this, but I guess I'll have to *get* used to it at least for this time," Tamma said ruefully. "Jovvi, I can tell that you're feeling dreadfully upset, and probably because you think you've been holding us back in some way. How am I doing using *your* ability?"

"You're doing a bit *too* well," Jovvi answered, feeling more than a little discomfited. "And I don't just think I've been holding us back, I know it for a fact. We've had a lot of trouble at various times that we might not have had, if I hadn't decided that I was the only one who could initiate the Blending."

"And that's supposed to be *your* fault?" Tamma countered, now sounding more angry than rueful. "We were taught only a single way to Blend, so what makes it your fault that we followed that way?"

"I knew better than most that Spirit magic was the last talent added to the Blending," Jovvi said, refusing to be comforted by an excuse. "I had that fact pointed out to me more than once while I was growing up, but I never even stopped to think about it. I also knew that nothing the nobles said or did could be trusted, but not once did I think to question the very important place they gave me."

"Neither did the rest of us, so what makes you so much better than we are?" Lorand put in, also sounding angry. "I love you very much, Jovvi, but you're blaming only yourself for something that all of us are guilty of. Don't you think we're *good* enough to be guilty right along *with* you?"

"Now doesn't that beat all," Tamma said before Jovvi

could tell Lorand that he didn't understand. "She believes she's the only one of us who can think, so all our failures are *her* fault. Does anyone else feel as insulted as I do?"

"Yes, me," Vallant said at once, joining Tamma in staring directly at Jovvi. "What about you, Naran?"

"Yes, definitely, I feel very insulted," Naran agreed as she also joined in the staring. "How do you see it, Lorand?"

"The same way you others do," Lorand said, but his stare wasn't quite as baleful. "Rion, have you been able to hear what's going on?"

"Yes, I have, and I certainly agree," Rion answered from the hearth. "Now the question is, what do we do about it?"

"That's easy," Tamma said, closing the circle she'd opened. "I say that Jovvi ought to be demoted from her previous place to one where she just calms and balances the rest of us. That is, if she can stop pitying herself long enough to do the job."

The last of Tamma's words were very pointed, and for a moment Jovvi felt a bit of outrage over the suggestion that she was too deeply into self-pity to conduct herself properly. Then Jovvi's practical side forced her to see the truth, and she smiled ruefully.

"Going from the most popular courtesan in my city to the central link in a Blending wasn't very difficult," Jovvi admitted with a shrug. "My ego didn't have to take any kind of a beating, so my sense of importance was untouched. Now, though . . . All right, missing the fact that I didn't have to initiate the Blending *wasn't* just my fault, but insisting it was gave me back the missing importance. I apologize to all of you, and I'll try to keep my ego under control from now on."

"See that you do, child," Tamma said in a deep and portentous voice, and then she grinned. "My goodness, but that felt *marvelous!* I never thought I'd get to chide Jovvi over being juvenile, so I didn't know how much I'd enjoy it. You can act childish again any time you like, Jovvi. I enjoy being more mature than you for a change."

"More mature, right," Vallant murmured with a teasing look of pain twisting his face, and the chuckling everyone had been doing turned to outright laughter. Tamma tried to be incensed over Vallant's comment, but she couldn't keep an accusing and angry expression on her face. After only a moment she was forced to join in the laughter, and Jovvi realized how incredibly lucky *she* was to be part of these people. She *had* been acting like an idiot, but instead of becoming seriously insulted they'd worked together to pull her out of the mood. She made a silent vow never to let them down again, even if she had to give up having an ego entirely . . .

"All right, our breakfast is ready," Rion called from the hearth. "Vallant, if you'll add moisture to this bread from yesterday before Tamrissa warms it a bit, the meal should prove adequate."

"I'll be glad to warm the bread, Rion," Tamma called back without turning, to keep him from seeing the pretended panic on her face. "But since you did the work in preparing the meal, we insist that you be the first one to taste it. It's only fair for you to eat first."

By then they'd all gotten to their feet and approached the hearth, which let them see Rion's immediate amusement.

"Meaning that if I fall dead from eating the food, that will save the rest of you," Rion said, and Jovvi could tell that his amusement was real. " 'Clarion' might have believed that your only interest was in fairness, Tamrissa, but I haven't been that innocent in quite some time. I'm able to understand your reservations, however, so I'll be glad to taste my efforts first."

Tamma tried to look shamefaced as Rion separated his omelet into six bowls, but she didn't make a very good job of it. It was now possible to smell the omelet, and the aroma seemed to be incredibly enticing. Jovvi thought about offering to join Rion in the test, but she looked up to see that her brother had already taken one of the bowls and a wooden spoon.

"Hmmm, yes, the consistency is right, but the seasoning is only just adequate," Rion pronounced after chewing and swallowing a bite. "My only excuse is that this house offered very little in the way of seasoning, so I was forced to make do. Would one of you others care to give *your* opinion?"

That invitation caused all the rest of them to reach for a bowl, and when Jovvi took the first taste she thought she was back in civilized surroundings and in a dining parlor. The omelet *was* cooked just right, and it had the kind of delicate flavor she hadn't tasted in a very long time. Jovvi closed her eyes in delight, hearing the same delight murmur through the rest of the group.

"Rion, you have my most sincere apologies," Tamma said after a long moment. "This could well be the best omelet I've ever tasted, so please feel free to cook for us at any time. Even if we do happen to fall over and die, at least we'll die happy."

Jovvi almost choked when she began to laugh, and she wasn't the only one. Leave it to Tamma to negate even the most sincere apology.

They all settled down to eat then, with Vallant and Tamma quickly seeing to the bread. Adding moisture and then warming the bread did make it seem fresh, and Rion hadn't forgotten to put up water for tea. Naran finished eating first and went to prepare the tea, and once Jovvi and the others finished eating they got cups and helped themselves. Jovvi felt very satisfied when she sat again with her cup of tea, and once Vallant was settled he looked around at them.

"I've been thinkin' while I ate, and I don't believe we ought to try Blendin' through Tamrissa just yet," he said. "We ought to tell the others what we're doin' first, and then have one of the other Blendin's keep an eye on the enemy. We'll have to give the enemy's Blendin' members a chance to rest before we challenge them, so we'll have lots of opportunity to practice before that time."

"It really annoys me that we have to be so fair about this," Tamma said, the annoyance she'd mentioned clear in her expression. "I understand why we have to be fair and I agree with the necessity, but I still don't like it. If the new way of Blending works the way we hope it will, there might not be much left of that enemy Blending."

"You won't find *me* weeping over the loss," Rion said from where he lounged with his own cup of tea. "I believe I've mentioned before how I feel about those who take delight in stealing the minds and lives of others."

"If possible, we ought to save at least one member of that Blendin'," Vallant said, obviously feeling nothing of the faint distress Jovvi did at the thought of destroying the enemy completely. "The slaves know little or nothin', but a Blendin' member ought to be able to answer most of our questions."

"You know, it should be possible to keep them all alive if we're able to destroy their talent," Lorand pointed out as he looked around. "They would no longer be a threat then, and each one of them may know something the others don't."

"And what do you expect we'd do with them after they answered our questions?" Tamma put in, but rather gently. "They aren't slaves themselves, or their Blending entity would hardly be as arrogant as it is. They're responsible for the deaths of hundreds if not thousands of people, Lorand, and they're ready and willing to kill even more. Do you really think people like that won't find a way to kill without talent if they're left alive?"

"I was about to suggest that they be locked up somewhere, but I withdraw the suggestion," Naran said with a sigh when Lorand didn't respond. "That option allows for the possibility of escape, and those people really are vicious. If they escape from confinement then innocent people will die, and the deaths will be *our* fault for not having the stomach to do the necessary."

"I'd love to argue for mercy, but I'm afraid I can't," Jovvi said, mostly to a forlorn-looking Lorand. "We have no right to put innocent people's lives in danger simply because we dislike the idea of killing. Happily, though, the matter will be seen to by those of us who have no qualms about doing the necessary. We'll have to take full responsibility for the action along with them, but we *can* avoid what we'd find painful if not impossible."

"And we don't mind," Vallant said as Lorand nodded despite his obvious reluctance, clearly speaking for Tamma and Rion as well. "As long as we know that the rest of you will tell us if we start goin' too far, we don't mind takin' care of the hard part."

Everyone reached out to touch Lorand then, showing him their love and support without words. Lorand clung to them for a moment before he straightened again, strengthened in spite of his continuing upset. Jovvi knew that Lorand would be strong enough to join the rest of them, and also knew that she would be the same. The one thing she didn't know was just how guilty she would feel afterward . . .

# EIGHTEEN

The village had a large, empty building that could have been a meeting hall, so we called our people in there to tell them what we meant to do. The new Gracelian High Blendings had taken the building over instead of using some of the houses, so they were the only ones who didn't have to send a couple of representatives. Everyone else *did* have to choose two attendees, otherwise we would have been five deep in each others' laps.

"Are you people serious?" Deegro Lapas, a member of one of my link groups, said once Vallant explained things. "Do you actually mean to tell us you've been doing things wrong all this time?"

"How can it be wrong if it got us *this* far?" I countered, shaking my head at the idiot. "You should know that we keep finding out all sorts of things about Blending that the nobles never knew—or simply didn't share—and this is just another of those things."

"Only a couple of days ago I would have said I wasn't up to trying your idea," Arinna said, looking delighted. Arinna was the Fire magic member of Pagin Holter's Blending, the Blending that was closest in age and strength to ours. "We were going through that phase of being exhausted all the time, but now we seem to be past it."

"And we're lookin' f'rw'rd t'hearin' each other in th' Blendin'," Holter himself added. "That ain't happened yet."

"But it will, and probably fairly soon," Vallant told him

210

with a smile. "We're thinkin' about chargin' you people for the warnin's we've been givin'. Without us you'd be flounderin' around the way *we're* doin'."

"Whatever you charge will be worth it," Arinna said with a laugh that Holter and most of the rest of the people in the building joined in. "You have no idea how good it feels to know what's coming, and because *you* don't, you have our sincere sympathy."

"We'll remember that the next time we think we're goin' crazy," Vallant told her with a wry grin, and then he grew serious again. "One of our Blendin's is keepin' an eye on the enemy, and their entity just came back to report. It seems our invaders are still gettin' their people out of the hole we dropped them into, but that chore is almost done. We expected them to have to fill in at least part of the hole to get their litters across, but apparently they cheated. The litters are already across the gap, so they must have used Air magic to give the litter bearers somethin' to walk on."

"Which means that after they've gotten the rest of their people out they'll be on their way here again," I said into the mutter of comments coming from our listeners. "You know that we wanted to wait until they were completely rested before we faced them, but that might not be possible now. They'll be resting in their litters as their force continues along the road, and if we wait too long they'll be here before we know it. We don't want to have to fend off murdering slaves determined to reach our bodies while we're Blended, or we won't be able to give a confrontation all our attention. For that reason I propose that we stop them about a mile away from here, and issue our challenge then. That will give the rest of you a chance to retreat if we still can't stop them. Does anyone have an objection to that plan?"

"I object to the idea of running away, but we're not the ones who will be doing the fighting," Arinna said when no one else spoke. "Since you're the ones whose lives will be on the line, I can't see that the decision is anyone's but yours."

Murmurs and mutterings of agreement came from all over the room, and the message was perfectly clear.

"You all seem to feel the way Arinna does," Jovvi observed aloud as she also looked around. "With that in mind I think we ought to end this meeting now, to give us a chance to practice Blending through Tamma."

That decision caused more commenting than protests as everyone turned to a neighbor to discuss what they'd been told. The meeting was over and no one was unhappy about it—with one possible exception . . .

"Stop worryin', you'll do fine," Vallant murmured to me, his arm coming to circle me. "I know you *want* to do it, and that's more than half the battle."

"I'll let you know whether that's true after we do our practicing," I muttered in return, really appreciating his support. "But I think I just had a better idea. Why don't we start with *you* initiating the Blending, and then you'll be able to tell me from personal experience just how easy it is."

Vallant started to give me one of those exasperated looks he'd gotten so good at showing, but Rion joined us before Vallant added words to the expression.

"I couldn't help overhearing your remark, Tamrissa, and although I'm sure you were joking you did give *me* an idea." Rion certainly did look thoughtful, and he smiled when he saw my raised brows. "What I mean by that is, I've just realized we *ought* to be able to Blend with *any* of us initiating the Blending. Once we've seen to the invaders, we really should try it just to see if there are any major differences each time."

"That's a very good idea, Rion," I said, seriously thinking about the suggestion. "If it works, the arrangement will make things easier for us. If one of us happens to see a situation where we need to Blend, we won't have to try to get Jovvi's attention."

"You're both right," Vallant agreed, looking as surprised as I'd felt a moment ago. "I'm rememberin' that time we were on our way back to Gan Garee, and I left that fancy inn the Guild people found for us and walked outside alone. The guardsmen were gettin' ready to attack us, but I couldn't think of a way to alert Jovvi without givin' away my position. If we were all able to initiate the Blendin', we could avoid situations like that."

By then the others had joined us, and they were just as enthusiastic about the idea. It felt mildly odd to be solving problems instead of finding new ones, and then Jovvi made me forget about pleasant things by touching my arm.

"Yes, it *is* time we got started with the practice," Jovvi confirmed my suspicion. "But just relax, Tamma, because initiating isn't hard at all. You'll be reaching out to the rest of us just the way you always do, but this time you'll be doing it first."

"That's not quite the tiny difference you're trying to make it sound like," I pointed out sourly, then took a deep breath and squared my shoulders. "Well, if we're going to try this, let's get to it. If it isn't going to work I want to know it for a fact, not just worry over the possibility."

Everyone seemed to be giving me nods and smiles of encouragement, so I took one last look at the rain outside the windows and then dove right in. I knew those people as well as I knew myself, so I closed my eyes and reached to all of them rather than to Jovvi first. In fact I left Jovvi for last, and suddenly I was the entity rather than just myself.

*This feels rather different,* the Jovvi part of me said after a moment. *I still lack full understanding of the difference, yet the oddity is certainly there.*

*Perhaps the observation is mistaken, but I seem to sense a good deal more strength,* the Rion part of me said. *This is definitely an arrangement that should have been attempted sooner.*

*I feel an approval of sorts,* I contributed as my own comment. *It seems as though something has been done to advance us as a properly integrated entity. I shall now dissolve our unity, so that our flesh forms may discuss the matter. Such a doing is necessary at the moment.*

The others knew that I'd spoken the truth, and then I was apart again and looking around. Everyone seemed pleased, but Vallant looked to be closer to delight.

"Yes, I was definitely feelin' a good deal more strength," Vallant said, mostly to Rion but to the rest of us as well. "If this doesn't make us at the very least equal to the invaders, I'm throwin' my hands up and goin' home."

"And the rest of us will be going with you, because we don't have anything else left to try," I agreed with a shrug. "Did you all notice that when we were Blended? That if we don't win now we never will?"

"I certainly did," Naran said with a sigh. "Our chances at victory have increased tremendously, but it's still up to us to turn the possibility into reality."

"You know, suddenly that doesn't worry me," I said as a revelation of sorts broke through. "We keep fretting over the fact that we aren't being guaranteed victory, but didn't we decide a long time ago that nothing is guaranteed until it actually happens? Even if the probabilities show everything stacked against us in the coming fight, there's still the chance that one of those litter bearers could trip and make the others drop the litter. Falling could break the neck of one of the enemy, and that would be the end of all the probabilities stacked against us. So let's not worry about the fight, only about where we put our feet."

"I think I'll take that excellent advice personally," Lorand said with a laugh while everyone else made sounds of agreement. "I'm probably the least graceful of all of us, so I *need* to take the advice. What are we going to do now?"

"We're going to have some tea and relax for the next hour or so," Jovvi said firmly before anyone else could answer. "Vallant will have one of our associate Blendings keeping an eye on the enemy, so we have nothing to do but gather all the strength we can. When the time comes, we'll then go out and put those invaders in their place. Does anyone think we won't?"

Jovvi looked so fierce when she asked her question that the rest of us simply shook our heads without showing our inner smiles. We *were* going to win, I knew we were . . .

Rion protected us from the rain on our way back to the house we'd slept in, and then he went off to think about what he would make for lunch. The rest of us got tea and sat down on our sleeping pads, but I, personally, found relaxing beyond me. I wanted to get on to the fight and have it behind me, but we couldn't even go out to meet the invaders at the place we'd decided on. Putting our bodies within reach of the enemy's slaves would have been colossally stupid, and we couldn't afford to be stupid . . .

"You know, I've been thinking about those invaders," Lorand said, appearing suddenly beside my sleeping mat. "They remind me quite a lot of your parents, Tamrissa."

"In what way?" Vallant asked, making room for Lorand on his own mat. "I didn't notice the enemy tryin' to fix her up with a husband."

"They've done everything *but* that," Lorand said with a chuckle as he sat and looked up again to see my faint smile. "They're just as arrogant as Tamrissa's parents were, demanding that we all do as they say, and they completely dismissed what *we* want. They also think we'll never find an effective way to argue with and resist them, and the whole point of their lives seems to be to get their own way no matter how many other lives are ruined in the process."

"I hadn't noticed that, but obviously you're right," I said with brows high. "Those people *are* just like my parents, going their merry way without once stopping to think about anyone else. And they need taking down just as badly as my parents did. Now I really can't wait until the fight starts."

I got to my feet and carried my tea over to a window, staring out into the rain as I enjoyed a sense of anticipation. I happen to love rainy days, finding the gentle confinement when indoors a snug and comfortable thing. If I have to go out in the rain the world seems different, as if it's enjoying its cleansing as much as I enjoy the smell of freshness. Yes, rainy days have always been special for me, and this rainy day would turn out to be more special than all the rest.

I lost myself in daydreams of sweet revenge for a while, thinking about the past and making plans for the future, and the sound of Vallant's voice came as a surprise.

"All right, brothers and sisters, the time for action has arrived," he said, his voice full of happy anticipation. "Our associate Blendin' tells me that the enemy is almost to the place we want them to reach, so it's gotten to be *our* turn to move."

"Yes!" I breathed, then headed back to my sleeping pad. "Okay, is everybody ready?"

"Not quite yet," Naran said, surprising me. "We don't know how long this will take, so a quick trip to the facilities is in order."

Everyone seemed to agree with her, and I discovered that that included me. We all took a turn using the facilities, but it still wasn't long before we were back to our sleeping pads.

"Okay, is everybody ready *now*?" I asked as I looked around. All I got in response was amusement, so instead of saying anything else I simply reached out to them. Their answering touches were immediate, and then it was the Tamrissa entity once again.

I knew the point at which I'd wanted the enemy to be met, so I flashed there without having to confer with our current guard entity. The slave flesh forms walking in advance of the enemy's litters were already in sight, so our arrival was just in time.

*The others are arriving behind us,* the Vallant part of me said. *Our associate entity informed them of the impending battle after reporting to us.*

*Good,* the Naran part of me said in approval. *Their presence is required in some way.*

*Our own presence is required to an even greater extent,* the Rion part put in. *Will it be necessary for us to announce our readiness to the enemy?*

*I believe my senses detect the beginning of their Blending,* I replied, pleased that the necessary awareness had now developed. *They should be with us in no more than a moment.*

—*You are too late*—the enemy entity announced an instant after it had formed.—*Clearly you thought to attack before this entity was prepared for you, but such an action*

*would not have been possible. This entity is more than pre-
pared, and so shall it ever be.—*

—*And you are mistaken,*—I told the enemy, annoyed by
its air of smug superiority.—*It was necessary that you be
fully prepared to face us, else we would have taken advantage of your earlier lack of attention. Our aim is to defeat
you where others may see your defeat, an aim which we now
mean to accomplish.—*

—*A pity, then, that it shall be this entity's aim which is accomplished instead,*—the enemy responded. And then that
roiling began inside it that indicated it was in the process of
gathering the power.

*It seems to be necessary that we allow the enemy to
strike first,* my Naran part informed me. *The reason for
such an action eludes me, yet am I not unsure.*

*Perhaps we must allow the attack so that we may be cer-
tain of what level of strength is available to us,* my Jovvi
part surmised. *In past attacks, we were merely able to withstand the enemy. Now we must also be able to reply.*

*We shall be able to reply,* I stated, my annoyance growing. *The enemy means to bend us to its will, and that I shall
not allow.*

My anger flared even as the enemy stuck, which was a
fortunate thing. The strength brought against me was as full
as it had been the previous times, and although I was able to
withstand the attack much more easily, I found I was still
unable to reply. The frustration of that truth added to my
anger as the enemy struck a second time, even more strength
behind the attack. I knew I lacked a certain knowledge, a
certain procedure . . .

And then the obvious finally made itself known. I had
very little experience as the initiator of the Blending, and
therefore still thought as a segment. Previously my place
had been to add my ability to that of the others, but now the
reverse was necessary. I knew I must add the ability of the
others to my own, in a *true* Blending of minds and talents.

As quickly as the thought came, that quickly did I act. My

Blendingmates had been . . . behind me, so to speak, but now I brought them forward in a full and proper union. I felt my flesh form breathe a sound of satisfaction, and then the enemy struck a third time.

—*This entity perceives that you have gained some small amount of strength,*—the enemy informed me smugly as I gave a whisper of distance to allow myself greater freedom of movement.—*You have, however, no hope of standing forever against my superior ability. When one or two of your flesh forms collapse, they and the others will then be mine to do with as I please.*—

And then a fourth attack came, harder than the previous ones and obviously meant to jar me back to my body. This time there was no reason to give ground or allow the attack to touch me in any way, and once it had washed past me harmlessly I couldn't hold back a very nasty smile.

—*Well, I'd say that that's all the chances* you're *going to get today,*—I sent, making sure the enemy was able to perceive my amusement.—*Now it's my turn, and I can guarantee I won't need more than just the one.*—

—*For what reason do you seem so strange?*—the enemy put with an odd quiver behind the question.—*Never has this entity seen such a thing before, and the perception distresses me. You are an unnatural freak, and therefore must be destroyed. Then all those behind you will be this entity's property, and they will be made to—*

The entity's comments broke off when I struck at it, and then it was gone. I was able to tell that most of the members of the enemy Blending were at least reeling if not actually unconscious, so I quickly turned my attention to the slaves surrounding the litters. It took very little effort to neutralize them and freeze them in place, and then I turned to my associate Blendings and our new Gracelian allies.

—*We'll have to move a bit briskly now, my friends,*—I sent.—*We don't want the enemy Blending members disappearing into the landscape before we have the chance to nail them down. Once we have* them *under control, we can free their slaves and decide what to do with them all.*—

Everyone's entity agreed with me, so I quickly dissolved the Blending. My Blendingmates sat staring at me wide-eyed and openmouthed for a moment, and then Vallant broke the stunned silence.

"Tamrissa, what did you *do*?" he asked weakly, still staring at me. "Everythin' was goin' the same as usual, and then suddenly it was just me instead of the entity. What did you *do*?"

"I have no idea," I answered with a small laugh as I got to my feet. "Whatever it was, it seemed like the right thing to do so I did it. Are you all just going to sit here with your jaws down to the ground and hand the enemy a chance to get over the battering we gave it?"

That comment made them snap their mouths shut at least, and a moment later they began to stand. It took another moment before we were all heading to the door of the house, but at least we didn't have to stop to saddle our horses. The horses had been prepared before we went to the confrontation, just in case it turned out badly.

Everyone else was either mounted or getting that way, so we headed toward where we'd left the invaders. The slaves were frozen in place, of course, leaving nothing to keep us from making our way to the five litters. The people standing to either side of each litter looked a bit worse for wear from what we'd done to them, but since they were also frozen in place it didn't matter.

One by one we pulled the Blending members out of their litters, and all but one were unconscious. That one snarled when we opened her litter and tried to use Water magic on us, but Vallant had no trouble smacking her down. She calmed after that and got out of the litter on her own, but her arrogance was definitely tinged with confused fear. She was about my size and faintly pretty with very light eyes and hair, her light skin even more pale than that of the slaves.

"Sit down next to your Blendin'mates," Vallant told her when she simply stood next to the unconscious bodies. "We have a number of questions, and you'll be answerin' them."

"I don't answer questions for slaves," the woman returned

as she looked off into the distance, obviously trying to ignore us. "I don't know why I even bothered to explain."

"You explained because you weren't given any choice in the matter," Jovvi said, her normally gentle voice showing a hard edge. "Your Blending had an advantage because it used techniques we weren't yet familiar with, but you as an individual have no more than average High strength. You won't be *allowed* to refuse to answer—or to disobey."

"How dare you speak to me like that?" the woman demanded even as she sat herself on the ground. Her accent was even more lilting than Borvri Tonsun's. She and the other, unconscious, woman of the Blending wore trousers of a sort like the men, flowing trousers of what looked to be silk in bright colors without decoration.

"You sound like the members of our former nobility, which isn't surprising," Lorand remarked as the woman fumed over the fact that she was sitting. "You've probably been in power long enough to think that you always would be, but now you're about to learn better. Our Spirit magic member has control of you, so you'll answer any and all questions put to you. What's your name?"

"I'm Blessed Hantiro Jogamme," the woman answered, anger flaring even higher in her very light eyes. "That means you have no right to even *think* about doing this to me, not to speak of actually doing it. When my mate-equals return to consciousness, we'll show you—"

"Ah, I see you just remembered," I said with a pleasant smile. "Your Blendingmates *were* awake and with you when we put you all in your proper places, so trying it again could be very bad for your overall health. How long have you and your friends been stealing other people's lives?"

"*We* are the only 'people' involved," Hantiro answered haughtily. "All the rest are nothing but unimportant savages born for no purpose other than to serve us. You and those others are the same sort of savages, and as soon as we discover what trickery you used to temporarily overcome us we'll take control again."

"Why is it always so hard for you people to accept reality?" I asked with a shake of my head. "We didn't use trickery we used ability, and if you could have matched that you already would have. You won't ever be back in control, and it's time you understood that."

"I already understand whatever I need to," the woman spat, looking at me with boundless hatred. "You're the freak who caused our downfall, spreading your freakishness among those others you consider your mate-equals. As soon as they truly realize what you've done to them they'll reject you, and then our superiority will once again come to the fore."

"Why don't you try holding your breath until that happens," Rion drawled to her as I discovered I couldn't quite find what to say. "A blue tinge to that fish-belly-white skin would be a definite improvement."

"Please don't lie to her, Rion," Naran said as I stared in puzzlement at my brother. "*Nothing* will improve her, not when she has no mind. When I think how little intelligence it takes to understand that Tamrissa is and always will be one of us, I wonder how this woman has intellect enough to come in out of the rain."

"But she *doesn't* have intellect enough to come in out of the rain," Vallant pointed out with amusement. "We're standin' under Rion's shield, but she's just sittin' there in the mud with the rain comin' down."

Jovvi and Lorand laughed and nodded agreement with Vallant's comment, as did Rion and Naran. For a moment I'd been afraid that my Blendingmates might have been really disturbed over what had happened in the Blending, but just that easily the question was answered for good and all . . .

# NINETEEN

For a brief moment Vallant worried that Tamrissa might take the captured woman's words as the truth, but then he saw Tamrissa smile. That smile said she understood the message Rion and Naran had begun and he had continued with, which was a great relief. Very odd things had been happening, but they would get around to those things once there was time.

"It's time we did somethin' more permanent with these people," Vallant said then to Jovvi. "We still have a lot of questions to ask them, and we wouldn't want them thinkin' about walkin' away before we get our answers."

"And I believe I'll enjoy questioning them more under better conditions than these," Jovvi responded with a smile. "I'll make sure they don't get the urge to leave our company, and then we can have their people bring them to the village. Once we have them safely tucked away, we can see to releasing all these poor people."

"I suggest that we release all these poor people only a few at a time," Tamrissa interrupted to say. "Remember what we agreed might be their reaction to being set free. If any of them are going to have hysterics, or try to take advantage of us, or even try to free their marvelous 'leaders,' we don't want them all doing it at once."

"Good point," Lorand said in agreement, putting an arm around Jovvi. "We do want these people to be free, love, but not at the possible expense of innocent lives."

222

"If you'll recall, I'm the one who understood that point even before you did," Jovvi said to Lorand with an impish smile that softened the words. "But let's get back to the village before we do anything else. Rion may be keeping the rain off us, but I still feel damp all over."

"So do I," Tamrissa agreed with a small grimace. "I'm tempted to remove the moisture from our clothes with a judicious amount of heat, but after everything we've gone through I have the feeling I may overdo it. Unless any of you would actually *prefer* to be left standing naked, I suggest we wait until we get back to the house and then let Vallant get rid of the moisture."

Vallant chuckled while the others hastily assured Tamrissa that they were more than willing to wait. The patient attitude was one he shared, but there was no need to be *too* patient.

"Jovvi, since we're goin' to be givin' orders to these people, why don't *you* initiate the Blendin'?" Vallant said. "I can tell that one of our associate Blendin's is here to back us up, but I think this needs to be done by us."

"I definitely agree," Tamrissa said, stepping closer to take Vallant's hand as she smiled at Jovvi. "I'm the one who does the beating-over-the-head. You're the one who uses more gentle methods."

"My methods may be more gentle, but in the long run they're much more destructive and not as honest," Jovvi said, her wry expression showing awareness with very little in the way of regret. "I may dislike controlling people, but at least I can tell when it's really necessary. All right, here we go."

Vallant suddenly became the Vallant entity, an entity that was well aware of what had to be done. It was the work of only a minute or two to place all the flesh forms of the enemy under firm control, and then the slave flesh forms were given precise instructions. Once that chore was completed, it was Vallant back again.

"I don't understand," Rion blurted before Vallant could say something of the same himself. "The last time we Blended, I became myself with no trace of the entity left.

Now, though, the entity was back as if it had never been gone. What *is* going on?"

"I have no idea," Jovvi answered, looking as perplexed as Vallant felt. "I was also expecting the entity to be gone, but obviously we were both wrong. And once we get back to the village, I think we'd better talk to our people even before we continue questioning the invaders. My entity self had no trouble noticing how . . . confused our people are."

"I don't blame them in the least," Lorand muttered, running a hand through his hair. "I just hope that telling them *what* happened instead of *why* it happened will help their confusion. Unfortunately, it isn't doing a thing to help mine."

Vallant muttered a definite agreement, and then they all got out of the way to let the slaves put their masters back in the litters. The woman Hantiro cooperated fully without speaking a word, but that was hardly surprising. They had put her and her Blendingmates under very tight control, and the five would not even be aware of their surroundings until they were told they could be.

Since Lorand had checked over the unconscious invaders when they were first taken out of their litters, there was nothing to keep Vallant and the others from heading directly back to the village. They passed the word that they would go directly to the meeting hall, and a few minutes after they got there they were joined by the same people who had attended the earlier meeting. Vallant used part of the waiting time to pull the moisture out of all their clothing, so it was a drier and happier six people who finally faced their associates.

"Most of you are controlling your distress, but some of you aren't," Jovvi said once their audience was more or less settled down on the hall's benches. "I'm filtering out the noise, but the Spirit magic users of our Gracelian allies are a bit new to the situation. I'm sure they would appreciate it if you helped to keep them from getting headaches."

"I think the best way for us to do that would be for *you* to tell us what happened during the confrontation," Arinna, Pagin Holter's Fire magic Blendingmate, put in at once. "Except for the . . . overall flavor of your Blending, everything seemed to be going just the way it usually did. Then something happened, and just before you dissolved the Blending we no longer recognized you. Our Blending entity took the whole thing in stride as nothing to get excited about, but we can't quite manage to do the same."

"You should have tried it from where *I* sat," Tamrissa said, taking over from Jovvi. "The enemy struck at us three times without our being able to respond, and then it suddenly came to me that I hadn't pulled my Blendingmates into a true merging. I was . . . standing in front of them, so to speak, instead of actually Blending, so I took care of the matter. That's when our entity . . . kind of . . . disappeared."

Exclamations came from all over the room, most of them composed of people echoing the word "disappeared." Vallant could feel how agitated they all were, so he rose from the bench Jovvi had returned to and stood beside Tamrissa.

"I can see we'll have to start chargin' *all* of you for this information," he said as he looked around. "If you don't think that these changes aren't harder on us than on people only watchin', then you deserve to be forced to pay through the nose."

"Yes, okay, he's right," Arinna said in a loud voice, standing and holding up both arms. "They *are* going through this first, so when it happens to us we won't have to wonder if we're losing our minds. But our Blending gets to go through it next, so you'd better get the staring and nervousness out of your systems now. If you look at *us* the way you're looking at them, I just might bash you all over the head to show how much I dislike your attitude."

A few people chuckled over the blatant threat, and a handful of heartbeats later people were beginning to settle down. That startled Vallant, who hadn't realized that a threat sometimes calmed people more quickly than gentle explanations.

"Yes, that's what you have to look forward to," Tamrissa said pleasantly to Arinna. "And once you reach that point, maybe you'll be able to tell *us* why our entity returned the last time we Blended. I seemed to have the impression that it was gone for good, but when we Blended to give orders to the invaders we found it back again."

"I don't even want to think about that," someone said from the audience. "My Blendingmates and I are thinking of going off somewhere quiet and peaceful until all you pioneer types have answers to the questions you keep coming up with. Then we can decide if *we* want to go through the same thing, only with advanced knowledge of what's in store."

"That sounds fine to me," Vallant drawled as even more people chuckled. "While you're gone, we'll have a chance to decide on what price to charge you for the information."

That comment caused outright laughter, and a glance at Jovvi confirmed Vallant's impression that just about everyone had gotten over their distress. That meant their most important chore was done, and it was time to get on to the second most important.

"Those litters ought to be here in a little while," Vallant said as soon as the laughter died down. "We're goin' back to our house for a few minutes to make a large pot of tea, and then we'll be bringin' the tea back with us. If any of you want to do the same, do it now so you don't miss any of the questionin'."

Everyone sounded as if they liked that idea, and a moment later people were standing and heading out of the hall. That meant Vallant and his Blendingmates had to wait their turn to reach the door, but waiting didn't bother them. Their associates and link group members were no longer looking at them as if they were strangers, and that was the important part.

Rion took the time to fry—sauté, he called it—a quick meal for them, which they ate with a great deal of pleasure before carrying their tea back to the meeting hall. The bearers were only just bringing up the litters, so their stopping for a meal hadn't delayed anything. It was time to question their prisoners, and once the questioning was over it would be time to start releasing the others from slavery.

*We'll be best off letting the others help with freeing the slaves,* Vallant thought as he watched his associates and the link group members filing into the meeting hall. *And the Gracelian people look bothered about something. We'll have to find out what the something is, and then we'll have to make plans about when we get to go home. Going home . . . Now* there's *a pleasant thought . . .*

Rion felt very pleased with himself, but tried not to let it show when the prisoners were brought in. The invaders were hardly likely to appreciate—or understand—why cooking a fairly good meal was of any importance to him. He now knew he had value even beyond being a part of the ruling Blending of his country, and his value would increase as his cooking talent did. For someone who had been told that he would have no value at all in life, Rion appreciated being able to prove differently.

But questioning the invaders would go more easily if they had scowling people in front of them rather than happily smiling ones. The five invaders being marched in would be at least as arrogant as Hantiro Jogamme had already proven to be, and needed to be taken down a peg or two right from the beginning.

"Jovvi, I suggest that we make our prisoners kneel at the foot of the dais," Rion murmured to his sister. "We don't want them to get the idea that they're in charge."

"They already have that idea, but I agree with you," Jovvi murmured back as the prisoners were brought forward. "They need to have their defeat waved in their faces, otherwise they'll hold back on everything they can."

Rion nodded his understanding. The invaders *were* strong High talents, and unless they were completely enslaved they would resist being controlled to a certain degree. Complete enslavement would make them answer all questions fully, but only the questions put to them with no additional comments. And it was the unguarded comments that would give him and his Blendingmates the most information . . .

"That's fine," Jovvi said as the prisoners were lined up in front of them. "Now you five may kneel."

The five former leaders did as they were told, and then Jovvi released a certain amount of control. The five all made sounds of outrage at the same time, and then seemed to be struggling.

"You won't be allowed to stand, so you might as well stop trying," Jovvi told them calmly while the audience of their associates quieted. "And we also won't bother asking your names. Only people who matter have names."

"We more than matter, because we're of the Blessed Ones," the man in the middle grated, the words slipping in and out of a growl. "Whatever trick you used to defeat us won't work the next time we face you."

"Your defeat wasn't a trick, so stop lying to yourselves," Tamrissa put in, her voice even harder than the man's. "You lost because we're better than you, and there won't *be* a next time that we face you. How did you fools get started with ruining people's lives?"

"We were born to rule in our own lands, and then were chosen to extend those lands," the man answered, pride and anger fighting in his tone. "The lives of lesser beings are unimportant when compared to our desires, as it is we who will civilize the rest of this barbarian-ruled world."

"I'll bet you were taught to say that when you were very young," Tamrissa commented with a sound of ridicule, the very thing Rion had also been thinking. "How many more of your kind were sent here to take over?"

"One group of mate-equals has always been enough to make any barbarian land ours," the man answered, arrogance back in his voice. "If your tricks are able to keep us prisoner, however, more than one group of mate-equals will follow after us. Tricks will *not* be successful with *them*."

"How long will it take those others to come after you?" Vallant put in, his tone making the question casual. "They should be givin' you enough time to kill or take over everyone in your path, I'd guess, so any followin' shouldn't be happenin' for a while."

"It was expected that this land would be ours within the half year," the man replied, this time sounding reluctant. "If we haven't announced our complete victory by then, the others will come after us."

"Which will give the High Blendings in this country more than enough time to practice and grow as strong as necessary," Jovvi said, looking out into the audience where the Gracelian Blendings sat. "And by then we ought to have things settled down enough in our own country to lend some High Blendings as support. How does that sound to *you* people?"

"It sounds like pure relief," Rangis Hoad, a member of one of the Gracelian Blendings said with a shaky smile. "We were worrying about how we would face one of these invader Blendings on our own, but we *have* been growing stronger every day. By the time any more of them show up . . . We *should* be strong enough to handle it, don't you think?"

"Yes, we do think so, as long as you're not stupid about the matter," Rion said, feeling it was time to underscore a particular point. "If you behave as your predecessors did and limit the number of Blendings in this country, you could well have a problem when the next wave of invaders appears. If, however, you continue to encourage the formation of as many Blendings of all strength levels as possible, you should have no difficulty coping."

"Why do you consider Blendings of other strength levels necessary?" Alesta Vargan, another Blending member, asked. "Won't it only be High Blendings who defend our country?"

"Countries require more than just defense if they're to prosper and grow," Lorand said, giving the woman an encouraging smile. "If you have nothing but High Blendings to look after things, chores will pile up and important matters will accidentally be left undone. Besides, don't you think that others are entitled to experience what *you* have? Even if they aren't able to do very much with their Blending?"

"He's right, but not just for those reasons," Hoad said to the woman wryly. "I don't know about you, but I spent a lot of time resenting the fact that there were only fifteen Blendings I might be able to force my way into—if one of the major talents didn't decide to cheat in some way. If we get to run this country, even for a little while, we'd be foolish to start out with the same kind of resentments piled up against *us*."

Most of the others around the two who had spoken nodded their agreement with what Hoad had said, Rion was pleased to see. If the Gracelians didn't suddenly come down with the "privileged noble" disease, they might make really good allies after all.

"It might eventually be worth our while to look into where these people are comin' from," Vallant said once it was clear the discussion with the Gracelians was over. "If and when a second wave of them gets here, we can see if we're in a position to take their ships back to where they started to make sure there's never a third wave. But we have time before that decision has to be made."

Most of their audience seemed to take Vallant's suggestion with interest, which brought the five invaders a good deal of agitation. Rion watched them begin to struggle again only harder, and then they all went completely still.

"I think they finally accepted the fact that they weren't bested by trickery," Tamrissa observed as she looked at the five people who were now completely controlled again. "The idea seemed to send them into a frenzy, as if their entire world was collapsing around them. I certainly hope they're right."

Rion chuckled his agreement along with everyone else who had heard Tamrissa's words, and then it was time to get to other things. There were a lot of slaves standing around waiting to be freed, and what happened after that would probably be the hard part.

The five leaders of the invasion were put into a small and dirty shed that had probably been used for storage of some kind, and then Rion and his Blendingmates joined everyone else in gathering up the slave forces. The slaves from the road had been ordered to continue on to the village and then await further orders, but it was Rion and his

Blendingmates who had to fetch the first group. They were still hidden in the nearby countryside, and had to be ordered back.

"And since you were the one who ordered them out there, Vallant, you ought to be the one who initiates the Blending this time," Tamrissa said with a wide smile. "But don't worry, I'm confident that you won't have any trouble."

"We're definitely goin' to have to do somethin' about that cruel streak of yours, Tamrissa," Vallant told her with a frown that Rion suspected wasn't entirely playacting, and then he sighed. "All right, I suppose it *is* my turn to try. And since you ladies did it first, I only have to follow *your* examples."

Rion joined Lorand in murmuring something encouraging while the ladies merely smiled. Rion had the feeling he would be just as uneasy when *his* turn came to initiate the Blending, and Lorand seemed to feel the same. Naran, however, looked far too calm and confident, which most likely meant she'd Seen something she hadn't mentioned.

In spite of Vallant's faint unease, however, the Blending formed with no trouble whatsoever. The Rion entity found himself fully prepared to do what was necessary, a mild and distant amusement present for some reason. The Rion entity reflected on the amusement for an instant, and then floated into the woods to see to his chore. The amusement was, for the most part, anticipatory, as well as an enjoyment of very satisfactory progress.

The slave flesh forms hidden in the woods were easily located and ordered to the village, and then the Rion entity took itself directly back. Rather than dissolving, however, there was an . . . adjustment within himself, the sort of adjustment the Rion entity had experienced only once before. There was the sense of increased satisfaction, and then his Vallant part spoke.

*Yes, that's much more like it,* the Rion entity heard. *This is the way it should have been all along.*

*And you did it exactly right,* Rion's Tamrissa part said. *Just as I knew you would. Aren't you glad you tried?*

*Yes, I certainly am glad, but now it's time we gave the others a hand,* the Vallant part answered. *If we make them do all the work, we could have a revolt on our hands.*

And then the Blending dissolved, leaving Rion alone again and fairly puzzled.

"Did any of you understand why that happened?" Jovvi asked, sounding as confused as Rion felt. "I experienced a change of some kind when Vallant adjusted our places in the Blending, and then it seemed that he and Tamrissa were no longer *part* of the Blending—even though they were. How did it feel to *you,* Vallant?"

"It felt as if the entity disappeared, and all that was left was me," Vallant said with raised brows as he looked at Tamrissa. "But you were right there *with* me, and I knew who you were and that you were there. It wasn't like hearin' everyone in the Blendin', it was somethin' else entirely."

"I think we need to find out just where all this is leading," Jovvi mused, then she glanced at what their associates were doing. "The first group of slaves has been freed, and there isn't anywhere near as much trouble as we were expecting. Let's tell someone that we're going to take an experimentation break, and then see what happens."

Since it was obvious that none of them disagreed, Vallant went over to tell their associates what they would be doing, and then Rion and his Blendingmates returned to the house they'd been using. The rain had stopped, leaving the day merely overcast, but an excitement of sorts crackled back and forth among all of them.

"All right, who wants to be next?" Jovvi asked once they were all settled on their sleeping pads. "It can't be me, because I have the definite feeling that I have to go last."

"Because of all the time you've *already* spent initiating the Blending," Rion said, distantly wondering how he knew that. "With that truth in mind, I volunteer to be next."

Lorand made no effort to put his own offer forward and Naran merely smiled again, so the matter was decided. Rion found the need to deliberately relax his body as he reached out to his Blendingmates, and then it was the Rion entity who looked about.

*Are you able to tell how far away the balance of us are?* the Rion entity's Tamrissa part asked. *Once you perceive the distance, you must draw us all closer.*

The Rion entity did indeed look about himself, and quickly saw that what had been said was true. His parts certainly were far too distant from him, therefore he drew them closer—and once again the world shifted.

*Nice going, Rion,* Tamrissa said, and Rion knew that she smiled at him. *And don't you two look handsome now.*

*You're not exactly an eyesore yourself,* Vallant came back, and Rion somehow saw his grin. In fact he somehow *saw* both of them, as themselves with no entity involved.

*Where has the entity gone?* Rion asked, now even more puzzled. *I can tell that what we've done is proper, but where did the entity go?*

*Maybe we'll find out after the rest of us have had a turn,* Tamrissa suggested. *Why don't you dissolve the Blending now so Lorand can join us?*

That was the logical course of action, so Rion did indeed dissolve the Blending. How odd that had been, to first be the entity and then—

"I don't know if I'm ready to try this," Lorand said after taking a deep breath. "I had a lot of trouble forcing myself to keep up with the rest of you, and I'm just afraid I might not be ready to take the next step."

"If you're not ready, then it won't work," Tamrissa said before Rion could think of something supportive to put in. "If it doesn't work, then we'll be no worse off than we are right now. What can we lose by trying?"

"Nothing, I guess," Lorand answered, clearly responding to Tamrissa's lack of accusation before he shrugged. "And since we have nothing to lose, I might as well give it a try."

Rion could see that Lorand wasn't quite as unconcerned as he'd tried to sound, but a moment later it was the Rion entity who looked about. There was a short delay as the Lorand part adjusted his perceptions and viewpoint, and then a jarring twist changed the picture entirely. It was now Rion, Vallant, Tamrissa, and Lorand who regarded one another, and then Lorand laughed an instant before the Blending dissolved.

"I had no idea that that would be so simple and—and—*easy*," Lorand blurted. "I wanted to say something to the rest of you, but then I decided to wait until Naran and Jovvi were with us. This is much too good to keep to ourselves."

"Yes, it certainly is," Tamrissa agreed with a gentle laugh while Rion joined Vallant in smiling. "And now it's Naran's turn, so let's get on with it."

"I was prepared to worry, but then I Saw that I would succeed," Naran said with the same calm smile she'd been showing all along. "With that in mind . . ."

Rion saw Naran close her eyes, and then there was a repetition of the experience with Lorand. The Rion entity formed, there was a jarring lurch, and then Rion *saw* the others with Naran included this time. They all smiled at one another, and then the Blending was gone.

"I'd still like to know why we start out as the entity and then the entity disappears," Rion said to Jovvi. "Do you have any idea why that is?"

"Maybe I'll understand once it happens to *me*," Jovvi replied ruefully. "I've done what I'm about to do a hundred times, but the entity has always been there."

"I think that's because you never brought the rest of us forward," Tamrissa mused, obviously considering the matter. "When I first initiated the Blending I did what *you* always did, but that put me out in front instead of meshed in with the rest of you. Once you do the bringing forward, it ought to work out the way it's supposed to."

"Then let's try it," Jovvi said with raised brows, clearly as encouraged as Lorand had been. For the third time the Rion entity formed, but there was a longer delay than previous. Then the Rion entity perceived a sound of pleased discovery, there was the familiar jarring lurch, and then—

"What happened?" Jovvi asked as she looked around at

all of them. "We were Blended, I brought you all forward, and then we *weren't* Blended. What went wrong?"

"You expect *us* to know?" Tamrissa said with a sound of ridicule. "When it comes to knowing what's going on, we're lucky we know what time of day it is. Why don't you initiate the Blending again, and maybe we'll get a clue."

"I might as well," Jovvi muttered, and Rion sat prepared to be swept up into the Blending. But a long moment passed with nothing happening, which couldn't possibly be a good sign.

"What's wrong, love?" Lorand asked a Jovvi who seemed to have gone pale. "Why aren't you initiating the Blending?"

"I'm trying, love, I'm really trying," Jovvi answered, tears clear behind the words. "For some reason I can't seem to do it, so I'd like one of you others to Blend us. I may be able to do it again after that."

They all agreed, of course, and Tamrissa was the first to try. When she failed then Vallant took his turn, but he wasn't any more successful. Rion made the effort when it became *his* turn, but there was nothing to be gained.

"It seems as though there's a—a—blank wall there instead of the Blending state," Rion said after the wasted effort, his insides twisting and churning. "Why is this happening?"

No one seemed able to answer his question, and no one seemed able to initiate the Blending. Each of them tried more than once, but finally they were forced to admit the truth.

Gandistra's Seated Blending was no longer *able* to Blend!

# TWENTY

Driffin Codsent stood in the room where Wilant Gorl, Oplis Henden, and the rest of their Blending, sat unmoving. Just staring at them wasn't doing the least bit of good, but Driff had felt the need to do it anyway.

"I almost asked if you were sure there weren't any clues here," Edmin's voice came from the doorway behind Driff. "But I do know what a foolish question that would be, so I won't make things worse for you by asking it."

"I don't see how *anything* could make things worse," Driff answered, turning away from the unliving Highs with a sigh. "It's as if something froze them in place all at the same time, and is now preserving them perfectly. Even after all this time, I can't sense anything actually *wrong* with them."

"Much like the same nothing our entity found," Edmin said, staring past Driff with a frown. "Nothing seems to be wrong with them, but if we can't find what's affecting them we can't bring them back to life. What about those books they're all staring at? Maybe if we looked at those books—"

"No!" Driff said sharply, and then he shook his head in apology. "I didn't mean to bite your head off, Edmin, but the servants tell me that everything was fine with the Highs until they started to read through those books. I can't imagine what could be in them that would do this not only to the ones reading but every other High in the city as well, but checking ourselves isn't a good idea. If this did happen because of

236

something in those books, we could end up in the same state the Highs are in."

"I don't think I'd enjoy that," Edmin said ruefully, rubbing the back of his neck with one hand. "Hopefully I'd have no idea it was happening, but on some level I *know* I would not enjoy it. So what are we going to do next?"

"We'll just have to get on with things, and hope that the Seated Blending gets back sooner rather than later," Driff said as he began to move toward the door. "I'm hoping that whatever is affecting these people is too subtle for my own talent strength, but not for theirs."

"But . . . what if the same thing happens to *them*?" Edmin asked, a question that stopped Driff just as he stepped out into the hall. "Since we don't know what's causing the condition, isn't it possible—"

"I don't believe I never thought of that," Driff said in horror, accidentally interrupting Edmin again. "But you're absolutely right, so we'll have to do something to keep the unaffected Highs out of the city until they can look around from a distance. It's a good thing you're here to do my thinking for me, Edmin. Obviously I need *someone* to do it."

"You're just being overwhelmed by the responsibility of being in charge, Driff," Edmin answered with a smile as he stopped to Driff's left. "And you're frustrated over not being able to help those people. The point would have come through to you as soon as someone reported the approach of the Seated Blending."

"I'm not sure you're right, but I still appreciate having you say it," Driff answered with a shake of his head and a clap to Edmin's shoulder. "But we do have to get on with things, and our next chore is to interview all those prisoners we took. Are you ready to get started?"

"I will be as soon as I take care of a chore of my own," Edmin answered, his own sigh rather deep. "As long as we weren't here in the palace, I could tell myself that seeing my father wasn't practical. Now that we *are* here, the excuse doesn't work any longer."

"Are you sure you have to do it alone?" Driff asked, somehow aware of the pain and disturbance filling his Blending-mate. "I know my presence won't do more than give you moral support, but if you'd like at least that much . . ."

"You have no idea how tempted I am to accept that offer," Edmin said with a grimace. "And I *would* accept it, except for the virtual certainty that my father would have a mar-velous time making you feel absolutely worthless. If you were there, it would just give my father and me something else to argue about, Driff."

"Since you already have enough things to argue about, I withdraw the offer," Driff said with a faint smile and a head-shake. "We'll be in that big meeting room once you've fin-ished with your visit."

"As long as the visit doesn't finish *me,* I'll be there," Ed-min said with the sort of faint smile he hadn't shown in quite some time. "Since those prisoners are still under control, you won't even have to wait for me to question them. I'll . . . see you later."

Driff nodded and then watched Edmin walk away, wish-ing all the while that there were *some* way he could help his Blendingmate. But facing his father was something Edmin had to do alone, and Driff didn't envy him. It would proba-bly be easier to face his own father, an effort Driff had no in-tention of ever making.

But Edmin had no choice, and as Driff turned toward the large meeting room he wasn't sure he even wanted to know how things went . . .

Edmin Ruhl, once a lord and the son of a High Lord, paused for a moment outside the room he'd been told his fa-ther was in. The old man had healed to the point where he was able to leave his bed for a short time every day, and had also begun to make himself unpopular with the serving staff. If the staff had had to obey the old man's demands, half of them probably would have quit by now . . .

But all those extraneous thoughts were just a way to put off what was necessary, so Edmin squared his shoulders, opened the door, and walked inside. Embisson Ruhl sat in a chair reading a book, and spoke without bothering to look up.

"I thought I made it clear that I wasn't to be disturbed," Edmin's father stated in the inflexible tone Edmin knew so well. "Get your carcass out of my sight, and do it this instant."

"But my carcass isn't *in* your sight," Edmin couldn't help answering. "You used to be a good deal more precise than that, Father."

Embisson's head came up fast to show a look of shock on his face, but the shock faded almost immediately.

"For the love of—! Edmin, get that door closed at once! If they find you here, the cell they put you in will be a good deal worse than *this* miserable room. I don't know how you found me, but you couldn't have arrived at a better time."

"Oh?" Edmin said as he closed the door behind him. "And why is my arrival at *this* time such a good thing?"

"It's a good thing because I was about to try escaping on my own," Embisson replied in a soft voice, gesturing Edmin closer. "We'll keep our voices down to make sure no one overhears us, but there are things I must know. How do you mean to get me out of here, and what point are the Nolls at? Are they likely to make their coup good before you and I can put our own plans in motion?"

"The Nolls are no longer a threat to anyone but themselves," Edmin answered, stopping in front of his father's chair. "They were allowed to do their best, and then they were all arrested."

"So they failed!" Embisson said with great amusement and deep satisfaction. "It serves them right, and now they'll be sent to join those other failures who dared to call themselves noble. But what did you mean when you said they were 'allowed' to do their best? Who allowed that, and how did you find out about it?"

"The various Blendings running this city knew all about the 'renegades,' " Edmin said, more than aware that he avoided the main issues but finding it impossible to do otherwise. "They could have arrested the Nolls at any time, but chose instead to let them make fools of themselves first as an object lesson to anyone else with the same idea. The days of a nobility running things in this empire are over."

"How can you speak such nonsense with a straight face, Edmin?" Embisson demanded, his tone trying to hide the dismay Edmin knew he felt on the inside. "The Nolls were nothing before the troubles, so their proving themselves failures means the same nothing. You and I are a different story, and I'll take a great deal of pleasure in proving that. Now tell me: How did you get in here, and how do you plan to get me out?"

"Obviously it's time we got down to it," Edmin muttered, feeling as well as seeing his father's intense stare. "I got in here without any trouble, because I'm now a member of a rather important Middle Blending."

"Edmin, that's absolute genius!" Embisson breathed, a wide grin quickly appearing on his face. "You've brought me a Blending to work with, and now our success is guaranteed. But how did you find enough of our people to make up a Blending? Were they all actually hiding here in the city?"

"Father, stop and think for a minute," Edmin said earnestly, hating the way things were going. "There aren't *any* of our people left in the city, and even if there were they would have no idea how to survive without servants to do things for them. Two members of my Blending do happen to have been born into our class, but they earned places for themselves in Astinda before they came back here. They're no more interested in seeing the nobility rise again than I am."

"You can't mean that," Embisson said, shocked horror echoing so strongly that Edmin probably could have felt it even without his talent. "Edmin, we're *nobles*, and it's the place of nobles to be in charge of the important things in life. If those important things are left for the peasants to see to, this country will fall to absolute ruin."

"This country was *about* to fall into absolute ruin when control was taken away from you and your friends, Father," Edmin stated, seeing no way out of the need to speak the truth. "Even if things had gone the way they usually did and your pet Blending was Seated, what do you imagine they would have been able to do against the ten Blendings from Astinda looking for vengeance? Ten *High* Blendings, not the useless Middles you and the others had control of. Do you really think you and the others would have been able to *buy* the Astindans off?"

"We would have handled the matter, just as we always handled things," Embisson muttered, now staring at the floor rather than at Edmin. "Gold speaks more loudly than talent, Edmin, and those Astindans would have taken our gold just as peasants always have."

"I won't let you conveniently overlook the fact that the Astindans could have taken your gold after you and everyone else was dead," Edmin said, feeling as though he batted his head against a brick wall. "Neither Gan Garee nor anyone in it would have survived the arrival of the Astindans, and all the excuses and blind stubbornness in the world won't change that fact. You have no business being in charge of anything, Father, not when you can't even admit the most obvious of truths. But you'd better accept *this* truth: You'll never be in charge of anything again."

"Are you really that afraid of me that you've come to warn me away from trying?" Embisson said, raising his gaze to Edmin's face as his arrogance reasserted itself. "You haven't the stomach for fighting the peasants yourself, so you're trying to make sure *I* don't do anything to embarrass you. Well, your efforts have been as successful as my own efforts to make you a real man. I *will* escape from this prison room, and I *will* find a way to take control again. And when I do—"

"Oh, spare me," Edmin interrupted, now more impatient than bothered. "When you make yourself a High Lord again, you'll do this and that and the other thing to make me sorry I 'betrayed' you. All right, Father, I can see it's time I called your bluff. Go ahead and show me all these wonderful things that a *real* man can do."

"You should know that I never bluff, Edmin," Embisson said with an oily smile. "I only promise, so when I find a way out of here—"

"But that part's already taken care of," Edmin interrupted again. "I'll tell the guards and servants to let you leave any time you care to, so getting out of here is already accomplished. Now tell me what you'll do after that."

"Why, I'll return to my house and gather my forces," Embisson said after a very brief hesitation, his emotions suddenly wavering. "I'm not fool enough to share the plans I've made with a newly adopted *peasant,* so you'll just have to wait to find out what they are."

"Point one," Edmin said, making sure his expression remained stony. "You no longer have a house to return to, as all property belonging to the former nobility has been confiscated. And even if you did have a house, how would you get to it? A public carriage driver has to be paid, and you don't even have copper, not to mention gold. The lack of gold should also take care of those 'forces' you mentioned, although how you would find anyone to follow you is another good question as well as being point two. The Nolls brought in more than three hundred men, but lost almost half of them as soon as the men had a chance to look around at what the new government is doing. Noll also tried to recruit the discontented, and ended up with less than a handful of incompetents. You expect to do better?"

Embisson sat frowning at the floor, but nothing in the way of cogent argument was forthcoming.

"Point three is the fact that you aren't able to take care of yourself," Edmin continued inexorably. "Even if you had a house and gold, I doubt if there's a servant in the city who would work for you. You have no gold, you have no place to live, and you have no skill to earn a decent income. No one in this city wants to bring the nobility back, so there isn't even anyone who will follow you. Do all those plans you've made take any of *that* into consideration?"

Embisson still had no answer, which didn't surprise Edmin in the least. He had no trouble telling that his father's mind now whirled with confusion and dismay, and words were completely beyond the old man.

"If you really are as superior as you claim, you'll eventually find it possible to come to terms with the truth," Edmin said after taking a deep breath. "If and when that time comes, have one of the servants send me word. But don't send for me because you've come up with yet another marvelous plan to take over control of the empire. I've learned that there are more important things in this life than being in charge, and if you're able to accept reality I'll tell you about them. Otherwise I won't waste my breath. I'm glad you weren't killed, Father, I really am."

With that, Edmin turned away from a still-unmoving Embisson and left the room. The time had been just as painful as he'd expected it to be, and although he wanted to believe otherwise he knew he'd be getting no messages from his father. Embisson Ruhl was still trying to find a way to deny the truth, and he probably always would. And chances were he'd never leave that room again . . .

Edmin was in a dark, depressed mood when he reached the large meeting room where the rest of his Blending were. One of the prisoners stood in front of the five people who were doing the interviewing, and Driff glanced up from where he sat when Edmin walked in.

"All right, we've heard enough," Driff said to the man in front of them. "You can now go to the room designated as room A."

The prisoner turned and headed for the door without a word or gesture to show he meant to acknowledge the order, but Edmin knew that the man would do nothing else. He was being *allowed* to do nothing else, conditioned almost in the same way that Edmin's father's upbringing had conditioned *him* . . .

"Edmin, come and join us," Idresia called from her place beside Driff. "We've only gotten through two interviews so far, and we're trying to decide if we ought to do the interviews individually instead of as a group. If we don't separate, we'll still be here doing the same thing next year."

"But is it right for just one person to decide the fate of these men?" Kail objected as Edmin moved to an empty chair beside Asri and sat. "What if the one interviewing takes a dislike to the man at first sight? Won't that dislike color whatever decision is made?"

"Why can't we compromise?" Edmin asked, overriding the comments made by the others that supported one or another of the points of view. "We can split up into three groups of two, and that way we'll work three times faster but there will be two people making the decisions instead of one."

"Do you all understand now why I said I would wait until I heard Edmin's opinion before I voiced one of my own?" Driff asked the group at large, his face creased into a smile. "Now I can say I support Edmin's suggestion, and I'd like to know if anyone can think of a really good objection to doing things his way."

"Really, Driff, even *I* support his idea, and I'm for turning thumbs down on *all* the prisoners," Issini said with a laugh. "But we ought to add that any prisoner our small group can't agree on will be interviewed by everyone together once the rest are taken care of."

"I agree with Issini," Kail said, echoing Asri's similar agreement. "Having us break up into groups of two will be much better than working individually."

"And having three groups working will get the job done faster," Idresia also concurred, apparently paying no attention to Driff as he rose and walked to the door. "I think we ought to get into the groups as soon as we can, possibly even right now."

"There's one more interview that needs to be done first," Driff disagreed as he came back from speaking to the guards in the hall. "And this is one we *all* need to be in on."

"I know who Driff means, and he's right," Asri said in support before Edmin could ask any questions. "This will be someone we all need to decide about."

Idresia, Issini, and Kail all started to ask who Driff and Asri were talking about, but Edmin thought he already knew. The answer had come almost as soon as the question had formed in his mind, and when the door opened to admit the next prisoner Edmin smiled to himself.

"Jost Feriun," Idresia said flatly as the former guard commander came to stand in front of them. "Yes, we do need to interview this one together."

"And I have the first question all ready," Issini said in a voice flatter and harsher than the one Idresia had used. "Tell us, Feriun, was gold the only reason you allied yourself with the renegade Noll?"

"Certainly not, although the gold played a large part in my decision," Feriun answered at once. The man hadn't been put under control at first, Edmin knew, but that had been taken care of after all the Nolls were in custody. "I decided to support the nobles so that I could finally have the place in life I deserved."

"And what place is that?" Kail asked, leaning forward just a bit where he sat.

"Why, as the man in charge of the empire, of course," Feriun answered without changing expression. "The noble was under the thumb of his wife, and *she* was too worried about how many servants she had to pay attention to the important things. Once they paid the men to put them into power, then I would have been able to make my own move. Hired men obey their commander without question, and my first order would have been to get rid of all six of the Nolls. Then I would have taught the peasants that they now had a real ruler to contend with."

"A real ruler," Edmin echoed, finding the phrase too close to one his father had used for casual acceptance. "And what do you consider a real ruler?"

"Someone who doesn't coddle the lower orders," Feriun answered with a distant undertone of derision. "That's the mistake the old nobles made, coddling the peasants who outnumbered them. My first command would have been to execute every hundredth man in the city, no matter who that was. Then the peasants would have been told that if they made any trouble, the next time it would be every fiftieth man who was executed. A third incident of trouble would have changed that to every tenth man, and after that the women and children would have been included. I really don't think it would have gotten that far."

"And if it *had* gotten that far?" Idresia asked while Issini hissed an unintelligible comment. "Would you really have murdered innocent women and children in cold blood?"

"Don't be ridiculous, of course I would have," Feriun said with a harsh laugh. "Why would I care *what* happened to peasants, especially when I would have already chosen the women I personally wanted? By then I would have brought in a lot of other men to be part of my guard force, so who could have stopped me?"

"Every man and woman in the city would have tried, you utter fool," Issini growled at the man, looking downright murderous herself. "You're obviously too stupid to realize that when people know they have nothing to lose, they often decide to go out with purpose rather than just standing around waiting for the end. At that point you would have had an empty city in the aftermath of a total bloodbath, and giving orders to the dead about running an empire doesn't accomplish much. Is there anyone who still thinks that this . . . animal deserves to continue living?"

"We still have a final question to ask before we make any decisions," Driff said, echoing Edmin's thoughts. "Tell us, Feriun: Is there anything that could make you give up these plans of yours? Is there anything that can make you understand how wrong you are?"

"But I'm not wrong," Feriun answered with a short laugh. "I was born to rule, and giving up my plans would be to turn my back on my destiny. What sense would there be in *that*?"

"He believes what he just said down to the very center of his being," Edmin told Driff with a grimace. "He *needs* to believe in his destiny the way other men and women need to breathe, and giving up the belief would be to give up all meaning and purpose to his life. He's completely insane, Driff, and as long as he lives he'll never stop trying to get what he thinks is his proper place."

"And I can't find anything physical causing the insanity," Driff said with a sigh. "Some people have an odd imbalance in their body's makeup, and once the imbalance is corrected they're sane again. But this man doesn't have the same thing, so I doubt if he'll ever be sane."

"And if he ever gets free to try again, a lot of innocent people will die," Asri put in. "He'll be stopped again, of course, but those innocent people will still be dead."

"In that case, I don't see that we have any choice," Kail said after taking a deep breath. "I won't be responsible for the death of innocents, so I stand with Issini in this matter."

"And I," Asri and Idresia said at the same time. Under other circumstances the two women might have smiled or laughed over having spoken together, but right now Edmin knew there was no laughter in any of them.

"Putting him down would actually be more of a kindness than a punishment," Edmin said when it was clear that Driff wasn't yet ready to speak. "As long as he remains alive, the man will suffer over not having 'attained his destiny.' The lack will eventually turn him even more insane, especially if he's somewhere he knows he'll never escape from."

"Thank you," Driff said quietly to Edmin, a faint smile of gratitude showing on the man's face. "You knew that I'm the one who has to put him down, so you tried to make the execution easier for me. I appreciate the attempt, and it does make a difference."

"But you *don't* have to be the one to put him down, Driff," Issini protested. "If the idea bothers you all that much, I can always do it. I really don't mind."

"I know you don't, Issini, and I appreciate the offer," Driff said with the same kind of smile. "I've appointed myself as executioner, though, and for one very important reason. If someone has to be killed, I think it would be better for all of us if the one doing the killing is reluctant. Otherwise we might get to the point of enjoying the job . . ."

Issini needed only a brief moment of thought before she nodded her agreement, a faint disturbance inside her clear to Edmin. He knew that Issini might be quick to decide that someone needed to die, but unless she were defending herself against attack she would later wonder if her decision had been right. Driff really was far wiser than the rest of them, Edmin thought . . .

"All right, no sense waiting any longer," Driff said, and then he looked at Feriun. The former guard commander sank slowly down to the floor as if he were falling asleep, and once he lay stretched out his breathing suddenly went ragged. Feriun gasped once, twice, and began to gasp a third time, but that was the end of it. All breath flowed out of the man in a single exhalation, making it perfectly clear that he was gone.

"And now I think we need to take a short break," Idresia said after a moment, her words brisk. "We had a perfectly good reason for not leaving Feriun for the Highs to judge, but it might be a good idea to put that reason into writing. Just in case they have any questions once Driff finds the way to bring them back."

Edmin joined the others in agreeing, which let them all rise and leave the room. Driff would need their support after seeing to his first execution, but Edmin paused outside the room to tell the guards to get rid of the body before he followed his Blendingmates. And it might be a good idea to find another room for Driff to use during the rest of the interviews . . .

Edmin had been hoping for something to distract him from the talk he'd had with his father, but *this* wasn't quite what he'd had in mind . . .

# TWENTY-ONE

Honrita walked into the shabby house to find that everyone had arrived before her, and that included Ayl. She was in a strangely clearheaded and oddly serene mood after all the thinking she'd done, so Ayl's scowl truly had no effect on her.

"You're late, Dama Grohl," Ayl said at once from the chair he sat in, the usual stiffness of his carriage suggesting he sat on a throne instead. "Should this happen again, your dereliction will be dealt with harshly."

This first room of the house was a sitting room of sorts, and someone had brought chairs and a table or two to partially fill it. The day before Honrita had used the kitchen to take control of Arbon Vand, but Ayl was apparently too good now to use a kitchen.

The rest of Honrita's proposed Blending also sat in chairs, Vand, Stelk Faron, and Seeli Tandor all holding themselves somewhat stiffly. Only Kadri Sumlow was fairly relaxed, probably because Honrita had taken full control of the Earth magic user as soon as she'd walked in.

"I hear no apology from you, Dama Grohl," Ayl said after a moment, his narrow, ascetic face showing nothing of the faint annoyance his tone—and mind—held. "Do you truly wish to test my patience?"

"Good morning, my friends," Honrita said to her future Blendingmates, giving each of them a smile. "I meant to be here earlier, but I was detained. Is everyone ready for our first try at Blending?"

Stelk Faron's nervousness increased, Seeli Tandor became faintly confused, and Arbon Vand looked sour. Since Kadri Sumlow was under Honrita's control she showed no reaction at all, but the same could not be said for Holdis Ayl.

"How dare you," Ayl growled as he got to his feet to glare at Honrita. "You will *not* ignore me as though I were of no importance whatsoever. First you will be punished, and then you will apologize properly. After that—"

"But you *are* of no importance whatsoever," Honrita interrupted to say, finally looking directly at Ayl. "It took me quite some time to understand that, but the truth finally made its appearance last night. You're exactly like my father: A useless incompetent with no talent other than frightening the helpless. You bully your way through life, forcing others to give you what you want, and then you decide to force your way into real power. But simple bullying isn't enough to gain real power, so you end up frustrated and insane—and a failure. That's all you'll ever be, Ayl, nothing but a poor, useless, failure."

"How dare you speak to me like that?" Ayl demanded, his eyes wide with frothing insanity. "I'm the one who found you and these others, and I'm the one who brought you together! You *will* obey me, else I shall—"

"Don't you know any other phrase than 'How dare you'?" Honrita interrupted again, pleased that her calm underscored Ayl's ranting. "I know it's inconvenient for you to remember things the way they actually happened, but *I* was the one who found *you*. You were going to use that pitiful specimen of a Spirit magic talent, but when I appeared you changed your mind. And you may have located the rest of these people, but I'm the one who brought them together. We'll be sure to throw you some silver for your effort once the city is ours."

Ayl sputtered and snarled, but nothing in the way of intelligible words came out of his mouth. Faron and Seeli now looked frightened, and Vand frowned at the goings-on. Then Ayl raised his hands and started toward Honrita, his intention to strangle someone clear in the bend of his fingers and the raging insanity in his eyes. Honrita had expected something like that, and her reaction was to say, "Kadri."

Speaking the Earth magic user's name was all it took. Kadri was completely under Honrita's control, and protecting Honrita was the woman's sole concern. Ayl took no more than two steps toward his intended victim before he staggered and gasped and went to his hands and knees. If his face had been pale before, now it was downright white.

"Thank you, Kadri," Honrita said with a smile before returning her attention to Ayl. "The reason so many people fear you, Dom Ayl, is because you're prepared to do violence and they're *not* prepared to defend themselves. I, however, am more than prepared. My Spirit magic may not be able to affect you, but other talents can—especially when you're not braced against them. Would you like me to have Dom Vand join the demonstration with his Fire magic?"

Ayl raised his head to look at Honrita, and the hatred in his madness-filled eyes was so intense that it widened Honrita's smile.

"You know, cutting *you* down to size is almost as good as it would have been to do the same thing to my father," Honrita told him. "I had a . . . discussion of sorts once with a High in Spirit magic and a very good healer. They made me understand that I didn't have to be afraid of everyone I met, because the only thing that let others bully me was my own fear. My taking control of the fear also took away the power others had over me, they said, but I didn't understand that completely until last night. Now that I do understand it, I'm free to forget about what others think and concentrate only on what *I* want. Kadri, you may release him now."

Kadri had clearly gotten a grip on Ayl's heart, and when she released him he closed his eyes for a moment. Honrita waited that moment to let Ayl's color start to come back, and then she cleared her throat.

"At one time I would have let Kadri kill you," Honrita said when Ayl reluctantly raised his head again. "I would have been too afraid to let you live, and because of that you would have escaped the punishment of having your nose rubbed in reality. You've done a lot of terrible things to a lot of people, Dom Ayl, and it's time you paid for some of it. Living with the knowledge that you'll never be anything but 'that crazy old man' ought to even things up a bit for your victims. Now get out of here."

Ayl silently pushed himself to his feet, staggered to the door, and left. The madness in his eyes was even more intense now, and Honrita had no illusions.

"Kadri, keep track of him with me and let's see if he really does leave," Honrita said. Ayl liked to get even with people, Honrita knew, and it quickly became clear that the madman wasn't even letting a near heart attack change his habits. Ayl made his way to the end of the shabby neighborhood's block and then he stepped around the corner, but that was as far as he went.

"He's waiting until we Blend, and then he means to come back and do something to us," Honrita murmured, as certain of that conclusion as she'd ever been of anything. "Kadri, I think Dom Ayl needs to be visited with an urgent call of nature. We'll be leaving here, and I don't want him able to follow."

Kadri's face still showed no emotions, but Honrita was able to tell that her suggestion had been acted on. Ayl was suddenly filled with desperation, and despite his clear desire to ignore the need he was quickly forced to give up his post. Honrita let her talent follow the man as he hurried away, and then she turned to the others.

"Come with me quickly, now," she said, taking control of Stelk Faron and Seeli Tandor as well. "I've found a much better place for us, and one that Dom Ayl isn't likely to locate very soon. Once we're safe, we'll be able to Blend."

Arbon Vand had no choice but to join the others in standing and following Honrita out. It was a small bit of a strain for Honrita to keep three people under full control and a fourth under partial control, but things worth having weren't meant to come easy. Honrita understood that now, and she was prepared to do whatever was necessary to make her dreams come true.

A hired carriage from the other side of the city waited two blocks away, and with Arbon Vand sitting next to the driver the carriage was able to carry them all. Once they were settled the driver got them on their way, responding to the buried orders Honrita had already given him. Once he left them at their destination, he would forget he'd ever seen them.

Their destination was the place Honrita had found to live, a fairly nice house that a fat and wealthy merchant of the city had given up when he bought one of the houses that the nobility used to own. The man who was supposed to be looking for a buyer for the house no longer remembered anything about the place, so Honrita knew they weren't likely to be disturbed here.

"See, I even had it furnished," Honrita said once she had her people inside, even though only Arbon Vand was truly able to understand her. "I think we'll be very comfortable here until the time comes for us to move to the palace."

"We haven't even managed to Blend yet," Vand pointed out sourly as she directed the others to the sitting room. "Unless and until that happens, talking about the palace makes you as crazy as that madman you tossed out."

"If I expected getting this group to Blend to be easy, I *would* be as crazy as Ayl," Honrita countered, clearly surprising Vand. "I'm going to have to talk to and work with our future Blendingmates first, and then we ought to be ready. And when we do Blend it will mostly be due to you, so please accept my thanks and appreciation."

"What are you talking about?" Vand demanded as he followed the rest of them into the sitting room. "I want no part of all this, so how can you say that *I* did anything to make it happen?"

Honrita simply smiled at him, not about to explain what she meant. She'd done a *lot* of thinking the day before, and after finally admitting to herself that she did want to bond with her male Blendingmates she'd had to admit something else. She did look like a skinny old maid, Seeli did look like a mindless and skinny old maid, and Kadri was a fat old

maid. Not one of them was truly attractive, and on top of that
Stelk Faron was so filled with doubts and uncertainty that
he'd probably be unable to perform.

So Honrita had decided to change her future Blendingmates a bit on the inside, and then would change them out-
wardly in each other's eyes. Stelk would be free of his
doubts, and Arbon would not find resisting really beautiful
women as easy as he expected. The fact that only he and
Stelk would see the women as beautiful was quite enough
for Honrita's purposes. Real beauty was on the inside, after
all . . .

Honrita smiled to herself as she headed for the kitchen to
make fresh tea. The next few days should prove to be *very*
interesting . . .

When Kail and the others reached the living quarters in
the warehouse, he wasn't the only one who collapsed into a
chair. They'd spent hours interviewing prisoners and still
weren't finished.

"Remind me to find those renegades before the Astindans
take them out of the city," Issini said in a voice that was
filled with as much weariness as Kail felt. "As soon as I get
enough sleep to let me stand straight, I want to beat the
Nolls over the head with a heavy length of wood."

"Why go looking for the Nolls when we have Edmin right
here?" Idresia countered in the same kind of voice. "He's the
one who hired all those men to begin with, and I've been
thinking about beating up on him for hours."

"If I thought I could stand up, I'd join you," Driff said to
Idresia as he sent Edmin something of a glare. "He deserves
everything we can think of to do to him."

"You seem to forget, brothers and sisters, that I'm already
being punished," Edmin returned, looking even more tired
than the rest of them. "My Spirit magic is letting me take on
more interviews than *you're* handling, so I'm even more
beaten down than you are. And don't worry about jumping
on me. If I survive the rest of these interviews, I plan to kick
myself up and down the length of the city."

"That sounds like a good idea," Kail granted with a nod. "Just make sure you let us know when you plan to do it so we can watch."

"But watching isn't what we need right this minute," Idresia said as the others chuckled. "What we need is a good meal, but I, for one, have no interest in cooking. If the rest of you feel the same, let's see if we can talk Driff into treating us to another meal in a dining parlor."

"Now there's another good idea," Kail said amid the eager agreement of everyone including Driff. "Just the thought of good food has given me the strength to get up and walk again, so let's decide where to go. How about—"

Before Kail could suggest the dining parlor that was quickly becoming his favorite, there was a knock at the door. Everyone looked as surprised as Kail felt, but Idresia still called out permission to enter.

"Idresia, I need to talk to you," a rather big man said from the doorway. He'd opened the door, but hadn't come in. "It's important."

"Well, don't just stand there, Jobry, come in and sit down," Idresia said with a smile. "We're getting ready to go out to eat, but we can spare a few minutes to listen."

"I'd like to think I'm not about to spoil your appetites, but I probably am," the big man said as he approached the large table and took an empty chair. Kail had thought at first that the man wasn't very bright, but that decision had been because of the man's looks. Once he began to speak, however, it quickly became clear that there was more to the man than his appearance.

"I don't like the sound of that," Idresia said, losing her previous amusement. "In case the rest of you don't know it, I haven't had my people stop looking and listening just because the Nolls are no longer a problem. I was hoping there would be nothing for them to look at and listen to, but the precaution seems to have turned out to be necessary. What have you found out, Jobry?"

"I was in the Tiger Tavern, pretending to drink," the big man replied at once. "A man came in alone and began to drink heavily, and before long he also began to talk to himself. A lot of what he said was slurred or mumbled, but he repeated himself enough that I probably didn't miss much if anything. He was drinking that heavily as a celebration of sorts, because 'the madman' had apparently found a different victim and now the drinker believed he was no longer on the spot. I say 'believed,' but I think it was more a matter of hoping desperately."

"Do you have any idea what madman he meant?" Idresia asked, her frown much like the one Kail could feel on himself. "And, for that matter, what spot he'd been on?"

"I couldn't very well let the matter go, so I pretended to be just as drunk as the mumbler," Jobry answered with a sigh. "I also used my Earth magic to keep the man just drunk enough to talk freely without passing out. It took some time to get the details, but the man has Spirit magic and he'd been running errands for Holdis Ayl."

"Not Ayl again!" Driff exclaimed, dismay clear in his expression. "They should have found and arrested him weeks ago."

"Well, they didn't, because Ayl is still trying to make trouble," Jobry said with a headshake. "He told the drinker that *he* would be the basis for a very special Middle Blending, one that Ayl meant to hand pick. The whole thing was supposed to be a secret, but Ayl still told the man that the special Blending would take over a High Blending one member at a time. Once all the members were under control, they would have the High Blending take over the government. Then the Middle Blending would run things, with the High Blending being nothing more than figureheads and guards for the real powers behind the throne."

"And Ayl would be the power behind the Middle Blending," Idresia said with disgust. "That plan is about a thousand times better than the one the Nolls came up with, and Ayl's six people would be worth that same thousand more than the three hundred guardsmen. We're just lucky that Ayl is so disturbed that he couldn't keep from boasting about the plan to the first person he picked out."

"Make that five people rather than six," Asri said with her own grimace. "I have the definite feeling that no Sight magic user would get involved with crazy people if they had the choice, and Sight magic gives you the choice."

"Not to mention the fact that Ayl probably can't spot someone with Sight magic," Issini put in. "He may be a renegade Guild member, but the Guild is only just learning to recognize Sight magic. Unless I'm mistaken, Ayl left the Guild some time before they began to learn that recognition."

"Jobry, did you get any idea of who Ayl got to replace the man you questioned?" Driff asked. "If we know that, it will save us a lot of work."

"The man knew nothing beyond the fact that his replacement was a woman," Jobry said with another headshake. "She also has Spirit magic, of course, and she *wanted* to work with Ayl instead of just being frightened into going along with a madman."

"That doesn't sound good at all," Edmin said, showing his own concern. "A Spirit magic user who isn't terribly enthusiastic about what he's doing can't possibly be as effective as one who wants to be involved. And the Spirit magic user is most likely the key to that proposed Blending, or else a different talent would have been chosen first."

"Because the first choice *would* be the key," Driff said, clearly agreeing with Edmin. "And since the first choice was Spirit magic, is it possible that the other choices weren't likely to be very enthusiastic either?"

"It's very possible, and that means the other choices might not go along voluntarily," Idresia pounced. "Or maybe I should say the others might not *have* gone along willingly. If the rest of the Blending members have been chosen, they might be missing from wherever they belong. A smart man or woman would have had the chosen ones come up with a good story before they left, but maybe Ayl and his girl friend are too arrogant to have done that. If we're very lucky, there will be reports of missing people to give us an idea of who the Blending members will be."

"Let's get the people who are running the classes involved

in this as well," Driff said after nodding his agreement with Idresia's idea. "They should have reports on everyone who's taken a class, and we might even get an idea of who that female Spirit magic user is. She has to be unstable to be willing to work with someone like Ayl, and the Spirit magic people kept very close track of everyone they trained. The talent allows for too many abuses if the person using the talent isn't completely well balanced."

"But there's one very large bright spot," Issini said after nodding her agreement along with everyone else. "If you can't quite see the brightness, think about what the major aim of that Middle Blending will be."

The man Jobry looked puzzled, but Kail found that he knew exactly what Issini meant. The madman's Blending would try to take over the members of a High Blending, but at the moment there weren't any Highs *available* to be taken over. All the High talents were frozen in place by something mysterious, and Kail could see that his Blendingmates understood that as well. Jobry alone seemed to know nothing about the problem, and Idresia smiled at him.

"Don't worry, Jobry, Issini is talking about something you don't yet know about," Idresia said. "It's also something we want to keep quiet, so please don't go digging around to find out. I know *you* can be trusted to keep what you learn to yourself, but your digging could very well give the information to someone who can't keep from telling 'just one or two people, people who know how to keep a secret.' "

"I know exactly the ones you're talking about, so I'll keep my curiosity to myself," Jobry agreed with a grin. "As long as you know that I *could* find out, and you do, I don't have to do any digging to prove the point. Would you like me to get people started looking for the information you need?"

"Yes, do, and recruit as much help as you need," Idresia answered, showing both amusement and approval before both emotions disappeared. "We need to get to the bottom of this as fast as possible, otherwise this entire city could blow up in our faces."

"Yes, I noticed that myself," Jobry said as he got to his

feet. "I'll make sure you're kept up to date, and if we learn anything I'll get it to you immediately."

After seeing Idresia's nod, Jobry smiled at the rest of the people at the table and then he left. Once the door had closed behind him there was a short silence followed by Driff's sigh.

"We still need to get that meal, and then we need to get some sleep," he said. "Now that we have something else to worry about, we can't spend all our energy on the interviews—or expect to be able to think clearly after a long day of work. And remind me to ask Jobry what he did about his informant. I certainly hope he didn't leave the man to walk around without someone watching him. If for some reason Ayl contacts him again . . ."

Driff didn't bother finishing the sentence as they all stood up and headed for the door. If the madman contacted the drinker again, it might be possible to solve the problem quickly and easily. Otherwise Kail had the feeling that they would be in for something of a struggle . . .

Holdis Ayl walked directly to the shabby little house and threw open the door, only to confirm what his rage already knew. The five traitors who had been in the house were gone, and it was extremely unlikely that they would be back. If that scheming little bitch hadn't meant to escape unnoticed, she would never have had the Earth magic bitch violate their master . . .

"And I *was* violated, because that whore hid behind surprise," Ayl snarled, picking up a small table and hurling it against a wall. The table broke into pieces, but the destruction only fed Ayl's rage. That miserable female had made him believe she had no idea that her Spirit magic didn't work on him, and then she'd come sneaking up behind him with Earth magic! Ayl, just like other Guild members, could slide the various talents past himself even as he assessed them. But he had to flex the part of his own talent that did the sliding, otherwise he was affected just like anyone else.

"And she had the Earth magic bitch touch me *twice* when

I wasn't looking!" Ayl screamed, pulling out a knife to slash at the chair he'd been sitting in. "I would have corrected my mistake if they'd stayed here to Blend, but she didn't *let* me correct my mistake! She took *all* of them, and now I don't know where they are!"

Ayl broke everything he'd had moved into that house, and then he slashed everything that was too large to break. His fury seemed unquenchable until exhaustion finally overrode everything else, and then he sat on the floor to breathe in gasps.

"I won't let her win," Ayl muttered as he fought for the air he needed so badly. "I *can't* let her win! My plan is perfect so it will work, but she can never be allowed to enjoy her victory. If I let her live then the rest of my followers will lose respect for me, and everyone *must* respect their master. I will be the master of everyone in this empire, so respect is of paramount importance. That means the whore must die, and so she shall. One way or another, she *will* die! I swear it!"

And with that vow Ayl got to his feet and stalked out to find the means he needed to kill a whore. A means that should even work for more than one whore, if the opportunity arose . . .

# TWENTY-TWO

Honrita came downstairs feeling much better than she had the day before, the day she'd brought her future Blendingmates home. She'd started to work with the original three at once, keeping them under full control while she probed them one at a time to find out what had made them the pitiful specimens they were. Ayl had *wanted* them to be pitiful so they'd be easily controlled, apparently having no idea that their weaknesses of personality translated to weaknesses in talent.

But *she* knew that Kadri, Stelk, and Seeli were liabilities in their present condition, so she'd tried to do something about their lacks. Kadri was the daughter of a merchant whose entire family consisted of snobbish, foolish people who thought that being overweight was a boast of their superior place in life. Honrita tried to loosen the hold those beliefs had on Kadri, but the woman clung to them so stubbornly that Honrita finally had to overlay the original beliefs with replacements of her own. Kadri now thought that pleasant agreeability and moderation at the dinner table were the signs of superiority, and she would continue to think so.

Stelk Faron had presented a different problem. Stelk had apparently had a father who was extremely critical of everything and everyone around him, especially his own children. Nothing Stelk had done had ever been even as good as acceptable, not to mention satisfactory. Stelk grew up to be just as critical, trying to emulate his father as closely as possible in an attempt to finally find some measure of success, but of course he never did. His mind was so filled with self-doubt and lack of assurance that he probably wouldn't have known success even if he'd found it.

Again Honrita had tried to change the man's inner beliefs, and again she found those beliefs too deeply entrenched to move. But leaving Stelk unchanged was out of the question, so Honrita made him believe that constructive criticism was his greatest strength—and that he was admired for his *diplomatic* suggestions.

Seeli Tandor had turned out to be the hardest one to work with. The women in Seeli's family had been strictly and firmly taught that women weren't ever to "push themselves forward." Apparently that injunction covered independent thought as well as action, and Seeli had learned to do as her mother and older sisters did without once questioning the validity of the stance. Seeli would never have been considered a brilliant thinker, but even the small amount of individuality she might have shown was completely buried under the constant demand to do nothing but obey.

By that time Honrita had begun to feel her weariness, so she hadn't even tried to change Seeli's convictions. Instead she made the Air magic user believe that emulating the new Kadri was the most acceptable of actions, right behind the desirability of obeying Honrita. Then Honrita had rested while the other two women made dinner, and after the meal she had sent the others to their rooms and had herself gone right to bed.

"But even now that I feel rested, I still can't think of anything else to do with Arbon Vand," Honrita murmured to herself as she reached the bottom of the stairs. "That personality of his won't let me change it even a small bit, so I'll just have to continue to control him."

"Talking only to yourself isn't very productive, Honrita," Stelk Faron said from the chair he sat in with a book open in his lap. There had been a teasing quality to his words, and his face wore an odd-looking smile. "If you have a problem, I'm sure the ladies and I would enjoy helping out with it."

"I appreciate that offer, Stelk, I really do," Honrita answered as she walked closer to the man. The change in him was amazing, and she basked in the glow of a job well done. "I was just observing that it would be nice if I could find a way to make Arbon more agreeable, but I don't think I can. Will he be too difficult for you to associate with just as he is?"

"Arbon doesn't believe that what we're going to do is possible," Stelk explained, his patient smile gentle. "Once he learns differently, he ought to be easier to live with."

"I certainly hope so," Honrita said with a sigh, and then she showed her own smile. "Has everyone had breakfast but me?"

"Actually, none of us has eaten yet," Stelk answered, putting his book aside before getting to his feet. "We decided to wait until you could join us, and only Arbon made a fuss over the decision. He's currently sitting at the table in the dining room and brooding."

"Then let's join him, but not in the brooding," Honrita said, taking the arm Stelk offered her. "This is much too pretty a morning to waste it on the dark emotions. Especially since after breakfast we'll be Blending."

Stelk nodded happy agreement and led Honrita toward the house's small dining room. *This is almost like a dream,* Honrita thought as she walked beside him. *Stelk looks strange on the inside where only I can see him, but on the outside he's the nicest person I've ever known. I now have a real companion, and I never truly realized how terrible it is not to have one. This is worth all the effort I put into it yesterday.*

Kadri and Seeli also sat at the table in the dining room, but they sat together at the end away from Arbon and ignored the man. When they saw Honrita they got to their feet, and each of them wore the same radiant smile.

"Good morning, Honrita," Kadri said as she stepped away from the chair at the head of the table. "I was just keeping your seat warm for you, and now that you're here we can eat. Is there anything in particular you'd like to have? It turns out that Seeli here is a truly excellent cook."

"Oh, I'm not *that* good," Seeli protested with a small laugh and a blush. "I just enjoy cooking, so I've learned what it's all about. *Would* you like something special, Honrita?"

"Anything you ladies prepare will be just fine," Honrita said, letting Stelk seat her at the head of the table. "Is there any tea ready?"

"I'll get you a cup while the ladies prepare our meal," Stelk said at once, and then he followed the women into the kitchen. Honrita made herself more comfortable in the chair, but suddenly Arbon voiced a sound of disgust.

"How can you stand to look at yourself in the mirror?" Arbon demanded from where he slouched in his own chair at the other end of the table. "You've stolen those people's personalities and made them over into something *you* consider better, but it doesn't seem to bother you. You're also keeping *me* a prisoner here, but that obviously bothers you even less."

"We're all here for an important purpose, so we all have to make certain sacrifices," Honrita explained to the scowling man. "I know it's easier to avoid doing your duty than facing up to it, Arbon, but isn't it time you stopped being a child and began to act like a man?"

"There—*is*—no—important—purpose—here," Arbon stated, speaking each word slowly as he leaned a bit toward her. "What you're doing can't possibly be your duty, because you'd never be able to run this empire even if you did become the leader of it. You can't even handle the people around you without changing them into grinning idiots. How do you expect to cope with an empire full of people who disagree with your decisions and don't beam at your appearance?"

"Just because your duty isn't pleasant, you can't decide not to do it," Honrita returned primly, wishing she could get through to the man. "I'll worry about dealing with what

comes up when it actually happens. Fretting over it before-
hand is a waste of time."

"Well, you're the expert on wastes of time," Arbon replied
as he leaned back again, but then he looked at her more directly. "You can lie to yourself about how what you're doing
is your duty, but don't bother *me* with that nonsense. You
can't simply decide that something like ruling an empire is
your duty. No one else *wants* you to run things, so it's a
whim you're working on, not a duty. If you really knew what
duty was all about, you'd be working against people like
yourself. We finally have a decent government in our country, and you're trying to bring it down. If you think you're all
that great, tell me what you'd do to make things even better."

Honrita frowned at the miserable man, trying to answer
his challenging question. The only problem was, the proper
words refused to come. Honrita *knew* it was her duty to take
over running the empire, but Arbon's accusations had scat-
tered all her perfectly good explanations. And as far as what
she would do to better things went, she would do a lot of
things. She just couldn't put any of those things into words
at the moment . . .

Stelk's return with a cup of tea diverted Honrita's attention for a short time, and after a sip or two she had managed
to calm herself. It had finally come to her that the Fire magic
user in their Blending *had* to be overly aggressive and un-
pleasant, otherwise their Blending would be ineffective. If it
made the man happy to think he'd asked questions and made
statements that Honrita couldn't reply to, then so be it. Having an effective Blending was the most important thing right
now; Arbon could be shown just how wrong he was once
they had taken over.

It wasn't long before the ladies brought out the food, and
they all enjoyed a very tasty breakfast. Honrita chatted with
her three true Blendingmates, finding the time immensely
satisfying. Arbon ate silently at his end of the table, refusing
to join them even with nothing more than words, but that
didn't matter. He was just as odd on the inside as the others

were, and Honrita felt confident that he would join them completely when the time came that it did matter.

They sipped tea for a time once they finished eating, but the excitement in Honrita refused to be held down for long. It quickly grew to the point where she couldn't bear it, so she put her cup aside and stood up.

"It's time, my friends," she said, smiling at all of them. "Let's go into the sitting room where we can be more comfortable."

Everyone including Arbon got up and followed her, and once they were all in the sitting room she turned back to them.

"I know we have to start out standing in a particular way," she said. "Arbon, please tell us in what order we have to stand."

"Fire first, then Spirit, then Earth," Arbon replied in a surly voice. "Air and Water stand to either side of Spirit."

"Are you sure?" Stelk asked Arbon with a small and thoughtful frown. "I was under the impression that there was a very specific place each of us had to be in, but your answer suggests that Air and Water can stand wherever they please. Shouldn't we—"

"It doesn't *matter* on which side Air and Water stand," Arbon interrupted in annoyance. "It doesn't really matter where any of the rest of us stand either, not when you get right down to it. The initial arrangement is simply to help our minds visualize what our talents will be doing."

"Then let's begin," Honrita said before Stelk could add to his objections. Stelk's lack of assurance was returning, but Honrita quickly smoothed it away. Nothing could be allowed to interfere with what they were doing, absolutely nothing . . .

"Now Spirit reaches out to the rest of us, and when we feel her touch we return it," Kadri said once they were all in place. "It's supposed to be really easy and completely natural, as well as being the most marvelous thing we'll ever experience."

Hearing those words gave Honrita the confidence she

needed to begin the effort, the most important effort of her life. More than anything she wanted to be part of something that was *important*, something that mattered. This *had* to work, it simply *had* to . . .

&bull;

"I have a list you need to look at, Driff," Idresia said, coming toward the table where Driff sat. He'd been going through reports until his eyes watered, but his efforts hadn't been very well rewarded.

"Another list?" Driff groaned, wondering if he would ever see normally again. "Just put it at the bottom of the stack, and I'll get to it as soon as I can."

"No, this list goes to the top of the stack," Idresia disagreed, stopping to stroke his hair with a clearly sympathetic hand. "There are five names of missing Spirit magic users on it, along with educated guesses as to where the five might be. Or should I say that there are guesses about four of them. The fifth seems to have disappeared completely, so we might be able to cross her name off right away. If she left the city, she can't very well be the one helping Ayl."

Driff took the piece of paper Idresia held out to him, wondering why he'd suddenly gotten a very odd feeling. The first four names on the list meant nothing to him, but the fifth . . .

"No, I don't think we'll be doing any fast crossing off," Driff said, staring at the name "Honrita Grohl." "I've met the missing woman, and I think it's very likely she's the one we want."

"You know the woman?" Idresia asked with brows high. "How did you meet her?"

"She's the last subject Gensie Landros and I tried to work with in the guarded residence," Driff answered with a sigh. "Gensie thought we'd cured the woman of her problem, but I remember being not quite as sure. It turned out that I was right after all, because as soon as we turned our backs on the woman she disappeared from the residence. Someone's Blending was supposed to go looking for the Grohl woman, but with everything we were involved with I forgot to follow up to see if she was found."

"Well, it looks like she *wasn't* found," Idresia pointed out wryly. "What was wrong with her that you think she's the one helping Ayl?"

"At first she was the meek and nervous sort who never said a word out of line," Driff explained, gesturing vaguely with one hand. "But taking classes that taught her how to use her strong Middle talent changed her personality, making her strut around with self-importance. But the feeling of self-importance also made her touchy, so that she considered a passing suggestion from someone an effort to 'tell her what to do.' "

"And she made trouble because of that impression," Idresia said after voicing a sigh. "I've seen that happen to people a time or two, and it's never pretty. They spend most of their lives being beaten down and bullied, and then they suddenly find something that takes them a step above the usual obscurity. That one step always looks a mile high to them, and encourages them to start their own pushing and bullying."

"Yes, well, Gensie and I worked together to heal the damage caused by her upbringing," Driff continued with a nod of agreement. "That healing seemed to bring out a completely different personality in the woman, one that wasn't hampered by doubt and fear and crippled by repression. She thanked us in a very sincere way for helping her, and Gensie's Spirit magic apparently confirmed the Grohl woman's interest in 'helping' our efforts with the rest of the people in the guarded residence."

"But you didn't agree with that opinion," Idresia said, giving her own distracted nod. "You probably felt the Grohl woman wasn't telling the complete truth, but a High in Spirit magic would find it hard to believe that a Middle in Earth magic might know better than her own talent. You didn't press the point?"

"Not when I wasn't all that certain myself," Driff said. "I didn't *know* something was wrong, I only suspected it, so I let Gensie's certainty make me think I was imagining things. Now the Grohl woman is probably after the importance she firmly believes ought to be hers, and she'll be coming at us with a Blending that might even be more powerful than our own."

"What makes you think that her Blending will be more powerful?" Idresia asked, looking at Driff with her head to one side. "If I recall correctly, every Middle Blending our entity has come in contact with so far has been a lot less than our own."

"You're right about that, but you're overlooking an important point," Driff said, reaching for the cold tea he'd been sipping. "Those other Middle Blendings—as well as our own—have all been put together by the people *in* the Blending. The Grohl woman's Blending will have people chosen by Holdis Ayl, a man who can tell the strength of a talent without having that talent himself. I can't quite believe that Ayl will have chosen people who aren't the strongest he could find."

"No, I *hadn't* thought of that," Idresia agreed, now showing a frown. "And you're right about the point making a difference. I wish we knew exactly who it was who'll be in Grohl's Blending."

"I think I may know who their Fire magic user will be," Driff admitted reluctantly. "A man named Arbon Vand has been reported missing by his family, and he's been described as someone who would never just walk away without telling people where he was going. He's a strong enough Middle talent in Fire magic that he was given a job teaching classes."

"Yes, he *is* a strong talent in Fire magic," Idresia said, surprising Driff. "He and I were in the same training class, and we never could decide which of us was stronger. He's a decent man who felt a lot of loyalty to the new government, but if that Grohl woman did something to him with her Spirit magic . . ."

"Then his normal loyalties won't matter," Driff said, finishing the sentence Idresia had just let trail off. "So we know that the opposing Blending will have a Spirit magic user who can fool a High talent, and a Fire magic user who is probably one of the strongest talents found so far. Do we really need to know details about the rest of the members?"

"That sounds like you found something out," another voice said, and Driff looked around to see their other four Blendingmates coming into the room. It was Edmin who had spoken, and now he added, "My share of those reports gave me nothing but eyestrain, so I'm glad at least *someone* has made some discoveries."

"Let's make that 'helpful discoveries,' " Kail amended as he closed the door behind all of them. "I've also found nothing of any real use, not when we don't know what it is we're looking for."

"At the moment we're looking for the balance of a Blending," Driff answered, then he began to bring them up to date while they and Idresia took seats at the table. "So we probably know the identity of two of our opponents, but we're still missing the rest."

"We may also know the identity of the Earth magic user," Kail said with an odd shake of his head. "A woman named Kadri Sumlow has been reported missing by her merchant father. From his description of her, it's fairly certain that she probably considers herself too important to simply run away. And the description also suggests it isn't very likely that she eloped with a man. The other reports of missing people don't feel the same."

"I think I may have come across one of the same sort," Edmin mused, leaning back in his chair. "A woman named Seeli Tandor was also reported missing by her father, who assured the guardsman taking the report that his daughter would never *dare* to simply go off on her own. She has duties at home, the father said, and because of those duties she's also never been permitted to become involved with men. But she was allowed to train her talent because that made her more efficient in carrying out her duties. She's an Air magic user."

"So if they haven't found a way to sneak up on a Sight magic user, that means we're just missing the Water magic member," Driff said. "But before I forget, let me ask Edmin a question. I know you've found a way to hide the strength of your talent, Edmin, but what about being able to lie? Do you think you could lie to a High talent without them knowing you're doing it?"

"Since I've never tried, I don't really know," Edmin answered with brows raised high. "Now that I think about it, though, I just might be able to. But that's only because I've spent most of my life hiding my true feelings from those around me. When you live a lie, the lie tends to become a . . . reality and truth of its own, you might say."

"That must be it," Driff said, nodding his understanding. "The Grohl woman spent her life being something other than what she was meant to be, so in a manner of speaking she was also living a lie. When her personality changed, all she had to do to hide herself was continue to behave the way she always had. But none of this tells us what *we* have to do to ruin Ayl's plans."

"I think the first thing we have to do is move a number of Middle Blendings into the palace who won't be allowed to leave," Edmin said slowly, as though he thought aloud. "Once they're safe from being tampered with, it will then be their job to examine every single person, guardsmen included, before they're also allowed in the palace. When Ayl's people can't find any Highs, they may settle for Middles."

"But what would they do with Middles?" Issini asked from where she sat beside Edmin. "They want to use Highs to take over everyone else, and a Middle by him or herself can't be used in that way."

"I don't know what they would use a Middle for, but we can't discount the possibility that *they'll* think of something," Driff said with a shake of his head. "I agree with Edmin, but we've got to take this one step further. We ourselves have been running to the palace on a regular basis, and that makes us just as vulnerable as anyone else. If there isn't some way for us to individually resist a Blending entity, and I don't think there is, we have to decide if we want to stay in the palace permanently or not go back until this problem is over."

That comment caused a lot of exclamations and a bit of confused discussion, but eventually one voice rose above the rest.

"Driff is right," Asri said firmly, looking around at the others. "The last time we went to the palace, I noticed that the guards were all behaving very deferentially toward us. A watching entity would notice the same thing, and then we'd be singled out. Do any of you think that *we* couldn't take over the empire at this point?"

"With no Highs around to stop us?" Kail said with a snort. "Taking over would be no problem at all, if we were silly enough to want to run things. But I just had an idea that might or might not solve our problem. In Astinda we found that combining talents produced all sorts of new ways of doing things, and that leads me to wonder how much an entity can actually do."

"How much in what way?" Driff asked, having heard Kail's description of what his Astindan group had accomplished. "How could new inventions stop Ayl's plans?"

"What if we'd be better off *not* stopping Ayl's plans?" Kail countered. "We already know what Ayl means to do, so forcing him to come up with something we *won't* know about doesn't sound very smart to me."

"Kail, you'd better start from the beginning," Issini said, just about taking the words out of Driff's mouth. "I'm having no luck at all in following you."

"Yes, you're right," Kail agreed, smiling wryly. "I really should start with my idea. It came to me to wonder if our entity could . . . put some kind of . . . invisible net around each of us. The net would be sensitive to the touch of another entity, and if that other entity did try to touch one of us our Blending would come into existence at once."

"Because we *are* the perfect decoys," Driff exclaimed as soon as he saw all the possibilities. "Just as Asri said, a watching entity would notice how the guards treat us and that would make us the perfect targets. Once our entity came into being we'd be able to face *their* entity, without our having to go to all the trouble of tracking them down. Yes, I think that's the answer."

"But there are still two more interesting answers we need to get," Idresia said as everyone else began to comment excitedly. "The first of those two, of course, deals with the question of whether our entity *can* put a net like that around us. If it turns out that the net can be provided, we come to the last and most important question: Will we be strong enough to defeat the enemy entity? If we aren't, any other success we have won't count."

Driff's excitement died away as he heard Idresia's very pointed comments, and everyone else quieted as well. They all had enough self-confidence under normal circumstances, but it wasn't death they would be facing. If they lost the encounter they would no longer be free human beings, and that thought frightened Driff more than death ever could . . .

# TWENTY-THREE

"But it *has* to be my fault," Jovvi objected for the hundredth time. "We didn't stop being able to Blend when the rest of you initiated the Blending."

Jovvi sat miserably on a bench with Lorand's arm around her shoulders, but for once Lorand's presence wasn't able to comfort her. Ever since Jovvi had done . . . *something*, they'd tried and tried, but no one had been able to initiate the Blending.

"Please stop blaming yourself, Jovvi," Naran said wearily, also for the umpteenth time. "If something like this was about to happen, I should have been able to See it. But there was no warning whatsoever, and I still don't See any signs of tragedy for us. Aside from the fact that I feel it's about to start raining again."

"You're right, Naran, and that's all we need," Tamma said in a grumble from where she stood with her fists on her hips. "More rain, and just when that group of riders is approaching the other side of the village. But at least *we* won't have to go out into the rain to see who they are."

"No, not when one of the other groups is startin' to Blend," Vallant said with a nod and a sigh. "At least whatever is affectin' us hasn't spread to the others."

"Wait a minute." Jovvi said, strangely gentle shock pulling her away from the misery she'd been drowning in. "I also know that it's about to start raining again, I can feel the approach of riders, and I know that a Blending is forming. I can also feel that the most likely probability of the identity of the riders is that they're High talents coming to be link groups for the Gracelian Blendings. If we aren't Blended, *how* do I know all that?"

Jovvi no longer sat slumped against Lorand now, so she was able to see that he stared at her in the same way the others did. Brows were high and incomprehension showed clearly in eyes, probably a perfect match to what *she* looked like.

"Well?" she prompted, continuing to look around. "Is there anyone who *doesn't* know and feel those things?"

Rion and Lorand raised their brows even higher, but neither one spoke up to say that he had no idea what she was talking about. Instead, it was Tamma who spoke.

"That's the best question I've heard today," the Fire magic user mused, now looking thoughtful. "I'm aware of everything I usually am when we're Blended, but when I'm the entity I can float through the wall and flash to the place I want to be—if I've been there before. Well, I've been to the other side of the village before . . ."

Tamma's voice trailed off as she took on the look that Naran usually wore when she checked probabilities, and then she exclaimed aloud.

"I don't believe this!" Tamma said excitedly, just about dancing in place. "All I did was decide I wanted to see what was happening at the other side of the village, and I *could!* Will somebody else please try this, so I'll know whether or not I'm dreaming?"

Jovvi felt Tamma's excitement so strongly that there was no hesitation about following Tamma's request. Jovvi decided she wanted to know more about what was happening on the other side of the village, and suddenly she could *see* what was happening! The approaching riders had been stopped by one of their associate Blending's entity, and the entity now questioned the people. She could hear the entity's questions and the answers being given, and also saw the entity as clearly as she saw the riders.

"This is incredible," Lorand said from where he sat beside

Jovvi. "I'm aware of everything going on over there, but I'm also aware of what's happening around my physical self. I'm looking at the other side of the village, but I'm also able to look back here in an instant."

"In other words, along with everything else our bodies are no longer at risk," Rion said, sounding as elated as Jovvi suddenly felt. "We can still function as a Blending, but we're no longer vulnerable in the way we were."

"I've got the sudden feeling that you're understating things, Rion," Tamma said, and clearly she'd withdrawn her attention from the approaching riders. Jovvi *hadn't* withdrawn all of her attention, but she still had no trouble following what was now going on around her.

"Okay, now it's time to test my next theory," Tamma said as Rion gave her a questioning look. "Naran, I want you to light a small fire in the air right in the middle of this very loose circle we're standing in. Go ahead, you should know how to do it."

Jovvi saw that Naran seemed ready to protest, but the words apparently died on her lips. Instead of speaking, the Sight magic user frowned at the place Tamma had indicated. A moment later a small length of fire appeared in the empty air, and Tamma laughed.

"See, I knew you could do it," Tamma said as everyone else—including Jovvi—exclaimed wordlessly. "Now watch me put the fire out with water."

A globe of water appeared just as suddenly around the length of fire, but the fire didn't go out. It continued to burn inside the globe of water, and this time both Tamma and Naran laughed aloud.

"You almost got me, but I saw at the last instant how to keep the fire alive," Naran said in delight, sounding for all the world like a child with a new toy. "I was able to experience this when part of the Blending, but I never thought I'd be able to do it at any other time."

"But that's the whole point," Tamma returned as the globe of water disappeared again. "I think it's obvious that we *are* Blended, but in an entirely different way. And right now I have just one more question: Jovvi, will you please try to *dissolve* the Blending?"

Jovvi might have been confused and distraught earlier, but now she had no trouble understanding and following what was going on. Without speaking she made the usual effort to dissolve their Blending, but nothing happened.

"Since I'm still feelin' and seein' everythin' I did a minute ago, I'd guess that our Blendin' is permanent now," Vallant remarked with an odd smile. "Obviously, it's a good thing we like each other so well."

"No, it's more than a matter of 'like,' " Lorand said, wearing the same smile. "If you'll remember, we all had to *love* each other before we could all be heard individually in the Blending entity. That came before we started to take turns initiating the Blending."

"How is it possible that no one knows that *this* is what the Blending experience is meant to lead to?" Rion asked with a shake of his head. "And even beyond that, how could anyone give up the possibility of achieving this by suppressing knowledge of how to Blend?"

"You're obviously talkin' about the nobles in Gandistra," Vallant responded, his smile having turned wry. "I think it's safe to assume that this only happens to a *complete* Blendin', otherwise our former enemies would have reached this point a lot of years ago. And so would the Gracelians, come to think of it. What we don't yet know is if their unbalanced Blendin's would have reached this point if they'd had Sight magic users added in."

"I have the feeling that that unbalance you mentioned would keep it from happening," Jovvi put in as she stood. "Balance comes from like joining like, and my guess is that any properly balanced Blending will reach this same point even if they don't happen to be High talents. If our training programs back home have gone as well as we hoped they would, we should have the chance to find out."

"But now we have to talk to our associate Blendings," Lorand said, also getting to his feet. "We have to let them know what's happened, but this time we really should charge them. Personally, I would have paid any amount to keep from being scared witless the way I was."

"You and me both," Tamma agreed as they all began to move toward the door of the house. "But after we talk to the others, we really need to do some more experimenting. I can't get rid of the feeling that there's a lot more we don't yet know about."

Jovvi knew exactly what Tamma meant, and the nodding of the others showed that they felt the same. As they walked out into the muddy street of the village, Jovvi got an idea. She really liked her soft riding boots, but going through mud was about to ruin them. So . . .

"Hey, what did you do?" Lorand yelped as Jovvi was suddenly three inches taller. His arm had been around her shoulders, which let him notice the difference immediately. "Are you somehow starting to grow again?"

"No, I'm just protecting my boots," Jovvi answered with a delighted laugh. "I don't want this mud ruining them, so I gave myself some hardened air to walk on. Rion, I had no idea how marvelous it was to be able to do this."

When Tamma and Naran heard what she'd done, they had to do the same. Then they also joined Jovvi's laughter while the men discussed whether or not to protect their own boots. They finally decided that it was very fitting for *all* of them to walk on air, and their laughter had turned more to juvenile giggling by the time they reached the place where their associates were.

"Have you six been drinking something other than tea?" Arinna asked with an indulgent smile once their rowdy group had gotten close enough. "Not that you don't deserve to celebrate your victory, but . . ."

"But we're gonna be havin' more rain purty soon," Pagin Holter said when Arinna let her words trail off. "Too many o' them slaves are comin' out of it feelin' scared, so we could use a hand settlin' 'em down b'fore we start drownin' again."

"I can help calm those people," Rion said with a wide smile as he looked over at the shivering, terrified group of former slaves. "Watch and see how easy it is."

The now-freed slaves began to calm even as Rion spoke, and a moment later they were straightening up and looking around in curiosity rather than with fear.

"Nicely done, Rion," Jovvi said with a good deal of pleasure. "I couldn't have done that better myself."

"What's going on?" Arinna asked as Jovvi and her Blendingmates began to laugh again. "You can't calm people with Air magic, so why are you trying to make us believe you can?"

"Rion didn't *use* Air magic to calm those people," Lorand said in a very bland way. "He used Spirit magic, which was only fair. After all, Jovvi used Air magic to keep her boots free of mud."

"How can you possibly be using each other's talents?" Arinna demanded, confusion clear on her pretty face before her expression changed to one of stunned amazement. "No, don't tell me! Something happened that made it possible. What was it? Was it something that we'll also be able to do?"

"How much is that information worth to you?" Naran asked as blandly as Lorand had spoken. "We did warn you that we were going to charge for information from now on, so you can't say we didn't."

That brought on another bout of laughter that Jovvi joined in, and by the time the amusement played itself out Arinna stood with a gold coin in her hand.

"If this isn't enough, I'll get more," Arinna said, holding out the coin. "Now *please* tell us what happened!"

"Let's take pity on them," Vallant said with a grin matching the one Pagin Holter wore. "They can pay us after seein' how much knowin' about it in advance is really worth."

Jovvi was the one everyone else deferred to, so she described what they'd done with taking turns in initiating their Blending. When she described her own final efforts and what had happened, Arinna looked horrified.

"You couldn't Blend again?" Arinna exclaimed. "But that's terrible! How did you finally overcome the problem?"

"We didn't," Tamma answered when Jovvi gestured to her. "What we did instead was realize that we *were* Blended, with everyone awake and aware of what was happening around us. We were also able to use each other's talents, just the way our entity was able to. We can also do a couple of other things our entity could do, but we don't yet know just how many more are possible."

"Then whut'r ya doin' *here*?" Holter demanded, his own expression looking stunned. "Why ain't ya back in thet house practicin'?"

"We came to tell *you* people what was going on," Tamma answered dryly, clearly noticing the way Jovvi had that Holter's accent had suddenly gotten thicker. "But if you'd rather we didn't say anything next time . . ."

"No, no, that's perfectly all right," Arinna assured Tamma quickly as she glared at Holter. "Pagin is just shaken up, and doesn't know what he's saying. We want to know about *everything*, as soon as you're ready to tell us."

"Since you're being so nice about it, we will," Jovvi assured Arinna, and then she turned to her Blendingmates. "Let's also take Pagin's advice and go back to experiment. After all, we don't really have to be here in order to help out. We can help as well as experiment, and still stay dry."

The others considered that a marvelous idea, so they began to retrace their steps to the house. There was an eagerness inside them all that Jovvi hadn't felt since the first time they'd Blended. They'd been through a lot since that first effort, but hopefully all the hard times were now behind them . . .

"All right, what are we going to experiment with first?" I asked when we were back in our house. "What could our entity do that we haven't yet tried alone?"

"You know, you should have asked that question before we left here," Lorand said, looking and acting as giddy as I felt. "Our entity could float along a street or road without using Air magic. Maybe we can do the same."

"That's a good thought, so I'll try it," I agreed with a laugh I couldn't hold back. "Let me concentrate for a minute."

I concentrated on the desire to rise up off the floor without using Air magic, but a very long minute passed and nothing happened. I thought about the failure for a very brief time, and then the obvious answer came.

"This is the wrong experiment," I said, getting the impression that most of the others had also been trying to rise into the air. "Our entity floated because it had no physical being, but we do. If we want to be up in the air we *will* have to use Air magic."

"You know, this isn't the first time you've had a definite answer to something, Tamma," Jovvi observed while Vallant and Lorand made very loud sounds of disappointment. "Since you don't seem to be guessing, I wonder where that certainty is coming from."

"Don't be silly," I started to say with a laugh. "I'm not—"

And then the laughter stopped when I realized that Jovvi was right. I *was* getting more than just ideas about things. Facts were coming that I had no doubt about at all.

"It could be happening because you're the 'oldest entity' among us," Jovvi mused, apparently seeing nothing of how momentarily upset I'd been. "Most of the new things have started with you, Tamma, but I wish I could be sure that we'll have access to the lost knowledge as well. There are still so many things I want to know about, including the question of where this knowledge can be coming from."

"Now *that's* a good question," Lorand said as I stared at Jovvi with raised brows and thought the same thing. "Our entity seemed to have access to memories that we didn't, and it never occurred to me to wonder where the knowledge came from. How does it work for *you,* Tamrissa? Are these things just coming to you?"

"Not really," I answered, actually thinking about the process for the first time. "It's as if I have all these different memories, ones I'm reaching for the first time. The information is just *there,* but now I'm wondering where 'there' really is. It isn't in my own mind, that's for certain."

"You might want to spend some time now and then thinkin' about it," Vallant suggested as he stepped closer.

"Our entity sometimes took a short while before it 'knew' things, as if it started a search and then let the search go on by itself. If the memories do work that way, you might suddenly find yourself with the answer."

"If I do, I'll be sure to let everyone know," I said, then dismissed a matter I couldn't do anything about right now. "But we were trying to think of a good experiment. Has anyone had any ideas?"

"I've had a thought," Rion said, speaking up before anyone else could. "When our entity looked at something, we could all see that something even though we seemed to be looking out of our own individual eyes. I've been wondering if we could all see what only one of us happens to be looking at."

"Now, that's worth trying," I said, knowing a good idea when I heard it. "I'll look at something, and at the same time I'll try to give the picture to the rest of you. But I think you'll have to . . . open up in some way for me to do that."

"You go ahead and try it, and we'll see if we can do the opening up," Jovvi said. "But don't tell us what you intend to look at. That way we'll know if we're seeing it ourselves or only through you."

That was another good idea, so I thought for a brief moment before deciding I wanted to see what our former enemies were doing. They'd been put into that shed under guard, and although they were also under control I thought it might be a good idea to check on them.

As soon as my mind was firmly made up, part of it seemed to . . . break off and flash away. The next thing I knew I had our former enemies in sight, watching as they snarled at one another. Each one seemed to think that their troubles were the fault of the others rather than themselves, the attitude rooted in a lack of true belief in their ability and talents. The accusations came from their individual fears, of course, and their Spirit magic user did nothing to calm his Blendingmates.

I looked around at the interior of the shed, but paid more attention to the workings of my mind. What I looked at was

being seen only by me, I knew, but then I realized that if I
made only a small adjustment . . .

"Oh!" Jovvi and Lorand said together, and I could feel
their excitement as Jovvi continued, "I just relaxed and
waited, and now I can see the invader leaders. Is that what
you're looking at, Tamma? Can the rest of you see them as
well?"

"Yes, that's what I'm looking at," I agreed as Lorand, Vallant, Rion, and Naran all confirmed that they saw the same.
"I'd say that this experiment was a success."

"Definitely," Naran said as I brought my attention back to
the house we stood in. "And now I have another idea that's
almost the same as two of the last ones. We know we can see
at a distance, but just how *far* a distance? What's the limit of
our range, so to speak?"

"Yes, that's definitely worth knowin'," Vallant said at
once with real enthusiasm. "You can't use your ability to its
fullest extent if you don't know what your limits are—and
aren't."

Everyone including me agreed with that, so the next step
in our investigations became obvious.

"Let's see if we can find out what our . . . 'friends' in
Liandia are doing," I suggested. "But let's all look at the
same time, to make sure we all have the same range."

"There shouldn't be any differences since we're supposed
to be a single being, but checking won't hurt," Jovvi said
with a nod. "First, though, I'd like to get a cup of tea and
make myself comfortable. Being able to drink tea while we
do things just may prove to be the best part of all this."

"I support that idea wholeheartedly," Rion said at once,
making the rest of us chuckle. "Being able to divide our attention *is* what I consider marvelous."

We took turns teasing Rion and Jovvi as we all got tea and
then went to sit on our sleeping mats, but I appreciated our
newfound freedom in a different way. With all the tea we
usually swallowed, being able to use the sanitary facilities at
any time was *my* idea of marvelous.

Once we were settled and ready, I sent that separate part

of my mind toward the city of Liandia. I suppose I expected there to be *something* in the way of hesitation in reaching so far or delay in finding the people I wanted, but there was neither. My vision flashed into Liandia, and then settled in what I recognized as the garden of Antrie Lorimon's house. Lorimon was there beside the man named Frode Mismin, and with them were Olskin Dinno, Satlan Reesh—and a depressed-looking Cleemor Gardan.

". . . continued to hope you all were wrong," Gardan was saying to the others. It surprised me for a moment that I could hear and understand the conversation, and then I realized there was no reason I shouldn't be able to. Our entity hadn't spent much time listening to people talk, but that was primarily because it had had other things to do instead.

"Well, of course you hoped we were wrong, Cleemor," Antrie said with a sympathy she really felt. "No man wants to believe the worst about the woman he loves, and Tenia is also your wife."

"Tenia *was* my wife," Gardan corrected, the words somewhat on the ragged side. "When I told her that even if the invaders are defeated I won't be a member of the assembly any longer, she suddenly stopped . . . showing herself off to me, is the only way I can describe it. I've always been very aware of her nearness and desirability, but as soon as she heard what I had to say, my intimate feelings for her came to an abrupt stop. She looked really annoyed and spent some time muttering to herself, then she developed a sad expression and informed me that she had to leave me. She assured me that her leaving was completely for my own good, and then she had the nerve to ask me if I knew who the new assembly members would be."

"She thought she had you under control again, and didn't know I was protecting you," Mismin told Gardan with a humorless smile. "Before she did that, it was only possible to know that you were being controlled. We couldn't tell for certain who the person doing the controlling was, but Tenia was kind enough to try her tricks while I was there as a witness. You should have heard her scream when I placed her under arrest."

"She'll scream even louder when her talent in Spirit magic is gone," Antrie said, her voice containing a hardness I couldn't remember hearing before. "We won't be members of the assembly once the High Blendings get here—if they do get here instead of the invaders—but until then we're still the only officials left. Olskin, can you handle the matter yourself, or will you need help?"

"I'll use my Blending to take her talent, and we can do it first thing tomorrow," Dinno replied as he shifted in his chair. "No matter *who* happens to be in charge of our country, it needs to be made clear that Spirit magic users won't be allowed to use their talent to take advantage of people. But possibly I should have said, I'll use my present Blending. Reesh and I have been looking around, and we've met a pair of lovely ladies of High talent who don't seem averse to the idea of becoming a Blending with us. We want to get to know them a bit better—and find a fifth—but we may just give those new Blendings a run for their money."

"The real miracle is that the ladies don't seem to find me objectionable in the least," Reesh said with an embarrassed sort of laugh. "They both decided at once that my shyness was 'sweet,' and I haven't been able to stop grinning since they said it. I let them see exactly what I'm really like, and they still think I'm 'sweet.' "

"That's because you've changed so," Antrie told him with a gentle laugh of her own. "You're no longer desperate to be accepted by others, so that acceptance is much easier to get now. And Frode and I have talked things over, and we've decided that we're also going to be looking for Blendingmates. Assuming we survive . . ."

Those last three words turned all of them somber, and it came to me with a small bit of guilt that we hadn't sent word to Liandia about our success. That gave me an idea, so I "moved" closer to the woman.

—*Antrie, can you hear me?*—I asked directly into her

mind the way our entity used to do.—*Can you understand what I'm saying?*—

"Who is it?" Antrie asked after almost dropping her teacup. "You seem familiar, but I'm not quite sure . . ."

"What is it, Antrie?" Frode Mismin said with abrupt concern as he touched her hand. "What's wrong?"

"I think I'm hearing one of the Gandistrans," Antrie said, still looking and sounding shaken. "But I don't know how it can be *one* of them when it takes a Blending to do this kind of thing . . ."

—*Don't worry about that part of it,*—I said into the woman's mind again.—*You'll find out all about the new discoveries we've made, but what you need to know first is that the invasion is over. Your people helped us to figure out how to face and best those "leaders," and now the five of them are our prisoners.*—

"She said the invasion is over!" Antrie exclaimed, delight beginning to fill her. "I know it's a 'her,' and I think it may be Tamrissa. She said that they've bested the invader Blending and now have them as prisoners!"

"Antrie, we *all* want the threat to be over, and you've been through some very hard experiences," Mismin said gently as he put a hand on Antrie's arm. "I'm sure that the Gandistrans will do everything possible to win against the invaders, so you don't have to—"

—*She isn't imagining things, so stop trying to soothe her hysteria,*—I said, now spreading my thoughts to all of them.—*We really did win, and in the process we learned a new thing or two. Once we have all the slaves freed, we ought to be able to head back to your city.*—

"They did it!" Reesh shouted, his face filled with joy. "They actually did it! Now we'll *all* have a chance to adjust to the new ways."

Even Gardan left off his brooding to join in the vocal celebration the other four were indulging in, so I withdrew my attention back to the house we sat in. I *had* been able to sip tea while I listened and spoke to the Gracelians, and my

Blendingmates and I exchanged grins over having passed on the good news.

But then I couldn't help wondering what *else* we would find we were able to do . . .

# TWENTY-FOUR

Honrita looked around fondly at her Blendingmates. The Blending experience had been as incredible as they'd been told it would be, and the second time had been even better than the first. Kadri, Stelk, and Seeli were still burbling to each other, but Arbon sat silent with heavy disturbance filling him.

"What's the matter, Arbon?" Honrita asked gently, drawing the man's attention. "You seem to be terribly disturbed when you really ought to be rejoicing like the rest of us."

"The rest of you are rejoicing because you don't know any better," Arbon returned, bleakness staring out of his eyes. "Achieving a Blending ought to be the greatest day in a man's or woman's life, not something you've been forced into to feed a madwoman's insanity. You have those other three under such tight control that they don't have any idea how much you've stolen from us, but I do."

"Why do you always have to see everything in such a negative light?" Honrita demanded, suddenly very annoyed. "Our Blendingmates there might have never had the chance to experience this marvel if not for me, and there's no guarantee *you* would have found four other people to accept you either. Why can't you see this as the opportunity you might otherwise have missed?"

"Well, for one thing there's your mention of *four* other people," Arbon said, his tone unrelenting. "You keep ignoring the point, but a proper Blending has *six* people in it, not

288

five. And how do you expect to take over an entire High Blending when their Sight magic user will probably See the danger and get at least him- or herself out of harm's way?"

"I love it when you criticize my plan," Honrita said with an honest laugh. "That tells me you really believe that it will work, and what you're trying to do is talk me out of putting the plan into motion. But you're wasting your time, you know. We'll be getting started first thing tomorrow."

"Do you mean we've reached the time when we get to strengthen our bond?" Kadri asked, eagerness clear in her dark eyes. "I've really been looking forward to this, but I was beginning to believe it would never happen."

"It had to wait for the proper time," Honrita told her, ignoring her own faint feelings of nervousness. "Now that we've Blended for the second time, we can get on to strengthening the bond. And since you've been looking forward to the time so eagerly, Kadri, you can be the one to go first."

"Do I also get to choose who I go first *with*?" Kadri asked, the archness she'd obviously been trying for coming across more ludicrous than sensual. "I really would like the choice, Honrita."

"Now, Kadri, you know there isn't supposed to be any kind of favoritism in a Blending," Honrita chided with a gentle smile. "These are our brothers, after all, and we'll be sharing ourselves with both of them. I've written Stelk and Arbon's names on these slips of paper, so you and Seeli get to choose one of the slips each. Then, afterward, you'll switch partners."

"But what about you?" Kadri protested, sincerely concerned with cooperation now that Honrita had taken a tighter grip on her mind. "Your bond needs to be strengthened the same way ours does."

"Yes, dear, but someone has to wait so it might as well be me," Honrita said with the same gentle smile. "You and Seeli have worked hard for this, and I really don't mind waiting."

"Let me translate that for you," Arbon said to Kadri just as the heavy woman's face took on a look of adoration. "Our great and generous leader over there is afraid to lie with a man, so she's going to use you and your skinny friend as sacrifices. If you two come through the experience without having hysterics, she *might* manage to get her courage up and try the same."

"Don't be silly, Arbon," Kadri answered with a small laugh while Honrita fought to overcome her stab of hatred for the horrid man. "She knows as well as we do that our Blending won't be as strong as possible if we don't strengthen our bonds, so of course she'll do the same. She *is* the one who most wants us to succeed, after all."

"I'm willing to put silver on the very strong possibility that your idol will suddenly decide that we're strong enough *without* her having to strengthen bonds," Arbon said with a vicious sneer in Honrita's direction. "Is there anyone foolish enough to bet against me?"

Stelk, Kadri, and Seeli moved uncomfortably in their chairs as they exchanged glances, but none of them said anything. Honrita was so furiously embarrassed that she was about to scream at Arbon, when the truth forced its way through to her. Arbon was filled with more anxiety than contempt, which meant that his comments were *supposed* to have infuriated Honrita. Arbon was still trying to ruin her plans, and his own plan had nearly worked.

But "almost" is simply another word for failure, Honrita realized as she calmed herself. The man didn't want their Blending strengthened, but he wasn't the one in charge. Honrita was in charge, and it was about time she proved that to him again.

So rather than speaking, Honrita reached out to Arbon Vand. Once she had the proper hold on him, she rose from her chair, walked over to him, and bent close to his ear.

"Isn't Kadri an incredibly beautiful woman, Arbon?" she murmured to the man who wasn't being allowed to resist her suggestions in any way. "Her face is flawlessly lovely, and her body is the sort of slender delight that's you've dreamed about for years. And she's just said that she's willing to lie with you! Isn't that what you've been waiting to hear?"

"Yes, yes it is," Arbon answered hoarsely, his breath beginning to come more heavily. "I've been waiting forever to give you my love, Kadri. Come with me now to my bedchamber!"

Kadri looked surprised as she glanced at Honrita for permission, which a smiling Honrita quickly gave her with a nod. Honrita had meant to use the slips of paper to see which of the women would lie with the more attractive Arbon first, but that procedure had now become unnecessary. The Fire magic user disliked Kadri more than he did Seeli, so it would be Kadri he sported with first.

Honrita let Arbon get to his feet and offer his hand to Kadri, who took the hand and stood before following the man out of the sitting room. Honrita paused a moment to make sure that Stelk and Seeli would wait quietly and patiently while she was gone, and then she followed Arbon and Kadri to his bedchamber.

Arbon's desire was easily fanned and inflamed by Honrita's talent, and by the time he and Kadri reached his bedchamber the man was actually panting. He led Kadri inside and would have closed and locked the door, but Honrita intervened to make him forget his intention. She *had* to see what would go on between the two, and no one would know about her watching unless she chose to tell them.

The man pulled Kadri close and kissed her, but the kiss didn't last very long. The two stood close to Arbon's bed, so Honrita moved quietly to a chair not far away and sat. By that time Arbon was already helping Kadri out of her clothes, and the heavy woman was making small sounds as if she were in some sort of pain. But the way she tore at her clothing said it wasn't really pain that she felt, and Honrita was able to confirm that in her mind. There was something else, something Honrita didn't understand, but she fully *meant* to understand.

Once Kadri stood completely unclothed, Arbon removed his own clothing. During his disrobing Arbon had urged

Kadri down onto the bed, so when he was completely bare he moved quickly to the bed and knelt across the heavy woman. The sight of his inflamed manhood had caused Honrita to gasp softly, but taking her gaze away from the pair seemed totally beyond her. There was a terribly compelling quality to what was being done . . .

Kadri had been whimpering where she lay on her back on the bed, and the sounds strengthened when Arbon finally came to her. The man spent a brief moment kissing Kadri again, but the frenzy in his mind made it impossible for him to hold off for any significant amount of time. He ended the kiss, put himself between Kadri's legs, and then positioned his manhood directly in a line with Kadri's womanhood.

Honrita had no true idea of what the procedure entailed, but when Arbon thrust himself inside Kadri so hard that the Earth magic user cried out, Honrita was appalled. There had been actual pain for Kadri, and now Kadri made sounds of distress under the kiss Arbon had begun as his hips moved hard and fast. Arbon's mind was lost to physical delight, but Kadri was extremely distraught over what was being done to her.

Honrita found herself abruptly on her feet and on her way out of the bedchamber. The emotions in the room were far too intense for her to cope with, most especially since her own emotions were nothing but a jangled jumble. Kadri had *wanted* to lie with men, but when the dream became a reality Kadri had wanted it to stop. If Honrita hadn't had the woman under such tight control, Kadri would probably have used her Earth magic to cause harm to Arbon . . .

It took a moment for Honrita to realize that she was back in the sitting room. Stelk and Seeli continued to sit where she'd left them, aware of nothing but Honrita's command that they wait. Honrita returned to her own chair and fought to calm herself, an effort more easily decided on than done. The struggle took a number of minutes, but once it was over Honrita discovered that certain decisions had also been made.

To begin with, there would be no other attempts to

strengthen their Blending. On the few occasions Honrita had thought about physical love, she had pictured it as something wonderful that brought great pleasure to those who indulged. What Kadri had felt had *not* been wonderful, however, even though Kadri had been openly looking forward to the experience. What the same experience would be like for someone—like Seeli—who faced the idea with trepidation was too terrible to be considered.

So there would be no more of that sort of thing to dismay the members of Honrita's Blending. She shifted in her chair as she wondered if she should have interrupted Kadri's suffering, even though the damage had already been done. But Kadri had been very insistent about wanting the experience, so the woman deserved to reap the fruits of her error. From now on, Kadri would know better than to insist on something Honrita was uncertain about.

But at the same time, Honrita knew that Arbon had to be made to believe that he'd lain with all three of the women. Anything less and the man would become even more insufferable, an outcome Honrita refused to consider. No, Arbon had to believe an untruth, but that would hardly be difficult for Honrita to arrange. As he'd already had his way with Kadri, allowing him two more encounters with her while thinking he had different women would see to the matter.

Honrita smiled as she realized that her problem was solved. Today would be used to quiet Arbon's endless objections, and tomorrow they would find and take over the first member of their puppet Blending. After that it would hardly matter *what* Arbon thought. As soon as Honrita was in full control of her puppets, she would look around for a more . . . manageable Fire magic user . . .

Issini Randos looked around at her Blendingmates and wondered if they were as nervous as she felt. Their entity had apparently put *some* sort of "net" around each of them, but they didn't yet know if the net would work the way they wanted it to. Rather than simply assume that they would have no trouble, they were now about to test the matter.

"All right, here we are, walking into the palace," Driff said as the six of them actually walked through the warehouse. "We have no idea that a hostile Blending is waiting to ambush us one at a time, and even if we did we would hardly know which of us would be chosen first. Whatever happens is going to be a complete surprise—"

Driff had been talking to distract them all, and the distraction had worked. Suddenly it was no longer Issini but the entity who stood—hovered—in the warehouse, facing another entity that had obviously touched one of its flesh forms.

*This entity is well aware of your presence,* the entity containing Issini and the others said to the other. *Your flesh forms seem well hidden, therefore must this entity search for them. There is a bit of data . . . Ah, yes, now the memory returns. The trail of dust . . .*

The entity almost smiled to itself at the use of the phrase "trail of dust." Actual dust had very little to do with the matter, nothing beyond a faint similarity to the true state of affairs. All Blending entities were . . . tied to their flesh forms, in a manner of speaking, the faint connection perceived as a line composed of what resembled dust motes. The connection was so visually faint that it needed to be consciously considered in order to be found.

Therefore the entity consciously searched for the trail, finding it after no more than a moment's questing. It took only another moment before the second entity's flesh forms were discovered sitting behind a distant stack of crates, and then the entity was gone and Issini was back.

"That wasn't hard at all," Edmin said with surprise in his voice. "First how quickly we Blended, and then how fast we found the other Blending's bodies. No one ever mentioned how easily that could be done."

"The lack of comments could be because no one ever tried this before," Kail pointed out, his own voice sounding pleased in the dimness of the warehouse. "And did anyone else notice that we had no trouble seeing in all this gloom?"

"Why should we have had trouble?" Driff asked, also sounding pleased. "Our entity doesn't use eyesight, after all.

And now that we know our plan will work, we have to get ready to go to the palace as soon as our . . . sentries send the word."

"A distant watch with Blending entities," Idresia said, and Issini could see her shake her head. "They'll be able to see any other entities close to the palace, and as soon as they spot one we'll be sent for. How will we know that it's the enemy they'll find, and why can't *they* take over the entity as soon as it shows itself?"

"Har, that's an easy question to answer," Issini said to Idresia. "Those are Middle Blendings doing the watching, not Highs. If they turn out not to have enough strength to best the enemy entity, the enemy will be warned instead of caught. And even besides that, what will we charge them with? Hovering near the palace isn't anything like a crime."

"Okay, so Arbon and I *will* finally find out which of us is stronger," Idresia conceded with a sigh. "It's just that he's a decent person, and became something of a friend. I really hate the idea of hurting a friend."

"But you're not going to be hurting him, you'll be helping him," Edmin pointed out as he moved to her side to put an arm around her shoulders. "We agreed that he can't be doing this voluntarily, so in effect he's been enslaved. If *you* were in his place, wouldn't you want to be freed even if it took pain to free you?"

"Yes, I would, so you're absolutely right," Idresia agreed, now sounding startled. "I hadn't looked at the problem like that, but now I can see it. Thanks for helping out, Edmin."

"My pleasure," Edmin returned, patting her shoulder before reclaiming his arm. At one time Issini would have felt a pang of jealousy seeing Edmin being so attentive to another woman, especially since she knew just how attractive Edmin found Idresia. But ever since they'd become a Blending, Issini knew for a fact that Edmin found *her* just as attractive as he found Idresia—and Asri. And Issini had to admit that her feelings for Edmin had spread to include Driff and Kail. It was amazing what Blending was able to do to ordinary emotions . . .

"Let's thank the other Blending and then go back to the kitchen and have a meal," Driff suggested as he also put a gentle hand to Idresia's arm. "We don't know when we'll be called, so we ought to be ready."

That *was* the best thing they could do, so they walked to where the members of the other Blending stood brushing the dust and dirt from their clothing. Now that it was too late, Issini realized they should have offered the other Blending members chairs or at least blankets to sit on. But the Blending members didn't seem to mind that they'd gotten dirty while helping out. They knew that *they* would not be the ones who had to face the enemy Blending, and their relief over that fact outweighed a bit of discomfort.

They took the other Blending members to the kitchen with them for drinks, and afterward Issini helped to make a meal for just their six. The other Blending members had gone home for their own meal, and had had no need of being reminded to stay away from the palace. The word had been passed to every Blending, Middle and Low, that was in the city: Stay away from the palace until word comes that it's all right to go back.

The rest of the day dragged on, but nothing in the way of word came from the Blendings watching the palace. After dinner they started a six-handed card game, but their usual enjoyment of the game was obviously missing. After only a couple of hours it became clear that no one had any interest in continuing, so they separated to go to bed.

Oddly enough, they broke up into their original pairs that night. No one had said a thing, but Edmin came over to Issini and smilingly offered her his hand. She took the hand and also smiled and stood, while Asri did the same with Kail. Then they all went to the sleeping quarters that had been arranged in the warehouse for them. The house that Driff had originally found for himself and Idresia would have been too small for the six of them, and they'd been looking around for something larger when the problem with the enemy came up.

Issini enjoyed Edmin's lovemaking as much as she always did, but afterward sleep wasn't as easy to find as it normally was. Edmin tossed and turned for a time as well, but eventually Issini drifted off.

The next morning Issini and Edmin walked into the kitchen to find that breakfast was already prepared. That was something of a surprise, and Idresia smiled wryly at them.

"I woke up early and couldn't get back to sleep, so I came out here and made breakfast," she explained. "For a little while I was afraid that the food would get cold, but not anymore."

Idresia's nod caused Issini to turn, and there stood Kail and Asri in the doorway. With Driff already seated at the table, that meant they were all up early.

Breakfast was a fairly quiet affair, with everyone else as sunk in private thoughts as Issini was in her own. They lingered over second and third cups of tea while Issini wondered what they would do to occupy themselves during the long hours of the morning, and suddenly Driff sat up straight.

"Yes, I do understand, and I thank you," Driff said to the empty air. For an instant it was Issini who didn't understand, but then her heart began to race.

"That's right," Driff said as he looked around at the rest of them. "One of the Blendings on guard just told me that there's an entity hovering near the palace. It looks like it's time we got moving."

"Yes, it's them," Asri confirmed, her gaze unfocused. "It's not a false alarm."

They were all on their feet instantly, and Issini couldn't keep from smiling her relief. No matter what happened during the confrontation, at least the *waiting* was over.

# TWENTY-FIVE

Vallant finished the meal that Rion had prepared, and sat back to digest it in comfort. The others were also finished eating, and Lorand gazed at Rion thoughtfully.

"You know, an interesting thought just came to me," Lorand said slowly. "Since we're still Blended, I wonder if Rion's ability to cook is now also *our* ability."

"I'd rather answer that question than test the theory that it might be true," Tamrissa said with a laugh. "Rion's ability with cooking is learned, and not part of his other, inborn, talent with Air magic. On top of that, our entity never tried to cook. In other words, if you're going to try your own hand at making a meal, I think I have plans to dine elsewhere."

"I'm not curious enough to want to poison myself," Lorand said with his own laugh. "That means I'll definitely show up for meals, but I'll be staying out of the way until the food is ready. But now that we're fortified, what's the next thing we can try?"

"I've been considering that point myself, and I have a suggestion," Rion said when Vallant joined the others in shrugging to show a complete lack of ideas. "My suggestion revolves around the fact that we were able to reach those people we know in Liandia."

"And I had no trouble speaking to their minds," Tamrissa said with a nod. "Did you want to try talking to or contacting someone else in the same way?"

"Actually, my suggestion is a bit more involved than that,"

Rion answered, his brow creased in a way that seemed to show he wasn't quite sure about his idea. "We found out that we couldn't rise up off the floor and float the way our entity did, simply because we have solid bodies and our entity didn't. What we *haven't* investigated, however, is the ability our entity had to . . . flash to a point it was familiar with. There was no floating involved in that, merely the desire to be somewhere else."

"Are you suggesting we might be able to go places without actually traveling to those places?" Tamrissa demanded, saying the same thing most of the rest of them did, only using different words. Vallant was no longer leaning back, and neither was anyone else in the circle. "I really don't think something like that will work."

"Are you offerin' an opinion, or are you accessin' that information we talked about?" Vallant asked at once. "Since I've had enough of travelin' by horseback for a good long while, I'm hopin' what you said was just an opinion."

"Truthfully, it was," Tamrissa said with her brows high. "Now I'm trying to find out if there's anything to suggest we can't try Rion's idea, but so far there doesn't seem to be anything. The last time I knew almost at once that floating wasn't possible."

"Let's give it another minute or two," Jovvi said, her expression wry. "I'd hate to find out we were wrong to try when we disappear here and end up not appearing anywhere else."

"I second that," Naran said while sending Rion an apologetic glance. "I'm sorry, love, but I'm still not as brave as you and Tamrissa and Vallant."

"But neither you nor Jovvi said we shouldn't try it at all, and I find myself agreeing," Lorand pointed out to Naran. "We three still seem to be the calming influence in our group, but at the same time we've picked up some of the boldness from our other members. I wonder if they've also picked up some of our caution."

"I think we have," Vallant said slowly while Tamrissa and Rion obviously paused to consider the question. "I'm all for tryin' the experiment, but not for rushin' into it. We *should* try, but carefully."

"Yes, that's the way I see it, too," Tamrissa said while Rion nodded his own agreement. "I like the idea of trying, but not of rushing into the attempt. So just *how* are we going to try this?"

"Cautiously," Rion answered with a grin for Naran, and then he grew serious again. "I think we need to look for a good place to go first, and once we know we won't appear inside a tree, or shrub, or chair—or a person—we try to go there."

"Now, that's a good idea," Tamrissa said just as Vallant thought the same thing. "First we look, and then we try to go. And I think I know *where* we can go. We all know Antrie Lorimon's garden, and in fact we just listened to a conversation there. The place is large enough and private enough that we shouldn't have any trouble if we succeed in getting there."

"I have one suggestion," Naran said, clearly studying the probabilities as she usually did. "Let's deliberately picture ourselves standing side by side before we go. If we just think about going, we might possibly end up all in the same place."

"Yes, that possibility is much too strong," Lorand said, showing the same distraction that Naran did. "It seems to be a danger we might have overlooked in our eagerness to experiment."

"Which means we all have to check the probabilities before we do anything new," Jovvi said, looking around at each of them. "Simply living life has pitfalls that need to be anticipated, and what we're doing now is a good deal more complicated than simply living."

"It would be safer if we had teachers, but it looks like we'll be the ones who do the teaching," Tamrissa said with a shake of her head. "Assuming we survive, that is. All right, are we ready to try this? I'm going to picture us in the same circle instead of standing side by side, which ought to make things easier. Let's all take a look first, and then we'll move our circle to a garden in Liandia."

Vallant nodded, at the same time willing his vision to see the garden they'd looked at a short time ago. No more than an instant later the picture of that garden was before him, only this time there were no more than two people sitting in chairs. Antrie Lorimon and Frode Mismin had apparently been left alone by their three former guests, and the two were holding hands and gazing at each other.

"I hate to interrupt at such a tender moment, but they can get back to holding hands later," Tamrissa said with a chuckle in her voice. "Is everyone ready? All right, let's move the circle."

Vallant clearly remembered how their entity had flashed to a place from where it was originally, so now he . . . took the same mental attitude, so to speak. The attitude was composed of a knowledge of where he was and an equal knowledge of where he wanted to go, combined with the *desire* to be in that other place. Reality seemed to blink, and then he sat in the same place in their circle that he'd been in, but only now he sat on grass instead of a sleeping pad.

"It worked," Rion said as he looked around with a stunned expression, and then his voice rose with gladness and excitement. "It really worked, and we're here!"

Vallant felt the same elation, but couldn't help flinching at the way Antrie Lorimon stood and screamed. Frode Mismin was also on his feet and just as disturbed, but Jovvi rose and turned to them.

"It's all right, don't be frightened," Jovvi said as Antrie seemed to be drawing breath for more screaming. "We've had something very wonderful happen to us, and we're experimenting with different aspects of that something."

"How can . . . *this* be considered even remotely human?" Antrie demanded, obviously calmed to a great extent but not really *calm*. "You six just appeared out of thin air!"

"It *has* to be human because humans are doing it," Tamrissa pointed out with clear amusement. "It seems to be a natural step in the development of a Blending, but you and your countrymen won't have to worry about it for a while, we believe. Apparently you have to be a *full* Blending before these new things start to happen."

"What do you mean, a *full* Blending?" Mismin asked at once, his own mind a good deal quieter than Antrie's. "I can see that there are six of you, just as there were when you first got here, but we all assumed . . . I think you know what we assumed."

"Yes, we do know, and we deliberately refrained from explaining," Naran said, her smile showing her own amusement which then disappeared. "But I'm a full member of this Blending, and you do need to know in what way."

Vallant watched Antrie Lorimon and Frode Mismin as Naran explained about Sight magic, and by the time the explanation was done the two Gracelians looked appalled. Vallant and the others were all on their feet by that time, and Antrie put a shaking hand to a pale forehead.

"I *knew* that policy was wrong, but I made no effort to change it," she muttered, turning to Mismin when the man's arm went around her shoulders. "It would have been politically inconvenient to speak in opposition, so I just kept silent. We were assured we were 'doing the right thing' by putting down those children 'without talent,' and now we get to pay a very high price for our lack of humanity."

"You're saying it wrong again," Tamrissa commented, and Vallant knew that his woman felt nothing in the way of compassion. "What you did was done by humans, so there wasn't a lack of humanity. Humans aren't perfect, Antrie, and trying to make it seem as if we should be is downright foolish. What you want to do is combine compassion with a bit of common sense, which isn't all that common. There will always be people around who want to do things for the 'good' of others, and they're the ones you have to watch out for. They're interested in control, not in good of any sort."

"You're absolutely right," Mismin conceded with a wry smile for Tamrissa. "Antrie wasn't the only one who disliked the policy of 'putting down' those without any obvious talent, but the rest of us kept just as quiet. From now on things will change, hopefully for the better."

"If it doesn't, you're the ones who will suffer," Tamrissa responded with a shrug. "Which is the way it should be, since we're supposed to learn from our mistakes. If the lesson is hard enough you learn to change your ways, and if you don't then you deserve to continue to suffer. That might sound harsh, but it's better than having someone else tell you the 'right' way to do things."

"Which *you* weren't doing, no matter what I said while we traveled together," Antrie put in with a weak smile. "You were simply showing us the right way of doing things and urging us to do the same. You left the choice of agreeing to us, and when we chose to continue with our old ways the suffering we experienced was of our own doing. I like to think I'm beyond that now."

"For your sake, I hope you are," Rion said, and Vallant knew that his brother agreed completely with Tamrissa—and himself as well. "But now I think we ought to be getting back. You can mention this visit or not, just as you see fit, but keep in mind how close you all came to losing your lives because of limitations and secrets."

Antrie looked disturbed, but Vallant paid very little attention to her or Mismin. He first looked into the house in the village they'd come from, and when it proved to still be empty he moved himself there in the same position in relation to his Blendingmates. In the blink of an eye he was standing on his sleeping pad instead of sitting, and an instant later his Blendingmates were also back.

"So . . . how much do you think we can charge Arinna and Holter and their Blendingmates for *this* piece of news?" Tamrissa asked, and then she laughed along with everyone else. Vallant's laughter contained his continuing elation, but one small corner of his mind wondered just how far these new revelations would take them all. Not to mention in what direction . . .

\* \* \*

Honrita finished her breakfast feeling extremely satisfied. Her little flock was behaving just the way they were supposed to, and even Arbon Vand was too distracted to give her trouble. Arbon believed that they'd all bonded, and so did the others. Kadri wasn't behaving as . . . outgoing as she usually did, and that was another benefit to the situation—at least in Honrita's opinion.

"Is today really going to be the day?" Stelk asked suddenly, holding his teacup in both hands just at chest level. "I've been thinking about it since I awoke this morning, because you said that today we'll be putting the plan into action."

"Yes, my dear, today is definitely the day," Honrita answered, smiling to show her increasing pleasure. "If things go right, and there's really no reason they shouldn't, by tonight *we'll* be in charge of the empire."

"There are any number of reasons why things might not go right," Arbon said, his unsmiling face staring directly at *her* rather than at Stelk. "Just because you refuse to see all those reasons doesn't mean they aren't there."

"Dear, dear, Arbon," Honrita said with a small laugh. "Every time you voice another protest, you're really telling me that you believe the plan *will* work. I can see you disagree with that truth, so why don't you tell me: What *are* all these reasons that you can see which I can't?"

"What if our entity isn't as strong as the High talent we pick out?" Arbon said after a brief hesitation, as though he meant to say something else and then changed his mind. "We *are* no more than Middles, after all, so it's possible that a High talent will prove stronger. What do you plan to do if *that* happens?"

"I don't plan to do anything, because it won't happen," Honrita explained slowly and patiently, enjoying herself quite a lot. "Our entity will find it easy to take over anyone we want it to, and once we have the first High we'll have no trouble getting all the others. Now, I know it's rather early, but let's dress and get over to the palace anyway. The sooner we're in position, the more quickly we'll be able to begin."

The other three rose at once in obedience, but Arbon

clearly would have stayed in his chair if he'd been given the choice. Honrita got to her own feet, annoyance coloring the pleasure she'd felt only a few moments ago. Arbon really was more trouble than she felt willing to put up with, but it would only be for a short time longer. As soon as that High Blending was tightly in her grip, Honrita promised herself that she would look around for another Fire magic user before she did anything else.

It didn't take long for any of them to dress, but Arbon was still the last one down to the sitting room. Honrita ignored the miserable man's tardiness and simply led the way out of the house, already knowing that the coach she'd arranged for now waited in the drive. The coach driver was as firmly under her control as her Blendingmates, and would take her wherever she wanted to go without knowing he was doing it. Honrita directed Arbon to join the driver on the coach box, and then she herself entered the coach with the rest of her Blending.

The day was a bit on the cool side and not as pretty as Honrita would have liked, but that was an unimportant detail. She watched out the window she sat beside as the coach moved toward the palace, excitement flaring up inside her. They were really on their way to their destiny now, the destiny that was *hers* rather than belonging to that fool Ayl. His madness had made him think he was certain to be great, but he'd had no true talent of his own. Honrita did have talent, and that was what made all the difference.

Honrita's thoughts drifted to what life would be like once she was living in the palace, and the ride disappeared behind those most pleasant of thoughts. Before she knew it the coach was slowing, and then it began to come to a stop in the place she'd picked out. The street was very close to the palace, but a building blocked them from the sight of any guardsmen. Their entity, however, would have no trouble seeing everything it needed to.

Once the coach had come to a full stop, Arbon climbed down from the box and entered the coach itself. There was room for him only on the floor between the two seats, but that position was somehow fitting. Honrita's most ardent opponent now sat at her feet, just as the rest of the empire would soon do.

Honrita set their coach driver to watching for the approach of anyone who might interfere, and then she initiated the Blending. In an instant it was the Blending entity who looked about, and then floated toward the large dwelling that was to be the object of its scrutiny. It knew that it must search out any approaching or departing High talents, and therefore set to work.

A fair number of flesh forms either approached or departed from the large dwelling, yet none of them were the High talents the entity was to have located. An unnoticed amount of time passed, and then the entity felt the strain in its own flesh forms. As newborn as the entity was, it still knew it could not remain aware for much longer—and then it was Honrita back again.

"We're no longer Blended," Stelk protested, sounding the next thing to whiny. "Why are we individuals again?"

"Maintaining the Blending any longer would have drained me completely," Honrita said, deciding to quiet the man without using her talent. "We'll rest for a short while, and then we'll Blend again. But I don't understand why there weren't any High talents going in or coming out. There were Middles and some Lows, but no Highs."

"Maybe the Highs all like to sleep late," Arbon drawled from where he sat on the coach floor, an expression on his face that was much too pleased. "I'll admit that's one possibility I didn't think of."

"Since they're in charge, they can sleep as late as they like with no one to tell them differently," Honrita said, grasping at the idea that Arbon had put forward only jokingly. "Yes, you've finally proven of use in some way, Arbon. The Highs aren't here yet because they're allowed to sleep late. By tomorrow it will be *us* who sleeps late, as late as we like."

Arbon shook his head before looking away from her, but Honrita didn't care what the man thought. The plan was a *good* one, a good one, and it *wasn't* going to fail!

It took a short time for Honrita to regain control of her

confidence. She had lived too many years in the shadow of failure in all things, and a ghost from those days still haunted her on occasion. But she'd had help in putting the attitudes of failure behind her, and now she knew that success had to be expected in order to be achieved. She *would* make the plan work, and very soon.

Once she felt rested, Honrita shifted to a more comfortable position on the coach seat and then initiated the Blending again. This time when the entity formed, it knew it must seek out *any* flesh form in seeming authority. As the High talents refused to come within reach of the entity's perceptions, the entity had no choice but to be guided to the location of the High talents.

A greater number of flesh forms now approached and left the large dwelling. None of them, however, proved to be High talents, therefore the entity began to look for one who might become a useful guide. A short time passed, and then six individuals appeared who were given more deference by those flesh forms around them than any previous flesh forms had been given. One of these Middle talents, then, would be the guide the entity required.

The entity floated quickly to the vicinity of the large dwelling where the six flesh forms were in the process of entering. Each of the six seemed odd in some way the entity wasn't able to define, yet its objective remained. It must take control of one of the six, and then instruct the flesh form to guide the entity to the High talents. The entity reached out toward the closest of the six, and then—

And then another, larger, entity suddenly confronted it. The new entity was barely older than the probing entity, yet it seemed much more complete in some way.

—*Your presence and efforts here are contrary to the well-being of the majority,*—the new entity informed the probing entity.—*The touching of the unsuspecting is not to be allowed, therefore are you to withdraw to your own flesh forms and retire from the scene.*—

The entity had been inspecting the newcomer as it spoke, surprised and pleased to discover that the newcomer seemed less than the probing entity despite the newcomer's air of superiority. The newcomer's Spirit magic segment was so faint that the lack was actually visible, giving the newcomer an unbalanced appearance. The entity had experienced faint trepidation at the sudden appearance of the newcomer, yet now full confidence returned.

—*Were you this entity's superior, it might well be necessary to retire,*—the entity informed the newcomer.—*You, however, are clearly inferior to this entity, therefore are you the one who must retire. Should you refuse, there will be battle between us that you have no hope of winning.*—

—*This entity has no wish to cause harm, yet is this entity willing to do so should it be necessary,*—the newcomer replied.—*You are small and weak and incomplete, and therefore is it you who has no chance at victory. Retire now, and all may be seen to without pain.*—

—*My purpose must be attained,*—the entity responded, and then it struck at the foolish newcomer. An entity as weak and unbalanced as the newcomer should have gone down immediately in the face of the unexpected attack, and yet the newcomer did not. Not all of the strength the entity had wished to use had been present in the attack, a matter the entity had no true understanding of. That, however, was the least of its lack of understanding.

Even with the lessened strength in the attack, the newcomer should have been staggered if not driven back. Instead, the newcomer held its place with what seemed like very little effort, and then an answering attack struck the entity. Its defenses should have been adequate, yet just as its attack had been less than was intended, so was the defense now erected. The entity staggered before it was forced back, and then—

And then it was Honrita, screaming in pain just as almost all of the others were doing. Arbon simply moaned where he lay, but his satisfaction was so thick that Honrita was able to feel it without the least effort.

"You traitor!" Honrita shrieked, kicking Arbon with all the meager physical strength left to her. "I don't know how

you betrayed me, but you won't get away with it! You're going to die *now,* and next time we'll have a *decent* Fire magic
user! Kadri! Kill this monster!"

The satisfaction in Arbon faded when Kadri looked at
him, the emotion coming to Honrita instead. She would
watch Arbon die in great pain, and once they rid themselves
of his body they would return to their house. After they'd
rested they would find another Fire magic user, and then—

"Honrita, I can't reach him!" Kadri suddenly blurted,
heavy distress in her voice and mind. "I'm trying hard, I really am, but I just can't reach him!"

—*None of you will find it possible to use your ability,*—a
voice said in Honrita's head, frightening her so badly that
her blood turned to ice.—*Your mind-sick efforts are now at
an end, and will not be resumed again.*—

Honrita screamed aloud at what she'd been told, refusing
to believe that the perfect plan had not been allowed to
work. She *would* try again, as soon as she got some rest, but
then there were uncounted numbers of guardsmen around
the coach and opening the doors, and hands grabbed her and
she screamed and screamed and screamed—

# TWENTY-SIX

"I think we all owe Edmin a large vote of thanks," Driff said into the insanity of gladness that he and his Blending-mates shared in the palace meeting room. "If he hadn't been using his 'I'm so weak' trick, that other entity might not have attacked us. If it hadn't, we would have had nothing to charge those people with beyond 'touching' someone. Proving they were touching with ill intent would have been almost impossible."

"I think that entity knew how unfinished and badly balanced it was, but wasn't being allowed to acknowledge its lacks," Edmin said with a smile when the others really did thank him. "The woman Spirit magic user was so twisted that she actually dominated the Blending to the point that their entity shared her madness-induced blindness. And the guardsmen are bringing them all in here right now . . ."

Driff turned toward the door just as the others did, seeing it open to allow the guardsmen to usher in the five people that had been found in the coach. Three of the five were babbling or shouting in utter confusion, which was perfectly understandable. Before they'd dissolved their Blending, Driff and his Blendingmates had freed the people Honrita Grohl had had under her control.

"Arbon!" Idresia exclaimed as she moved toward a man who looked tired but delighted. "You wonderful, talented man! How did you manage to hold back during that attack and the defense afterward when you were under complete control?"

"Idresia, it's good to see you again," the man called Arbon responded with a warm smile. "And to answer your question, I'm not completely sure how I managed the trick. I only know that I was so totally opposed to being a part of that woman's insane plan that she wasn't able to control my inner mind. I suppose I used my stubbornness to fight her, that same stubbornness that most people think so little of."

"The stubbornness we were both yelled at for showing," Idresia agreed with a laugh as she touched the man's arm. "Once you're back to your teaching job, you're going to have to add that trick to what you teach other Fire magic users. We'll all do what we can to keep Spirit magic users from betraying their talent the way this one did, but having Fire magic users able to resist anyone who gets around our safeguards will help enormously."

"It certainly will," Driff said with his own smile as he joined the small group. "Since attack and defense is in the Fire magic user's province, any future attempted coup should be stopped before it starts. But let's get those other people calmed and out of here. They need to go home to the people worrying about them, and then we'll have time for a visit."

Idresia and Arbon nodded, so Driff turned away toward the other three victims of madness. The heavy woman and other man now stood quietly, which showed that Edmin had already done his part. Edmin himself stood and talked to the thin woman, and despite an odd expression on her face she nodded her head slowly.

"Well, now that you're no longer involved in someone else's plots, you're free to leave," Driff said to the two people who stood looking at him. "But first I need to ask you a question. Holdis Ayl wasn't in the coach with you, and we found no trace of him in the area where the coach had stopped. Can you tell me where the man went?"

"We haven't seen that horrible man in days," the heavy woman responded, a faint disturbance behind her haughty words. "The Grohl woman threw him out, and then made sure he couldn't follow us to the new house. We don't know where Ayl is and I, for one, don't *want* to know. May I go home now?"

"Some of the guardsmen will escort you back to where you belong," Driff said, gesturing toward the door. "You're free to leave any time you wish."

The heavy woman nodded once and then headed for the door, and after a brief hesitation the man followed her. He seemed vaguely disturbed about something, and Driff made a mental note to have someone with Spirit magic visit the victims in a day or two. They might have problems they would find it difficult to get over, and there was also the reason they were chosen by Ayl in the first place. Lack of stability might be one of the things Ayl had looked for in addition to strength of talent . . .

"Thank you," Driff heard the thin woman say, and then she was also heading for the door. Her words had been addressed to Edmin, who stood watching her leave with a heavy sense of satisfaction.

"What was that all about?" Driff asked Edmin once the woman was gone. "What was she thanking you for?"

"Well, I asked her if she was content to simply go back to the life she left," Edmin replied, showing an odd smile. "I asked in the first place because I had the impression she wasn't, and that turned out to be true. Her father uses her and the rest of his family as slaves to his whims, but she didn't know how to free herself. I helped her out with that, and now she'll be able to leave home and live on her own. I also promised to see what we could do to free her sisters."

"I think we're going to have to interview everyone in this city to find all the petty tyrants and bullies and advantage-takers," Driff said with a sigh. "The first step will be for those of us who are obviously stable to check on the members of all Blendings, and then we can use the Blending entities to do the interviews. Even the entities of Low Blendings ought to be able to accomplish the interviews, so hopefully the project won't take forever."

"But it's a very necessary step," Issini said as she came

over to join Driff and Edmin. "People with serious personal problems have no business being in charge of children, even if the children are their own. We don't need any more twisted individuals that have to be coped with, and we'll need to talk to the Seated Blending as soon as they get back—and it's safe for them to be here because we've solved the problem holding the Highs."

"Speaking of twisted individuals, what are we going to do with the one we have at the moment?" Driff said, turning to study Honrita Grohl where she stood with her hands clasped and a resolute expression on her face. "I don't need Spirit magic to know that she still believes she has a chance to make her plans work."

"Yes, you're right," Edmin confirmed with his own sigh. "She's completely determined to accomplish what she set out to do, and I have no idea how to change her mind. I think that I really must enroll in one of those classes at the first opportunity. I *should* be able to do something for the woman, but I don't know where to begin."

Driff parted his lips to answer, but a sudden flurry of shouts out in the hall distracted him and the others. Whatever was causing the noise sounded serious, and Driff headed for the door with the sinking feeling that even more trouble had found them . . .

We discovered that mind-traveling was really rather tiring, so after telling Arinna and Pagin Holter that we'd just visited Liandia we went back to our house to rest. We were chuckling over the reaction we'd gotten from Arinna and Pagin, a kind of openmouthed shock and awe that quickly changed to the realization that they would soon be able to do the same thing. They'd run off screaming for their Blending-mates, leaving the freeing of the invader slaves to the rest of the Blending members.

"Holter's Blendingmates aren't the only ones babbling about what's been happening to us," Lorand observed after we were all sitting down with cups of tea. "Apparently the word's been spreading like a fire deliberately started by

Tamrissa, and all of our people are jumping up and down like children on Feast days."

"But I noticed that the Gracelian Blendings aren't as down-in-the-mouth as I would have expected," Jovvi observed with a thoughtful look. "Considering the fact that it will be a while before they can do what we have, I wonder why that is."

"I would guess that they're not despondent because some of the members of my link groups spoke to them," Naran put in with a smile. "My link group people have apparently Seen the very strong possibility that some of *our* people with Sight magic will be visiting here in the near future. Making the innocent people in this country wait years before they can be complete Blendings would be in no one's best interest."

"That's very true, and I'm relieved to hear about it," Jovvi said with one of her beautiful smiles. "If the Gracelians had to wait years, many of them would be nursing more grudges against *us* than against their own people for 'putting down the useless.' And if they weren't consumed by a reasonless urge to 'get even,' their envy would probably be at least as bad if not worse."

"Which means we may actually avoid a war with this country," I put in, enjoying the idea. "If it ever comes to war we'll have to help out even if we're not the Seated Blending, and if I never come back to this place I won't miss it for a minute. What I want more than anything right now is to go home."

"Not without me," Vallant said with a smile, beating the others to similar comments by only an instant. "But we'll be goin' home really soon now, so we can start lookin' forward to bein' there."

"I think I'll first start looking forward to making dinner," Rion said as he rose to his feet with his teacup still in his hand. "I've *been* looking forward to going to bed, but since we have to eat first we might as well do it in as tasty a way as possible."

"If you need any help, just let us know," Lorand said to

Rion's retreating back without moving from where he lounged on his sleeping pad. "If not, you'll find us right here when the food is ready."

I leaned back myself then, finding that I was too tired even to think about what our next experiment ought to be. There was so much it might be possible to do, but before we could do any of it we'd first have to think about it all in detail. If we missed something, there was a good chance we'd never stumble across the missing item by accident . . .

No one seemed very interested in conversation, and I nearly dozed off before Rion turned to announce that dinner was ready. Considering the fact that he'd cooked the meal in the room's fireplace, the formal announcement of dinner was almost amusing. I thought about laughing, then decided that I was too tired to make the effort.

The meal was only a quick stew with some bread, but it filled the hole inside me and increased my sleepiness. Vallant and Lorand volunteered to clean up after the meal, which made Jovvi, Naran, and me love them even more. I saw Jovvi take off her boots and settle down alone just as I was doing, Naran snuggling up to Rion as she closed her eyes, and then . . . sleep . . .

There are times when you know that you've slept longer than just a few hours, and when I woke up I knew it was one of those times. I felt much too well rested for an ordinary night's sleep, but I also felt lazy. I didn't want to sleep anymore, but enjoying the comfort of the bed was something else again. It really was *so* comfortable—

"Bed?" I suddenly said out loud, my eyes opening instantly with the word. "How can I be in a bed? And why is it so dim in here when there aren't any curtains on the windows?"

That was when I took a closer look at my surroundings, and for a moment I was certain I had to be in the midst of a dream. The dim room *did* have curtains as well as drapes on its windows, and it was very familiar for an excellent reason. Somehow I was back in my own house, in bed in my own bedchamber.

"But that can't be," I said in a very reasonable voice as I

sat up to look around even more. "I'm in Gracely right now, and I only *want* to be home. Flashing to Liandia is one thing; going all the way back to Gan Garee just isn't possible."

I agreed completely with that summation, but my surroundings refused to cooperate. They kept insisting that I *was* back in my house, and even standing up and walking to the door didn't change matters. I opened the door, peeked out into a dim sitting room, then closed the door again to lean on it with one arm and my forehead. I'd stubbed my toe on the way to the door, and the faint throbbing in my foot was as disturbing as the solidity of the door I leaned on.

"So what do I do now?" I asked the air with a sigh as I straightened again. "I suppose I have to go back to that little house where the others are, and soon enough to keep them from getting frantic. But it would be really nice if I could bathe and change into clean clothes first. That would make *me* feel better, and might even convince them all that I wasn't simply imagining things."

I really didn't like the idea that I'd transported myself in my sleep, but that was a worry best left for another time. The first thing to do was get a clean outfit to wear, and then heat the water in the bathing house. I walked to the wardrobe and opened one door, then opened the other even as I remembered: All my clothes had been moved to the palace, and not even an old, worn outfit was left.

"Rot," I muttered, knowing I had a choice to make. Either I went back just as I was, or I took a quick trip to the palace to do my bathing and changing. I really didn't want to go back as I was, not when there was an opportunity for a real bath so close to hand. That meant I had no real choice at all, but at least there was no need to waste a lot of time. I sent my new vision into my wing of the palace, found it empty, then moved myself there.

Moving from place to place so easily was still a bit startling, but it was even more satisfying. I'd put myself in my bedchamber, so it took only a minute or two to get out clean clothes, which I then carried to the bathing room. The water in the bath was both clean and hot, and the hardest part of the bath was keeping it from lasting for hours.

But I did let myself soak for a short time, and while I did an odd thought came. Wilant Gorl and his Blendingmates were sitting in for us, so they should have been occupying the various wings. We'd all agreed that if they had to do the work, the least they were entitled to was a few of the pleasures. Having servants around to do things for you was more than nice, but I hadn't seen any sign of the servants who should have been in the wing. And my bedchamber had looked as though no one had used it for quite some time . . .

"All of which means I really do need to take a quick look around before I go back," I murmured as I finished dressing. "If there's a problem, it might not be able to wait for us to get back here in the ordinary way."

That decision carried me out of the bathing room and into the corridor that led out of the wing and into the public part of the palace. There was no sign of a servant until I reached that public area, and then I was stared at by a man whose mouth was hanging open.

*Surprise, surprise,* I thought as I walked toward the gaping servant. *Now, how am I going to explain where I came from? . . .*

Deslen Voyt felt as if he were strutting even when standing still. He'd finished his training class and then expected to be put out in the streets as a guardsman, but instead had been assigned to the palace. Since everyone seemed to know his origins as one of the renegade's men, the amount of trust in him showed by his placement in the palace was both incredibly encouraging and horribly daunting. No matter what happened, Deslen knew he *had* to prove himself worthy of that trust. Even though it did make him want to strut . . .

"Well, will you look at that," Jeemar, Deslen's training partner, murmured from Deslen's left as he stared to their right. "How did the Seated Blending get back without us knowing about it?"

Deslen looked over to see a pretty woman with reddish hair heading toward the servant who stood not far from Jeemar and him.

"She's one of the Seated Blending?" Deslen asked, feeling a shadow of disappointment. The woman was really attractive, and he wouldn't have minded asking her out to dinner.

"Yes, she's Tamrissa Domon, the Fire magic user," Jeemar confirmed with a shake of his head. "I still don't know how she got into the palace without us knowing about it, but where are the others? She couldn't have come back without the rest of her Blending."

Just as Deslen was about to suggest that the others must be in their individual wings, everything began to happen at once. A tall, thin stranger appeared from somewhere behind the pretty woman and began to walk toward her. The servant scrambled away to the right with a cry of alarm, because the tall man held two knives.

Jeemar must have seen the knives at the same time, and the guardsman didn't hesitate. He ran forward with a shout, actually pointing at the tall man, the pointing most likely an aid to using his talent. Jeemar had Earth magic, Deslen knew, and was a fairly strong Middle talent. The tall man should have gone down at once, but instead he paused to throw one of his knives, and then it was Jeemar who went down with a knife in his chest.

Deslen wasn't the smartest man ever to be born, but it didn't take much intelligence to see that using talent wasn't working on the tall intruder. Deslen had tried using his own Water magic, and the intruder had acted as if nothing at all was being done. That meant force had to be used rather than talent, but there wasn't much time. The intruder had moved his remaining knife to his right hand, raising the knife as he neared the pretty woman. The woman had begun to turn toward the intruder, but if talent didn't work against the man she was as good as dead.

Which meant that Deslen didn't hesitate. The pretty woman was one of the Seated Blending, one of those who had changed everything in Gandistra. That change had given Deslen a chance to make a life he could enjoy and be proud of, and now someone was in the midst of trying to kill one of those who had made his new life possible.

"Not while I still live," Deslen growled even as he moved faster than he ever had in his life. He reached the pretty woman an instant before the intruder, grabbed her by the arms, and spun her around. That put Deslen's back toward the intruder rather than hers, but even as he felt the terrible pain of the knife plunging into him he didn't regret what he'd done. He pushed the woman feebly, to get her as far from the intruder as possible as he whispered, "Run!" and then everything went black—

The first guardsman had screamed when Holdis Ayl's knife hit him, but the second only whispered "Run!" before he collapsed to the floor. Everything had happened incredibly fast, but suddenly I felt rage fill me as it rarely had before.

"I don't know where the others are, but you'll do for my purposes," Ayl said to me, the bloody knife still in his fist. "With you dead your Blending is finished, and that will prove that no one can expect to rule this empire without *my* permission. And I'll certainly get out of here as easily as I got in. Those fool guardsmen gave so much attention to capturing the cretins trying to use their Blending that I was able to walk in here without notice. While everyone stands around screaming over your death, I'll be able to walk out the same way."

"Guess again," I growled as the knife came flashing down toward me. At the end of the swing Ayl stumbled, mostly because his knife no longer had a blade. I'd melted the steel so fast that he hadn't even realized the blade was gone, and then I added the touch I'd learned from Rion. A block of hardened air struck Ayl even as he stumbled, and then he was facedown on the floor and mostly unconscious.

I used Lorand's way of putting the madman into a deep sleep, and then I quickly turned my attention to the guardsman who had tried to give *his* life for mine. I crouched over the man's body and saw that he still lived, but that wouldn't hold true for long if something wasn't done.

"What's going on out here?" a male voice demanded, and then a group of people came hurrying out of a nearby meeting room.

"It's already handled," I answered without looking up, working to heal the guardsman I crouched near. "Go and see if you can do anything for that other guardsman."

"This one is dead," a second male voice reported, sounding as concerned as the first. "You'd better help her with that one, Driff."

"Yes, he's badly hurt," the first man, apparently named Driff, answered as he crouched on the other side of the guardsman. "Let's work together, girl, and we ought to be able to save him."

The healing talent I had from Lorand was doing a fair job of pulling the guardsman back from the brink, but suddenly a different talent joined the one *I* used. It wasn't quite as strong as Lorand's ability, but in an odd way it was even more effective. The guardsman's healing went at a much faster rate even as my inner eye watched, and a few moments later the smallish man crouching opposite me looked up.

"He's out of danger now," the man named Driff said as he studied me. "And with that being the case, how about telling me now what happened and who *you* are."

"Holdis Ayl was a Guild man, so he knew he could shrug off the use of talent against him," I said, gesturing to where Ayl still lay unconscious. "He was too far gone into madness to understand that talent can be used in more than one way, something my Blendingmates and I learned really well. He intended to kill me, but it didn't work out like that."

"Ayl?" the man Driff exclaimed, straightening to stare down at the ex-Guild member. "How did he get into the palace? Edmin, get some servants to send for more guardsmen. And we need to get this wounded man bandaged and into bed."

One of the other five people nodded and hurried back into

the meeting room, and my curiosity refused to be held down any longer.

"All right, now it's time for *you* to answer some questions," I said, putting my fists to my hips after I also straightened. "You seem to be giving the orders here, but Wilant Gorl and his people are supposed to be in charge. Who are you, and what happened to Wilant and the others?"

"You still haven't told me who's asking," the man pointed out, sounding significantly more reasonable than I had. "I'm Driffin Codsent, and my Blendingmates and I are in temporary charge. Would you like to tell me who you are and why Holdis Ayl tried to kill you?"

"I'm Tamrissa Domon, Fire magic," I answered without thinking much about what I said. "Ayl wanted to kill me because he thought that would cripple my Blending, but he was wrong on any number of counts. Now tell me what happened to Wilant and the others."

"Why does your name sound so familiar?" Driffin Codsent muttered instead of answering me. "I know I've heard it before, but—"

"Sir, she's one of the Seated Blending," the servant who had dodged out of Ayl's way put in, his voice still quivering noticeably. "We had no idea that the Excellences were back, otherwise their wings would have been properly attended. We offer our most abject apologies—"

"That's it, of course that's it!" Driffin exclaimed, pointing a finger at me. "We've never met, but the Highs have mentioned your name often enough—The Highs! And *you're* a High! We've got to get you out of here as quickly as possible!"

"What are you babbling about now?" I demanded, moving my arm to keep him from grabbing it. "And you'd better tell me where Wilant and his people are before I ask again in a way you definitely won't like."

"Every High talent in this city is in some sort of trance," Driffin answered, now looking even more harried. "It happened to them all at the same time, and I've been trying to

*Sharon Green*

break them out of it but can't. Since all High talents seem to be in the same danger, we have to get you out of here before whatever got them comes after *you*."

"A trance?" I echoed, feeling my eyes narrow. "And one that left no one but Middles to run things? I think I'd better get my Blendingmates here as soon as possible."

"But how can you take the chance of all of you being here?" Driffin demanded. "If we lose you as well, I don't think any of us will be able to stand it. But how can you be here if the others aren't? And you said you had Fire magic. Ayl has been *made* unconscious, and that guardsman was being healed even before I touched him. How can someone with Fire magic do all that?"

"Those are questions that will take time to answer, and we don't have the time," I told him, quickly making up my mind. "I'm going back to my wing for a couple of minutes, and then we can start to get everything straightened out."

*At least I hope we can get things straightened out,* I qualified silently as I hurried back in the direction I'd come from. It had just come to me that my Blendingmates might not be *able* to join me in the palace. Most of the changes had happened to me first, and if the others weren't yet ready to move themselves as far as I had—

I didn't even want to think about what would happen then . . .

# TWENTY-SEVEN

Vallant felt frantic, and the others weren't doing any better. They'd awakened to find Tamrissa gone, and it hadn't been possible to locate her anywhere in the village or even in Liandia. She could certainly take care of herself, Vallant knew, but that wasn't the issue. Where she could possibly be was the question, and whether or not she'd gone voluntarily.

"She would never just up and walk away without letting us know," Jovvi said for the tenth time, worry fairly radiating from her. "Tamrissa just isn't that uncaring or thoughtless."

"But if someone has taken her against her will, who could that possibly be?" Rion countered, the same worry coloring his words. "Can you imagine how powerful some outside force would have to be to just . . . steal her away without the rest of us noticing?"

"And without her bein' able to do anythin' about it," Vallant agreed, his thoughts now going grim. "But if somethin' did take her, they won't have the same luck with me. If I get my hands on them . . ."

It was clear that Rion agreed with Vallant's unspoken threat, but before anyone could say anything else Lorand appeared in the doorway.

"I found something out, but I don't know how helpful the information will be," Lorand said at once as he entered. "Tamrissa's link group members remember being partially awakened during the night or early this morning. They found themselves linked and having their strength drawn on, and then they weren't linked any longer. Most of them thought they'd been dreaming, so they went back to sleep."

"That does nothing to help me See any more than I already have," Naran complained, her gaze still unfocused. "The probabilities are acting as if nothing has changed, as if Tamrissa is still here with us. I'm sure that means something, but I have no idea what the something is."

"Well, wherever she is, we know she's all right," Jovvi said with a shake of her head as she paced back and forth. "If anything terrible had happened to Tamma, we'd all know about it."

Vallant realized that that was true, but it was only a small consolation. He still had no idea where Tamrissa was, and he couldn't let that state of affairs continue. He was about to ask again if anyone had any idea at all when he felt something odd. It was as if someone were trying to say something to him . . .

"Wait a minute," Vallant said as the others began to make comments or voice opinions. "I think someone is tryin' to contact me, but can't quite reach me. Maybe if I—"

Vallant cut off his words as he reached out toward his link group members. He knew exactly how to link them together to give him more strength, and once he'd done so he thanked whatever agency had given him the idea.

. . . *can you hear me?* came what sounded like Tamrissa, but from a great distance off. *Vallant, please try to hear me. I'm doing this alone, so you've got to do something to hear me.*

*Now I can hear you,* Vallant responded, relief flooding over him. *Tamrissa, where are you? Tell me what happened.*

*I woke up to find myself back in Gan Garee,* came the equally relieved answer. *I meant to come back before the rest of you woke up, but I wanted to get a bath and clean clothes first so I went to the palace. Now I realize that I wouldn't have been able to come back, not without the help of other Highs acting as my link groups. And at the moment there aren't any other Highs available here.*

*Why not?* Vallant asked, worry suddenly returning. *There ought to be more Highs than you need, right there in the city.*

*Ought to be, but aren't,* Tamrissa replied. *Something took all the Highs at once, and they're all in a trance of some sort. There's a Middle Blending handling things right now, but they're very anxious to hand the reins back. Do you think you and the others can follow me here in the same way I used to get here? Preferably without falling asleep first . . .*

*We'll tell the others, and then give it a try,* Vallant promised her, more than aware of how alone she felt. *Don't try to do anything on your own. Wait until the rest of us get there. Where are you now?*

*I'm in my wing of the palace,* came the answer. *Be careful, but come as fast as you can.*

*We will, so be patient,* Vallant said, then turned to the rest of his Blendingmates.

"That was Tamrissa, and she says she woke up in Gan Garee," Vallant told them, then waited only a moment for the exclamations to die down. "She also says that all the High talents in the city have fallen into some kind of trance, so a Middle Blendin' had to take over. She asked us to follow her there, goin' the same way she did. I told her we would try, but first we have to tell the others."

"Let's do that telling now, and then get our link groups together," Lorand said, his expression showing a bit of relief along with a different kind of worry. "If Tamrissa managed the trip we should have no trouble, but even she obviously needed her link groups to get there. I just hope this isn't one of those things that she can do but we aren't yet able to."

"We won't consider failure until and unless it actually happens," Jovvi said briskly as she looked around. "From what I can See, there's nothing to suggest that we won't be able to do exactly as we wish. Naran, do you See anything that I'm missing?"

"No, nothing more or even different," Naran said, and now she no longer studied the distance. "With the help of our link groups, we ought to be able to do just as we please."

"Then let's get to it," Vallant said, a heavy burden now gone from his shoulders. "We don't want her to get bored waitin' for us and start to look into the mystery of the trances by herself."

The others agreed with a laugh, then followed as Vallant led the way to the door. They'd all talked about how much they wanted to go home, and now they were on the verge of doing it. Only not precisely in the way they'd expected to . . .

". . . so that's what you have to look forward to," I said to the six people having tea with me in my sitting room. "Once a complete Blending gets to a certain point, life really starts to become interesting."

"I don't know if 'interesting' is the word I would have used," Edmin, their Spirit magic user, said wryly with an odd smile while the others simply looked stunned. "But you believe that even Middle Blendings will have the same experiences?"

"There's no reason why they shouldn't, and every reason they should," I answered, the knowledge coming into my mind the way it had been doing lately. "In fact, even Low Blendings ought to experience the same, assuming their members are really close to each other. It's the closeness—called love—that turns the trick."

"Well, we've certainly discovered that kind of closeness," Driff put in with a fond glance for his Blendingmates. "I can't imagine ever Blending with anyone but my sisters and brothers."

"I can see now that your Blending has taught us an important lesson," I said, again accessing that odd information. "Even people who once considered themselves enemies can achieve the necessary mix, if their motives are as sincere as yours obviously are. And a second lesson is that we may not be holding those competitions for strongest High Blending in a year's time. Having one Seated Blending running everything now strikes me as unnecessary, especially the part about limiting the office to Highs. You people aren't Highs, but you've done a marvelous job keeping things running smoothly. Instead of strength, I think the Blending in charge ought to have a *talent* for running things."

"You'd better add 'desire' in along with 'talent,' " Driff told me dryly with a grin. "Wilant and Oplis and the rest of their Blending did a great job sitting in for you and your Blendingmates, but they weren't any happier about being in charge than we were. As soon as the rest of your Blendingmates get here and help to bring the Highs back to themselves, there's a good chance you'll never see them or us again."

"Actually, I think we want to *avoid* people with the desire to run things," I said after joining the others in a laugh. "My people and I are no more eager to run things than you or Oplis and his group, and that could well be the key. If you have capable people doing the job they don't want to do, you can promise to let them loose in a certain amount of time if they perform really well. That gives them the motivation to do the best they can, and saves you the trouble of having to fight to get them to turn loose the reins of power. Giving power to people who live for nothing else is just asking for trouble."

"You can say that again," Idresia agreed with a wry smile, but then her amusement faded. "But talking about people who live for power, I'd like to ask what you think will be done with that Grohl woman and Holdis Ayl. Will you spend time trying to help them, or simply put them down?"

"Where the Grohl woman is concerned, I've decided that I agree with our neighbors in Gracely," I said slowly, finding that I really had come to a decision. "Her final disposition will be made by the courts, but we can't afford to let her keep her talent. She's already shown that she has no qualms about taking over innocent people, and Driff said that one effort has already been made to help her past her problems. If she gets loose again the way she is, too many more innocents can be hurt."

"So there's a third option beyond keeping her under control and killing her," Kail said with a somber nod. "I can't say I like it any better than the first two options, but I also can't deny the necessity. Making other people pay for our squeamishness can't be considered fair."

"Not when we ourselves have nothing to worry about," I agreed. "Honrita Grohl can't take over any of *us,* so we feel tempted to be lenient to spare our consciences. But it's better to have an aching conscience than to leave those who *can't* protect themselves to be victims to someone's madness."

"But what about the man Ayl?" Issini asked, just as concerned as the rest of her Blending. "Is it possible to take away *his* talent?"

"I'm not certain, but I don't think it matters," I answered slowly. "Holdis Ayl is so deeply insane that we probably won't be able to do anything to reclaim him. He's very much a danger to those around him, and due to his previous actions the courts will probably have him executed. I can't say I'm sorry."

Most of the others nodded their agreement, but that was all the time we had to talk. Suddenly there were five other people in the room, and the rest of us got quickly to our feet.

"How about that, we made it," Lorand said happily while Vallant headed straight for me. "We all had to really believe we *would* make it, but once we got past the doubt there wasn't a bit of trouble. Would you like to introduce us to your guests, Tamrissa?"

"I'll be glad to," I answered, really enjoying the feel of Vallant's arms around me. "Driff, Idresia, Edmin, Issini, Kail, and Asri, these are my Blendingmates."

"And now it's fairly obvious why you're the Seated Blending," Asri said as she and the others stared with wide-eyed expressions. "Even if other Blendings *will* be able to do the same, you can do all these things right now."

"But we won't be the only ones for long," Jovvi said with a smile as she came over to touch my arm. "We'll have to have the classes pass on what we've learned, or we'll have a lot of panicky Blending members descending on us when their own changes start. But right now we have a different problem, so how are we going to tackle it?"

"I've been thinking about that, and I've decided that we shouldn't all go together," I said, reluctantly stepping away from Vallant. "I'll go and take a look at Wilant and his Blendingmates, and if I'm not immediately frozen, then I can send what I see back to the rest of you. Until we know that I won't be taken, we shouldn't make an attempt to link up."

"Why do *you* have to be the one to go?" Vallant said, rather predictably, I thought. "I can do any lookin' around as easily as you can."

"But I'm still our primary protector," I pointed out, touching his face in silent thanks. "We may all be able to use each other's talents, but the one who had the talent originally is still the strongest wielder of that talent. Which means that I'm the one who has to go."

"I was about to voice my own protest, Vallant, but it has come to me that Tamrissa is right," Rion said as Vallant parted his lips to argue. "She *is* the Blending's protector, and for that reason has the best chance to resist whatever it was that took the other High talents. Our own chances would be just that much less, which might make the difference between success and failure."

"And we can't afford to fail, not with so many lives in the balance," Vallant said after a brief hesitation, obviously hating the conclusion but still making it. "All right, I withdraw my objections."

"Thank you, love," I murmured with a kiss to his cheek, and then I turned to Driff. "All right, now's the time I get to see Wilant and the others lying down on the job."

"Sitting down, actually," Driff corrected with a faint smile. "As far as I can tell they're all still in good health, but that can't continue for much longer. If you find that we can help in any way, just tell us how."

"If I can figure out what help to ask for, you'll be the first to know," I assured him. "But give me a moment and I'll be right with you."

At first I'd intended to simply walk out, but I quickly realized that I couldn't. Instead I went to my loved ones, and spent a moment giving each of them a hug and a kiss. I'd missed them terribly even during the short time we'd been apart, and they seemed to feel the same about me. The reaffirmation of our closeness strengthened me, so that once I finished with Vallant I really could turn and walk out.

It wasn't far to the meeting room where Wilant and the others sat unmoving. Two guardsmen with strong Middle talent stood in front of the door, both of them firmly in touch with the power. I realized then that almost everyone in the palace now touched the power constantly, but then the door to the meeting room was opened and all other thoughts left my mind.

Wilant Gorl and his five Blendingmates sat around a large table, each one looking down at a large book as though immersed in reading. But no one ever got *that* engrossed in a book, not to the extent of looking as though they were covered with dust.

"You see?" Driff said from just behind me. "They're still in perfect health, but even our Blending entity can't get through to them."

"There's a very good reason for that," I said as I stared at the six victims. "You probably can't see it because you didn't mention it, but there's a . . . shell of some sort around each of them. Now all we have to do is figure out who put them in those invisible shells, and convince the someones to take the shells off again. Should be nothing to it."

Driff and the others behind me exclaimed in surprise, but learning about the shells wasn't the last startling revelation. Even as I watched, the shells faded and disappeared, and Wilant Gorl suddenly looked up.

"Hey, it's Tamrissa!" Wilant exclaimed, starting to get to his feet. "If *she's* here, then the others also ought to be—"

His words broke off as he fell back heavily into his chair, clearly finding it impossible to stand up.

"Just stay there until I can have a good look at all of you," Driff ordered as he moved past me into the room. "You can't expect to move so quickly, not after all the time you've been sitting in one place."

"But it's only been five minutes," Oplis Henden protested

after failing at his own attempt to stand. "And how did you and the others get back here without anyone knowing you were coming, Tamrissa? What *is* going on?"

I parted my lips to answer him, but suddenly the room began to swirl around me until everything went dark.

# TWENTY-EIGHT

But I didn't lose consciousness, and an instant later there was light again. In fact I was back in my sitting room, and my Blendingmates were standing all around me. My sudden arrival startled them, and then we were all put off balance when a complete stranger appeared only a few feet away. The stranger was male and a bit smaller than our own men as well as a few years older than us, with brown hair and eyes and showing a friendly smile.

"Good morning, brothers and sisters," he said, his voice as friendly as his smile. "I'm delighted that it's finally time for us to meet."

"I'm glad *someone* is delighted," I said, beginning to get really annoyed. "Would you like to tell us who you are before I show my own *lack* of delight?"

"Now, now, Tamrissa, let's not lose our tempers," the stranger scolded with his amusement increasing. "I'm not quite up to your strength either in attack *or* defense, so I would prefer to keep this meeting amiable. My name is Drees Allovin, and I'm here to answer some questions for you."

"Then let's start with the most obvious question," Jovvi said, her usual outgoing calm conspicuously absent. "Your comment to Tamma suggests that you know us, but we've never seen you before. Would you like to clear up *that* little mystery?"

"That's what I'm here for," Allovin agreed in what

seemed to be his usual open and friendly way. "Why don't we get some tea and then sit down? This could take a while."

"Why don't we get some of those answers first instead," Vallant said, his tone making it clear that he wasn't going to be moving from where he stood. "We're still waitin' to hear how you know us."

"I know you because I've been watching and helping out when I could ever since just before you all came to Gan Garee," Allovin said, and his own tone had turned gentle. "I wasn't alone doing that, but I *was* put in charge after the first ones saw you safely to that point. The first ones were getting on in years, so they let younger people take over then."

"When he said 'first ones,' I got an odd flash," Naran put in suddenly, her gaze unfocused. "Did anyone else see the same?"

"Yes, I did," Lorand agreed with a frown. "It looked like someone moved aside a curtain I didn't know was there. What does it mean?"

"It means that we no longer have to hide from your formidable talents," Allovin said with a very wide smile. "It took quite a few of us to keep you from finding out about our presence, but there are very good reasons why we couldn't let you know we were there. If you thought you were chosen to lead the people of this continent into their birthright, you never would have become as close as you have."

"There's that word 'chosen' again," Rion said, the sour annoyance in his voice an excellent match to the way *I* felt. "Are you trying to suggest that the Guild is right about our being 'chosen'? We don't happen to agree."

"But the Guild *is* right, only not in the way they believe," Allovin said, his smile still strong. "It was your ancestors who were chosen, brought together on purpose so that they would eventually produce the Blending members that would be needed at this time. Our people knew that only the strongest and best would be able to succeed in this time of upheaval and change. We needed *you*, but before I get to the details I'm going to sit down."

He walked to a chair and sat, then heaved a sigh.

"This would be easier with a cup of tea in my hand, but your suspicion is understandable," he said. "Everyone has been trying to use and/or manipulate you since you first got to this city, and trust won't come easy. Let me start by saying that I come from a place that has almost nothing but full Blendings, and our society has been around for hundreds of years. And now you should be asking yourselves why you've never heard of us."

"We're not the only ones who have never heard of you," I pointed out. "Those invaders we just defeated never heard of you either, not even when they were killing and taking over all those innocent people. If you and your people are full Blendings, why didn't you stop them?"

"We were just about to, when some of us realized that we couldn't," Allovin said, all amusement suddenly gone. "If we'd stopped them then they'd never have been able to try spreading out to this continent, and two things would also never have happened: the Gracelians would never have been forced to change their political and social arrangements, and you six would not have pushed forward at the rapid rate that you did. Without antagonistic opponents possessing great strength and using a different method of Blending, how long would it have taken you to find what Blending is really meant to be?"

He looked at each of us in turn when he asked that question, but there weren't any quick answers offered back.

"I think you can see more of the whole picture now," he said with a nod. "Or at least more of it than you did. It's fine to talk about the 'greater good,' but it's hard to remember that millions of lives are involved while you watch hundreds and thousands die. The only reason we were able to stand by and simply watch those invaders take over various places is that the initial killing stopped rather quickly. They were— and are—more interested in taking slaves than lives, using the initial slaughter only as a tool to terrorize. When the terror spread, conquering became much easier."

"What about now?" I asked, still not quite convinced. "Since the invaders have already served your purpose, will we be able to go after them where they live once a few more of our people have reached the point we already have?"

"Sorry, but my own people have a prior claim on that pleasure," Allovin said, his smile back and very wide. "We've already started to move after those pathetic cripples, and in a little while they'll all be captives instead of rulers. Freeing their slaves and returning them to their interrupted lives will take an enormous effort and a lot of time, and you six don't have any effort and time to spare."

"You've decided we have something else to do?" Lorand put in, his expression showing nothing of his feelings. "What might that something else be?"

"We're not the ones who have made the decision," Allovin said, holding up one hand. "What you have to do is continue on with what you've already started, which is spreading knowledge of Blending techniques and building on that foundation. I can't tell you much about what you'll discover, because we don't want to limit the possibilities. We'll give you a hand every now and again, and if you come up with something *we* don't have we'd appreciate being able to share it. But there *is* one point you'll never have to worry about again."

"What point is that?" Naran asked while I tried to decide whether I believed the man. "The possibility that our lives will ever be free of complete chaos?"

"No, and that's another thing you won't have bothering you," Allovin said behind a small laugh. "Things will begin to settle down for you very soon now, and you'll be able to guide those coming after you to full Blending—and investigating what can be done with the state. The point I meant involves making your offspring and those of your supporters into something other than a spoiled nobility."

"You're willing to tell us how that can be done?" Jovvi asked, only just beating me to asking the same. "If you do, *I'm* willing to forgive quite a lot."

"There's no need for you to buy the information, because you already have it," Allovin said, and his smile had turned warm and sharing. "It's the state of full Blending itself that will provide everything you need. Your children and those of your followers will be raised with love and the standards of fair play, two essential ingredients for producing people who are healthy in mind as well as in body. You'll accept your children for what they are rather than what you or someone else imagines they should be, and you'll be proud of even their smallest accomplishments. In that way they'll grow up expecting to surpass what their parents accomplished, but if they don't the lack won't bother them. They'll know they're loved and accepted anyway."

"It can't be that easy," I said, the words coming out flat. "If it was, there would be a lot more people having untroubled children."

"But it just *may* be that easy," Vallant disagreed before Allovin could speak. "My own parents raised competent, lovin', and capable children, and we all knew they were there for us even if they happened to be away visitin' somewhere. One of my brothers wasn't quite as . . . all-around capable as the rest of us, but that never mattered. My father worked with him until he found somethin' my brother *was* good at, which happened to be nothin' more than keepin' things neat. So our father found my brother a job goin' from business to business in town, tellin' people the best way to keep their places neat. It worked out well, and my brother did the same for *us* without charge."

"Proving that even the smallest of talents can be put to good use if someone takes the trouble to try," Allovin said with a nod and another smile, but then the smile disappeared. "The only ones you'll have trouble with are those who, for some reason, are born with . . . odd differences inside them. You'll find it possible to heal some of those children, but the ones you can't . . . You'll have to decide for yourselves what to do with them, but one thing you won't be able to do is let them live among you. It won't be good for you *or* for the children."

"Let's not think about that right now," Lorand said once we'd all exchanged uneasy glances. "We've had enough trouble lately that we don't need to borrow any from the future. Instead let's get back to getting some of our questions answered. Allovin, you said that our ancestors were chosen instead of us, but just how did your people do that? And what about those 'signs' that were supposed to indicate the Chosen Blending? Were your people responsible for those?"

"Yes, we were the ones who produced the 'signs,' all of them," Allovin admitted with a chuckle. "The first sign had to be public so that you would have the support of the Guild when you needed it, and the rest of the signs came when you six needed the bolstering. Even Naran experienced some signs, although I know she never talked about them. At first she didn't realize their significance, and later, when she did, she decided not to make the rest of you even more upset than you were."

"You used the Sight to guide you," Naran said abruptly, as though just realizing the truth. "You knew we would need help when we came back to Gan Garee to face the usurpers, so you provided for that help well in advance. Can your people really see that far into the future?"

"It's less a matter of Seeing than of separating out the probabilities," Allovin told her, and now his smile looked encouraging. "The method takes a lot of people working together, and then the probabilities have to be linked to their various possibilities. Once you understand that . . . taking a drink of water at the wrong time, for instance, can lead to the deaths of a hundred people, you start to learn what to do and what not to. We'll get you started on the right track with that, as soon as you have enough full Blendings to get somewhere with the method."

"Does that mean you determined you'd get the Blending members you needed if certain people were paired off?" I asked, having been thinking about the question. "If so, you're saying you forced people together for your own ends. And that's your idea of doing something good?"

"No, that isn't our idea of doing something good, so we didn't force anything," Allovin stated, all amusement now gone. "We determined which pairings would produce the best results, and arranged for the individuals involved to

meet. We did that with ten times the number we actually
needed, because we knew that not all the pairings would be
made. We did that over and over for two hundred years, and
at last got the members of *your* generation. You may have
noticed that you're not the only ones who are third level
High talents. You just happen to be the strongest of them,
and we did have a hand in bringing all of you together. If
you hadn't matched each other so well, we'd never have encouraged the arrangement. But you blended as individuals
before you ever Blended formally, and that's when we knew
we'd found success."

"I just remembered something," I said, feeling the new
frown I wore. "While we were on the way to Gracely we
were all approached by people who felt 'attracted' to us, but
when we tried to find those people they'd disappeared. I
have the definite feeling that those people were yours rather
than a group working for the Gracelians, and I'd like to
know why you sent them. We had a really bad time because
of those 'advances.' "

"No, Rion and Naran had the really bad time, not all of
you," Allovin said, nothing whatsoever of amusement showing. "That particular issue had to be forced, to keep it from
turning around and biting *all* of you at some later time. Rion
had to learn that associating only with his sisters was his
*choice,* not something forced on him by circumstance.
Naran had to learn that loving someone isn't the only thing
life has to offer, and Lorand had to start gaining a more
complete understanding of his own situation. The time may
not have been pleasant, but it was certainly necessary."

Rion, Naran, and Lorand exchanged glances, but none of
them seemed prepared to argue what had been said. Their
expressions were rueful, but since they weren't complaining
bitterly on their own behalf, I couldn't quite continue to be
insulted *for* them.

"I think I'd like to clarify something," Jovvi said in an obviously deliberate change of topic, her gaze directly on
Allovin where he sat. "You and your people started us on
our way, so to speak, but you're all done with 'arranging'

things from the shadows now. From this point on we're free to do as we think best, without anyone manipulating events to force us in the direction they want us to go. Is that right?"

"Your conclusion is right, even though you didn't quite state the situation properly," Allovin told her, still showing full seriousness. "We didn't do a lot of the manipulating; we just helped along much of what would have happened anyway, only in a less optimum way. If you six hadn't met, where would the people of Gracely, Gandistra, and Astinda be today?"

That question put an end to my urge to laugh in the man's face over his claim that he and his people hadn't manipulated us. If my Blendingmates and I hadn't met and gotten together, the usurpers might still have been on the Throne when the avenging force from Astinda reached Gan Garee. At that point almost everyone in the city would have died, not even counting those who would have been killed when the Astindan forces left Gandistra again.

We also wouldn't have been there to help the Gracelian assembly members face the invaders, so Gracely would have fallen. After that the people of Gandistra would have been conquered, and then the Astindans would have had their turn. No one would have been left their freedom on the entire continent, and all that had been avoided because—

"All right, maybe manipulation isn't a horrible perversion under *all* circumstances," I granted in a grumble. "But what I don't understand is why your people didn't just step in and avoid all the trouble before it started. You could have stopped the invaders before they took over wherever they come from, visited the Gracelians and told them what they were doing wrong, made the nobility stop being stupid here in Gandistra—"

"Ahh, I think you've just seen the light, Tamrissa," Allovin said with a return of his widest grin. "Of course we could have done everything you suggested, and we could even have made everyone involved listen to us. But you could also have forced the Gracelian assembly members to do things your way, only you didn't. Full Blending can only be achieved by fair-minded people, and it isn't very fair to take over the lives and minds of those around you. You have to give them the chance to do the right thing on their own, or to stay with what's demonstrably wrong and live with the consequences. Besides, how closely would *you* have listened to strangers who moved in and took over running your country?"

"Not very closely," Vallant granted the man when I just shrugged to show I couldn't argue with what he'd said. "And instead of listenin' and learnin', we would have spent our time figurin' out ways to get you out of our lives. This *was* the better way of doin' things."

"Although I feel a good deal of personal reluctance, I also must agree," Rion said, voicing a sigh. "A difficult childhood is of relative unimportance when compared with the various benefits eventually obtained by myself and others. But we've left our companions a far distance from here in another land. Much as I would enjoy remaining here and not have to face the long overland trip back, in all fairness we can't simply abandon the people who have supported us so well."

"Well, actually, you won't *have* to abandon them," Allovin told us with badly hidden amusement when the rest of us groaned our agreement with what Rion had said. "You six aren't strong enough to transport more than yourselves yet, but my people and I have been using the trick for a good deal longer. Once you straighten out the confusion here, I'll go back to Gracely with you. By then all the former slaves ought to have been freed, so we'll be able to get you and all your people back here for good."

"I think I may eventually learn to love you," I told Allovin after shaking my head. "We'll have to wait to find out, but I just thought of another couple of questions. Why did you transport me here in my sleep? And why did you and your people freeze all the Highs in the city in one place for so long?"

"Actually, we had nothing to do with transporting you here to your old house," Allovin said with another grin. "You and your Blendingmates have been yearning toward the time when life was less complicated for you, the others all sharing *your* dream of being home again. Once you learned how to consciously transport yourself a short distance, your inner mind seized on the technique, used your link groups for the needed strength, and took you where you so badly wanted to go. But don't worry, you'll be taught how to keep something like that from happening again."

"*Now* I'm delighted," I answered, referring to his original comments. "But you haven't said why you did what you did to the Highs in this city."

"There were two reasons," Allovin replied, this time voicing his own sigh. "The first was because of those damaged people who were just recently captured. The chances were too good that they would succeed in taking over a High Blending, and that would have made for unnecessary bloodshed and death. You six would have been able to defeat them eventually, but not without the loss of too many lives. The second reason was to teach something it took *us* far too long to learn: It isn't only those with High talent who have something special to offer to the world. As you said, Tamrissa, the strong possibility exists that there won't be any competitions held a year from now. By then a large number of you will have learned that strength isn't everything."

"That should also mean that *we'll* be off the hook," I said, looking at my Blendingmates with true delight. "No one can insist that we stay in charge if being in charge isn't restricted to the strongest."

"Now, *that* I like," Lorand said with a laugh that the others shared in. "Once we get things started up the right path, we'll be free to become private citizens again. And we can find out if more of us than just Rion has a talent for cooking."

"Don't look in *my* direction for that talent," Jovvi said with her own laugh. "I'm much happier just eating what those with true talent provide. And speaking of eating, will you take the noon meal with us, Drees Allovin? We're certain to think of other questions by then that need answering."

"It will be my pleasure," Allovin replied, standing to give

Jovvi a smile and a bow. "My reward for having to watch you flounder again and again without helping is to give you what help I can now. If you don't mind, I'll get myself some tea while the six of you go off to take care of calming things down among your other people. It shouldn't take long, and I'll be right here when you get back. And during the meal, I'll teach you how to get in touch with my people and me if and when you need to."

The man *seemed* to be telling the truth, but it didn't make much difference even if he were lying and intended to leave as soon as we were gone. I had no idea how we would keep him from leaving if he chose to, and an exchanged glance with my Blendingmates showed that they felt the same. Either Allovin would be there for lunch or he would be gone, so we left the sitting room to see to things we *did* have some control over.

Outside in the public part of the palace, we found mild chaos. The High talents who had been frozen in place had found out just how long they'd been out of things, and more confused Highs were staggering in to demand answers as soon as they were able to move. Driff and his Blendingmates were arranging to get the Highs fed as quickly as they appeared, but getting them calmed down was something else entirely.

It even took *us* a while to establish some kind of order, and we had to repeat the explanation of what had been going on three times before enough people heard it that they could do the repeating themselves. We were also brought something to eat, but by the time noon approached we were ready for a meal that wouldn't have to be taken standing up.

"Sneakin' out of here ought to be possible now," Vallant murmured to the rest of us while people argued about what they believed and what they didn't. "Driff and his Blendin'- mates just got back, and they look like they've been fortified with food. Let's go get some fortifyin' of our own."

If anyone had argued with that idea I probably would have flattened them, but of course none of us was *dim* enough to argue. We left the room without anyone noticing that we were going, but once out into the hall we ran smack into Lavrit Mohr, High Master of the Guild. There was another man trailing after Mohr who looked faintly familiar, and the High Master beamed at us.

"Excellences," he said, bowing to all of us. "I only just heard that you were back, so I hurried over at once. I have someone you're certain to want to meet."

"To tell the truth, High Master, we're a bit pressed for time right now," Lorand said smoothly at once. "Surely the introduction will wait until we're free again?"

"Well, of course it will," Mohr said, looking downright crestfallen. "After all the time the man has waited, I suppose another hour or two won't matter that much. They *are* extremely busy men and women, Dom Gallaine. You can understand that, I hope?"

"Sure, I can understand it," the man with Mohr said, his disappointment so sharp that it nearly made me gasp. "Just tell me: Which one of them is he? If I know that much, I can wait as long as I have to."

"A reasonable request," Mohr granted, decision suddenly firm in his mind. "This man here is the one known as Rion Mardimil, originally called Clarion Mardimil."

Mohr pointed to Rion, but Rion was already staring at the stranger behind Mohr. Rion's frown was perplexed, but suddenly I understood exactly what was happening.

"I think lunch can wait awhile," I said, feeling happy tears come to my eyes. "Rion . . . unless I'm completely mistaken, that man is your father."

"Why, yes, I am, and my name is Aldrin Gallaine," the man said, his gaze unmoving from a stunned Rion. "I had no choice about letting my child be stolen from me, but I still feel as if I abandoned him. If he doesn't want to know me now I'll understand, but I still had to see with my own eyes the fine man he's become. His mother would have been so proud if she'd lived, as proud as I am . . ."

By then Rion had moved closer to the man, and then they were hugging with tears in both their eyes. Jovvi and Naran cried openly with silly smiles on their faces, the kind of silly smile I probably wore as well. Vallant and Lorand showed broad grins, but I thought I detected a bit of moisture in their eyes as well.

"Ah, so much happiness brought about by a fortunate accident," Lavrit Mohr said as he dabbed at his face with a handkerchief. "One of my people, a man or woman whose name I don't even know, learned that Dom Gallaine was supposed to be the true father of the Excellence Rion. The information was passed on to me along with Dom Gallaine's location, and I arranged to have him returned here to Gan Garee. I really must find which of my people gathered the necessary information, and reward him or her properly."

"So you found Rion's father purely by accident," I said, looking around to see that my Blendingmates had gotten the same idea I had. "You may have trouble locating the one who sent you the information, Dom Mohr, but if so don't worry about it. I think we can pass on all our thanks to the proper parties."

"Yes, probably over lunch," Jovvi said with an amused smile. "Of all the gifts we could have been given, this one has to be best—and the best gauge to measure some new acquaintances. You can usually tell what people are like by what they do in an effort to please you."

"Then let's go tell a new acquaintance how pleased we are by the effort," I said, my arm around Vallant's waist as his was around my shoulders. "Rion and Naran and their guest will certainly want to have lunch in their own wing, Dom Mohr, and you've definitely earned the right to join them. The rest of us will go on to that meeting we mentioned, and we'll get back together later."

Mohr didn't quite understand everything I'd said, but Vallant, Jovvi, and Lorand had. We left Rion to his happy reunion and the chance to introduce Naran to his new-found father, and headed back to the sitting room in my wing. We had some thanks to give, and the future had never looked brighter.

We hope you've enjoyed this Eos book. As part of our mission to give readers the best science fiction and fantasy being written today, the following pages contain a glimpse into the fascinating worlds of a select group of Eos authors.

Join us as beloved sf author Sheri S. Tepper recounts an intelligent, witty, and deeply human tale of first contact. As fantasy author Sharon Green reveals the true fates of the Chosen Blending, six courageous men and women whose talents stand between the evil and the innocent. As Holly Lisle introduces a magical world so close to our own that both destiny and disaster spill through the world gates. And as acclaimed editor David G. Hartwell brings us the very best science fiction stories of the year.

Spring 2002 at Eos.
Out of This World.

# THE FRESCO

Sheri S. Tepper

*Available in February 2002*

Along the Oregon coast an arm of the Pacific shushes softly against rocky shores. Above the waves, dripping silver in the moonlight, old trees, giant trees, few now, thrust their heads among low clouds, the moss thick upon their boles and shadow deep around their roots. In these woods nights are quiet, save for the questing hoot of an owl, the satin stroke of fur against a twig, the tick and rasp of small claws climbing up, clambering down. In these woods, bear is the big boy, the top of the chain, but even he goes quietly and mostly by day. It is a place of mosses and liverworts and ferns, of filmy green that curtains the branches and cushions the soil, a wet place, a still place.

A place in which something new is happening. If there were eyes to see, they might make out a bear-sized shadow agile as a squirrel, puckering the quiet like an opening zipper, rrrrip up, rrrrip down, high into the trees then down again, disappearing into mist. Silence intervenes, then another seam is ripped softly on one side, then on the other followed by new silences. Whatever these climbers are, there are more than a few of them.

The owl opens his eyes wide and turns his head backwards, staring at the surrounding shades. Something new, something strange, something to make a hunter curious. When the next sound comes, he launches himself into the air, swerving silently around the huge trunks, as he does when he hunts mice or voles or small birds, following the pucker of individual tics to its lively source, exploring into his life's darkness. What he finds is nothing he might have imagined, and a few moments later his bloody feathers float down to be followed by another sound, like a satisfied sigh.

Near the Mexican border, rocky canyons cleave the mountains, laying them aside like broken wedges of gray cheese furred with a dark mold of pinion and juniper that sheds hard shadows on moon glazed stone, etched lithographs in gray and black, taupe and silver.

Beneath feathery chamisa a rattlesnake flicks his tongue, following a scent. Along a precarious rock ledge a ring-tailed cat strolls, nose snuffling the cracks. At the base of the stone a peccary trots along familiar foot trails, toward the toes of a higher cliff where a seeping spring gathers in a rocky goblet. In the desert, sounds are dry and rattling: pebbles toed into cracks, hoofs tac-tacking on stone, the serpent rattle warning the wild pig to veer away, which she does with a grunt to the tribe behind her. From the rocky scarp the ring-tailed cat hears the whole population of the desert pass about its business in the canyon below.

A new sound comes to this place, too. High in the air, a chuff, chuff, chuff, most like the wings of a monstrous crow, crisp and powerful, enginelike in their regularity. Then a cry, eerie and utterly alien, not from any native bird ever heard in this place.

The peccary freezes in place. The ring-tailed cat leaps into the nearest crevice. Only the rattler does not hear, does not care. For the others staying frozen in place seems the appropriate and prudent thing to do as the chuff, chuff, chuff moves overhead, another cry and an answer from places east, and west and north as well. The aerial hunter is not alone and its screams fade into the distance, the echoes still, and the canyon comes quiet again.

And father south and east, along the gulf in wetland that breeds the livelihood of the sea, in the mangrove swamps, the cypress bogs, the moss-lapped, vine-twined, sawgrass-grown, reptile-ridden mudflats, night sounds are continuous. Here the bull gator bellows, swamp birds call, insects and frogs whir and buzz and babble and creak. Fish jump, huge tails thrash, wings take off from cover to silhouette themselves on the face of the moon.

And even here comes strangeness, a great squadge, squadge, squadge, as though something walks through the deep muck in giant boots on ogre legs, squishing feet down and sucking them up only to squish them down once more. Squadge, squadge, squadge, three at a time, then a pause, then three more.

As in other places, the natives fall silent. The heron finds himself a perch and pull his head back on his long neck, letting it rest on his back, crouching a little, not to be seen against the sky. The bull gator floats on the oil surface like a scaly buoy, fifteen feet of hunger and dim thought, an old man of the muck, protruding eyes seeing nothing as flared nostrils taste something strange. He lies in his favorite resting place near the trunk of a water-washed tree. There was no tree in that place earlier today, but the reptilian mind does not consider this. Only when something from above slithers sinuously onto the top of his head does he react violently, his body bending, monstrous tail thrashing, huge jaws gaping wide . . .

Then nothing. No more from the gator until morning, when the exploring heron looks along his beak to find an intaglio of strange bones on the bank, carefully trodden into the muck, from the fangs at the front of the jaw to the vertebra at the tip of the tail. Like a frieze of bloody murder, carefully displayed.

# DESTINY
## Book Three of the Blending Enthroned

### Sharon Green

*Available in April 2002*

"What's happenin' now?" Vallant asked, and there was almost accusation in his tone. "I leave the bunch of you alone for no more than five minutes, and you find somethin' else to worry about as soon as my back is turned. So what is it now, and just how dangerous will it turn out to be?

"Flux has been keeping me from seeing more than bits and snatches," Naran said with a sigh. "I'm being surprised by everything but what we absolutely have to know."

"You know, that's exactly the way it *has* been," I said, hit by a flash of revelation. "You haven't been able to see much of anything beyond the completely essential, and that can't possibly be a coincidence either. Someone has to be deliberately blocking you."

"Could the enemy really be strong enough to reach all the way here to block Naran without us being aware of it?" Lorand asked, worry widening his eyes. "If they are, we have even more trouble that we thought."

"It can't possibly be the invaders," I said while everyone else just came up with exclamations of worry and startlement. "Naran's had this trouble since before we left Gan Geree, and if the invaders are *that* strong we might as well just stand here and let them take us over. No, someone else is responsible for blindfolding us, and I'd really like to know who that is."

"Who *could* it be?" Vallant countered, but not in a challenging way. "I'd be willin' to believe that Ristor Ardanis, leader of those with Sight magic, is behind the blockin', but he and most of his people are a long way away from here. Naran, are you absolutely certain that the people in your link groups are workin' *with* you rather than against your breakin' through?"

"Normally I might not be absolutely certain, but once I'm part of the Blending there's no doubt," Naran answered with a nod. "My people are trying as hard as I am, but something is keeping us from breaking through."

"It certainly can't be the Gracelians," Jovvi said, her distracted gaze saying that her mind searched for an answer. "The Gracelians don't *have* anyone with Sight magic, so they can't possibly affect it. Who does that leave?"

"No one but the Highest Aspect," I said, finding it impossible to keep the dryness from my tone. "If the enemy isn't doing it, the Gracelians aren't doing it, and Ristor Ardanis's people aren't doing it, there's no one left."

"But there *is* someone left," Rion disagreed slowly, his gaze as distracted as Jovvi's had been. "We haven't mentioned the fact in quite some time, but there's still a mystery in our lives that we haven't solved. Those 'signs' the Prophecies spoke of . . . We've denied that they ever happened, but they did happen and we still don't know who was responsible for causing them."

"And we don't know who was responsible for bringing us all together," Lorand took his turn to point out. "A minute or two ago we were refusing to accept all those dreams as a coincidence, but we never questioned the even bigger coincidence that we all ended up in the same residence. We are each of us the strongest practitioner of our respective talents, and we all just *happened* to end up in the same residence and made into a Blending? If you can believe *that*, then you must also believe that the Highest Aspect leaves a copper coin under our pillows as a reward for having gone through the five-year-old tests successfully."

"It looks like someone's been makin' a *lot* of things happen around us," Vallant observed, vexation showing on his face as strong as I felt it inside me. "So there's some group, large or small, makin' these things happen, but we don't know if they're friend or foe. Until we find out just what their aim is, we can't call them one or the other."

"Well, one of their aims *was* to bring us together," I suggested, thinking about it even as I spoke. "If they're friends of ours, they did it so that we could win the throne and get rid of the nobility. If they're enemies, they did it to put us all in the same place so we could be gotten rid of with a single effort. If *we* get taken down, everyone knows that no one else is as strong as we are and so they might not even put up a token struggle. By winning over us, the enemy would win over everyone else at the same time."

"I see a flaw in that logic," Lorand said, another of us almost lost to distraction. "These unknown someones have obviously known about us since before we got together in Gan Garee. Putting us all together just to conquer us at the same time makes no sense, not when they could have killed us one at a time before we knew what we were doing. If they had, there would *be* no 'others' to worry about, only the Middle Seated Blending the nobles picked out. Even an arrogant enemy would never go to such lengths just best six people."

"I'm force to agree with that," Vallant said even as Jovvi nodded her own agreement. "What's the sense in havin' almost a dozen more enemies, when killin' a few people will give you no enemies to speak of at all? These invader leaders just rolled over all opposition until it was crushed, and then it took over the people and used them for their own purposes. That means there's definitely someone else in the game.

# MEMORY OF FIRE

## Book One of the World Gates

Holly Lisle

*Available in May 2002*

Molly McColl woke to darkness—and to men dragging her from her bed toward her bedroom door. The door glowed with a terrifying green light.

She didn't waste her breath screaming; she attacked. She kicked upward, and felt like she'd kicked a rock—but she heard the satisfying crack of bone under her bare heel, and the resulting shriek of pain. She snapped her right elbow back into ribs and gut, and her hand broke free from the thin, hot, strong fingers that clutched at it. She twisted and bit down on the fingers holding her left wrist, and was rewarded with a scream. She clawed at eyes, she kneed groins, she bit and kicked and fought with every trick at her disposal, with every ounce of her strength and every bit of her fear and rage.

But they had her outnumbered, and even though she could make out the outlines of the ones she'd hurt curled on the floor, the rest of her assailants still dragged her into that wall of fire. She screamed, but as the cluster of tall men around her forced her into the flames, her scream—and all other sounds—died.

No pain. No heat. The flames that brushed against her didn't hurt at all—instead, the cold fire felt wonderful, energizing, life-giving; as her kidnappers dragged her clawing and kicking into the curving, pulsing tunnel, something in her mind whispered "yes." For the instant—or the eternity—

in which she hung suspended in that place, no one held her, no one was trying to hurt her, and for the first time in a long time, all the pain in her body fell away.

She had no idea what was going on; she felt on the one hand like she was fighting for her life, and on the other hand like she was moving into something wonderful.

And then, out of the tunnel of green fire, she erupted into a world of ice and snow and darkness, and all doubts vanished. The men still held her captive, and one of them shouted, "Get ropes and a wagon—she hurt Paith and Kevrad and Tajaro. We're going to have to tie her." She was in trouble—nothing good would come of this.

"It's only two leagues to Copper House."

"She'll kill one of us in that distance. Tie her."

"But the Imallin said she's not to be hurt."

Other hands were grabbing her now—catching at her feet, locking on to her elbows and wrists, knees and calves.

"Don't *hurt* her," said the one closest to her head. "Just *tie* her so she can't hurt us, damnall. And where's that useless Gateman the Imallin found to make the gate? We still have people back there! Send someone to get them out before he closes it!"

Molly fought as hard as she could, but the men—thin and tall, but strong—forced her forward, adding hands to hands on her arms and legs until she simply couldn't move.

When she couldn't fight, Molly relaxed her body completely. First, she wasn't going to waste energy uselessly. Second if she stopped fighting, she might catch them off guard and be able to escape.

Someone dragged a big, snorting animal through the dark toward her, and rattling behind the animal was a big wooden farm-type wagon. But what the hell was the thing pulling it? It wasn't a horse and it wasn't any variety of cow—it had a bit of a moose shape to it, and a hint of caribou, and some angles that suggested bones where bones didn't belong in any beast of burden Molly had every seen. And its eyes glowed hell-red in the darkness.

The whole mob of them picked her up and shoved her into the back of the wagon, and most of them clambered up there with her—bending down to twist soft rope around her ankles, and then around her wrists. When they had her bound, they wrapped blankets around her, and tucked her deep into bales of straw. Instantly, she was warmer. Hell, she was warm. But as the wagon lurched and creaked, and began to rattle forward, she heard lines of marching feet forming on ether side of the wagon. She knew the creak of boots and pack straps, the soft bitching, the sound of feet moving in rhythm while weighted down by gear and weapons. She remembered basic training all too well—and if Air Force basic was pretty easy compared to the Army or the Marines, she'd still got enough of marching to know the drill. She had a military escort.

What the hell was going on?

But the people who had come to get her weren't soldiers. They were too unprepared for resistance, too sure of themselves. Soldiers knew that trouble could be anywhere, and took precautions. More than that, though, she couldn't get over the feel of those hands on her—hot, thin, dry hands.

She decided she wasn't going to just wait for them to haul her where they were going and then . . . do things to her. She'd learned in the Air Forced that the best way to survive a hostage situation was to not be a hostage. She started to work on the rope on her wrists, and managed by dint of persistence and a high tolerance to pain to free her hands. She'd done some damage—she could feel rope burns and scratches from metal embedded beneath the soft outer strands, and the heat and wetness where a bit of her own blood trickled down her hand—but she wasn't worried about any of that.

Fold and wrap a blanket around each foot and bind it in place with the rope, she thought. It won't make great boots, but it will get me home. Turn the other blankets into a poncho, get the hell out of this place and back home. She could follow the tracks in the snow.

Except there were the niggling details she hadn't let herself think about while she was fighting, while she was getting her hands and then her feet untied, while she was folding boots out of blankets and tying them in place. She hadn't heard an engine since she came out of the tunnel of fire; she hadn't heard a car pass, or seen anything that might even be mistaken for an electric light; nor had she heard a plane fly over. In the darkness, she could make out the vague outlines of trees overhead, but not much else—not a star shone in the sky, which felt close and pregnant with more snow.

She had the bad feeling that if she managed to escape the soldiers that marched to either side of the wagon and succeeded in tracing the wagon tracks back to the place where she'd come through the tunnel of fire, that tunnel wouldn't be there anymore. And she was very, very afraid that there would no other way to get home.

She listened to the speech of the men who drove the wagons, and she could understand it flawlessly—but if she forced herself to listen to the words, they were vowel-rich and liquid, and they didn't have the shape of English. The hands on her arms had felt wrong in ways besides their heat, their dryness, their thinness. When she closed her eyes and stilled her breath and forced herself to remember, those hands had gripped her with too many fingers. And when she'd had been fighting, her elbows had jammed into the ribs that weren't where ribs were supposed to be.

When the sun came up or they got to a place with lights, Molly had a bad feeling that she wasn't going to like getting her first clear look at her kidnappers. Because when she let herself really think about it, she had the feeling that she wasn't on Earth anymore—and that her captors weren't human.

# YEAR'S BEST SF 7

### Edited by David G. Hartwell

### Available in June 2002

The tradition continues! The YEAR'S BEST SF 7 collects the best science fiction stories of 2001, never before published in book form, in one easy-to-carry volume. Previous volumes have included stories by Ray Bradbury, Joe Haldeman, Ursula K. Le Guin, Kim Stanley Robinson, Robert Silverberg, Bruce Sterling, Gene Wolfe, and many more.

With tales from both the grand masters of the field and the rising new stars, the YEAR'S BEST SF is rapidly becoming the indispensable guide to science fiction today.

## Praise for the YEAR's BEST series:

"Impressive."
—*Locus* magazine

"The finest modern science fiction writing."
—*Pittsburgh Tribune*